THE APPRENTICE PRINCE

THE *WOLVES OF DUMNONIA* SERIES

AVAILABLE NOW

Book 1: The Shadow of Fenrir

Book 2: A Thrall's Crown

Book 3: Wolf of Dumnonia

Book 4: The Apprentice Prince

FORTHCOMING

Book 5: The Monk's Sword

THE APPRENTICE PRINCE

Peter Fox

ELTERWATER PRESS

This book is a work of fiction. Apart from a small number of historical persons and events, the majority of characters and incidents portrayed in this novel are the work of the author's imagination, and as such any resemblance to actual persons, living or dead, is purely coincidental.

THE APPRENTICE PRINCE

First published in paperback in Great Britain in 2022
by Elterwater Press Ltd, Cumbria

www.elterwaterpress.com

A CIP catalogue record of this book is available from the British Library.

ISBN 978-1-912689-16-3 Paperback

Typeset by Elterwater Press in 11/15pt Sabon
Printed and bound by Amazon

For the two Katies in my life,
who have - from opposite sides of the planet -
supported me on this journey
with great patience and humour.

Contents

Part I

Westseaxna Ríce (Kingdom of Wessex)
Late Summer, 823 AD

1 Sloppy footwork

Heremund's Smithy, Scirburne, Wessex

'*Turn sideways!* the Devil commanded. *Lead with the shoulder! Drive with the right foot! Watch the man, not the blade!*

Saeric, former slave and recent apprentice to Heremund, blacksmith of Scirburne, stumbled backwards in the dusty yard, barely maintaining his balance as he ducked under the swinging blade. Sun flashed on polished steel as his opponent's sword scythed the air where his head had just been. Saeric swore at his assailant, swinging his own blade in a poor defensive parry. The iron band on his head slipped as he ducked, and he only just managed to shove it back into place before it fell. Ealdorman Eadwald had been true to his word and had insisted that Saeric wear the uncomfortable circlet whenever he was in his presence, including sword practice. It was the only time he wore it, mind, for neither Saeric nor the Saxon general wished to signal Saeric's heritage to anyone outside the tight circle of Saeric's mentors. As far as Saeric knew, even Carwyn remained ignorant of the truth. For those outside the group who asked, Eadwald explained that the crown represented all of Dumnonia's ousted nobility, whom Saeric had vowed to avenge collectively.

Saeric adjusted the band again as Eadwald attacked, cursing as he struggled to hold the stupid thing in place while defending himself. If he let his crown hit the ground, he would forfeit the bout. He had already lost three sessions today.

Hopeless! railed the Devil, forcing Saeric's body into what he considered a better stance.

'What the Hell?' cursed Saeric, fighting back, but the Devil was having none of it, and he drove Saeric onto his front foot. He lunged at his attacker, a better effort this time to be sure, but he was still no match for his opponent.

Your sword skills are terrible! complained the Devil. *How have you let yourself get so bad?*

I'm better with a ploughshare, Saeric thought angrily, wishing he could have another go at it, but his tutor had flatly refused to let him anywhere near the thing. 'No acolyte of mine is going to run about bludgeoning people to death with a lump of iron,' Eadwald had said with contempt.

Saeric sprang sideways to avoid another lunging swing, and then his body leapt forward on the offensive, Saeric having little choice but to follow the Devil's lead. Much to Saeric's surprise, his attack succeeded, earning a blurted exclamation of disbelief from his adversary.

That's how you do it. Watch and learn.

Saeric went on the offensive again, pressing hard and fast, forcing his opponent onto the back foot, and suddenly the tables were turned. To his astonishment, Saeric found himself holding the point of his sword in his opponent's startled face.

Take that! came the voice in his head again, and Saeric realised it could not be the Devil, at least not the version he had grown used to. This voice was young and brash.

Who are you? Saeric demanded.

Saeric's opponent was saying something, but it was the voice inside his head that Saeric heard.

I told you, said the cocky newcomer. *I'm a better version of you.*

'Saeric?'

Saeric blinked at his mentor, then he lowered his sword, muttering an apology.

Eadwald, commander of the King's western fyrds and tutor to Saeric of Scirburne in his spare time, frowned at his pupil. 'Where did that come from?'

'I don't know,' Saeric answered, unsettled by the intrusion of this different character in his head. A part of him felt a thrill at hearing that voice; a voice he'd heard before, only it had been in his dreams in the past. This was different. This had been real, as though he had been standing right beside him. *What does this clarity mean?* he wondered. *Are you, in fact, alive? Could you be somewhere nearby?*

'Well, whatever it was, do more of it,' Eadwald said. When Saeric didn't respond, Eadwald added, 'perhaps that's enough for today. Sorry about striking you.' He nodded at Saeric's left shoulder, which fortunately was cloaked in high-quality chainmail armour on loan from Heremund.

'It's fine,' Saeric said, rolling his left arm to prove it.

In truth, it did sting a little, but the wound was well-healed now, despite Heremund's fears that it would come to hinder his apprentice. Nearly two months had passed since the disastrous outing with Leofwynn, and whilst his shoulder had healed, Saeric's spirits had not. He simply could not shake the guilt he felt for his failure to save Leo. Leo's father, Dunstan, had, predictably, banished Saeric from his household, which was unjust, given Dunstan's utter disinterest in his daughter and her welfare prior to her death. The thegn had not bothered to return from wherever he was in the north for the funeral. Instead, he'd sent instructions by way of a dispatch rider from the campaign. Whilst that was not unusual in itself–particularly for an inconsequential younger daughter–Dunstan's banishment of Saeric was more evidence that Dunstan hated his brother's apprentice for no other reason than Saeric was a Briton; a Godless, lower form of human deserving of his brutal treatment at the hands of his superiors.

How could two brothers be so different from one another? Saeric had wondered, as Heremund had read the eulogy at Leo's service in Scirburne mynster. Carwyn had said it was because Dunstan was forced to live in his older brother's expansive shadow and therefore hated Heremund for it. Saeric belonged to Heremund; thus, he was also despised. She had gone on to explain that no matter what efforts Dunstan had made to ingratiate himself with the men of Ecgberht's court, someone always had a better tale about Heremund to surpass Dunstan. Perhaps more galling was that Dunstan had only managed to earn the rank of thegn. In contrast, Heremund had been granted a prestigious earldom, bringing a vast tract of land in Dumnonia that Heremund had not even bothered to take up. 'Surely an insult to the king?' Dunstan had often complained. Yet Ecgberht had not seemed to mind.

As a result, the younger sibling had decided it was all the fault of the Dumnonians, upon whom he poured his considerable spite. 'You are not the only Briton he reviles,' Carwyn had told Saeric during his recovery. 'I am sure that Dunstan thinks Heremund married me just to spite him, to score another point against his insecure little brother in their fraternal battle.'

Saeric had needed to ask what fraternal meant. Occasionally, his cruelly truncated education revealed itself when Heremund or Carwyn used an unfamiliar word. 'It means a brotherly battle,' she had explained, 'and Dunstan is wrong. Heremund married me because we love one another.'

Saeric had agreed that he could not imagine Heremund being so dishonourable, but then he remembered that Heremund was the same man who had led the Saxon fyrds to overthrow his kingdom. 'How can he be the Iron Fist?' Saeric had asked, still unable to reconcile the man he had grown to like with the horrible revelation that Heremund had, by proxy at least, ousted and murdered his family. 'Why have you done that to me?' he had asked the Devil. 'Why did you send me here to be saved by my enemy? I don't want to hate Heremund, but I must.'

'You don't have to hate him,' Carwyn had disagreed, startling Saeric because he hadn't realised he had spoken aloud. 'And God brought you here because he wanted you to find hope and restoration through forgiveness. For without forgiveness, there can be no healing, and we would be perpetually at war with one another. As Jesus himself said from the cross, "Father, forgive them, for they know not what they are doing."'

'But how can I forgive Heremund?' Saeric had countered, 'and how can you? Heremund knew exactly what he was doing, and we lost everything because of him. Before he died, I vowed to my brother that I would avenge our family if I survived. But here I am sharing an ale with the man who helped Mael take Dumnonia! I have betrayed them, Carwyn. Every day that I eat at your table, I betray them!'

'Do you really believe that killing Heremund will remove your pain and guilt? I think you know that it would only add to it.'

'It would make me feel better,' Saeric had muttered.

'Would it? Truly? Forgiveness comes at a great cost, Saeric, but with it can come great reward. Heremund and I love one another deeply, and our boys are growing up knowing that it is possible to share blood from either side of the Exe. Are we that different, Briton and Saxon? The only thing that I can see is that we speak different languages. Otherwise, we both hate, love, laugh, eat and shit the same way. We even worship the same God.' She had paused then and looked him in the eye. 'The reason you struggle with this is because all that guilt and hatred you carry around with you is not who you truly are.'

'It is,' he had argued, feeling threatened by Carwyn's observations. It had to be. For what else, if not his desire for revenge, had kept him alive through all those horrendous years of brutality and deprivation at Eanswith's hands? That and the belief that Caelin was out there somewhere, alive but lost.

Carwyn had shushed him. 'My husband is a sound judge of character, Saeric. He would have thrown you out to fend for yourself had he not seen past the layers of hurt to the worthy soul hidden within.' She paused, searching for a way to better explain herself. 'You are like a cabbage....'

'A what?' Saeric had exclaimed, laughing, despite himself.

Carwyn had laughed too, the tension broken by the absurd image. 'Well, perhaps not a cabbage. An onion? That has layers. No, that's not right either; the middle is the same as the outside.' Her eyes glinted with sudden insight. 'You're a chrysalis; that's what you are. A caterpillar hidden inside your hard shell to protect you from the harsh world around you. You're waiting for the right conditions to break free and reveal the real you; the same beauty and goodness that God can see within your heart and which you reveal from time to time, no matter how hard you try to suppress it.'

Saeric had shaken his head at her, certain he was no caterpillar or any sort of grub for that matter. He had also wondered whether she was alluding to his true identity, hidden deep within that same, hard shell.

'Lord Eadwald sees it too,' Carwyn had continued. 'That's why he helps you, and I can assure you that Eadwald is not a man to waste his valuable time on the unworthy. Although I do admit I am a little surprised that he has taken such an interest in you, even considering his friendship with my husband.'

Saeric had nearly responded with an unkind comment about the Saxon general's ulterior motives. Still, he had stopped himself, taking her statement to mean that Heremund had not shared the revelation of Saeric's remarkable heritage with his wife.

'Saeric? Ahoy there! Are you with us?'

Saeric blinked away the memory to find himself standing before his mentor. He sheathed his sword and backed away from Eadwald. 'You're right,' he said. 'I need a rest.'

Saeric's instructor nodded and handed his sword to his attendant, then he tugged off his gloves and handed them over too. Saeric unstrapped his own sword and scabbard and leaned it against the wall beside him. Moments later, Heremund's two red-headed twins burst into the yard and scuffled for the right to carry Saeric's weapon back to the house.

'Let me help you out of your mail, Saeric,' came a voice from his right. Saeric turned to Gerard, former sergeant-at-arms to Heremund and, more recently, Saeric's aide-de-camp. The thick-haired Saxon fyrdsman had taken it upon himself to act as Saeric's chamberlain ever since the attack on Leo, despite Saeric's repeated protestations that Gerard owed him nothing. 'I owe you my life,' Gerard had countered simply, 'and God knows you need someone to straighten you out.' And that had been the end of the matter.

Despite the seriousness of his injuries, Gerard had been expelled from Scirburne Hall by Dunstan for his failure to protect his charge. Dunstan had threatened to execute Gerard for his wrongdoing, but Heremund had forcefully intervened, further intensifying the enmity between the two brothers. Saeric had questioned the extremity of Dunstan's actions, but Heremund had advised Saeric to stay well out of it, for there was a long and unhappy history between Gerard's family and Heremund's own. This only piqued Saeric's curiosity, and he promised himself that he would raise it with Gerard at a more opportune time.

Soon afterwards, Heremund had grumpily embarked upon an extension to his hall to accommodate his growing band of adoptees. Both Gerard and Saeric had received near-mortal wounds that required lengthy convalescence, but Gerard suffered most from his injuries. The arrow puncture in his arm had recovered well, but the Saxon fyrdsman had remained bedridden for a whole month and two weeks while his lungs and ribs healed. For a time, they feared the worst as he struggled to breathe, but the old soldier had refused to give in, and here he was now, alive, if not altogether restored to full health. Alas, Gerard still found himself running short of breath if he overstrained himself, and just today, Saeric had caught the soldier wincing as he had helped Saeric into his chainmail armour.

Saeric plucked off his iron circlet, then he bent over and held out his arms so that Gerard could pull the heavy garment over his head. He was more adept at it now, having practised the technique with Gerard and Heremund for the past week. Saeric had not yet felt ready for sharp-edged sword practice, not least because his injured left shoulder continued to trouble him, but Eadwald had been insistent. Saeric remained mediocre at best with the sword, hence the heavy chainmail. He'd nearly broken his neck the first time he'd tried pulling it off on his own, having stubbornly refused Gerard's assistance. However, Saeric was fast coming to learn that any advice Gerard offered should be respected, but it still bothered him that he was learning the ways of a warrior from his sworn enemies.

'We aren't monsters, you know,' Gerard had grinned after a particularly arduous session, amused by Saeric's irritation over his reliance on him. 'Like it or not, you've got a lot to learn.'

'If you people hadn't come and overthrown my kingdom, I wouldn't need all this training!'

'And if you people had been better prepared in the first place,' Gerard had said, 'perhaps we wouldn't have been able to trounce you so easily. It's time to put the past behind you, Saeric,' Gerard had continued, cutting Saeric off before the Briton could flare into anger, 'and catch up on all that you have missed. You will be a worthier man for it, and better still, you will have learned the ways of your enemy.'

Of course, Gerard knew the truth about Saeric's ancestry, but the wily Saxon soldier never spoke directly about it nor treated Saeric any differently. Saeric had thus allowed himself to be guided by the experienced soldier, following his instructions without complaint. Today, however, Saeric took the weight of the sweat-dampened chainmail as they draped it over its stand. Gerard offered a nod of gratitude, prompting Saeric to say, 'you need to be more careful and not push yourself. I know what to do now.'

'Time for ale,' Gerard announced, refusing to acknowledge Saeric's well-intentioned advice. He shooed away Beornwald, who had lost the battle with his twin brother for the right to carry

Saeric's sword. Saeric handed him his iron circlet instead, and the young boy pranced off to the house after his brother, cooing in triumph. Gerard, meanwhile, began lecturing Saeric on the proper care and maintenance of chainmail, warning him of the special Hell that kinked chains brought the careless. On another occasion, he'd spent nearly an hour on the merits of oiling to avoid rust, another of a Saxon soldier's Great Sins, apparently. Gerard was bound to return to that topic today, given how much bodily fluid Saeric had left behind on the iron, thanks to his gruelling session with Eadwald. The ealdorman, by contrast, was irritatingly composed, with only a few tell-tale beads of sweat glistening on his brow. Saeric peeled off his tunic and undershirt to let the air cool his bare skin.

'You're not listening to a word I'm saying, are you?' Gerard said.

'Huh?' Saeric muttered, his thoughts having drifted back to the youthful intruder who had helped him in practice. He felt a tingle in his spine. *It has to be Caelin.*

'Hurry up, girl. I'm parched!' Gerard shouted in the direction of the house.

They were soon joined by Gerard's daughter, Hildelith, who bore a large jug of ale and three mugs. 'Why are you thirsty, father?' she asked. 'Saeric's the one doing all the work.' She winked at Saeric, and the Briton felt his face redden.

Why does she have that effect on me? he thought irritably, annoyed at his body's betrayal of him.

Hildelith equalled Saeric in height, and her clear, hazel-brown eyes suggested a sharp, inquiring mind. Her attractive face was framed by thick waves of blond hair, falling to broad shoulders. She often tied her hair in a braid, but she wore it loose today. Her jaw and chin were her most striking feature, almost masculine, but offset by full lips and high cheekbones. Her face suited her forthright character, and Saeric had found himself wondering which had come first, her formidable looks or the personality that filled them. Whatever it was, there was no doubt that he had come to find her company agreeable.

She had appeared after the routing of the brigands at the ford, settling into Heremund's house to care for her father. The two invalids – Saeric and Gerard – had been tended by Carwyn and Hildelith as they recovered from their respective wounds; Gerard happy to receive the care and attention, Saeric at first resenting it. He'd survived all this time without the need for cosseting, so why had it felt so good to receive it? It had made him feel strangely uncomfortable to receive care without ties, and he had remained uneasy for fear of the payment that would likely be extracted. It had been a considerable leap of trust to accept that Hildelith and Carwyn sought nothing in return for their nurturing of him. Thus, he had relented to Hildelith's ministrations, realising too late that Hildelith and Carwyn had deftly swapped responsibilities.

You are a fool, the Devil had scolded him at the time, and that judicious warning returned to him now. Saeric held Hildelith's gaze and reminded himself he could ill afford to trust her. Despite all the evidence that she bore him no ill will, she was nevertheless a Saxon. He'd been enthralled by a strong Saxon woman before, and his body and soul bore the countless deep and painful scars of that coercion. Never again, he had vowed to himself on that first, rain-swept night following his escape.

What Eanswith had forced him to do had been profoundly sinful. Still, it had been the reason he had survived all those years – not because he was a useful hand around the burh – but because she had developed a potent bond with him, a tie driven by a base desire that it seemed could only be satisfied by Saeric. *It kept me alive whilst all around me succumbed to their callousness*, he reminded himself, *but at what cost?*

'What about me?' protested Eadwald, breaking into Saeric's thoughts. The ealdorman took one of the tankards from Hildelith and held it out whilst she filled it from the jug. He glanced at Saeric. 'What happened just now? It was as though you connected with some new part of yourself.'

Yes, I did, Saeric thought, taking a mug from Hildelith. He took a long swig of the frothy drink, gulping it down to quench his thirst. The day was muggy with oppressive heat. He frowned, still troubled by the unexpected intervention in his head. *No,* he cautioned himself, *it's a delusion invented by your desperate mind*. 'I'm not sure what happened,' he answered.

'Well, it worked,' the ealdorman said. He cocked his head and considered his pupil for a moment, then came to a decision. 'I believe it's time you forged your sword.' He leaned past Saeric and called for Heremund.

There was a clatter from within the smithy, then the tall, broad-shouldered blacksmith appeared and strode over to the yard, rubbing his hands on his apron. 'What may I do for you, my Lord?' Heremund asked, winking at Saeric.

'He is ready,' Eadwald said, clapping Saeric on the shoulder.

Heremund nodded thoughtfully. 'Very well,' he said, then noticed Hildelith standing behind them. 'Oh, ale.' His face lit up at the prospect of refreshment. His face fell when Hildelith tipped the jug upside down to show it was empty.

'I'll get some more,' Hildelith said with a grin.

Heremund watched her go, and then he turned to Saeric. 'She'd make a fine wife, you know,' he said, far too loudly and with another wink.

'Heremund!' Saeric protested.

'I'm just saying,' the smith said, 'Hildelith is a woman of stature, with excellent breeding and advantageous connections.'

'You'd like that, wouldn't you?' Saeric said, a smile playing on his lips. 'Marry me off to a Saxon and get me even more tightly bound in your grip?'

'Naturally,' Heremund grinned.

'But she's Gerard's daughter,' Saeric countered, feeling uneasy that he might somehow be taking advantage of Gerard due to the debt the soldier owed him.

'Should I be offended?' Gerard asked.

'She's a good age, too,' Eadwald added, enjoying Saeric's discomfort. 'A little old at nineteen, perhaps, but you aren't the type to suffer giggling fillies, are you?'

Saeric turned to Gerard for support. After all, it was his daughter they were discussing. Unhelpfully, the retired soldier smiled in apology. 'I'm hardly going to object to my daughter marrying a nobleman, even if he does have a questionable pedigree.'

'Would you stop...' Saeric began, then he gave up, knowing it was pointless arguing with them about his ancestry. 'I'm not ready for this,' he said instead, and in a rare moment of candour, continued, 'she intimidates me.'

Heremund laughed at that. 'Aye. She'll have you knocked into shape faster than you can blink.'

'I don't need another woman to bash me into shape,' Saeric said, waving a hand over his body. 'I've already tried that.'

Heremund realised his insensitivity and nodded in understanding. 'No,' he said, his eyes falling onto Saeric's scarred chest. 'Of course you don't. Yet again, my mouth blunders into tactlessness before I can stop it.'

The awkward moment was dispelled by Hildelith's reappearance, holding a tankard in each hand. Carwyn followed, carrying a tray of thickly cut bread and a large pot of chunky broth.

'Ah, lunch,' Heremund announced, sounding relieved. He beckoned the others to follow him to the table beneath the great oak. Saeric glanced up at the leaden clouds banked to the northeast, threatening to swoop down and blot out their sun.

'Will you join us before you return to Sceaptesburh?' Carwyn asked the ealdorman.

Eadwald looked up at the sky and shook his head. 'I'd best be on my way,' he said. 'I rather suspect I'm going to get drenched by that storm as it is. Still, we could do with the relief. It's staying hot this year.' He saluted Saeric and waved at his attendant to prepare the escort for departure. 'Keep practising,' he said to his pupil. 'We are finally seeing improvement.'

Heremund swept the table clean with his arm and indicated everyone to sit. When the family had settled, he retrieved a cloth bag, which he dumped with a solid clunk in front of Saeric. 'Eadwald says you are ready, and I am a man of my word. You have earned the rest of your iron.' He nodded at Saeric to open it. 'This is Frankish steel; the best you will find. If that sword is to do all the work you will ask of it, it will need to be as strong as the man who wields it.'

Eanswith frowned up at her companion, peering into his playful blue eyes.

'What?' he asked, raising himself onto his elbows to better see her face, but he stayed on top of her, still hard and still moving, ever so slightly. It was a warm summer's afternoon, and they lay in the long, soft grass on the riverbank beyond the burh, her body shuddering with delight in the afterglow of their lovemaking, but her mind remained restless. God only knew how she'd managed to capture this alluring young man with his infectious grin and boundless energy. He was younger than her, inappropriately so, but nicely developed in all the right places, not especially bright, and entirely in her thrall: a perfect companion.

'So, you know what to do?' she asked again.

He nodded thoughtfully, as though her instructions had been complex and deserving of great deliberation. *Thank God he is good in the hay*, she thought, wondering whether she might need to repeat her directions one last time. Until this newest conquest, Eanswith had struggled to find a new partner in play since Sugu's escape. To her surprise, Edward's boy was not to her taste, despite him being uncommonly beautiful and well-versed in the commixtion arts. If Edward was to be believed, the little pervert had been trained by his former master, which should have boded well for her, but it transpired she liked men now, not boys.

The youth lying upon her, with his nicely shaped arms and smooth, muscular chest, was barely a man himself, but she found his company revitalising after the brooding intensity of Sugu, or Saeric, as he now called himself. Strange how she still yearned for him. It irritated her to varying degrees, sometimes greatly, for Sugu could be relied upon to make an appearance in her thoughts whenever she was indulging her womanly needs with her young paramour, who was so far removed from Sugu in every way that it was absurd, or pathetic, depending upon her mood. This new lover had – so far at least – shown a distinct aversion to her more extreme proposals, but he made up for it with his impressive stamina, enthusiasm, and imagination. Truth be told, though, sex just wasn't the same without a sharp blade in her hand and the taste of blood on her tongue. Perhaps it was time to lock this boy in a collar and irons so that he would have no choice but to do as she bade.

She sighed. *Why bother with Sugu at all?* she wondered, then let out an involuntary cry when the boy thrust at her without warning, then laughed at her startled response that quickly turned to irritation. He did it again, so she grabbed his neck and dragged him down onto her. She bit his ear hard, and he let out a cry.

Let Sugu go, she told herself. *I have a new plaything now*. But her jilted heart stubbornly reminded her that Sugu had betrayed her; not by escaping, although that was irksome, certainly. It had always amazed her how he had managed to stay alive all that time, despite the brutal treatment he had endured at her father's and brother's hands. Nor had he attempted to get away from them. Of course, other slaves had tried to escape, and a few had succeeded, but most were hunted down, executed, and fed to the dogs and pigs. She liked to think it was because Sugu had come to need her as much as she did him, so he did not want to leave. That could be the only explanation, surely?

No, your mistake has been finding yourself another woman, she thought. *Time to fulfil my promise. The dish is cold.*

Time to strike.

'Heremund is right. Saeric *is* very strong,' Hildelith said, admiring how the muscles in the Briton's arms and shoulders flexed as he hauled on the bellows to keep air up to the forge. The young man was stripped to the waist, and his powerful upper body glistened with sweat in the searing heat of the smithy.

'He does have a fine physique,' Carwyn agreed, smiling knowingly at the younger woman.

'Pleasant to the eye, certainly,' Hildelith grinned, distracted from her sewing. The two women sat beside one another in the shade of the great oak, enjoying each other's company while their men worked together at the forge. It was yet another hot, unsettled day – too hot for working in the smithy in Hildelith's mind – but Saeric was determined to make his sword, no matter the conditions. Heremund was shaking his head at Saeric and explaining something to him. Saeric was, in turn, frowning back at his master, one hand on the bellows handle, the other holding his blade in a pair of long-handled pincers. Crafting a sword was evidently no simple task.

Saeric lifted the glowing blade from the fire and turned to the anvil, then, under Heremund's direction, began pounding it with a heavy iron hammer. Hildelith watched him in silence, marvelling at his strength and the speed of his recovery. He seemed untroubled by the wound in his left shoulder, yet the now-puckered entry and exit holes remained fresh and angry-looking and most definitely painful in appearance. *What do you think of these latest additions to all the other scars that mark your body?* she wondered. She had also pondered what had driven him to stay alive in the face of such dreadful maltreatment. She knew that Carwyn believed Saeric to be somehow blessed by God and granted some form of immortality. Seeing him bashing that unyielding iron so soon after receiving a wound that would have killed any other man did lend credibility to that claim. He certainly seemed immune to pain and injury.

'Why does he deny his nobility?' Hildelith asked Carwyn.

The older woman looked up from her darning and tilted her head in thought. 'He does not deny it. Rather, he rejects it because whatever status he and his family may once have held, it was swept away during the overthrow of our kingdom. Saeric is an orphan with no home and no family. That is why he has such an uneasy relationship with Heremund.'

'Father says that is why he came here. That he sought revenge against the Iron Fist for his part in the conquest of Dumnonia.'

'Aye, Bishop Ealhstan wonders whether Saeric might even be an escaped rebel, and those scars are the marks of his torture from his captors in Escanceaster.'

'A rebel?' The prospect intrigued Hildelith, and it would certainly explain Saeric's occasionally surly attitude towards his new Saxon masters.

'There are some in the far west of Dumnonia who still desire a return to the old days,' Carwyn said. 'From time to time, the Kernowyon cause trouble, but invariably they are caught and executed. Is Saeric a rebel? I don't think so. I believe his tale of enslavement to that diabolical family. But whatever his past, I am certain that his coming here was no coincidence, yet my husband insists that Saeric did not know he was the Iron Fist until after the attack at the ford. When Bishop Ealhstan raised the matter again recently, Heremund pointed out that Saeric has been with us since St Agatha's Day and could have slit our throats on one of a hundred nights thereafter. He saved your father's life and was grievously wounded trying to save Leo's. If he wished ill toward us, why go to such lengths to defend us?'

'I suppose you must be right,' Hildelith said, 'but if he hates us so much and is so angry about what happened to him and his family, why does he stay here?'

'I told you. He has nowhere else to go to.'

'But he's Dumnonian. Why doesn't he just go back there?'

'I imagine it is because he fears that all he'll find upon his return will be the charred bones of his family scattered in the burnt-out ruins of his home.'

'Lady Carwyn!' Hildelith protested.

'I was in Escanceaster on the day it fell, Hildelith, and so was he. He is tormented by memories of that time. Imagine what it must have been like for a little boy, for that's all he was, separated from his family, surrounded by flames and slaughter, hearing the screams of the women and children as they were hacked to pieces in home after home, the stench of blood and smoke suffocating him….' Her voice trailed off as she remembered the horror of that most debased of days. She crossed herself and muttered thanks to God for having had pity on her.

'Oh, Lady Carwyn,' Hildelith said, seeing the distress she caused. 'I am so sorry. I should not have said anything.'

'No, for that very reason, Heremund offered Saeric a place in our household. It is a small measure of atonement for my husband's part in those violations.'

'Even though Saeric came here intending to hurt you?' Hildelith sighed. 'You are remarkable people; much better than Lord Dunstan.'

Carwyn let out a wry laugh. 'That would not be difficult.' She paused and put aside her sewing. 'I suppose I like to think that Saeric stays because he finds some measure of peace here in Heremund's and my partnership, even if he doesn't know it himself.'

Hildelith thought about that as she watched Saeric hammer away at his sword, wondering what it might be like to feel those strong arms wrapped around her waist.

Clang, clang, clang.

'I think you are right, Lady Carwyn. You are Dumnonian yourself. He finds solace in that too, I am sure.'

Hildelith watched Saeric for a while, contemplating what life with him might be like, and wondering what fate may have held for him had the new Dumnonian king not won his battle against Cadwyr. She turned back to Carwyn. 'One thing I do not understand; not one part of him is unscathed. If he was so defiant to require such punishment, why not just get rid of him?'

'Because those are not the marks of disobedience, Hildelith,' Carwyn said, more harshly than she had intended. 'That woman used him in all the cruellest ways you can imagine. He was her plaything: a living, breathing doll that she could torture to satisfy her wicked desires. She had him in a collar with a chain attached, like a dog. You've heard the story of the star on his chest. He does not speak of it, but it is obvious that he suffered the most dreadful torments for years. He knows nothing of intimacy. Lovemaking to him means sodomy, pain and terror.'

Hildelith's expression darkened. 'I would like to meet that woman,' she said coldly.

'Saeric won't let Heremund seek her out. He believes that she and her family are servants of the Devil and possess powers that make them untouchable. Having seen what they have done to him, I do not doubt it. Saeric is terrified of her. He is safe out of her reach here, and he is keen for it to stay that way.'

'What they have done is repugnant.'

'They do say that about the Devil's work.'

'Well, Saeric is free of her now, and I shall show him that we are not all born of evil.'

Carwyn smiled at the younger woman. 'Does Saeric have any say in this?'

'My father is of noble stock, as you know, my Lady,' Hildelith said defensively, 'and I am tired of being overlooked because of palace intrigue. Despite all his flaws, I can't help that I like him.'

'Who, your father?'

'No, my Lady,' she replied testily. 'Saeric.'

Carwyn chuckled. 'Your father was in the wrong, Hildelith,

and it is only thanks to the intervention of Earls Heremund and Eadwald that he kept his head.'

'Father was innocent! And why should that mean I be forever doomed to spinsterhood? No one has ever proved that my father killed the king. It was Eadburgh who poisoned him. At least father got his revenge on her. I've heard that she is still alive, begging in the streets of some Frankish town.'

'*Queen* Eadburgh, Hildelith,' Carwyn reminded her, 'and you should not be so quick to find joy in her fall. One misstep and you could easily find yourself in the same circumstances.'

'She got what she deserved,' Hildelith said, unrepentant. 'She killed my great uncle.'

'Oh, Hildelith, I'm not sure your family squabbles are entirely to blame for your lack of suitors, do you?' Carwyn added, her expression softening.

'Lady Carwyn!'

'Gerard is right when he says you are, what is it, forthright? And you prefer manly pursuits. Most noblemen I have met fancy a wife who understands her place in society and his household. The wife's role is to do all she can to make her man shine, not the other way around.'

Hildelith threw down her sewing, crossed her arms and glared at the British noblewoman. 'Poppycock, and that's rich coming from you, my Lady, who happens to work as a blacksmith.'

'I am an artisan, a maker of fine jewellery. Blacksmiths are like those two; all muscle and brute force, bashing and clattering their way through the day like a thunderstorm.' On cue, there was a distant rumble from the storm to the northeast.

'That still doesn't make what you do a womanly chore.'

Carwyn let out a sigh. 'Your father has done you no favours indulging you in the way he has. You must learn to be more courteous when speaking to your superiors.'

'I don't *mean* to be rude, Lady Carwyn,' Hildelith said, frustrated, 'and what is so wrong with being taught to read and write? You make it sound as though it is a mortal sin.'

'There are many who believe that the only women who should read are nuns, and even that is questionable. Writing is the preserve of men. And given that the vast majority of noblemen can't read *or* write,' Carwyn said pointedly, 'no husband will permit you to pursue that interest lest it makes him look inferior, which it will, because you won't be able to help yourself.'

'You're jealous!' Hildelith protested. 'You're angry because you can't read, whereas the rest of us can, even Saeric.'

'No, I am not,' Carwyn replied, exasperated. 'I am perfectly satisfied with the small amount of Latin that I can understand. I am sad for you because you are a bright, beautiful woman whose options in life have been severely limited by your father's poor choices and his overindulging of you.'

'Well, that's all going to change because I have found a man worthy of my attention.' She frowned up at the smithy, and to her surprise, Saeric turned and looked at her. He was panting from the effort of hauling on the bellows and hammering the iron, his broad chest heaving attractively as he paused in his work. He smiled at her, and Hildelith felt her desire flare. The moment passed when Heremund barked an instruction to his apprentice, and Saeric returned to his blade.

'He likes me, I am sure of it,' Hildelith said, as much to convince herself as Carwyn.

'Which brings me back to the start of this conversation,' Carwyn said. 'He does like you, but you need to be careful with him.'

Hildelith frowned at the older woman. 'I can look after myself,' she assured her.

'He bludgeoned five men to death with a ploughshare, Hildelith. His raw brutality frightened Gerard, and if you won't listen to me, pay heed to your father. He says that the man who killed those brigands was not the Saeric you so admire. He bore the face of Saeric, but his violent actions were those of someone or something altogether different. You know that Brother Donagh thinks him possessed by a demon.'

'You just told me *not* to listen to my father,' Hildelith scoffed, 'who we all know is prone to exaggeration, and as for old father Dummer....'

Carwyn shook her head. 'I have seen that face your father describes. It is certainly not the Saeric you so desire.' She paused, shuddering at the memory of Saeric on that day when Bishop Ealhstan had visited. 'Heremund knocked him out before he could do me any harm, but I knew what he intended, Hildelith. His eyes were those of a madman.'

'What are you saying, Lady Carwyn?' Hildelith asked, annoyed that Heremund's wife could not just say, "good luck," or "yes, he is a fine-looking fellow," or any one of a hundred things a woman might say to encourage a sister in love. 'Surely you don't believe him possessed?'

'I don't know what to think, Hildelith. Sometimes I think of him as some kind of avenging angel, working on the side of good, and at other times I wonder if the bishop is right and we are harbouring a monster. Saeric hears words in his head that he says are the voice of the Devil. What I do know is that he frightened himself as much as he did me when he threatened me. That is why he avoids you, indeed all of us. He is afraid that he might hurt us. But you are a good soul, so perhaps you will find a way through his pain and fear of himself. But you must be patient and vigilant.'

Hildelith said nothing in reply, mulling over Carwyn's cautionary words as she watched Saeric at work. *And yet he chose to save my father*, she reminded herself, *and he killed those men in defence of Leofwynn, so he cannot be all bad?* 'Well, I shall heed your words, Lady Carwyn, and I shall earn his trust and perhaps even his love one day.'

Carwyn softened and smiled at the young woman. 'If you manage it, I am sure it will be the making of him.'

Hildelith looked long and hard at Carwyn, but the noblewoman appeared to be speaking honestly. 'Well then,' Hildelith said, 'I shall start immediately.' Abandoning her sewing, she rose and walked across to the smithy.

2

A sword of kings

Heremund's Smithy, Scirburne, Wessex

Hildelith's plan came awry as quickly as she had decided to execute it. Her first chosen task was to clean up Saeric's sleeping place, starting with his clothes, which were, in her opinion, badly in need of a good scrubbing.

'You don't have to do that,' Saeric said from the other side of the forge.

'It is no bother,' she replied.

'I don't need others to serve me,' Saeric said, pausing in his work, clearly intending to come over to take his clothes from her.

'But I *want* to, Saeric,' she countered, holding firm.

'Why?' he frowned, apparently bemused.

'Because she fancies you, numbskull,' Heremund offered. 'Which demonstrates unwise judgement in my view, but there's no accounting for love.'

'Lord Heremund!' Hildelith scolded.

Saeric's reaction mirrored Hildelith's indignation, and the burly smith laughed at them both. 'It's too late to back out now, Saeric,' Heremund said. 'And why the fuss? You've let her care for you these past few weeks, and I've not heard a peep out of you.'

Saeric ignored Heremund, took his clothes from Hildelith, and dropped them onto his bed. 'Thank you, but no. I don't have time for a wife.'

Hildelith raised her hands in contrition and backed away, not wanting to further upset Saeric.

Heremund shook his head at his apprentice. 'Would it be so bad to allow a woman through your defences?'

'What, like the one who did this to me?' Saeric snapped, jabbing at the star on his chest. 'Or how about the old villein who fattened me up to sell me into slavery in the first place?' He turned to Hildelith. 'I don't want your kindness.'

'Well, thank you,' flared Hildelith, 'I'm glad I went to all that trouble to look after you. You ungrateful dalcop.'

'I didn't ask for it,' Saeric said.

'And that's your problem,' Hildelith countered. 'You don't ask for anything, but trust me, you need help. Lots of it.'

'So, what is it *you* want?' Saeric demanded, dropping the iron blade on the anvil with a clang and throwing the pincers onto the bench. They landed amongst the other tools with a loud crash. 'I know you're after something.'

'Calm down, Saeric,' Heremund warned his apprentice. 'She cares about you, as we all do.' He turned to the young woman. 'Perhaps you should go, Hildelith.'

'Not until he apologises to me,' Hildelith said obstinately, unable to let it pass. 'I am not like that other woman.'

Saeric glared at them both, but it was clear that he knew he had gone too far.

'Damn you, Saeric,' Heremund said. 'This has gone on long enough. I am going to put this to rest once and for all.'

'How?' Saeric said. 'She is a demon, born of Hell itself.'

'All the more reason to shove a stake through her heart!'

Saeric shook his head and retrieved the pincers from the bench, then he snatched up his iron, rammed it into the coals, and pulled hard on the bellows. The fire roared to life, and the coals crackled and glowed.

'Saeric, this is not something you can do when you're angry.'

He pulled out the glowing metal and then slammed the mallet on it. Clang!

'Saeric!'

'I will put all my anger and hurt into this blade,' he said.

Clang!

He bashed harder and harder, then suddenly, he stopped mid-strike, let out a wail and dropped the mallet. The raw blade fell to the floor with a clank, and Saeric sank to his knees, his face twisted in distress.

Heremund at first thought his apprentice had hit his thumb, but he quickly realised that something more serious afflicted Saeric. The smith hurried around to the young Briton, who had dropped to the ground, his face screwed up in agony. Saeric cried out again and clenched a hand over his heart.

'Saeric!' Heremund shouted. 'What is it? What's happening?'

'Alrik!' Saeric cried. 'Alrik, no!'

Heremund reached out to take Saeric in his arms, but the Briton staggered to his feet, shaking his head. He stumbled out into the yard, wailing inconsolably.

'What in God's name is happening?' Heremund said, following his charge out of the smithy and waving at Hildelith to get out of the way. That it was another of Saeric's turns was evident, but this was the worst he'd seen yet. He called for Carwyn, but she was already there.

Saeric began walking in small circles in the yard, his eyes closed, fists clenched, repeatedly crying 'why?' to himself. He was utterly lost to them. Carwyn moved to touch him, but Heremund called her away.

'One of you fetch my sword,' he instructed his boys, who had appeared as soon as they'd heard Saeric's screams, 'and the other find Gerard. Does anyone know where he is?'

'He's up at the mynster,' Hildelith said.

'Of course he is,' muttered Heremund, 'with his nose buried in a bloody book, no doubt. Get him down here, quick!'

None of them could get through to the Briton, who stumbled about the yard like a drunkard. He walked into the wall, staggered sideways, and tripped over the cooling barrel, toppling it and spilling dark water onto the ground. He lurched a few more steps, then sank to his knees, breathing heavily, his arms wrapped around his shoulders. He rolled onto his side, drew in his legs, and curled up in the mud beside the upturned barrel. He lay like that for a long time, whimpering, his eyes closed, his face twisted in torment.

Gerard arrived, panting from having run across town from the monastery, but the danger was over, for the time being, at least. Heremund handed his sword to Gerard and crouched down beside Saeric. He rested his hand lightly on Saeric's arm.

'Saeric, it's me. Do you know who I am?'

Saeric looked up at Heremund, at first not recognising him, then his eyes came into focus, and he nodded. He looked like a small, vulnerable child. The air had taken on a chill, and the sky was darkening with the oncoming storm.

'Let's get you inside,' Heremund said, and he put his arms around his apprentice and hauled him to his feet. Saeric did not resist, allowing himself to be led back to his bedplace in the smithy. Gerard brought him a mug of warmed mead while Heremund shooed the women away. Carwyn and Hildelith retired to the hall reluctantly, but Heremund firmly resisted their objections.

'Did I hurt anyone?' was Saeric's first question.

Heremund let out a long breath. 'No. What happened?'

'I don't know. One moment I'm working on my sword, then....' He turned and looked for the blade. Heremund had, of course, picked it up from the floor.

Heremund followed his gaze and assured his apprentice the iron was fine. 'It's a little bent, but you can straighten it out easily enough.'

Saeric took a sip of the mead, and then he drank the entire mug. He put it aside and drew a breath. 'It has something to do with my brother. I think I was feeling what he was feeling. Something terrible has happened.'

'You called out a name,' Heremund said. 'Orlric or something like that?'

Saeric closed his eyes and saw the tear-streaked face of a blond-haired youth. He shuddered and blinked away the image. 'I think someone has died.'

'Your brother?' Gerard asked, shocked.

Saeric shook his head. 'No. It was a young man dressed the same way as Caelin. I think it was him who died, and I was feeling my brother's distress. He must have been important to Caelin.' Saeric still felt a strong sense of loss and despair, and he knew that it would take very little for him to fall back into that bleak place. 'I can still feel him now. It's stronger than ever before.'

Gerard looked behind him and spotted Heremund's ale jug. He poured a full measure for Saeric and handed it to him.

'How often do you… feel Caelin?' Heremund asked. 'It seems to be happening more often.'

'I think it was him showing me what to do during sword practice the other day,' Saeric said. He looked up at them both, then let out a short, ironic laugh. 'You must think I'm mad.'

'No,' Gerard said, his tone thoughtful. 'You did seem to leap straight from walk to canter. It's the first time you've caught old Eadwald off guard.' He poured himself an ale but only got half a mug from the jug before it ran out. He peered into it, momentarily disappointed, then shrugged and drank it down, dregs and all. 'So how does it happen?' he asked. 'How does he tell you what to do?'

Saeric frowned in thought. 'He was speaking to me, in my mind. I fought it for a bit, and then I let him take over. I thought it was the Devil at first. That's who usually talks to me.'

Gerard and Heremund exchanged glances. 'Well, let him do it some more,' Gerard said. 'Your brother knows what he's talking about.'

Saeric let out a sigh. He felt utterly drained by the whole episode. 'I wish I knew how to find him.'

'If he really was taken by heathens,' Heremund said, 'then you have no hope whatsoever of locating him. They arrive in their demon ships from Hell and vanish again before anyone can go after them.'

'Then I have to find one of those ships and get on it. They will take me to him.'

'No, they'll cut off your head and throw your body overboard, or worse, take you to Hell with them.' Heremund leaned forward and looked into his apprentice's troubled face. 'Saeric, listen to me. You made a vow to yourself and your family. You must not lose your way.'

'I've already lost my way, living this easy life here,' he objected. 'I should have acted sooner.'

'No, you were not ready; you're still not ready. We've been through all this. You are on the right path, but you must be patient. You have help. Here, now. Caelin, if he is alive, which I very much doubt, will have to make his own way.'

'He is alive, and it isn't Hell. They are people like us. I am sure of it.'

'No, they are monsters who wreak destruction on our towns and sacred places–'

'Then where is God? Shouldn't He be protecting His churches from the demons, if that's what they are?'

Heremund let out a sigh. 'Very well then. Consider this. Caelin was a newborn babe when he was taken. Let's pretend they are men, not demons from Hell. The chances of him surviving the journey back to wherever they come from are nil. Why would they take a baby as a slave? What possible use would a bairn be?' He stopped, a horrifying realisation coming to him. He'd heard the rumours of them roasting babies on spits. Was that Caelin's fate? To be a meal on the sea journey back home or a treat for the feast on arrival? Or some other diabolical sacrifice on the altar of their blood-hungry heathen Gods?

'What is it?' Saeric asked, seeing Heremund's troubled expression.

'Nothing,' Heremund said, grunting as he got back to his feet. He began to put away the abandoned tools from the forge and workbench. 'You will have to trust that Caelin will find you when he is ready or when God ordains it, just as you came to us. There are clearly greater forces than us at work here, and you must learn to have faith in them. Now, do you want your dinner brought out here, or will you join us in the house? I think we shall take the afternoon off, yes?'

'Have you told Carwyn and Hildelith who I am?' he asked.

'No, and you must keep your brother's name to yourself too. We must keep your identity a secret, Saeric. If Talec or Mael get any hint of your reappearance, they will come after you in force. I think you know that. As far as everyone is concerned, you are one of the many Dumnonian nobles who lost their home and title after the fall of Cadwyr. Which is the truth, is it not? You just happen to be a little nobler than the rest.' He rubbed his chin in thought. 'Carwyn and the Bishop are convinced you came here to do me harm, but that God turned you from that destructive path, and instead, you have chosen to accept my offer of a place in this household as atonement for my part in your pain and suffering. Your saving Gerard's life explains his devotion to you, so I think your story is perfectly plausible.'

Gerard nodded in agreement.

'What about Eadwald?' Saeric asked, frowning.

Heremund let out a long breath. 'That will require more thought, methinks. He was once my subordinate, so perhaps I have asked him to take you under his wing. But you are right; we need to be careful that we do not draw the wrong kind of attention to you simply by virtue of those who mentor you. I shall talk to Eadwald about this. In the meantime, we will avoid mention of your noble past. I think you should also stop wearing that ridiculous thrall's crown of Eadwald's.'

He got no argument from Saeric. It was bad enough that Heremund and Gerard knew his identity, let alone Eadwald, the

Westseaxna King's master-at-arms, for God's sake.

'And stop being so hard on Hildelith. I know that she is far from conventional; you can blame her father for that,' and Heremund threw a disapproving glance at Gerard, 'but if you trouble yourself to get to know her, I think you will fast come to appreciate all that she can offer you.'

Saeric shook his head. 'I don't need anyone to look after me.'

'Yes, you do,' Heremund said. 'There is only so much that Gerard, I or Eadwald can do, and you can't have Carwyn because she is already taken. But you need not worry; your latest outburst will have driven Hildelith away.'

Saeric sighed. 'I know it was wrong to say she is like Eanswith. She is nothing like her.'

'Listen, Saeric,' Heremund said, 'it is perfectly understandable that you would not want anything to do with another woman after all you suffered at that witch's hands. I am sorry for making light of it. Now, you need to rest, and we need our dinner. We can talk more about this another day. In the meantime, if you want to honour your brother, you must finish that sword.'

Eanswith shifted position, unable to get comfortable thanks to the gnarled tree roots pressing into her knees. It wasn't an ideal hiding place, crouched beside the small brook that ran past the smithy, and she would need to move on soon lest she be spotted. She moved the wicker washing basket out of the way and shuffled sideways like a crab, frustrated that the shrubbery obscured her view, no matter where she knelt. The movement brought an unpleasant waft of sour sweat and body odour, and she wrinkled her nose in disgust. Her disguise as a lowly housemaid had been an excellent last-minute plan, but now she regretted paying the stupid girl for her basket and filthy clothes. God only knew what awful things inhabited the rags. She scratched her side in a reflexive action, imagining the mites crawling around her skin and biting her with their tiny fangs. The smarter play would have been to cut the girl's throat and take what she needed; the accursed villein wench was probably crowing right now to her equally disgusting villein mate about the well-dressed noblewoman who had paid so handsomely for her clothes and wash basket. *I can be so stupid sometimes*, Eanswith thought, then she reflected that leaving a naked body with a slashed throat down by the river would have created all manner of problems. *Damn you, Sugu, why don't you just come to your senses and return to me?*

She had, of course, come here against her brother's bidding. Edward had again told her in his most contrary tone to leave alone that which cannot be hers, and he had refused to help her. *Idiot. I should have wrung that new slave's neck when I had the chance.* Thanks to the dark-skinned little fiend, Edward had no interest in Sugu anymore. *Very well. All the better. I shall have Sugu to myself.*

She had watched her former scortum working away in the smithy, her desire manifesting itself as a deep ache in her chest and a tingling in her loins. He had grown so deliciously powerful in both body and fury, but his vulnerability had seemingly grown alongside them; a potent combination that Eanswith found difficult to resist. Most interestingly, what she had always thought to be a response to her ministrations on him – some kind of release of pent-up rage driven by the demon that evidently possessed him – now appeared to be rather more than that. At least Earl Heremund and that old soldier felt them significant, from what she had overheard of the conversation in the aftermath of Sugu's fit. Curiously, they did not think it the work of a demon, although they had known him for only a few months; what would they say had they witnessed him with Eanswith? She shuffled back to her previous position, from where she could at least see Sugu's face. He was sitting alone now on his pallet in the smithy, staring out into space. Why on earth he insisted on sleeping there was a mystery to her, but he had always been an odd one, that was for sure. She had wanted to bring him into the house, but he had refused, preferring the shit-smeared floor of the byre. She so desperately wanted to go to him now; he would probably fly into her arms in his current state, but she would never get him away from here in broad daylight.

Through the screen of leaves, she could see a snippet of his broad chest and left shoulder, pleasingly filled out and well-muscled thanks to his newfound profession and a more fulsome diet. Her star-shaped brand above his heart remained reassuringly distinct on his skin, and she smiled in memory of that day. Despite cursing her brother for his intervention at the time, she was pleased Edward had put a stop to her game. She hadn't intended to kill Sugu at all, but her excitement had got the better of her, so it had been just as well that Edward had dragged her off Sugu when he'd seen what she was doing.

She caught a glimpse of Sugu's new woman near the house, and a nasty smile played on her lips. *You may desire him, foolish girl*, she thought, *but you won't know how to satisfy him, and he will likely break your neck on your first outing. What you have just witnessed is nothing!* This thought calmed her, but she still felt the hot sting of jealousy, and it had taken a considerable effort of will to prevent herself from leaping from her hiding place to wring the girl's neck as she cooed about Sugu. Sugu was clearly interested in her, despite his outward spurning of her attentions, so perhaps mitigating action was required. *Or should I allow fate to run its course and let Sugu unleash his worst upon her?* The problem was that this Hildelith wasn't a silly girl at all. Far from it, it seemed. Nor should it come as any surprise that Sugu had sought out a strong-willed woman like Eanswith. *So, a threat to be dealt with*, Eanswith decided. *After all, did she not say that she wanted to meet me? Shall I arrange that?*

She tilted her head in thought, still mindful of her previous disastrous attempt to kidnap Sugu's earlier girlfriend, companion or whatever she had been. Surely not his lover, at any rate. *What had I been thinking?* It had always been a terrible plan, but Edward had, as usual, caved into her demands. Unfortunately, the spectacular failure of that mission had hardened Edward against her. She leaned back for a moment, easing the pressure on her aching knees. *I will deal with her myself, with a little help from my new devotee*, she thought. *He must have arrived by now. I wonder how he is settling in?*

She frowned in thought, her eyes returning to Sugu. He hadn't moved, and his face also bore a thoughtful expression. Her neck tingled as she looked upon him, wondering if what she had suspected for some time now might not be as far-fetched as she'd told herself, although how on God's Earth he had ended up in her hands was beyond comprehension. It was so improbable that there had to be some greater hand at work here. God certainly worked in highly mysterious ways sometimes. Or was it the Devil? Sugu had said that the two of them were his servants, and she readily believed it, for God would not have sanctioned the games the two of them had partaken in, particularly those in which her brother had also participated.

Sugu had had the occasional episode like this when he had been her slave, and she had learned from those ravings that he'd had a brother, more than one, perhaps. But the name he had returned to over and again was this Caylin. Somehow Caylin had been his responsibility, but Sugu had failed to protect him so that Caylin was now with the Devil too. Not dead, though, because Sugu had insisted that Caylin was alive, taken by heathen raiders if her understanding of the conversation she had just overheard was accurate. But what was most interesting was that Earl Heremund seemed to know this already. He had shown no surprise. Instead, he seemed to know of this Caylin, and he knew that the name meant danger for Sugu. And so her mind now turned back to the long-discarded myth of the Dumnonian royal family: that the two youngest boys had supposedly survived the rout but had never been heard from since.

What if one of the children was named Caylin? And what, then, is your name? she wondered, peering at Saeric. She knew it wasn't Saeric, that was certain. *I must find out,* she decided. Her heart quickened at the thought that she had one of the Dumnonia crown princes in her thrall. No wonder he'd had such a fierce desire to live! But then her mind turned to the puzzle that lay before her. If Sugu really was one of the lost princes, then why in God's name was he here, of all places? Why did he seek the hospitality of his enemy? It made no sense at all, other than the obvious reason of revenge. But she saw no evidence of such an intent. *Unless you are a truly devious monster*, she thought, impressed and excited by that prospect. She imagined the shock that would ripple through King Ecgberht's court when the news came one day that Ealdorman Heremund and his family had been inexplicably murdered and strung up by their entrails by their Dumnonian adoptee.

Sugu lifted his head and stared right at her. She let out a little gasp. His frown deepened, and he stood up, peering into the bushes. Eanswith held her breath and stayed dead still, like a rabbit caught by a wolf's nose; smelt but as yet unseen. *Hardly surprising given what I'm wearing*, Eanswith thought, annoyed. *Or can you sense me?* she wondered, certain that he could. She knew he'd been aware of her presence back at Easter. They seemed to share some strange bond in that way; he had certainly known when she was needful of him, and she felt that carnal urge now, strongly. Again she resisted the temptation to go to him. It would be madness, she knew, but her body's yearning for him was remarkably strong. *He rejected me*, she reminded herself, angry that she was fawning like some pathetic teenage girl over the object of her wrath.

She waited. Sugu stood there, glaring at her, his nostrils flaring as he sniffed the air, just like the wolf he imitated. Then the flame-haired twins broke the spell, bursting noisily into view, bearing

Sugu's meal. Sugu blinked and turned away, releasing Eanswith, who drew in a long breath. *Time to go*, she thought, knowing it would be perilous to stay a moment longer. She carefully retrieved the basket and backed away down the burn, keeping her eyes fixed on Sugu as she went. He looked up at one point, peering in her direction, but the connection had been broken, so she made good her escape.

You are too comfortable in your new life, she thought as she hurried back to her horse, keen to rid herself of these filthy garments. She was sure she could feel the nits crawling deeper into her hair, and she cursed and vigorously scratched at her scalp. She took one last look back up the hill towards the smithy, but it was hidden by the trees and shrubs that cloaked the path down to the river.

It's time to get you back.

Four days after Saeric's fit, he and Gerard were working up a sweat in the outer yard, practising swordplay. Heremund, Carwyn and the boys were up at Dunstan's burh sharing a meal with Burghild. Gerard and Saeric remained outcasts from Dunstan's Hall, so they had decided to take advantage of the dry weather and get some exercise. Saeric welcomed the diversion because he had been unable to shake the foreboding impression that Caelin was in distress, which in turn upset Saeric because he was utterly unable to offer any help or solace to his brother. He was also troubled by the niggling sense that Eanswith had been nearby, although he knew that had to be impossible. And yet...

It was Saeric who spotted Hildelith leaning against the smithy wall, arms crossed, watching them. Worryingly, she wore riding trousers and a sword. Only then did Saeric see one of Hildelith's attendants holding the bridle of a horse over by the gate.

Saeric raised his hand to stop the bout, and Gerard turned to see what had distracted his trainee. He let out a grunt of surprise when he saw who it was.

'What are you up to?' Gerard asked, walking over to his daughter, panting a little.

'You need to take more care of yourself, father,' she scolded. 'You know you shouldn't over-exert yourself.'

'I am perfectly fine, my dear,' he said testily, 'and don't change the subject. Why are you here?'

'He is still in thrall to that woman,' Hildelith replied, pointing at Saeric. 'I intend to put this matter to rest since you won't.' She paused, then caught Saeric's eye. 'You need to come with me.'

'Don't be ridiculous,' Gerard snapped. 'Return to your grandmother's and stay out of this. You don't know who she is or where she comes from, and Saeric won't tell you or show you.'

'I don't need him to,' Hildelith replied haughtily. 'Unlike you, father, I have taken the trouble to find out. It wasn't particularly hard.'

'What? How?' Saeric blurted.

'I am well aware of her identity,' Gerard said. 'You will not go there.'

'I'm not afraid of her,' Hildelith said.

'You should be,' Gerard warned. 'They are not a house to be trifled with.'

'You can't go there,' Saeric agreed.

'Really?' Hildelith asked caustically. 'Afraid I might get hurt? If anyone's in danger of injury, it isn't me. Give me that,' she said, nodding at Saeric's blunted practice sword.

Saeric hesitated, glancing at Gerard.

'Must I take it off you?' Hildelith asked.

Saeric reluctantly handed his weapon to her. She tested it and shook her head with distaste.

'Hildelith, stop this,' Gerard said in a vain attempt to control his errant daughter.

Hildelith drew her sword and handed it to Saeric. 'A wager then. You beat me, and I will leave that woman alone. If I win, you, me and my father will pay her a sociable visit.'

'I'm not going to fight you,' Saeric objected, 'and your sword is blunt. The one you've given me is sharp.'

She struck him hard on his sword arm with the practice sword. 'It still hurts, though, doesn't it?' she said.

Saeric spat out an expletive and inadvertently dropped his sword.

'Hildelith!' Gerard snapped. 'That's enough!'

'Stand aside, father,' she said. 'None of you has been able to knock sense into him, so it's my turn.' She picked up the fallen sword and held it back out to Saeric. 'Ready, or are you afraid of me like you are that witch?'

Saeric took the sword and stepped away from her.

'Hildelith,' Gerard warned again. 'Saeric will hurt you. You don't understand what you're doing.'

'Hold it like this!' Hildelith said, ignoring her father. She stepped forward and grabbed Saeric's wrist, rotated the sword slightly in his hand, and then let him go. 'I am beginning to wonder if your ineptitude is not because of a lack of training but that you are, in fact, genuinely stupid.'

'I'm not stupid,' Saeric said.

'Prove it,' Hildelith teased. She flicked the practice sword deftly in her hand. 'Come on then, beat me. That's what you want to do, isn't it? You want to hurt me, so let's see if you can.'

She lunged at him. Neither combatant wore any protection, which was not lost on Saeric. Hildelith immediately had Saeric on the back foot as she pressed forward in attack, and she danced around him like a spring lamb annoying a grumpy old ram. Saeric lashed out to no effect, and suddenly she dove in and slashed him on the thigh with a heavy blow. It left no cut, of course, but had the sword been sharp, Saeric would have lost the use of his leg.

'Hildelith, stop this at once!' Gerard snapped, but she ignored him, instead attacking in a flurry of short, sharp jabs and lunges, forcing Saeric backwards. She struck him again, this time on his upper sword arm. He cursed and swung at her neck with a growl, aiming to take off her head. Incensed, Hildelith went for him, her blade crashing again and again against Saeric's sword as he held it up in defence against her onslaught. She let out a shriek, then slammed her sword so hard at Saeric's that his weapon was wrenched from his hand, and he stumbled backwards, falling onto his back in the dirt. Hildelith pounced on him, kneeing him in the stomach to wind him, then she sat on him and pressed her sword to his throat. They glared into each other's eyes, both panting from exertion.

Hildelith saw the glint of excitement and anticipation in Saeric's eyes and could feel him hardening beneath her.

She sprang off him, her suspicions confirmed. 'Christ's Bones,' she swore. 'You are still in thrall to that woman.' She threw the practice sword down and retrieved her blade. She rammed it back into its scabbard and then stalked over to her father. 'We need to deal with that witch.'

'I am well aware of that,' Gerard growled, 'but this is not your business, and nor will you act on this alone. Her house is not well disposed toward us.'

'Don't worry, father, I know I am but a woman,' she said sarcastically, 'and I'm not going anywhere without *him*.' She pointed at Saeric, who still lay on the ground, staring at her, shocked.

Gerard shook his head at his daughter and walked over to Saeric. He reached down to help the Briton to his feet. 'I can only apologise. Hildelith decided from an early age that she wanted to be a boy, or at least enjoy the training and privileges due to a first-born son. She's an only child, you see.'

'But women aren't meant to....'

'Aren't meant to what?' came a sharp retort from behind Gerard. Hildelith stood with her arms crossed, her expression dark. A stripe of blood ran down her right forearm. 'I suppose you expect me to stay home, bake bread and meekly bear your children?' she asked.

'Um... I... who said anything about children?'

Saeric took Gerard's outstretched hand, and the old soldier hauled the Briton to his feet. Saeric winced as his thigh protested, and Gerard mirrored his pupil as he strained his chest and lungs.

'Well?' Hildelith said, walking back over to Saeric. 'You haven't answered my question.'

'I daren't,' Saeric said. She wasn't going to let him off, standing beside her father with her hands on her hips, her forearm bleeding quite badly, now that Saeric could see it more closely. 'I'm just not ready for this,' Saeric went on. This was a completely different side to her. He was utterly thrown, and he found it exhilarating.

Hildelith's eyes narrowed when she realised that he was looking at her expectantly. She slapped him.

'Hildelith!' Gerard cried. 'What are you –'

She grabbed Saeric's face and kissed him hard on the mouth. He kissed her back.

Hildelith pulled away, her lips pursed. 'So, that's how to get to you,' she said quietly, then she left Saeric to it and returned to her horses.

Saeric stared after her, confused and frustrated.

'Saeric,' Gerard said firmly. 'Go and prepare the forge while I deal with my daughter.' He waited until Saeric had gone into the workshop, then he walked over to Hildelith, who was making ready to leave. 'What in God's name is the matter with you?' Gerard demanded.

'I was testing a theory.'

'What theory?'

'That the witch has cast some kind of foul spell on him. Saeric *wants* me to hurt him. You saw the way he looked at me. Violence excites him.'

'That's ridiculous. Saeric was the witch's scortum. She terrorised him. He is afraid of her, plain and simple.'

'And yet he still hankers after her, or at least for whatever wicked games she devised for him.' Hildelith tugged at her mare's girth strap, then added, 'Saeric may have run away from her, but he is not yet free.'

Gerard sighed. 'There may be other reasons he does not wish to court you, Hildelith,' he said.

'Such as?'

'Your intimidating behaviour for a start. You humiliated Saeric just now. I thought you liked him?'

'I do, but I've no chance of winning his heart until he is exorcised of that woman.'

'Damnation, Hildelith. Stay out of this!'

Hildelith considered Gerard for a long moment, then she sprang up onto the saddle and settled in for the ride back home. 'Don't worry, father, I won't act without your consent. But you do agree that something must be done?'

Gerard let out a long sigh. 'Yes, I will talk to Eadwald about it, but Saeric is very fragile, Hildelith. Would you not be better off with someone less… um… complicated?'

Hildelith gently nudged her mare's flank and turned the horse towards the road. She offered her father a wry smile. 'Simple means boring, father, and you know how much I hate being bored.'

Fashioning the sword was hard work, and it took all of Saeric's concentration to ensure he didn't ruin the blade. His mood was made a thousand times worse by the close observation of both his master and aide-de-camp, and, following a particularly irritating critique from Heremund, Saeric snapped at both men, 'do you want to make it?'

'No,' Heremund replied. 'This is something you need to do for yourself, with our help to be sure, but this blade must be forged by your hand.'

By the end of the third day, Saeric had almost completed the initial raw forging. Still, it would be more days yet before the superheated metal began to take on a familiar shape and length as he hammered, dunked, pounded and dipped. Gerard and Heremund would, from time to time, check the balance of the raw blade, making suggestions on how to improve it.

On the fifth day, the blade was ready for grinding and polishing. Eadwald appeared on the afternoon of that day, accompanied by a troop of soldiers, none of whom Saeric had seen before. All wore the standard of Ecgberht, and all seemed to be of high rank. Saeric felt uncomfortable in their presence, but their interest was primarily amusement that this determined Briton was to be taught by their ealdorman in the ways of a Saxon soldier. This angered Saeric. 'The whole of Westseaxna Ríce and therefore Dumnonia will know about me by the time you're done telling everyone,' he complained when the men were out of earshot. 'I'll be lucky to finish this before Mael sends his assassins after me.'

'Best work quickly then,' Eadwald replied, grinning. 'Don't worry,' he added, 'your secret is safe. They have no idea who you are.' The ealdorman led Saeric out into the yard and held his hand out to one of his attendants, who duly handed his lord a sword. Eadwald drew his own blade and then gave it to Saeric. 'I know you're wondering why it is taking so long to get this blade right, but you have some while yet to go. Here is why. One – mine – is properly balanced. This was made in Francia. You may have held its cousin, perhaps, back in Dumnonia. Feel how well balanced it is. Come out and swing it. I know you've held it before, but you will appreciate my point this time.'

Saeric did so, flicking and thrusting it in a series of moves that Eadwald himself had taught him. The men watched with interest. To Saeric's relief, he didn't make a fool of himself and instead was delighted by how natural the sword felt in his hand. It was a magnificent weapon, much finer than the sword that Eadwald usually wore during his training bouts with Saeric. Saeric turned the blade over, marvelling at its quality and balance. He realised that the fine pattern-welding in the polished steel was, in fact, the same as his father's sword: the sword of a king.

'No, you can't have it,' Eadwald said, grinning and holding out his hand for its return. Saeric duly gave it back and swapped it for the other blade. 'Now do the same with this one.'

Saeric did. It was horrible. It felt heavy, clumsy, with none of the fluidity of the other blade. The other had felt like an extension of his arm. This one was simply what it was: a heavy lump of iron with a handle at one end and a sharp point at the other.

'You see the difference, yes?'

Saeric nodded, handing back the sword. 'It's terrible.'

'It's one of yours,' Eadwald said.

The men chuckled. Saeric flushed angrily, not appreciating the humiliation. Heremund, likewise, harrumphed with displeasure.

'Don't be offended,' Eadwald smiled. 'It's no different from what most of my men carry. It does the job, but that's all it does. It's a utilitarian piece.' He handed the lesser blade back to his attendant, then he rested a hand on Saeric's shoulder and looked him in the eye. 'You are making a special sword for an important purpose,' he said quietly but earnestly. 'Mine was gifted to me by a king; yours will become the sword of kings.' Eadwald smiled. 'You have a talent in this, which may stand you in good stead if your quest doesn't turn out as you plan. So, to my next observation in your lessons: you are impatient for the wrong things. Yes, there are times for urgency and speed, but equally, there are occasions for care, attention and perfection. This is one of them. Take your time fashioning this weapon. You will be glad of it one day.'

With that, he mounted his horse and led his men away.

Nine days after Saeric had first dropped the ingots into the searing heat of the hearth, Eadwald returned to check on Saeric's progress. This time he had left his retinue in Dunstan's burh so that Eadwald could speak more freely. The Briton handed his freshly hilted sword to his master. The burnished blade flared in the sunlight as Eadwald inspected Saeric's handiwork. Eadwald made several thrusts and swings, then he smiled and nodded, returning it to its maker. The ealdorman turned to Heremund. 'You'd better watch out, old friend. He'll put you out of business if he sets up in competition.' He turned back to Saeric. 'How much for a score of these? No, make that two score.'

Saeric had no idea what to say.

Eadwald smiled at him. 'I mean it, I want you to make me more of these. In the meantime, however, your martial lessons start next week in Sceaptesburh. Young man, you've got a great deal more to learn beyond swordsmanship.'

'Sceaptesburh?' Saeric frowned, not at all keen to leave the security of Heremund's compound.

'I need you somewhere I can keep an eye on you, and I also need you to be out of Dunstan's reach because he will be returning soon for the winter, assuming Mercia behaves itself. Besides, Heremund has been far too soft on you. You'll be working hard over the coming months, Saeric. Depending on how well you progress, we may consider plans for the next stage in your journey. But you've got a long way to go before we set out on that road. Therefore, you will present yourself to the burh commander on Monday evening. I presume you'll be walking?'

Saeric nodded.

'You really need to learn to ride,' Eadwald said, shaking his head at the Briton. 'Everything about you shouts, "peasant." Which reminds me, don't bring your crown. Heremund is right; it might prompt too many questions.' He tapped his temple and raised his eyebrows. 'Where is it, by the way?'

With a pang of alarm, Saeric realised he wasn't wearing it. 'I didn't know you were coming,' he said, 'and Heremund said I didn't need to wear it anymore. He said it would draw attention to me.'

Eadwald's smile broadened. 'We made each other a promise,' he reminded his charge, 'and that hoop was part of our bargain.

But Heremund does have a point, I suppose. You can leave it off while you are training with my men.'

'What am I to say to them when they ask who I am?'

'You are Heremund's apprentice, and your master has asked me to knock some discipline into you.' He waved in Gerard's direction. 'You'd better bring him along too. I need someone on hand to stop you from turning native and slaughtering all my men.'

So it was that Aneurin, crown prince of Dumnonia, formally began his training in the princely arts of warcraft with one of his enemy's greatest generals, within the palisades of a Saxon fortress, amongst scores of Saxon soldiers going about their business as if nothing were out of the ordinary. Whilst in the fort, Eadwald made no observations or comments about Saeric's past but instead focused on his inadequate education, sloppy footwork and poor agility.

'The way you move, you'd be better off with a mace,' he said, smacking Saeric on the hip with the flat side of his blunt practice sword. 'Stop relying on all that brawn and start using your brain. And before you say it, no, you are not going back to your ploughshare.'

It was hard. True, Saeric had grown strong during his time as a blacksmith's apprentice, but it was all in his upper body. The furthest he'd had to move at any one time was about six yards from one end of the smithy to the other, and in most cases, that was carefully and slowly, as invariably he had a hot piece of metal clamped in his pincers. He'd developed good leg strength from lifting heavy weights; he'd been taught how to do that and keep his back straight, but again this was all brawn, not agility. As a result, much of his physical training regime involved running and jumping and climbing to improve his dexterity, and he was required to join the men in their daily military drills.

Saeric slept and ate with the garrison, and by the time autumn had set in two months later, he knew all their names, and despite himself, he couldn't help but like them. Most, in turn, came to like him, too, although there were the predictable few who treated him with the scorn due a vanquished native Briton. For the most part, however, the men treated him with respect. He'd had a head start, for, long before he arrived at the fort, the men had heard the dramatic tale of Saeric the warrior angel, who had saved the life of Gerard, who now served as Saeric's aide-de-camp by way of repaying that debt. They learned the truth behind Leofwynn's death from Gerard, countering the scurrilous lies that Dunstan had spread about the debased Briton. They instead heard a tale of exceptional valour, albeit tragically in vain, and of his brutal routing of every last one of the bandits armed with nothing more than a rudimentary farming implement. It instantly cemented Saeric's reputation amongst the fyrdsmen, who also suspected that the Briton was someone special, for why else would Eadwald be tutoring him? Rumours and speculation abounded, some of it alarmingly close to the truth, but Saeric denied all, assuring the men he was just another British refugee who, like so many of his compatriots, loathed his traitor king and wanted to avenge his murdered family. The men settled on that story, amused that they were in all probability aiding and abetting another rebel in the making. For his part, Saeric pleaded with the men to stop speculating so openly about him as his fears grew that word would somehow get back to Mael. Gerard laughed at his comrade, assuring him he had nothing to fear from that quarter. 'Your old enemy grows fat on his throne in Escanceaster, more concerned about filling his coffers with tithes and levies than any rebellion. He's long forgotten you and your family, I guarantee it.'

Some seventy or so miles to the west, a tall, lean man with a long face and dark, wide-set eyes stood on a riverside pier, arms crossed, shaking his head. 'Wrong answer,' he said, his voice calm and quiet. He wore a long, ankle-length tunic tied at the waist with a coral-studded, silver-tipped swordbelt. Today he wore no blade because he did not need one. Six of his personal guard stood in a wide arc around the subject of his attention: a slightly shorter but altogether stronger man; the stocky sea captain of a fine merchant ship tied up to the pier. A thick, damp fog enveloped them so that the furthest of the guards had taken on a ghostly form, sometimes clear, sometimes shrouded and indistinct.

'I assure you, my Lord, I paid my dues,' the captain replied, standing his ground.

Yes, but to whom? mused the King's Master-of-Coin. He perfectly understood the captain's dilemma. He obviously wouldn't admit to robbing the King of his rightful import tithes. That would end badly for him. He had undoubtedly paid a tax of sorts, but alas, it hadn't made its way to the King's coffers. So, the captain had decided to pit his word against the reeve's, hoping that he might somehow prevail. Today, he had made the right choice.

'My Lord, he lies,' the reeve in question insisted.

'Hmm,' said the Master-of-Coin. 'Throw everything overboard,' he ordered, nodding at his sergeant. A group of soldiers appeared from the mist and made their way onto the ship, clomping noisily up the gangplank onto the deck. They proceeded to rip up the decking timbers to access the goods stowed in the shallow hold.

'My Lord!' the merchant cried in dismay, holding up his hands in entreaty.

The Master-of-Coin ignored him and instead turned to his reeve, who was watching the cargo being tossed into the river, his expression smug. 'Can you swim?' the Master-of-Coin asked.

The reeve looked confused for a moment, and then his eyes widened at the same moment his master shoved him hard in the chest.

'My Lord?' the reeve bleated, echoing the merchant captain as he stumbled backwards towards the pier's edge. 'The Frank lies!' He clutched onto his master's arm in a desperate attempt to save himself from pitching into the muddy waters of the Tamar.

'Yes, he does,' the Master-of-Coin agreed, 'but so do you.' He punched the reeve in the nose with his free hand and snatched away his other as the reeve yelped in pain and shock. The Master-of-Coin followed up with a punch in the stomach, and the reeve fell backwards into the river. It was too deep to stand by the pier, and the Master-of-Coin watched his pitiful servant splash about in the water like a landed fish, struggling to breathe through his bleeding nose. Uninterested in his subordinate's fate, he turned back to the merchant.

'Be glad I've spared your life today, Frank. Go back and tell your friends that no one robs King Mael of Dumnonia.'

The merchant stared at the nobleman, then he turned to his ship, crestfallen. The last of his precious cargo was being hurled out into the river, the barrels and sacks floating a few yards out of reach. Soon they would be carried out to sea by the receding tide.

'You will leave now,' the Master-of-Coin instructed.

'But my Lord, the weather is turning, and this mist is unfavourable. It hides all manner of dangers.'

'Can you swim?'

The merchant stared at the nobleman. 'Of course I can swim,' he answered.

'Then you needn't fear your ship foundering. Take yourself out of my waters this instant, or I will tie you to your mast and set your boat afire. Your choice.'

'Lord Talec?' The tentative voice came from the mist somewhere behind him.

'What?' the nobleman snapped, his eyes still locked on the merchant.

'Dispatches from Westseaxna Ríce. There was one I thought you should hear.'

'Leave,' Talec ordered the merchant, then he turned and held out his hand to receive the report. 'Well?' he growled.

The courtier stepped forward, but he did not bear any parchment or tablet. 'My Lord, a West Saxon informant has word that a former slave, a Dumnonian, is being trained in warcraft by none other than Lord Eadwald himself.'

Talec laughed. 'Eadwald? Ecgberht's Master-at-Arms? I sincerely doubt it.'

'My Lord, the source is sound. I, too, did not believe it, so had it verified by a second source.'

Talec frowned, irritated by this fatuous interruption to the vital business of state, namely the collection of customs duties and the weeding out of corruption from amongst the King's tax collectors. 'Does this Dumnonian have a name?' he asked, his tone revealing his displeasure.

'Saeric, my Lord.' The man said it as though it should mean something to Talec.

'Never heard of him,' Talec said, turning his attention back to the trader, who was being helped with his preparations by the guards. 'Careful now,' Talec scolded his sergeant as the burly soldier slammed the captain's face against the mast. 'I need him to get back to Francia with his teeth intact so that he can pass on our message to his fellow guildsmen.'

The soldier released the captain and shoved him in the back so that the Frank fell to his knees on the deck. Talec watched as the Frankish trader hastily corralled his crew to rig the sail. It was utterly pointless as there was no wind at all, but with the tide's turning, the river current was picking up now, and all the Frank needed to do was push away from the dock, and his boat would be swept seaward.

Something about that limp sail reminded Talec of another foggy estuary, further to the west and further back in time. He wondered why the conversation he'd just had with the messenger had thrown up that memory, and he wondered why his mind was connecting the two entirely unconnected things.

He paused in his thinking, unsettled by the news and this unexpected association. Could this Saeric and the rebel who had appeared two months ago be the same person? What if the rebel had ridden not west but east, and had somehow inveigled his way into Eadwald's favours? Talec frowned. That made no sense at all. Eadwald was their ally and had faithfully honoured Mael's arrangement with Ecgberht, despite Mael's sometimes flagrant breaches of the pact. If that was the case, then who the Hell was this Saeric? The informant had to be mistaken. The fellow was probably Mercian, which would make more sense. And yet...

'Lord Talec?'

The nobleman's sergeant was trying to attract his attention. Talec turned from the fog-swathed river and scolded himself again for his overactive imagination. *Sixteen years. They're dead. Gone.* He turned to his adjutant and wrenched his mind back to the present. 'Who's next?'

3

Spelling mistakes

Sceaptesburh, Wessex

'See, I told you it would come in useful,' Eadwald said as he watched his pupil insert a new rivet into the nose guard of a fyrdsman's helmet. The ealdorman had arrived from Wiltun earlier that morning and had insisted Saeric show him his improved sword skills. Instead, he was receiving a lesson in smithing. 'You need to be careful. You might accidentally come to like us Westseaxna wealas.'

'Is that your plan?' Saeric asked, carefully tapping the rivet into place. The men of the fort had soon learned of Saeric's skills as a blacksmith, and before long, Saeric was mending all manner of items, much to Gerard's and Eadwald's amusement.

'Partly. Whilst I don't mind you chopping off a fellow Briton's head, I don't want you turning around and swinging your blade at us poor innocents.'

'Innocents?'

'Spring lambs.'

Saeric leapt up and snatched his sword from the bench beside him, but Eadwald had anticipated the move and was already on the attack by the time Saeric had taken up position on the practice ground. Saeric parried Eadwald's blow, pivoted on his heel and took a swipe at the ealdorman as the older man followed through. Eadwald ducked and flicked his blade up as he turned and danced out of harm's way. He cast his student a grin and beckoned him to try again. Saeric accepted the challenge and threw himself at the general, taking a hefty swing at the ealdorman's head. Eadwald parried expertly, entirely untroubled by his opponent's powerful but ill-directed attacks. He, in turn, counter-attacked, and Saeric barely managed to deflect the rapid flurry of blows as he was forced backwards by Eadwald's assault. Neither wore any armour, but both fought with sharp-edged blades.

Their bout quickly attracted the attention of the men, who had also noticed that neither swordsman wore any form of body protection. They gathered around the two combatants, forming a loose circle on the edges of the parade ground, watching Eadwald fend off Saeric's heavy blows with skill and ease, untroubled by the keen-edged blade that flashed barely a handspan in front of his face. No one uttered a word, for who would dare champion the wealh in the face of Wessex's commanding general? And who in their right mind would fight the unprotected ealdorman with a sharp edge?

'Come now, Saeric. You'll have to do better than that,' Eadwald mocked.

Now's your chance, said the Devil.

To do what? Saeric angrily thought as he brought his sword up to fend off yet another thrust from Eadwald. I *can't strike him even if I wanted to. He's too good, the bastard.*

He mocks you in front of all these men. You are weak. Unworthy.

Tell me something I don't know, Saeric responded, sidestepping Eadwald and launching his own attack. He swung hard and wide and fast, but no matter how violent his onslaught, the ealdorman deftly and confidently avoided Saeric's heavy blows. *Sard it, where is Caelin when I need him?*

Suddenly, in a sharp, unexpected movement, Eadwald stepped into Saeric's attack, pirouetted on his left foot and slammed his sword into Saeric's own. The force of the impact ripped the weapon from the Briton's grasp. The blade scythed in a flashing arc over the ducking heads of the onlookers and fell with a clank onto the dry earth. The men applauded the two combatants for a fine fight, but the clapping was muted; the men unsettled by Saeric's apparent lack of regard for their general's safety and, equally, Eadwald's willingness to put himself into danger. They fell to silence as they awaited Eadwald's response.

The Saxon ealdorman rested his hand on Saeric's shoulder, completely unruffled, and smiled in apology to Saeric.

His pupil stood opposite him, panting.

Eadwald surprised Saeric by offering a compliment. He nodded. 'A lot better. You still have a long way to go before you trouble me, mind, but you are improving. Keep up the good work.' He turned to Gerard. 'Don't let up on him. I must go to Wintanceaster for a spell, and then we'll see how he has come along after that. I don't need to tell you that he needs to apply less brute force and more footwork. And then I suppose we'll have to send him back to Heremund, or the old goat will complain that I've stolen his apprentice and demand compensation.'

Afterwards, when Eadwald had left the burh and the men were settling in for their supper – considerably more relaxed now that their commanding officer had gone – Gerard said in a low voice, 'what the Hell were you thinking, drawing your sword on him like that?'

Saeric shrugged. 'He provoked me, but it didn't make any difference, did it?'

'But you were trying to hurt him, weren't you? Everyone knew it, not least Eadwald, for Christ's sake.'

Saeric shrugged, and then he smiled. 'He knows I've little chance of hurting him, Gerard. He was just showing me how much further I've got to go. And he was showing his men that he is not afraid of the blade.'

'So you don't hate him then?' Gerard pressed.

Saeric frowned at the Saxon, again unsure how honest he could afford to be. The older man had shown no cause for Saeric to mistrust him. *Hell, I saved his life*, Saeric thought, *and he didn't shoot me when his Lord ordered him to.*

'No, of course I don't hate him. I...' He stopped. *What do I feel about him, then? Yes, he makes me angry sometimes, but why?*

Because you are reliant on his help, said the Devil. *Because he knows who you are, and he holds that knife to your throat as a constant reminder of his control over you.*

No, it's not that, Saeric thought. *Is it because I like and respect him, but shouldn't?* Something else occurred to him, and he suddenly felt uncomfortable. *Is it because he reminds me of my father? Do I wish he was...?* He sighed. 'It's complicated,' he said at last.

Gerard nodded thoughtfully. 'Aye, I suppose it is,' he said. He rose and grabbed their mugs to top them up with more ale. He paused. 'You're safe here, you know,' he said, 'and you needn't worry about King Mael. It's like our commander says, this is not something to do lightly. You need to grow stronger and smarter if you want to win your kingdom back.'

'What will they say when they find out who I am, who they've been helping?' Saeric asked, waving his hand at the other men sitting at the tables, talking loudly and happily, enjoying the camaraderie and security of peacetime on their western border. *Will they see me as their enemy or their ally?*

Gerard smiled at the Briton's troubled expression. 'Your secret's safe for the moment,' he said, 'but given enough time, I'm sure you'll do something completely stupid or heroic or both that sets tongues wagging.'

He winked and left to refill their tankards.

Two weeks later, one of the fresh recruits of the garrison, Selwin – a handsome seventeen-year-old Saxon with unruly dark hair and a wide smile – received a summons sealed with an impressive wax stamp. It was actually addressed to the camp commander, but as the commander was away in Wintanceaster with Eadwald, Selwin was unsure what to do with it. It was written in Latin, of course, but none of the men could read it. Saeric, on hearing of the summons, asked Selwin if he might read it. One of the men scornfully said, 'what, the hero wealh can read Latin too?' The men's laughter fell quickly to silence when the Briton did just that, reading the intimidating summons aloud. Then Saeric stopped mid-sentence.

'Well?' the soldier who had first spoken said, his eyes narrowed. 'Pah, you can't read it, can you? Feel good making fun of people, does it, wealh?'

Another soldier cast his fellow fyrdsman a cold stare. 'He *can* read it. He just doesn't want to share Selwin's troubles with you and the rest of the garrison.'

But they were both wrong. Saeric had stopped because he had seen who had signed it. He swallowed, feeling a cold chill in his heart. The summons bore the seal of Talec, Earl of Escanceaster.

'Saeric?' It was Selwin. 'What is it?'

Saeric shooed the onlookers away and then handed the summons back to Selwin. 'Did you do it?' he asked bluntly.

'Do what?' Selwin asked. 'You haven't finished reading it to me.'

'It says there was an attack on a Dumnonian royal transport some months ago that contained two chests of tribute destined for Wintanceaster. You were one of the Saxon escorts on the wagon but miraculously escaped the ambush. You said you were lucky, but they're now charging you with treason because a recently-captured rebel claims that you are one of them; a supporter of the cause who conspired with the rebels to make off with the king's taxes. There's a whole page of accusations here, Selwin. It ends with an order to arrest you for trial in Escanceaster.'

'That's all lies!' the young soldier protested. 'I didn't steal that money, and I don't support any rebel wealh.' He spat on the ground for emphasis.

'Well, it's a good thing *we* have this summons, not the

commander,' Saeric said, 'and thank Christ there are no filthy Dumnonians in our presence.'

'What can I do?' Selwin asked, distressed and frightened, missing Saeric's rebuke entirely. 'I'm a villein carpenter's second-born son, sent to serve in this fyrd as has been the tradition in our family for generations. I've no riches, no land, nothing! And I did not take that wergild!'

'But you were on that escort?'

Selwin flushed. 'Yes,' he said.

'What happened?'

Selwin looked down at his feet, ashamed. 'I hid.'

'What?'

'I was afraid,' he said, his voice rising with his distress. 'I was barely sworn in. I never wanted to be a soldier, Saeric. I'm not like you. I don't want to die.'

'I don't either.'

Selwin looked at Saeric. 'You're so strong and unafraid. Everyone knows about what you did for Lord Gerard and that girl. You're…' he stopped and looked away again. 'I'm not like you.'

'Well, you should be safe enough here. I'm sure Gerard will be able to help. Where is he, by the way?'

Selwin didn't know. 'What should I do?' he pressed.

'I'd have said burn it,' Saeric answered, 'but everyone knows now. Let's wait for Gerard to come back.'

Why? interjected the Devil. *Is Gerard your master now? You know what to do.*

And what would that be?

Help the boy.

How?

You can write, can't you?

No, I mustn't provoke him.

Why are you afraid of Talec? You keep saying you fear no one.

It's not the right time.

If these Saxons have their way, it will never be time. Do you know what Eadwald calls you behind your back? Aneurin the Unready, although I think Aneurin the Afraid is better. Don't you?

Sard off.

Precisely. Tell him to sard off.

Fine. You want me to poke the snake?

Saeric turned and frowned at the commander's quarters; little more than a shingle-roofed hut with a covered porch and single door opening onto the inner court of the fort. 'Do you suppose he has any parchment?' he asked, mainly to himself.

Selwin took it upon himself to find the necessary materials to compose the letter. Soon, he and a goodly number of men gathered around Saeric at one of the tables in the refectory hall to watch him write to the Dumnonian Earl.

Saeric's first attempt at a response was ruined when he smudged the ink with his palm, but Selwin saved face, stating this was simply a practice, to get all the words just so.

What the Hell am I doing? Saeric wondered. *I'm meant to be laying low.*

You're taking back your independence, the Devil assured him, *and you are righting an injustice.*

The Briton turned his attention back to his reply. He decided to keep it simple because he knew he was reaching beyond the limit of his abilities.

He wrote, "*Erl Talec, you acuse my fyrdsman, Alwerd of Nywetone of stealing yor wergild. He denys this charg, which is a charg against both his onor and mine. If you wish to take this mater further, then you must send all futur corispondis to me and I will deel with yor conserns myself. – Saeric of Bur Scirburn.*"

When he'd finished, he re-read it several times, wondering whether his spelling of correspondence was correct, whether his tone was too rude, his letter too short, and what right he had to say any of what he'd written. Most importantly, what would he do if Talec turned up at Scirburne – or worse, here – demanding retribution? *Is that your plan?* he asked the Devil. *Am I playing into your hands and giving Talec an excuse to come here looking for me? Heremund will have a fit, and Dunstan will come baying for my blood. Why am I doing it at all? This boy is a Saxon soldier who hates Dumnonians. Let him lose his head.*

Coward.

'Well?' Selwin asked pensively.

Saeric read out what he'd written. Selwin blinked at him while one of the other men let out a low whistle. 'Well, it's to the point.'

'I don't think you can say that,' Selwin said. 'He's an ealdorman. Look at that seal. I don't think we should send it.'

'Did you steal the money or not?' Saeric asked bluntly, then suddenly wondered whether Selwin was, in fact, sympathetic to the Dumnonian cause, and his hatred of Britons was an act to throw everyone off his scent. *Wouldn't that be ironic?* he thought, amused. He resolved to challenge Selwin about it later.

'No!'

'Then let him come,' Saeric said. 'I'm not afraid of him.'

Yes, you are, taunted the Devil.

'I need some wax, and we need to find something with a gryphon on it.'

As the men searched for an appropriate stamp for the seal, Selwin frowned at Saeric. 'Are you sure about this?' he asked. 'The gryphon is Heremund's mark.'

'And I'm Heremund's apprentice and a member of his household. I've signed as me, not him.'

Selwin opened his mouth to argue but was interrupted by the men, who arrived with a surprising collection of items bearing a gryphon. Saeric settled on a ceremonial swordbelt buckle. He melted the wax in a pewter ladle.

'We need to make it red.'

Without hesitation, Selwin pulled out his knife and cut his left hand. 'How much do you need?'

The blood turned the wax pink, but no matter how much

Selwin let drip into the ladle, it refused to deepen to the rich maroon colour of a typical wax seal. Saeric told him to stop, confused.

'The red colour in a seal is made from ground cinnabar,' one of the men said. 'Not blood. The commander is bound to have a stick of sealing wax somewhere in his office.'

Saeric looked up at Selwin hopefully. The young fyrdsman shook his head. 'He keeps that sort of thing locked up, unless you want to break into his chest.'

'No,' Saeric said. 'Better not.' He stirred it one last time, poured a good dollop of the wax onto the folded parchment, and pressed the scabbard buckle into it. It left a better-than-expected impression of the gryphon. Saeric blew on it to cool and harden it. It was nowhere near as impressive as Talec's and certainly nothing like Heremund's actual seal, but it would have to do. He handed it to Selwin. 'You'll have to work out how to get it to him.'

One of the men said he would sneak it into the dispatches. Selwin was enormously impressed, as were many of the other fyrdsmen, for Saeric's ability to read and write Latin, his willingness to stand up for one of them, and his audacity in telling the powerful Dumnonian ealdorman to sard off.

'Best not tell Gerard about this,' Saeric warned.

'He's off at his mother's,' said a fyrdsman named Drefan, nodding to the east and grimacing. 'He'll be back by tonight, though, for sure,' he added with a smile. 'They don't get on.'

When Saeric frowned at him, the soldier smiled back. 'You've no idea who he is, do you?' he asked, amused.

Saeric shook his head, intrigued.

'So, when you saved his life, who was he to you?'

Saeric shrugged. 'Gerard. A soldier in Heremund's burh. Brigands were attacking him. I just fought them off, that's all.'

The fyrdsman smiled. 'And in return for that service, he is now your aide-de-camp? What if I told you that Gerard is his middle name, which he uses now because he has been forbidden from uttering his given name, and there was once a time when people addressed him as "your grace", including Ealdorman Eadwald.' He laughed on seeing Saeric's dumbfounded expression. 'He has fallen a very long way, Saeric,' he said, 'but my advice is to forget you ever heard that. He doesn't like to talk about it. The last person who made light of it lost his head.'

So, I'm not the only one with a secret, Saeric thought, his mind racing. Such an honorific was only used when addressing nobles of high standing, such as bishops, ealdormen or æthelings. *So who were you?* he wondered, *and what did you do to fall so far out of favour?* He resolved to find out, although he knew he would have to be careful, as Drefan had warned.

Gerard returned to the fort that evening in a foul mood, so Saeric kept his distance, hoping no one would mention the summons. Predictably, however, word got back to the old soldier by the time the supper bowls were being cleared away, and Gerard stomped over to his charge bearing a face as dark as a thundercloud. 'So that's why you have been avoiding me,' he growled. 'I step away for one day, and you go and do something unbelievably stupid. What exactly did you write?'

Saeric winced, not sure he wanted to admit to his folly. *Why did I do it?* he wondered, knowing it had been foolish beyond measure. He shrugged, trying to detract from his actions. 'I wrote a letter on Selwin's behalf.'

'In response to…?'

'A summons.'

'From?'

Saeric suddenly flared to anger. 'You know who, so why are you asking me these questions?'

'Because I am trying to understand why you have been so… so reckless! What in God's name were you thinking, writing to Earl Talec of all people?' He grabbed Saeric by the arm, hauled him to his feet and dragged him out of the hall and away from prying eyes and flapping ears. 'Do you want to be found?' he growled. 'Are you so impatient for glory that you ignore everything we have told you and throw all our good work away so that you can bring Talec's assassins here to slit your throat? Is that what you had in mind?'

'Obviously not,' Saeric hissed back.

'Then why?' Gerard asked, spreading his arms in entreaty. '*Why?*'

Saeric didn't know what to say. *Because the Devil told me to*, was what he wanted to say, but Gerard simply wouldn't understand. 'I'm sorry,' he said.

To Saeric's surprise, the Saxon's shoulders slumped, and he let out a long sigh as he pushed his anger aside. His eyes glinted in the torch's flickering light beside him as he considered his charge. A horse in the stables nickered, then all fell silent again.

'Well, it's done now. I suppose it was unrealistic of us to expect you to stay cooped up for so long, especially with such a tempting challenge from your nemesis. It's my fault because I wasn't here to stop you from doing it. I'm sorry, Saeric, I've failed you. We'll just have to deal with whatever comes of it, but please promise me you won't do anything like this again. We can't afford your secret to get out. Not yet, anyway.'

They returned to their duties and drills, but as the days went by without even a hint of a response, Saeric's regrets flourished, and he began to worry about the ramifications of his impetuous actions. The Devil remained frustratingly silent on the matter, and Gerard grew more taciturn as the days wore on. For his part, Selwin avoided Saeric thanks to the harsh reprimand he received from Gerard for dragging Saeric into his troubles.

Saeric's fears took a turn for the worse at the close of a particularly chilly day when he found himself alone with Selwin, tidying up after an archery drill.

'Saeric?' the young man asked tentatively.

Something in the young recruit's tone set Saeric's hairs on end, and he paused, setting down the half-dismantled target he had been holding. 'What's the matter?'

They stood outside the fort in the shadow of the southern wall, and Selwin's blue eyes darted this way and that as he checked that they were alone. 'Some of the men say you were once a nobleman in Dumnonia. Is that true?'

Saeric took a sharp breath, unsure how to answer. He had grown to like Selwin in their time together at Sceaptesburh, but Saeric's actions to defend Selwin had been motivated by a selfish desire to rile Talec. That he now regretted those hot-headed actions was beside the point. He'd done it and would have to face whatever consequences arose. At least he'd finally taken some form of action against the despicable traitor. But in doing so, he had dragged Selwin into his fight with Mael and his collaborator. There was also the fact that Selwin was accused of treason against both Dumnonia and Westseaxna Ríce, to which, until now, Saeric had not given much thought.

Are you a sympathiser, he wondered, *or a simple thief?*

Selwin was undoubtedly no innocent, despite how he behaved among the garrison's men. Saeric had noticed how Selwin used his potent combination of good looks, youthful self-confidence and a quick smile to inveigle favours around the fort. But he wasn't work-shy; he threw himself into all their drills with vigour and took equal delight in winning contests as losing them. He'd more than once thrown away a victory by selflessly coming to the aid of one of the other men. All of which made Saeric a little suspicious of the boy's motivations. There was something ingenuine about him, which didn't make sense in the face of all the evidence otherwise, but nevertheless, Saeric had been careful to remain guarded in his presence. That was until Talec's summons had arrived, of course.

'I was born into a good household,' Saeric answered, 'but I was only nine when Mael killed my family, and since then, I've been a slave. I hold no title now.'

'Some even say you were a prince of some kind.'

Saeric stared at the young man, anger and fear rising in equal measure. *How does he know that?* 'I am no prince,' he said scornfully, then bent down to pick up the target.

'Drefan says that you're biding your time, and one day when we least expect it, you will turn on us. He says you plan to kill Lord Eadwald.'

Saeric dropped the target and launched himself at Selwin. He grabbed the startled youth by the scruff of his tunic and shoved him up against the rough, limewashed wall.

'I am no traitor,' he growled, 'and Drefan had better watch his mouth.' He leaned in close to Selwin's terrified face, baring his teeth at him like a wild animal. 'What is it you want?'

Saeric could see in Selwin's eyes that the boy's fear was genuine, so he let him go. Selwin dropped to his knees, gasping.

Saeric crouched down opposite him. 'Did you take that wergild?'

Selwin shook his head. Then he closed his eyes and grimaced. 'I… I helped them take it.'

'What? Helped who?'

Selwin looked up at Saeric, his blue eyes glistening with tears. Saeric felt a flush of shame for his violence against this poor boy. 'You people,' Selwin said. 'Dumnonian rebels.'

'You're Saxon. Why help them?'

Selwin looked away, evidently ashamed.

'Selwin?'

'Don't hit me!' the youth said, lifting his hand to defend himself.

Saeric let out a sigh. 'I'm sorry I did that,' he said. 'I don't like people prying into my past.'

Selwin looked at him for a moment, then he said, 'I did it for a Dumnonian girl.'

Saeric blinked at him, not expecting that answer, but why do most men do what they do if not for power, wealth or love?

'I know,' Selwin croaked, rubbing his neck. 'It's pathetic. She probably doesn't even love me, but....' He trailed off, embarrassed.

Saeric couldn't help but smile. 'So, for the sake of a roll in the hay, you've brought a world of trouble upon yourself, and now me.'

'It wasn't just some fling with a milkmaid. We'd been seeing each other for months. I'd been posted to the garrison at Escanceaster. I didn't know anyone there. She was nice to me.'

I'm sure she was, Saeric thought wryly.

'I'm afraid, Saeric. I came here because I thought I would be safe, but I'm not, am I?'

'No,' Saeric said, regretting sending the demand more than ever. 'The best we can hope is that my letter either doesn't reach Talec or is ignored if it does.'

'But what if he takes you seriously?'

'We'll cross that bridge when the time comes, if it comes.' Saeric held his hand out to Selwin and helped him to his feet. 'But I promise that whatever the Turncoat does, we will face it together. In the meantime, don't tell anyone what you just told me. You had nothing to do with any of it, understand?'

Earl Talec's response did arrive, but it was another two weeks later and in an entirely unexpected form.

Eadwald appeared at the burh on a blustery October morning to check on his charge and assess his progress. He instructed Selwin to fight Saeric. The two men set out for the practice ground, but Eadwald shook his head. 'Sharp edges, please,' he said. 'Just as you did with me.'

'But my Lord...' Selwin began, then stopped when he saw the stern expression on the ealdorman's face.

The two men ran through their practice drills, taking care not to inadvertently strike one another, until Eadwald ordered them to stop. He called them over.

'I thought you hated wealh scum like him?' the king's general demanded of the young fyrdsman.

'Well, sir, I....'

'That was a perfect opportunity to inflict a little hurt, a cut or two here and there, all in the name of practice. I can see that you're a much better swordsman than him. Why did you hold back?'

'No, Lord, I assure you I didn't,' Selwin said nervously. 'Saeric has improved.'

Eadwald raised an eyebrow. 'So, you wouldn't be returning a favour then?'

Selwin shook his head, and then he stopped, his eyes widening with understanding.

Eadwald held his hand out. Saeric only now saw that Eadwald's attendant held a leather dispatch pouch. The aide opened it and took out a letter that he handed to his master. Eadwald unfolded it in front of the two young men.

'I'm curious,' he said, addressing Saeric. 'What precisely do you mean when you say, "I will deal with your concerns myself, Saeric of Burh Scirburne?"

Saeric swallowed, his impetuous confidence swept away. In that moment, he felt like a naughty boy being chastised by his father for a gross misdemeanour. The worst of it was that Talec had clearly not received the letter. God only knew what would happen now. A thousand things flashed through Saeric's mind. *What will Selwin think of me? What will the men think?*

That you're a fool, the Devil offered. *A fraud.*

Saeric had no idea what to say.

'A few days ago,' Eadwald continued, 'Heremund received an unexpected visit from the recipient of this letter. An emissary from Earl Talec arrived unannounced, accompanied by a not insignificant retinue. He asked all sorts of questions about you, Saeric. If his summons were intended to draw you out, it succeeded!'

So the letter had got to him? Saeric thought, feeling a burst of smug satisfaction at that revelation. He heard Selwin draw in a sharp breath beside him.

'Wipe that grin off your face, Saeric,' Eadwald growled. 'You have overreached yourself. You are an escaped slave, a fugitive in law, and you have no right whatsoever to threaten an ealdorman, especially this one.' Then he turned on Selwin. 'And you? Are you guilty of Earl Talec's charges? I understand you have recently arrived in this burh? Hiding from justice, perhaps?'

Selwin swallowed. 'No, my Lord. I swear by the mother of Christ that I am innocent, my Lord.' He bowed again, clearly terrified by the likely ramifications of his misconduct.

Eadwald gave him a long, cold stare, then turned back to Saeric. He held up the letter and tapped the remains of the wax seal, which had mostly fallen away with all the handling the letter had received. 'Do not write to anyone in this manner again. And most absolutely do not ever impersonate Ealdorman Heremund again.'

Saeric began to protest, to say that he signed his own name, but Eadwald rounded on him.

'I know exactly what you were doing!' He snapped. 'You are his apprentice! That is your place in his household, nothing more! You do not go about threatening people in Heremund's name, especially not Earl Talec. You are fortunate his man went to Heremund, and not one of the other ealdormen or worse, the King himself. And what would you have done had his emissary come here? Do you have the faintest idea how incomprehensibly stupid you've been?'

When Saeric failed to respond, Eadwald rounded on Selwin again. 'You let him write it. What do you have to say for yourself?'

'I, I didn't think, my Lord. I...'

'No, you didn't think, and nor did he. I am deeply unhappy that you have used Saeric in this way. Deeply. We will talk of this further when I feel less inclined to slice off your head and stick it on a pike.'

'He didn't use me,' Saeric said angrily. 'I offered to write it. And you can't punish him for it.'

Eadwald's expression darkened, and he drew Saeric way from Selwin and the growing band of onlookers. 'Are you telling me how to run my affairs now?'

'He didn't even know I could write.'

'You can't,' the general said caustically. 'This letter is as good a declaration of war between the fyrds of Wessex and Dumnonia, who, I might add, I have grown a great many grey hairs ensuring stay friendly with one another. And then you do this! You'll be lucky if Heremund welcomes you back, and if Dunstan hears of it, he will come after you, cut off your hands, and dig out your eyes.' He paused, then his eyes narrowed. 'If I didn't know you better, I might even wonder if that had been your intention. Effective means of getting revenge on us, to pit us against one another.'

'Then what should I have done?' Saeric retorted. 'Signed it with my real name and title?'

'Do you want to fulfil your vow or not?' Eadwald snapped, 'because stunts like this will ensure that you don't. Two months ago, you were wailing about being found out, yet now you go and do this!'

'What was I meant to do? Ignore it? He was threatening one of your men.'

'Which is my business, not yours! Your naivety is terrifying. You've lived your whole life in your little burrow in the back end of nowhere, ignorant of all that has happened in my kingdom and yours. What this shows me,' and he shook the letter in Saeric's face, 'is that you are far from ready to take on the responsibilities of the role you would have yourself fulfil.'

'Not my whole life,' Saeric said, aware that every man in the fort was watching the argument, even if they could not hear it, and knowing that any other soldier would have been condemned by now to the lash – or worse – for talking back so disrespectfully to one of the highest-ranking men in the King's armies.

'Remember who and what you are, Saeric,' Eadwald said in a low voice. 'Do something like this again, and your dreams will stop dead. Understood?'

Saeric glared at his mentor, shaking with fury. 'I know exactly who and what I am.'

'Do you?' Eadwald shoved the letter into Saeric's chest, but Saeric let it fall onto the dirt at his feet. 'And who and what is that exactly?'

Kill him! shouted the Devil.

Saeric glared at his mentor, too angry to speak, rendered impotent by the knowledge that every word spoken by Eadwald was true.

'You have much yet to learn before earning your title,' Eadwald snarled. 'You can start by learning to spell. For your information, Scirburne is spelt with an 'e', honour has a silent 'h', as does burh, and I won't even try to explain how to spell correspondence....' He stopped for a moment, then went on. 'Given how badly it was written, I'm astounded that Earl Talec paid it any heed.'

'It wasn't the writing he was paying attention to,' Saeric muttered.

Eadwald's eyes narrowed, but he checked his temper, aware of the damage this argument was inflicting upon his authority. 'I have to go. Thanks to you, I've got a diplomatic fiasco to sort out. Report to Brother Sigebert in the mynster tomorrow where you will recommence your education, ignorant wealh.' He shook his head in disgust, then he addressed Gerard, who stood in silence by Saeric. 'And where were you in all this?' he growled. 'You were meant to be keeping an eye on him.'

Gerard began to answer, but Eadwald cut him off. 'Forget it. We'll talk about it later.' Then he turned on his heel and marched out of the camp, snapping his fingers for his attendants to join him.

The whole burh was silent, and all eyes were on Saeric. Saeric picked up the letter and walked back over to Selwin.

'My Lord,' Selwin began hesitantly, horrified that he had been the cause of the terrible scene, and knowing now that Saeric was far more important than anyone – not least Saeric – had let on.

'I told you, I'm no Lord,' Saeric replied.

'I am... so sorry, Lord Saeric. I... I should never have let you do that for me.'

Slowly a grin formed on Saeric's face. 'Well, at least we know it worked,' he said, allowing himself to feel pleased that his letter had borne such dramatic results.

'How... how are you still alive?' Drefan said, asking the question that was on everyone's lips. 'And how is he?' He pointed at Selwin.

'Pfft. Don't mind old Eadwald,' Saeric said, his confidence returning now that his surrogate father had left them. He was aware that Drefan was still staring at him.

'What?' Saeric asked.

'Who the bloody Hell *are* you?' Drefan asked, astounded. 'You know he has cut off people's heads for far less?'

'You heard. I'm an apprentice to a blacksmith, a rubbish swordsman and an ignoramus.' He handed the letter to Selwin. 'You should put this with the other one. I'd better get back to my practice before I get into more trouble from father.'

He strode off to fetch his sword, smiling as he heard Drefan muttering to one of his cohort, 'did he just say, "father?"'

Saeric's grin broadened. *That'll get them talking*, he thought, amused. *In fact, why haven't I thought of it before? It was perfect. Saeric: the illegitimate son of one of the greatest ealdormen the kingdom has ever known. The big secret is revealed. And it will put old Talec off the scent.* He laughed out loud. Today was a good day indeed.

You missed an opportunity, said the Devil.

For what? Saeric demanded.

The Devil remained silent.

Later, as the men gathered for the evening meal, all talk was inevitably about the day's excitement and speculation as to the identity of their British conscript. Saeric refused to be drawn on the matter, except for declining to deny that he'd referred to Eadwald as 'father'. He also refused to accept Selwin's apology. 'You have nothing to be ashamed of. We righted an injustice, and Eadwald won't punish you.'

He was wrong. Eadwald appointed a new training master for Saeric, a powerfully-built, balding brute of a man by the name of Rodor, who held a particular hatred for Britons. It turned out they had slaughtered Rodor's family in retaliation for a raid on the borderlands. 'A Dumnonian rebel put that scar on his forehead and took off half his ear,' Eadwald said when introducing Saeric to his new training master. 'I have instructed Rodor to oversee your training in my absence. He will take over from Gerard immediately and start by devising suitable punishment for your insubordination. Fitting, no?'

'My what?'

'Disobedience. I presume you're familiar with that word?' Eadwald dropped his voice. 'I've just heard an extraordinary rumour circulating amongst the men that you're my son, which explains my uncharacteristic tolerance for your outrageous behaviour.'

Saeric shrugged. To all intents and purposes, Eadwald was his father, bizarre as the idea seemed on first speaking. Who else would have taught him the ways of the court and kingship? Eadwald had filled Cadwyr's place with ease and thus far was as uncompromising as his birth father had been to his nine-year-old son. 'You're definitely annoying enough to be my actual father,' he agreed.

Eadwald's face broke into a grin. 'I'll take that as a compliment. And I think we should fan these flames. It is a perfect pretext for our association. It emerges that the childless general has a son, albeit a debased mongrel wealh, whom he wants to make into a decent soldier, a man befitting his father's station.' He stood back and looked Saeric up and down as a general might appraise one of his soldiers. 'You might even get there,' he said, nodding as any proud father might. 'Time for me to go. More trouble to sort out.'

He smiled at Saeric's unasked question. 'No, from the north. As if fending off this new heathen scourge from over the seas isn't enough, I fear our Mercian neighbour may be planning some sort of trouble for our King. If you remain in this fort for much longer, you may be called upon to join your comrades in that conflict. On the upside, you will have the opportunity to kill as many Saxons as you like with your ploughshare. You might even want to try out your newfound skills with the sword in battle; think of it as a trial for the real thing.'

He clamped a hand on Saeric's shoulder. 'You will take your punishment, as there can be no favouritism in my ranks, son or no.' He spoke loudly enough for the men nearby to hear, and then he took his leave. 'I'll be back in a few days, and I expect you to have begun your lessons with Brother Sigebert by the time I return. Oh, and Gerard, you're coming with me. You and I have much to discuss.'

Rodor relished his instructions by setting a variety of gruelling physical tasks, forcing both Saeric and Selwin to drill until they were exhausted. Rodor genuinely hated Saeric; that was clear enough, made all the worse because Saeric was a half-blood. 'And you'll get no coddling from me just because you're his bastard spawn,' the Saxon warned. Obviously, even he had swallowed the father-son tale, and Saeric was not about to refute it, so he accepted his punishment and played along. All the while, he wondered what Talec had learned through his emissary's visit to Heremund. Saeric wasn't the least bit concerned that Heremund might have given him away; the general was far too wise for that, but what had been behind Talec's letter in the first place?

Selwin's story seemed genuine enough, but Saeric had a nagging feeling there was more to this than mere coincidence. *Is this all a cleverly planned ruse to lure me out and give Talec an excuse to come sniffing around?* Saric wondered. *Is Selwin all he seems?* One thing he did know: sending that letter had been a colossal mistake.

Let him come, gloated the Devil.

On the eighth day of their punishment, young Selwin collapsed, but Rodor lashed him and demanded he get up. Just as he had months before, Saeric grabbed the tail of the whip and tried to wrench it from the soldier's hand. But Rodor was wise to him and held on tight.

'That's enough,' Saeric growled.

Rodor's dark eyes narrowed. The two men stood face to face, Saeric the taller and stronger; one held the whip handle, the other with the thin tail wrapped around his hand. 'What are you going to do, Saeric of Scirburne?' Rodor growled. 'Ram this down my throat like you did that innocent huscarl?'

That would be fun, the Devil said. *Shall we?*

'Well, before you do,' Rodor continued coldly, 'remember that your father instructed me to punish you, and I am your superior officer.'

'You may be right on the first point,' Saeric responded icily, 'but you are mistaken on the second. I do not answer to you.'

Rodor's eyes narrowed, but he knew this to be the case. Despite his relationship with Eadwald and the men, Saeric had not been formally inducted into the fyrd, so in theory, none of the men could order him around. 'Perhaps it's time we changed that,' the Saxon said.

'You've made your point,' Saeric said. 'I wrote the letter, so if there are any more lashes due, give them to me.'

'That will be my pleasure, wealh.'

Saeric released the whip and stood up against the post. Again, all eyes had turned to the two men, and soon the burh fell silent as the commander unleashed his fury on Saeric. The Briton bore the punishment with gritted teeth but refused to give the Saxon any ground. The Saxon hit him harder and harder, no longer tempering his blows, trying to extract a cry from Saeric. He failed, and the lashing stopped. Saeric did not turn around. Instead, he went over to Selwin to check on him. The teenager was struggling not to cry, and Saeric wondered if this was the first time that the boy had received such harsh punishment. He had noticed the lad's skin had been unmarked before today; indeed Selwin was quite particular about maintaining and showing off his fine physique. Rodor was quite the opposite. *As am I*, Saeric thought ruefully. For his part, Selwin was horrified that Saeric had taken such severe punishment for him. Saeric saw the guilt in the young Saxon's eyes as the other shook his head at the lines of blood that striped Saeric's back and sides.

'I'm fine. This is nothing, trust me,' Saeric said.

Selwin stiffened and saluted over Saeric's shoulder.

Saeric turned to find Eadwald standing there, bloodied whip in hand.

'Now then, what lessons have we learned?' Eadwald asked them both.

Selwin murmured something suitably humble, his eyes firmly fixed on his feet.

Eadwald turned to Saeric.

Saeric wanted to say something clever about poor spelling, or how much the Saxons like the lash, or a thousand other retorts, but instead, he offered what he knew to be true: 'I am not ready, father.'

'Hmm,' Eadwald muttered. He handed the whip back to Rodor, who stood glowering at Saeric. Gerard stood three paces behind, watching Saeric, his expression one of deep concern.

'They tell me you remain a poor marksman with the bow,' Eadwald said. 'I want you to try this one. An East Saxon thegn recently brought a couple to Wintanceaster. The Franks have been using them to great effect, apparently. Quite timely given the growing heathen scourge. I can't even draw it, but then I thought of my brawny blacksmithing boy.'

He gave a flick of his fingers, and a soldier stepped forward, carrying a tall, heavy bow. It was almost twice as long and far sturdier than any Saeric had seen in the fort. Saeric took it, his back still bleeding, and tested its weight and tension. The bowstring was more like a thin rope and had been well waxed. He held his hand out for an arrow. He grunted at its size; the shaft was double the thickness of an ordinary arrow, and the same could be said of the fletching, which ran some way down the shaft. It bore a larger-than-usual leaf-shaped iron point, mounted and stuck fast with sinew binding and resin. A brutal weapon fit for a brute.

Facing Eadwald, he nocked the arrow and drew back the bowstring. It was strung tight. Eadwald was right when he said it needed superior strength to pull it. The yew wood creaked under the tension, and the multiple slashes across Saeric's back screamed at him as he drew the weapon. The arrow was pointing between Eadwald's legs. Saeric met the ealdorman's gaze, then, straining against the taut bowstring, the Briton raised the bow so that the arrow pointed at his enemy's chest. At this distance, the arrow would rip straight through the ealdorman, clothes and all, and just as likely tear his heart out with it. The men gasped and began murmuring in alarm.

Eadwald didn't blink. Saeric released the Saxon's gaze, then, in one smooth movement, swung on his hip and loosed the arrow. It slammed into the target mannequin by the south tower with a heavy thud, burying itself far up the shaft. The manikin rocked backwards under the impact, tipped beyond the point of no return, and hit the ground with a dull thump. Saeric let out a satisfied grunt, and then he claimed another arrow from Eadwald's attendant. He took a shot at a second mannequin, and the arrow burst through the neck, spraying straw as it decapitated the target and slammed into the wooden palisade beyond with a loud thwack. A few of the men uttered expletives.

This is an excellent weapon, the Devil said, impressed.

Yes, it is, Saeric agreed. He turned to Eadwald, a wry smile on his face.

Eadwald cocked an eyebrow. 'I think we have finally found a weapon that suits you. From now onwards I want you to practise with this. And more swordcraft. You will never hold your own on the battlefield if you cannot handle a sword competently.'

'That was you, wasn't it? With the whip, at the end.'

'Rodor was holding back. All the men here hold back for you. It does you no good. It holds you back.'

'You're an arsehole, do you know that?'

Eadwald smiled. 'Thank you, my son. Now, back to your drills. Oh, and why haven't you started your lessons?'

Saeric stared at Eadwald, infuriated. '*He* hasn't let me!' he said, pointing at Rodor.

'Well, I'm taking him with me so that you can get started straight away. Gerard can accompany you.' Eadwald turned to Selwin. 'Pack your things. You're coming too.'

'What? No!' Saeric protested.

Eadwald raised his hand for silence. 'It's not up to you to decide Selwin's fate. The fact remains he has been accused of treason and must answer to those charges.'

'But it's not true!'

'And you can prove that how? Were you there to bear witness, were you?'

'Saeric,' Selwin interrupted, 'Lord Eadwald is right. I don't have a choice. You did your best.'

'Tell him what you told me,' Saeric urged.

'He can tell the reeve in Escanceaster,' Eadwald said. 'You have a choice, Selwin. Wait here in custody, and I will collect you on my way back, or come with me now.'

'I'd rather wait here if it pleases you, my Lord,' Selwin said, his eyes on his feet.

'I'll keep an eye on him,' Gerard said.

'Like you did, Saeric?' Eadwald growled. 'I want him tied to that pole. Rodor?'

'With pleasure, my Lord,' the broad-shouldered fyrdsman said, grabbing Selwin by the arm and wrenching the young man off his feet so that Selwin's back painfully twisted as he was hauled away to the lashing post. Saeric followed, demanding Rodor treat the boy more carefully.

Eadwald opened his mouth to call Saeric back, but Gerard gripped the ealdorman's arm firmly and turned Eadwald around to face him.

'What exactly are you hoping to achieve, treating Saeric like that?' Gerard said angrily. 'You've torn his back to shreds!'

Eadwald gave the other soldier a long, hard look, then he pulled his arm free and said, 'I am reminding him that he is beholden to me, and he must do what he is told. He most certainly cannot go about applying his initiative on half-baked antics like that letter. You and I both know that this was a ruse from Talec to draw Saeric out. My question to you is what was Selwin's part in it? That boy might claim innocence, but he's up to his neck in whatever is going on here.'

'You are too hard on Saeric,' Gerard said, ignoring the warning about Selwin.

'I don't need him to like me,' Eadwald countered.

'There is a good man beneath all that hurt and anger. He's barely in control of himself as it is, so why are you so Hell-bent on setting him back?'

'Have you gone soft because he saved your life? I want people to fear him, and I, in turn, want him to fear us. He must know his place, which is as my subordinate.'

'*Your* subordinate?' Gerard growled, eyebrows raised.

'I am sorry, your grace,' Eadwald said sarcastically, dipping his head in mock entreaty. 'I forget myself.'

'He will never fear us, Eadwald. Hate us, absolutely,' Gerard went on, letting the ealdorman's disrespect pass. He shook his head in disgust at his cousin. 'Do you truly think that being feared will make him a better king?'

'A better fighter, certainly. His brutality and lack of humanity are qualities that will be useful to us. I am hoping that some of it might rub off on you.'

'The men in this burh like and respect him because of his good qualities, not because they are frightened of him.'

'Then we have more work to do, don't we?' Eadwald snapped.

'You do know that one day you will wake up to find Saeric standing over your bed, holding a sword at your throat, but you won't be able to call for help because he'll have slaughtered the rest of us beforehand.'

'Then we must ensure that doesn't happen. Remember, all of this is for your benefit.'

'No,' Gerard hissed. 'This is my mother's scheme, not mine, and drawing Saeric into it is a mistake.'

'Time will tell,' Eadwald said. 'Saeric was delivered into our hands for a reason, and I believe it is to aid our cause. God knows we need all the help we can get. How ironic that God should choose you – a book-loving pacifist – to take up your father's banner.'

'I've seen my share of battle, cousin,' Gerard growled. 'That I don't share your lust for blood is a virtue, not a sin.'

'Hmm,' Eadwald said, looking over Gerard's shoulder. 'Your underling returns, and I must go. Keep him tightly leashed, won't you?'

The ealdorman stalked off to round up his entourage and soon found himself arguing with Rodor, who evidently did not wish to be relieved of his duties. Not long afterwards, they left the burh, Rodor riding alongside Eadwald, a deep scowl darkening his face. Saeric enjoyed sending him off with a fittingly rude gesture.

'Good riddance,' Gerard said, but he was not speaking to Rodor.

Saeric looked at Gerard, surprised at the passion behind the older man's words.

'Don't ask,' Gerard said. He glanced at the Dumnonian's shredded back. 'We need to get you seen to. I've sent for Hildelith; only try to be a bit more appreciative this time, yes?'

'I'll try,' Saeric said with a wry smile. He looked over at Selwin, who was bound tightly to the lashing post. 'Does he have to stay there?'

'He stands accused of treason.'

'Against Mael.'

Gerard let out a snort. 'So?'

'That makes him a hero of the rebellion. *My* rebellion.'

Gerard let out a sigh. 'You're a pain in the arse, Saeric.'

'Lend me your dagger.'

Gerard rolled his eyes. 'You know that Eadwald will tie you up to that post himself if you let Selwin free?'

Saeric smiled at Gerard. 'Let him try,' he said, but there was no humour in his voice.

4
Marked by the Devil

Sceaptesburh, Wessex

'Lord Eadwald did this?' Hildelith asked, shocked by the welts that scored Saeric's back. She had led Saeric and Selwin over to a bench by the stables to better inspect their wounds. Saeric insisted she tend to Selwin first. Selwin, in turn, refused, but Saeric won, and Hildelith started on the seventeen-year-old. The young fyrdsman held his eyes shut and his mouth clenched, but Saeric saw tears seeping from his eyes.

'I'm sorry I got you into this,' Saeric said. 'I wasn't expecting him to be so angry with me.'

Hildelith tutted as she dabbed Selwin's welts with a dampened cloth. 'It's one thing to punish you, but why take it out on this poor lad?'

'It was my fault,' Selwin said between clenched teeth. He looked at Saeric. 'Maybe you're right, and I should tell your father what happened.'

'No,' Saeric said. 'I was wrong before. It'll only make things worse for you.' He looked across the fort to Gerard, who was deep in conversation with Drefan, undoubtedly discussing Saeric's latest act of insubordination in freeing Selwin. The burh was abuzz with it, but no one dared challenge Ealdorman Eadwald's son, especially as Gerard had not done so. 'I think we should ask Gerard what to do,' Saeric said. He turned back to Hildelith. 'Father was making a point,' he said, answering her original question. He involuntarily flinched as she moved to him. She did not have the same light touch as Carwyn. Rather, she approached his care efficiently and without fuss, like everything else she did. 'He's right,' he went on. 'I was stupid. I sent that letter for the wrong reasons. I need to rise above my feelings somehow.'

'And him whipping you taught you that?' Hildelith stopped dabbing for a moment, indignant on Saeric's behalf. She looked into his eyes, frowning. 'Is he really your *father*? It certainly explains a lot about you.'

Saeric's immediate reaction was offence, and then he softened. He nodded, feeling a little ashamed that he was lying to her. 'Is that a good thing or bad?' he asked.

She paused and tilted her head, giving the question more thought than Saeric felt was warranted. 'I've yet to decide,' she said eventually. She tutted again. 'Why would a father do that to his son?'

'Because he wants the best for him,' Saeric answered, surprising himself with that insight, but it rang true. Saeric really did believe that for whatever reason, Eadwald was doing this out of a genuine desire to help the Briton grow into a better person, a leader no less, someone who might one day be worthy of the title king. King. It sounded so odd, so wrong. *Me, a king?* For the first time, Saeric understood the full weight of that word, that title, that responsibility. He smiled to himself. Eadwald truly was a master at this game. In the short time he had met Saeric, Eadwald had shown the Briton how simplistic and childish his intentions had been and how unprepared he was to deliver on his promise to himself and his family.

'Saeric?' Hildelith was peering at his face.

'Hm?' the Briton muttered, his mind still drifting. Around them, the Saxon fort was preparing for the evening watch. He was vaguely aware of the westering sun sinking below a thick bank of clouds on the horizon. The gates were open, and the atmosphere was relaxed and calm. This was a time of peace. Here, at least, the men were content and unconcerned for their future, their duty to defend a trouble-free western border. His thoughts turned to the time before the conquest when life had been similarly calm and happy in his home at Caer Uisc; at least for a spare prince who would never see responsibility, free to run about the city with his low-born friends, showing them how to fight as he himself had been taught by Berec. How strange that he had not carried those skills into manhood. *Perhaps I was not as good as I believed back the*n, he thought, amused by that prospect.

He had paid scant attention to the boring lessons delivered in monotone by old Brother Cerdic in the mynster, and he barely remembered his father's lectures on how one must behave as a prince of Dumnonia. The lessons had been so tiresome as a nine-year-old who had just wanted to get back outside the fort's walls to be with his grubby friends down in the densely packed township that sprawled in all directions from the citadel. But had it really been that simple? His father had made no secret of his distaste of Westseaxna Ríce and had railed at the vassal status of what had once been an important, independent kingdom. King Cadwyr had often spoken of returning to the glory days of old, when Dumnonia's very own son, Arthur, had fought off the Saxon invaders and, for a time at least, had brought together the disunited British kingdoms to fight a common enemy. But that had been so many generations ago, and so much had changed since. Saxons ruled most of the land now. Berec had always feared Cadwyr's unapologetic dislike of the West Saxons, and he had warned that the ascension of the new King Ecgberht to the Westseaxna throne marked a dangerous new time for the outlying Britons.

He was right, and Ecgberht began showing interest in Dumnonia of the wrong kind, which prompted Cadwyr to invite his brother to return from the Brythonic lands across the sea. Everyone knew what happened next. Had Mael been plotting with Ecgberht all along, for they had both been in exile in Francia, or was Mael an opportunist who had simply made Ecgberht an offer he couldn't refuse? *You will pay for your treachery*, Saeric thought darkly, *and Dumnonia will return to independence, just as father had intended.*

His thoughts turned to his younger brother, who always remained in Saeric's consciousness, sometimes dimly, sometimes rising to the surface like a tumbling twig in a stream, only to be drawn back down again as something from Saeric's more immediate surroundings drowned him out. He imagined himself and Caelin standing together on the west tower of Caer Uisc's walls, their wolven banner flying over the city. Such an impossible dream, yet one that was within reach, if only he could find the discipline and faith to follow his mentors' directions. Where are you now? he wondered. He had not experienced any further fits since the distressing episode in the smithy, but he had remained faintly aware of him, or his temperament at least, which was dark, sad and desperate. Caelin was still alive, of that Saeric was certain, but his brother remained frustratingly unreachable. *Where are you, brother?* he asked in his thoughts, but he received no answer.

He turned back to the here and now, to the fort and the closing of the day. *If people are happy, why seek to wreck that peace? What good will come of it? But Eadwald has a plan, and I am now a part of it, whether I want to be or not. What exactly is he up to?* Eadwald and Gerard had had a long talk before Eadwald left, and now Gerard was heading their way with what appeared to be mugs of ale.

They are your enemies, warned the Devil.

Are they? Saeric wondered.

'Saeric?' Hildelith was still trying to get his attention. 'What were you thinking just now? You were far away.'

'Sorry,' he said, smiling at her, pleased she was attending to him, and knowing he needed to try harder with her. 'And I'm sorry about before,' he said awkwardly, aware that Selwin was sitting next to him. 'I... I don't know what happens to me sometimes. It's not that I don't appreciate the help you all give me.'

'Including your father?' Selwin said, a wry smile on his face.

'What's my father...?' Saeric began, then remembered that Eadwald now filled that role. This was going to be hard to get used to. 'Yes, and Eadwald,' Saeric said.

Selwin and Hildelith both waited for Saeric to continue.

He shrugged. 'I suppose I'm not used to all this kindly attention,' he said, 'especially since you are Saxons.'

'You're half-Saxon as well,' Hildelith reminded him.

Saeric frowned at her, offended by that statement, yet he would have to get used to that too if this story was going to stick.

'Sorry,' she said, seeing his annoyance, 'but it's true.'

'That doesn't make it alright,' Saeric said. 'Most of my family were killed during the betrayal. I've no idea what happened to my mother. I was raised by a pair of...' he paused, anger returning as he thought of the two old peasants who had found him and cared for him, only to sell him on as soon as he was of suitable age and fitness. *I will be sure to pay you a visit one day*, he thought darkly.

Hildelith paused in her dabbing and met his gaze, her eyes revealing her sympathy for his plight. He felt a stab of desire, which surprised him, and he looked away, embarrassed.

'One thing I don't understand, though, is how Lord Eadwald came to be your father?' Hildelith said. 'You talk of your family as though you had siblings and, well, you know...' she trailed off awkwardly, but Gerard's arrival saved her. The old soldier handed the two men a mug each, then apologised for not bringing one for his daughter.

Saeric's mind raced as he considered Hildelith's question. Maintaining this lie was fast becoming complicated, and sooner or later, he was bound to make a mistake.

Perhaps you should have given this a little more thought before rushing to claim Eadwald as your sire? observed the Devil helpfully.

Saeric was about to speak when Gerard intervened. 'When Escanceaster was being sacked, Saeric's mother told him the truth about her and Eadwald. I imagine she would never have said anything had things been different. She was a noblewoman in Cadwyr's court.' He shrugged. 'She caught Eadwald's eye, despite her being married. Saeric had an older brother and sister, you see. Saeric's father was not the kindest of men, and I suppose Saeric's mother was flattered to have attracted the attention of a handsome young Saxon warrior. Saeric is the result of that brief affair.'

Saeric blinked at Gerard, impressed with the tale. Gerard continued.

'Eadwald won't tell me if it was something that went on for more than one, erm, encounter, but Saeric's mother hid the truth of her son's siring, and presumably, her husband went to his death none the wiser.'

'But how did you learn the truth?' Hildelith asked Saeric.

The Briton felt a momentary flash of panic, and then the answer came to him. 'When it was clear that all was lost during the rout, my mother told me to flee not into the west but eastwards and seek out a Saxon fyrdsman named Eadwald from Scirburne. When I asked why, she said he was my father.' He shrugged, then regretted it as his welts protested. 'I was just a child. I didn't know what she was talking about. I certainly didn't believe or understand her. But I went east because that's what she'd told me to do. I didn't get very far. In the aftermath of the attack, I was found, fattened up, and eventually sold into slavery. As the years went by, I came to hate my Saxon sire, and I vowed that I would get my revenge. I learned that he was a friend of the Iron Fist, so I decided that I would seek them both out if I could escape.' He shrugged. 'You know the rest. Luckily for me, Eadwald didn't cut off my head and throw my body down a pit when I told him who I was.' He let out a small sigh. *At least that part is true*, he thought. 'So, I guess I am a nobleman of sorts,' he said to Selwin.

'I had a good life in Dumnonia, which was wrecked by Mael when he took over.'

'Ironic that your father was part of that same ruin,' Selwin said.

'Selwin!' Hildelith protested. 'How could you be so insensitive?'

The young Saxon blushed and muttered an apology.

Saeric sighed, fighting back another surge of sadness for all that had been lost. 'He's right. I told Eadwald that I wanted to kill him for it. Heremund too.'

Hildelith stared at Saeric, shocked, then looked to her father for confirmation.

Gerard nodded, grinning. 'He did try to take off Heremund's head with the ploughshare, but Eadwald arrived in the nick of time to save his old friend.'

Selwin gaped at Saeric. 'You tried to kill Lord Heremund?'

Saeric nodded. 'I think things would have been a bit different had I been successful,' he said, smiling. 'I'd have been shoved straight down that pit. In pieces.'

'Well, thank the Lord you were not,' Hildelith said, shaking her head at him.

'Don't worry,' Saeric said. 'I know how lucky I am to have been adopted by those two..., three,' he corrected himself, looking at Gerard. 'As I said, it's Mael and Talec who I want to make pay for their treachery.'

Hildelith tilted her head at Saeric. 'I don't imagine Lords Eadwald or Heremund would support you in that quest. And you're just one man.'

'They don't,' Saeric said, 'but there are others who want the same as me.'

'Do you mean the rebellion?' Hildelith asked. 'I thought it was over long ago?' She looked to her father. 'Didn't Eadwald help crush the rebels back in 815?'

'Now you're being insensitive, dear,' Gerard said. He shrugged. 'There are still a few old men in the west who grumble about days long past,' he added, earning a scowl from Saeric, 'but Saeric here remains determined to vanquish his nemesis all on his own.'

'I made a vow,' Saeric muttered.

'We'll help,' Selwin said enthusiastically.

'That would be treason, young man,' Gerard reminded the Saxon fyrdsman, 'something you seem to be drawn to. King Mael is King Ecgberht's vassal and has our protection as a result. I do keep reminding Saeric of that.'

Selwin retreated in the face of Gerard's stern expression. 'Sorry,' he muttered. 'I just want to put things right.'

'I suppose it is reasonable that you would seek some form of reckoning,' Hildelith said to Saeric. She dropped the cloth into the small pail beside her to rinse out the blood.

'Lots of people were betrayed, Hildelith,' Gerard said. 'Treachery is found in Saxon halls, too.'

'Yes, well, you know all about that, father,' she said irritably.

'Hildelith!' Gerard barked, startling Saeric with his sudden forcefulness. 'There will be no more talk of betrayal, treason or vengeance. They are all mortal sins.'

'So you keep saying,' Hildelith muttered angrily.

'Saeric is Eadwald's son,' Gerard pressed on. 'He has chosen to acknowledge him and train him in the ways of a Saxon nobleman. That is a fine path.'

'So he intends Saeric to be a general in the King's army, just like him,' Selwin observed. He turned to Saeric. 'You could do a lot worse, especially since you were a slave before.'

Saeric considered Selwin for a moment, looking for malice, but the youth had spoken plainly and without spite. He was right, of course. It was a fine aspiration for an ealdorman's only son and would most likely have been his destiny had his fate been different, albeit for a different king and kingdom. Would being an ealdorman in Wessex be such a bad thing? *Why walk an impossible path fraught with endless tribulation and pain when a clear route to certain glory lies ahead of me?*

And you speak of others' treachery? said the Devil. *Do you really think that Eadwald would let you abandon his plans for you? He wants you to be king so he can control you, and through you, Dumnonia.*

Hildelith patted Saeric on the arm. 'I've done as much as I can. You both need to be careful not to twist your backs for a while. And I don't care what you say,' she added. 'Eadwald is too hard on you.'

'Not hard enough,' Saeric replied.

The following day, Gerard dragged an unwilling Saeric to the mynster to commence his education and distract him from the pain in his back and his anxious musings about his quest. There was no question of physical exercise, at any rate.

'I have to run an errand for our good friend Eadwald,' Gerard said, as they walked across the market square to the mynster, 'so I'll be away for a few days. Can you promise me that you will behave while I am gone?'

Saeric shrugged. 'That depends on whether anyone provokes me,' he responded.

Gerard paused, then asked, 'have you seen Selwin? I can't find him anywhere.'

Saeric smiled. 'He was facing trial for treason. Where do you think he's gone?'

'That sarding little bastard,' Gerard growled.

'He's not a traitor. He's just stupid. He fell for a Dumnonian lass who was obviously a rebel and who tricked him into helping them.'

'Still a traitor,' Gerard said bluntly. 'And when were you going to tell me he'd talked to you?' He stopped, something occurring to him. 'You encouraged him to run?'

Saeric smiled. 'He is a friend of the cause, even if it was unwitting.'

'For Christ's sake, Saeric. Do you want Eadwald to lash you again?'

'Eadwald's made his point, and if Rodor comes anywhere near me again, I'll introduce him to my ploughshare.'

That drew a snort from Gerard. 'I'll gladly hand it to you,' he said.

'What happened between you and Eadwald yesterday?'

The Saxon stopped for a moment, looking at his British companion in thought. 'Eadwald and I have differing views about your education,' he said at last. 'Eadwald leans towards the blade, while I prefer the calefactory.' He shrugged. 'It's probably for the best, you know. There's no one better to teach you military tactics than Eadwald.' He looked up. 'We're here. Now, I want you on your best behaviour, Saeric.'

Sceaptesburh's mynster was smaller and poorer than Scirburne's monastic complex, but it was nevertheless a place of learning, with its own modest library of books and a well-appointed calefactory. The monk there was at first reluctant to give Saeric lessons at all, citing the Easter Heresy. 'I have no wish to anger God by allowing a heathen Dumnonian into this house. This Briton must repent his sins before I can permit his attendance here.'

That will take some time, Saeric thought grimly, wondering how long this disagreeable old man had been a monk. Brother Sigebert was, in fact, so ancient that Saeric wondered what kept him moving. Sigebert was bent over so much that he had to hold his head at an odd angle so that he could see ahead of him, but he was unable to look so far up that he could see into Saeric's face; the highest he managed was the Briton's broad chest. He was so thin that he resembled a mummified skeleton. The barest breath of wind would surely blow him over, especially with the sail of a habit he wore.

The monk was droning on about something called the latercus cycle, which the heathen Dumnonians had continued to insist on using to determine the date of Easter, despite the Synod of Whitby demanding they subscribe to the Pope's edict to follow the Alexandrian computus. Fortunately, with the pagan Dumnonian king having been ousted, there was now hope that the inbred British would finally accept the will of the Lord and His Servants and adopt the correct means of calculating the date for Easter.

'Saeric?' It was Gerard, trying to get his attention.

'I've no idea what he's talking about,' Saeric said.

'It is far beyond your wit, pagan,' said the monk. 'Do not trouble yourself over it, lest it turns your mind to jelly.'

'I'm not a pagan,' Saeric growled. 'I worship God, just like you.'

The monk let out a snort of disbelief.

'Are you going to teach me to spell or not?' Saeric said angrily, but deep inside, he wondered whether the cleric could see the dark stains of sin in his soul.

'What do you mean he didn't take the bait?' Eanswith snapped. She sprang from the bench and strode angrily to her blue-eyed paramour, who had just arrived from Sceaptesburh. They stood within the gates to Baldwyn's burh, waiting for the stableman to come and take the horse for feed and water. 'That summons cost me a goodly amount of silver and an unpleasant favour. The monk assured me it was as close to genuine as you can get.'

The young man nodded. 'Oh, he believed it alright. He asked me to tell my side of the story, which I did, just like you told me. I even pretended to deny it all, just like any real rebel would.'

'And?'

'He wrote a letter.'

'He *what...*? Eanswith stopped, speechless. *What does he mean, "wrote a letter?" Who would do that? And Sugu can't read or write.* A creeping sense of fear began to crawl its way up her spine, but she quickly quashed it. *Of course he can't. He got a notary to do it for him, as I did.* 'Who wrote it, and what in God's name did it say?'

'Saeric did, and he told Earl Talec to sard off because he didn't think it fair that someone with so much power should make false accusations and try to crush an ordinary man like me. But the main reason he wrote it was to upset Talec, who he hates more than anyone else in the world.'

Eanswith stared at the seventeen-year-old, astonished. She had not expected this at all, although it did bolster her suspicions about her scortum. 'How was it signed? What name and title did he use?'

'Saeric of Burh Scirburne.'

'But it wasn't dispatched, obviously. You made sure of that?'

The fyrdsman winced in apology, which earned him a slap on the cheek.

'Idiot!' she hissed. 'You're as useless as my brother. If that letter should get to Earl Talec....' She recoiled at the thought of the Dumnonian's response upon reading it. At least it could not easily be traced back to her, but what would Talec do in reply? What if he troubled himself to make proper enquiries?

'It already did,' the young soldier said.

'Christ's bones!' Eanswith swore. This was getting worse by the moment. Perhaps her brother was right. *I am too clever for my own good. Why did I sign it from Talec? I could have made up any name!* 'Did Earl Talec come to Sceaptesburh?' she asked hesitantly. It seemed improbable, but how would her own father react if someone flagrantly impersonated him and made false accusations in his name? He'd not rest until he'd flayed them alive; the more publicly, the better.

'No, he sent someone to Lord Heremund to demand an explanation. Lord Heremund sent him away, but I don't know what passed between them. What I *do* know is that Lord Heremund got word to Lord Eadwald about what Saeric had done.' When Eanswith remained silent, he added, 'what did you expect to happen?'

'Exactly what I planned: that Sugu would confide in you and

reveal his true identity on hearing you were a rebel sympathiser. You would get close to him and tell him of your hopes for a new Dumnonia, and he would tell you about his past. You would then earn his trust so that he would ask you to help him, so that you could bring him back to me. Was that too much to ask? I didn't expect him to pick a fight with the Earl, for God's sake. You should have stopped him.'

He smiled at her, then, without warning, grabbed her shoulders and planted a firm kiss on her mouth, then he danced out of her reach, laughing. 'Glad to see you too, my green-eyed witch,' he said. 'I did exactly what you told me to, but you were wrong. He isn't one of the lost princes.'

'Yes, he is,' she said, still reeling at Sugu's unexpected response to the summons.

'No, he isn't. Your plan worked but in a different way. He's Lord Eadwald's son.'

'He's *what*?' Eanswith exclaimed, struggling to maintain her grasp of the compounding revelations.

'The ealdorman himself confirmed it in front of everyone. That's the big secret, my Lady. Saeric is Lord Eadwald's bastard son. Saeric sought him out after escaping from here, intent on revenge. But Saeric was never going to best Eadwald. The amazing thing is that instead of breaking his son's neck and shoving him down a cesspit so that nobody would ever know, the Earl decided to acknowledge him. He's childless, you see. It would make more sense if you'd seen how the two of them treat each other, as I have. They are obviously father and son.' He smiled at the memory of the bickering pair. His expression changed when he saw that Eanswith's face had paled. 'My Lady?'

Eanswith moved back to the bench and sat down, fighting to control the rising sense of panic that gripped her chest so tightly that she found it difficult to breathe. *Why hasn't Eadwald come here to seek retribution for his son's maltreatment? Has Sugu not told them? Or are they still planning their revenge? Regardless of whatever Saeric had or hadn't told his father, a man as powerful and well-connected as Eadwald would soon uncover the source of the fake summons. My father's fyrd is a decent size, but will he stand behind me against the king's master-at-arms? I will have to deal with that monk*, she thought, *and quickly*.

'He's not the bad villein you say he is,' her lover said, breaking into her thoughts. He pulled off his shirt.

'Not here, idiot! Father is in the house, and he'll cut off your manhood if he finds a common fyrdsman bedding me.' She let out a gasp when he turned his back on her.

'Lord Eadwald flogged me raw thanks to my part in your plan,' he said, but his tone held no rancour. 'But it would have been far worse were it not for Saeric's defence of me.'

'His name is Sugu,' Eanswith corrected, frowning at the youth, 'and don't you dare get fond of him.'

He laughed. 'But you told me to!' He raised his hands in entreaty when she glowered dangerously at him. 'Everyone likes him. He's so strong and unafraid of anything and anyone! And you should see what he can do with those big new bows from Francia.' His eyes glittered with adulation.

'Stop it!' Eanswith snapped. 'You're making me ill.'

He grinned back at her, undeterred by her irritation. 'You'll be pleased to know that they like him best for thwarting your attack on that young noblewoman. A righteous hero,' he added, placing his hand dramatically on his bare chest.

'He didn't thwart it. The bitch died. Now get out of here before I flog you too.'

He looked back at her, disappointed.

'You're getting no reward from me,' she said coldly. 'Go back to Sugu and find out what plans he has for me.'

'He wants to kill you. He calls you a debased witch, but fortunately for you, he is afraid of you. In fact, I think you're the only thing he *is* afraid of.'

'Is he now?' Eanswith said, pleased with that piece of news.

'He doesn't know you were behind the ambush on the noblewoman or that you're the source of the letter. Why do you still care about him, anyway? You've got me now.'

He sounded genuinely hurt, which surprised Eanswith. *Stupid boy*, she thought, but she nevertheless felt her desire flare when she looked into his impossibly blue eyes and disarming smile framed by that wild mop of hair. 'I don't care about him,' she lied. 'I care about me. Try to use that simple brain of yours and think about whose son he is. Lord Eadwald, Ealdorman to King Ecgberht. What do you think Eadwald will do when he finds out who kept his son enslaved for most of his life?'

'Oh,' the young fyrdsman said, the implication finally dawning.

'My family and our fyrd – which includes you – are in danger, Selwin. Sugu must be planning his revenge.' She stood abruptly and pushed him towards his horse, which stood obediently near the gate. He began to protest that he'd only just got here, and his horse needed rest, and so did he, but Eanswith was unrepentant. 'I need to know what Sugu and Lord Eadwald, or anyone else for that matter, are planning.'

'Well, you'll need to find someone else to do that. I can't go back there.'

'Why not?'

'I'm wanted for treason, remember? I ran away. Saeric helped me escape.'

'Then you'll need to run back there.'

'They'll execute me!' he protested.

'Get your new friend Saeric to protect you, as he did with that sarding letter. Oh, and I want to know more about that woman of Sugu's. Hildelith, is it? Now get along.'

Selwin let out a long sigh, but he did as he was told. He pulled on his shirt and gathered up his mount's reins. The gelding made his reluctance known by stepping sideways when Selwin moved to put his foot into the stirrup, and Selwin had to snap at him to behave himself.

Eanswith frowned up at the young fyrdsman, her mind conjuring a host of exciting and painful delights to reward his diligence, a goodly part of her wanting very much to drag him off his horse and take him right there on the ground, but that would show weakness, and she was not weak. *Am I not?* she wondered, surprised and alarmed by this boy's effect on her. A voice from within warned her that it was not Selwin who was caught in a spell.

The young soldier made one last adjustment to the reins and then turned on his hip to bid his mistress farewell. 'What are you going to do now?' he asked. 'It's only a matter of time before they come for you.'

She met his clear blue gaze and felt another sharp pang in her chest, but behind it came a wave of fear to swamp her desire. *Sugu is Lord Eadwald's son. We are in peril. It was bad enough that Heremund had taken him in, but now I know why he did.* Her mind swirled with the muddy waters of uncertainty, the dirty mixing with the clear so that all became clouded. 'I'll think of something,' she said. 'In the meantime, stay close to him, and let me know the instant you hear anything about him coming for me.'

She watched Selwin ride back down the road, her confidence shattered. *I must clean up this mess*, she thought, her mind racing as she considered the potential mitigations for this unfolding disaster. How swiftly the tables had been turned. *I am the hunted now.* She frowned at her lover's back and reluctantly came to a decision. *The notary first, and then you.*

❧

The lessons were hard, and as the days dragged by, Saeric grew to vehemently hate the monk and his inexplicable prejudice against Dumnonia and its representative. One day, Brother Sigebert questioned Saeric about Eadwald being his father. It became another reason to be loathed by the cleric; Saeric was a bastard son, a halfling, as though the British part of him was somehow a demonic parasite to be exorcised. *If only you knew how close you were to the truth*, Saeric thought.

'What business is it of yours?' Saeric said instead.

'Leviticus tells us that thou shalt not let your cattle breed with a different kind,' the monk responded. 'Thou shalt not sow your field with two kinds of seed, nor shalt thou wear a garment of cloth made of two kinds of material. You are an abomination, wealh.'

And so it went on, day after day, until Brother Sigebert made the mistake of hitting Saeric with his walking staff when the Briton made yet another error on his practice slate. It was the first and last time the monk struck his pupil. Uttering an expletive, Saeric sprang up, snatched the staff from Sigebert and whacked him with it as hard as possible. There was a snapping sound, and the tiny man toppled to the floor, shrieking.

Yes, yes! encouraged the Devil. *Beat the nasty little ferret. Snap its mean little bones.*

Saeric stood over the monk, holding the staff in his hand, looking into the terrified eyes of the old man and fighting the temptation to succumb to the Devil and unleash his anger. He became aware that someone was shouting, and he looked behind him. A lay brother stood just inside the doorway beside another monk, both of whom bore terrified expressions. The lay brother held out some kind of gardening implement with the sharp end pointing at Saeric.

Saeric dropped the staff onto the floor beside Sigebert. 'You've nothing to teach me,' Saeric said.

He strode towards the door, prompting the two monks to scurry along the calefactory walls in opposite directions.

Hildelith found Saeric out on the practice ground, firing his big bow. She had heard about the commotion in the mynster, and in the absence of her father, had gone in search of Saeric, worried that the Dumnonian might continue to vent his anger in the fort. Saeric stood bare-chested in the cold air, firing the heavy missiles into one of the practice dummies. The straw-filled target bristled with so many arrows that it was falling apart. Creak, whoosh, thud. Another arrow slammed into the target, and Hildelith shuddered at the thought of one of those missiles striking another man. The power with which Saeric fired them was both astonishing and disturbing.

'You should not have attacked Sigebert,' she said cautiously.

'He made me angry.'

'Saeric!' Hildelith said, shocked. 'He is a frail old man. What did he do to deserve your wrath?'

'He hates and mocks me for no reason other than my birth.' Creak, whoosh, thud. 'And he hit me.'

'So you decided to hit him back?' Hildelith scolded. 'You are a hundred times stronger than him. You could have killed him.'

'Is he dead?' Creak, whoosh, thud.

'Is he…?' she let out an exasperated breath. 'No, he isn't, which is pure luck, I expect. And firing those arrows will hurt your back.'

'Will it?' Creak, whoosh, thud. An arm fell off the target, and wisps of straw drifted to the ground after it. Saeric nocked another arrow and drew the string back.

'Do you not feel even the slightest bit of remorse for what you've done?'

Saeric eased his grip on the bow and let the string go slack. He turned to Hildelith. 'What do you want me to say?' He went to reset the arrow, but Hildelith snatched it out of his hand and threw it aside.

'What is wrong with you?' she demanded. 'What has made you so angry all of a sudden?'

'I can barely read or write. I know nothing about my own kingdom. And every day that monk mocked me for it. It's not my fault I'm illiterate. It's your fault for destroying my home and putting me into slavery. What chance have I – little better than an ignorant serf – of ever recovering what was taken from me? You pretend to be my friend, but you're no better than the rest because you're one of them.' Saeric reached down to the quiver for another arrow, but Hildelith kicked it away, sending arrows scattering in a fan across the grass.

'None of that is my fault,' she said. 'I didn't choose to be born this side of the Exe. Why does that even matter?'

'Because your father was in Dumnonia when my family were murdered by the Traitor and his allies, the Westseaxna. How many of my kin did he cut down in Mael's name?' Saeric shoved the bow at Hildelith and walked away, distressed not by the pain of his uncle's betrayal but by his inability to forgive and accept Gerard and his daughter, whom he liked very much. Compounding his suffering was the guilt he felt for befriending these Westseaxna, which itself was a betrayal of his family and his kingdom, to say nothing of the responsibility he felt for failing to save Leo, who he shouldn't feel guilty about because she was Westseaxna too. He stumbled toward the gatehouse, confused, distressed and disoriented.

'He wasn't any part of it, Saeric,' Hildelith called after him. 'He wasn't a soldier back then. In fact, he wasn't anywhere near Dumnonia when all that happened.' Hildelith hurried after him, catching him on the other side of the fortress' wall. 'Saeric, stop! I'm sorry. I didn't mean to upset you. I am just trying to understand.'

He kept walking.

'Saeric! Where are you going?'

'Home,' he called, without looking around, then he quickened his pace.

That's a long walk, observed the Devil, choosing that moment to re-join the conversation.

The wind rattled the dry autumn leaves in the trees as he

turned towards Scirburne. Saeric paused, realising the Devil had meant Caer Uisc, but Saeric had been thinking of Heremund's. He let out a curse and walked on.

Hildelith wasn't letting go. She hurried after him, and for a moment, he was tempted to run, but he felt stupid. *What am I running from?* He paused and waited for her to catch up with him. She stopped a respectful few paces away.

'Saeric, I'm sorry. I can be stupid and insensitive sometimes. I didn't mean to hurt you.'

Sometimes? he thought.

'Having Eadwald as a father cannot be easy.'

'He's *not*...!' Saeric said emphatically, and then he clamped his mouth shut.

She frowned at him. The wind was tousling her hair into her face. She brushed it away, annoyed. 'He's not what?'

'Eadwald...' Saeric paused, not knowing what to say and wishing he'd not come up with this sarding idiotic ruse. It felt like a further betrayal of his family and kingdom.

'He has acknowledged you, Saeric. That must mean something to you?'

'Of course it does!' Saeric snapped.

'Then you are most fortunate. Lords Eadwald and Heremund are both good men. As is my father.'

'I'm not sure luck has anything to do with it,' Saeric said, an edge of bitterness in his voice.

You're quite right, the Devil confirmed.

'Saeric, why won't you trust me? You trust my father.'

'No, I don't trust any of you.' The leaves swirled around their ankles as the wind gusted from the northwest. Bad weather was on the way.

'Then why did you fight those brigands and save my father's life?'

'Because I could,' Saeric retorted. 'Because he was about to be killed, and I could stop it. It was instinctive, that's all. I'm not the hero that everyone thinks I am, and he owes me nothing.'

Hildelith frowned at him. 'You do know they were after my father, don't you? The attack was an assassination attempt, and you waded in and foiled it.'

'What? Why?'

'You haven't a clue who father is, do you? Has no one told you?'

Saeric stared at her. What in God's name was she talking about? 'They were thugs robbing a merchant. We just stumbled upon them. I did what anyone would have done.'

Hildelith let out a long sigh. 'No, not anyone. You put all of them down, Saeric. With a plough. But if that means nothing to you, why then did you stand in and take the lash for Selwin?'

'Because I got him into trouble. It was my fault, and I had to make things right.'

'But can't you see that all this makes you special? You acted with honour and courage. Many would have let Selwin take the lash.'

'Then they would be lesser men for it!' Saeric flared. 'Why are you doing this? Why won't you let me be?' He spat out an expletive and started walking westwards again.

'Because I like you!' She called after him. 'A lot.'

He slowed down, then stopped and turned to look behind him. Hildelith hadn't followed. She stood in the middle of the road, a few yards back, her arms spread wide, shaking her head at him.

'How can you like me?' he asked. 'I am broken, a sinner. You've seen what they did to me.'

'Yet you are a good man. You don't accept injustice. You stand up for what is right, no matter who is challenging you, even when it is one of the kingdom's most senior noblemen.'

He walked back to her. 'I am *not* a good man,' he said, his voice harsh.

'No one has an ill word to say about you.'

'I can think of a few.'

'Who?'

Saeric glared at her, furious and grateful at the same time. *My family*, he thought. *My brother, sister, mother and father. And Caelin, who I promised I would look after, but who I left to be taken into a heathen Hell. They all remain unavenged while I live a life of comfort amongst my Saxon enemies.*

'Why do you hate yourself so much?' Hildelith asked. The first raindrops had begun to fall; large, wet and cold. Hildelith reached up and put a hand to Saeric's face, but he jerked his cheek away from her. She pressed on, undeterred. 'I know that you were treated horrendously by that thegn and his family, and nothing will ever take that hurt away. But that doesn't mean you are unlovable or that love cannot find a place in here one day.' She put her hand on his bare chest, and he felt the warmth of her palm on his skin. 'For now, let that love rest here,' and she took his right hand and placed it on her own chest, 'and maybe one day you will be ready to take some of that love into your heart again. But do not ever believe you are unworthy of love, Saeric.'

Saeric shook his head, tears in his eyes. 'You're wrong,' he said. 'I am marked by the Devil for what I have done.'

'No,' she argued. 'You were a little boy, an innocent lamb taken by the Devil. That woman and her kin are evil. The Lord has a place in His heart for you.'

'No, I tell you, he doesn't!' Saeric said. 'He put me into her hands and left me there so that she and her brother could do their worst with me. They did it for years, Hildelith. I belong to the Devil, not God!'

'Then we must put away those Godless demons so that you can be exorcised of them. Let my father and Heremund deal with them!'

He wrenched his wrist from her grip and growled, 'I told you, she and I are as brother and sister in mortal sin. How do you kill someone who has already given over their soul to Satan?' He turned and walked into the gathering darkness as the rain began to thunder down.

'Where are you going?' she called after him.

'Away from you!'

'I am trying to help you!'

'And I you,' he said. 'Stay away from me if you want to remain unpolluted by sin. You deserve better than me.'

He stalked off, fists clenched, his distress roiling inside his belly like the storm clouds above. *What is wrong with me?* he wondered, struggling to understand the change in his mood and the inexplicable grief he felt deep within his heart. It seemed to be more than just Eanswith. He cast his mind back through the day, wondering what had triggered it. *Caelin?* he wondered. *Are you the reason I am so distressed? Are you showing me what Hell is like because I doomed you to an afterlife of torment and sin? Is that to be my punishment for my failure to fulfil my promise to you and mother?* He took a deep, shuddering breath, realising with horror that this must be the explanation behind his visions and his fits of rage. *You are trying to drag me down into your world, where we can be together once again, only it will not be the glorious reunion I had imagined.*

He paused and looked back at the fort, all at once yearning for the security of its walls and the company within, but at the same time hating himself for it.

I *tried, Caelin, but it is as Hildelith says: I was just a boy. Surely you know that? Why are you so angry with me? Shouldn't it be Mael or Talec you seek to destroy, or even father or Berec? How could I have made a difference in the outcome?* He tried reaching out to his brother but felt only distress and pain in return, mirroring his own anguish. Another thought occurred to him, one which was even more disturbing than the idea that Caelin might be behind this. *What if I'm wrong? What if these feelings are not Caelin at all but, like the voice of the Devil, are simply another sign of my madness; insanity brought on by the extremity of my suffering?*

The rain was pouring down now, throwing up spatters of mud and dirt as it splashed into the earth around him. He stared up at the grey, rain-misted sky, feeling utterly helpless and alone.

I'm never going to be King. I'm probably never going to set foot in Dumnonia again. Caelin is long dead and lost in the fiery torments of Hell, and I will not be long in joining him.

He stumbled along the road into the gathering night, the rain hammering his head and shoulders, his tears mingling with the rain on his cheeks.

5
A purseful of pennings

Sceaptesburh, Wessex

Gerard found Saeric the following morning, curled up and shivering in a byre amongst the cattle. Saeric had made a nest of hay for himself, just like he'd done when he had been a slave at Baldwyn's.

'Jesus Christ,' Gerard swore, upset to find his charge in such a sorry state. He tried to rouse Saeric, but the Briton told him to go away and drew his arms tighter around his knees. He was wet and cold and wanted to be left alone.

I'm hopeless, Saeric thought. *Too weak and afraid to do what I should have done years ago – rammed a dagger through my heart to bring an end to this life of sin and self-delusion. I was never going to get my kingdom back, let alone avenge my family. How could I, after so many years of slavery and isolation, of living in ignorance of the world around me while I indulged in acts so vile and debased that even God turned his face away in disgust? How could I ever have believed myself worthy of wearing my father's crown?*

'Up you get,' Gerard said and grabbed Saeric roughly by the arm and hauled him out of the hay. Saeric tried to resist, but his exposure to the frigid night had weakened him, so he allowed himself to be manhandled by his Saxon comrade. He had not gone too far along the road because the storm had quickly worsened, forcing him to seek shelter. As Gerard and Drefan half-led, half-carried Saeric back to the fort, Saeric noticed the debris littering the road where the gale had stripped the trees of the last of their autumn leaves.

They soon had him sitting before the fire in the barracks hall, a blanket wrapped around his shoulders. Gerard handed Saeric a mug of warmed mead and placed a bowl of steaming broth on the bench beside him. 'What am I to do with you?' the Saxon said, smiling and shaking his head.

Saeric took a drink from the mug, savouring the warmth and sweetness of the mead. There was nothing much to say, so he shrugged.

'At some point, you'll have to accept our fellowship,' Gerard said.

Saeric looked around him. The soldiers of their cohort variously chatted, played dice, and laughed as they regaled one another with stories. They paid scant attention to Saeric, other than to confirm that he was unscathed by his latest adventure. He finished off the mead and picked up the bowl of broth.

'I know I keep saying this,' Gerard went on, 'but you can't achieve your dream without our help. Unless you're still planning on raising an army of your own and arming them with all those buried swords and pitchforks?'

Saeric remembered having that conversation weeks ago with Eadwald and Heremund. He frowned at the fyrdsman, keeping his voice low so he could not be overheard. 'I will seek help from Kernow. Their king will gladly come to my aid. He was vassal to my father.'

'Alas, they didn't do too well during the rout, if I recall,' Gerard observed. He paused, frowning at Saeric. 'Do you even know who the peninsula king is now?'

Saeric scowled back at the irritating Saxon, trying to remember the vassal king's name. 'Hernam,' he said.

'Nope. He's dead. His son Hopkin ascended the throne a couple of years after the fall.'

Saeric thought the name sounded familiar. Perhaps he had met him in Caer Uisc. It was too long ago, and those memories were now blurred. 'He will rally to my call.'

'I doubt it. The stragglers who fled west after the fall convinced Hopkin to lead a rebellion against Mael some years after your lot were thrown out. In return, your dear uncle Mael led an army, swelled by his West Saxon allies under Ecgberht himself, that swept to the very end of your lands, crushing all resistance and forcing Hopkin to accept vassalhood to Dumnonia and Westseaxna Ríce. That was eight or so years ago now, and we've not heard a peep from him since.'

'Yes, Heremund told me all about it,' Saeric grumbled, 'but I'll wager Hopkin wishes nothing more than to take off Mael's head for his betrayal. He'll be planning his revenge.'

'I doubt it. Hopkin has a small fyrd and few resources; certainly nothing compared to the might of Wessex, particularly after they lost so many men in their failed uprising. They were required to pay a hefty wergild for their insurrection. The only way you'll get your kingdom back is with our help, not Hopkin's.'

Saeric let out a long breath. 'You're wrong. The men of Kernow have always been strongly independent. I remember my father complaining about their stubbornness.'

'Ah, the Easter heresy,' Gerard said.

'Not that again? Why is it so important?'

Gerard did his best to explain the centuries-old rift between the Celtic and Eastern Roman churches, but Saeric failed to understand why the church of Kernow was so determined to dig its heels in for something so trivial. 'It's not trivial, and it's one of the main reasons that the Pope supports Mael,' Gerard said. 'Your uncle accepts the Pope's decree. Hopkin does not. It greatly annoys King Ecgberht because he thought all that was settled by your ancestor Gerontius' submission a hundred or so years before to King Ine.'

'What a stupid reason to go to war,' Saeric said, then he paused and frowned at Gerard. 'How do you know all this stuff?'

Gerard spread his hands and smiled. 'I was fortunate to receive a good education, although my father disapproved of my scholarly indulgences. And contrary to what you might believe of me, I was forced into military service, and I hated every moment of it. But I'm retired now, and I find history a rewarding pursuit. Heremund chose smithing, and I chose books.'

Saeric took another spoonful of broth, and then it occurred to him. *Books?* 'You can *read*?'

Gerard's smile broadened. 'And write. In three different languages, in fact,' he added, obviously immensely proud of this achievement. 'Four, if I include Greek, but I'm not very accomplished in that, so I'm not sure it counts.'

Saeric shook his head, surprised again by Gerard, and annoyed that he was, like Heremund and Eadwald, better educated than Saeric. 'Hopkin *will* rally behind me, and no one can speak *four* languages.'

Gerard put down his mug and frowned at Saeric, his face showing concern. 'He really won't, Saeric. He is an intelligent man, and he knows when he is outnumbered.'

'Meaning?'

'Put yourself in his place. What do you bring him, other than a thirst for revenge?'

'I am the rightful king of Dumnonia,' Saeric said, glancing around to make sure no one could hear him.

'And Hopkin is the rightful king of Cornubia – sorry, you call it Kernow – who, I might add, still has his crown. You do not. What are your plans for him? He failed utterly to defend Dumnonia. How can you allow him to remain your vassal? That's what I'd be thinking if I were him. Don't be so sure he'll come running into your arms, his eyes glistening with tears, joyful that you are alive.'

'Fuck you,' Saeric said, standing up and heading for the door.

'The Dumnonia you knew is gone, Saeric,' Gerard called after him. 'That's what Heremund and Eadwald keep trying to tell you, and that's what's making you so angry.'

Saeric went outside, picking up his bow and quiver on the

way. He was soon slamming more arrows into the two remaining targets. Thanks to his earlier fury, the other mannequins lay in shreds on the ground. He wished he was back in the smithy so that he could take out his frustrations at the forge. There was something profoundly satisfying about using all his strength to bash metal into and out of shape; no matter how hard he hit it, it willed him to strike it again.

Gerard came out, bearing ale. 'Listen, Saeric. At some point, you'll have to sit down and hear us out so that we can fill you in on a little of the history of Dumnonia since... since you were taken. I know how painful that is for you, but....'

Saeric turned and pointed the bow at Gerard, just as he had previously done to Eadwald. And just like Eadwald, Gerard appeared unconcerned. The Saxon's lack of regard for his wellbeing annoyed Saeric so much that for a fleeting moment, he thought about releasing the arrow. 'You'll just tell me whatever lies you need to protect your precious peace.'

'Peace *is* precious, Saeric. That's what you don't seem to understand. I get it, you are angry, rightly so, for the wrongs that you have borne, but you need to start looking around you. It was a long time ago now. No one wants another war. It's bad enough that Mercia is picking fights with Ecgberht. Most of us here don't want to go off to fight another battle. Some of the fresh recruits like Selwin do, of course, because they've never seen combat. They don't know the smell of blood or the kind of fear that makes you shit your pants. Let them go to war. Me, I'm happy where I am.' He reached out and gently pushed the arrow aside with the mug, then offered the drink to Saeric. 'Direct your anger at Mael, not us. I will keep saying this until you accept it: we are not your enemy.'

Saeric refused the ale but did release the string. 'I want Mael dead. How do you propose I overthrow him without a fight?'

'Oh, there might be a little skirmish over that, but if you truly are who you say you are, I think we can manage a transition with limited bloodshed. Most people will be smart enough not to argue with Wessex.'

'And I become your vassal king.'

'And we all live happily ever after,' Gerard agreed, smiling.

'I want to go home.'

'You said it yourself: you're not ready.'

Saeric realised that Gerard thought he had meant Caer Uisc too. He let out a wry laugh. *That's the second time I've done that*, he thought. *I really have been turned.* 'I meant Scirburne.'

'With an e?' Gerard joked, offering the mug again. 'You have lessons,' he reminded Saeric.

'Sard the lessons. And Brother Sigebert is unavailable.'

'All joking aside, Saeric, you should not be so offhand about what you've done. He is an important member of the Church, and Bishop Ealhstan will seek reparations.'

Saeric frowned at Gerard. 'You don't seem to mind so much.'

Gerard shrugged. 'Sigebert and I were not… close,' he said cryptically, 'and you still have much to learn. Don't you want to know about Dumnonia and her history?'

'Seems like you can teach me all that I need to know. After all, you can speak *four* languages.'

'It is true that one of the best scholars on Dumnonia resides in Scirburne. You've met him: Brother Donagh.'

Saeric smiled. 'The one who thinks I'm a demon?'

'That's him. Might be fun, no?'

Saeric relented and took the ale. 'Just who were you before you joined the fyrd?'

'There are two paths to scholarship, Saeric; nobility and the church. Which do you think it was?'

Saeric frowned at Gerard, recalling the exchange between Gerard and his daughter and how Eadwald had responded to Gerard in their argument after the lashing. He had seen Eadwald's unexpected genuflection. He felt a tingle in his spine as he realised to his shock that he had completely underestimated the affable fyrdsman.

Gerard smiled at Saeric and nodded. 'You and I are more alike than you imagine,' he said.

'How?'

'The principal difference between us is that you want your kingdom back.'

Saeric blinked at Gerard. 'You're a *prince*? Drefan said as much, but I didn't understand what he was saying to me. What happened?'

Gerard grinned at Saeric, then he clacked his mug against Saeric's and swigged his ale down in one go. 'That, your grace, is a very long tale,' he said, 'but it will have to wait. Right now, we need to deal with your ignorance, and the best place to do that is Scirburne.' He turned and started walking back to the barracks.

'Where are you going?' Saeric asked.

'To pack. Are you coming?'

Saeric and Gerard rose early the following morning. Gerard would not be drawn on their earlier conversation, despite Saeric's best efforts to extract more from the fyrdsman about his past. 'All in good time,' Gerard had said, not bothering to hide his amusement at Saeric's confusion and discomfort. 'But don't worry. You saved my life, which is a debt that I will not forget, no matter what happens in the months to come.'

'You speak as though one day we might cross swords.'

'That will be up to you,' Gerard said. 'We're taking quite a gamble helping you in your quest, after all, and that assistance will not come free of obligation. We trust you will not turn on us as soon as you win back your crown.'

'You know I wouldn't do that,' Saeric said, somewhat hurt by Gerard's implication.

'Ah, but you do not yet know what will be asked of you in return for our help,' Gerard said. He was not smiling.

Those words did little to reassure Saeric, and he stole a glance at the Saxon as they carried their travel kit toward the fort's gatehouse. *Who the Hell are you?* Saeric wondered.

Hildelith was waiting outside the gates with three fine horses, saddled and ready for riding. Saeric swallowed, wondering what to say to her. She looked magnificent atop her horse, and he felt like an awkward adolescent as he approached her. 'Why are you here?' he said clumsily.

'I sent word,' Gerard explained, then realising Saeric was probably wondering how on Earth Hildelith could have got all the way from Scirburne in such a short time, went on, 'she has been staying with her grandmother, who has a small house just outside town. That's where she came from the other day when you had your tussle with Sigebert. Did you not know this?'

Saeric judged from Hildelith's wry smile that the house was anything but small. Her horse and tack also suggested that she, or her family at least, were people of considerable means, which confirmed that Gerard was indeed a man of wealth and influence too. On reflection, there had been a host of small hints of Gerard's nobility. *I am so blinded by my own afflictions that I cannot see what is in front of me*, Saeric thought.

'Yes, it's bigger than Heremund's burh,' Gerard confirmed, smiling at Saeric's expression. 'Bit of a sore point. Best not mention it. Now then..., what in God's name is he doing here?'

Everyone turned to where Gerard was looking. Standing half-hidden behind a large elm tree was Selwin.

'What are you doing there, boy?' Gerard demanded. 'Come here. Now.'

Selwin didn't move.

'Let me talk to him,' Saeric said, dropping his travel pack and walking up the road to where Selwin waited.

'Lord Saeric,' Selwin said in greeting. He was nervous and kept glancing over at Gerard.

'What are you doing?' Saeric asked. 'I didn't cut you free so that you could come back to be arrested.'

'Where are you going?' Selwin asked.

'Scirburne. Why?'

'Can I come?' Selwin asked. 'I want to clear my name, but you're the only one I trust to make sure I get a fair hearing.'

'I can't guarantee you that,' Saeric said, 'and Eadwald will likely order your execution the moment he sees you. You've seen how much attention he pays to anything I say.'

'Well, it's better than being tied up here on my own,' Selwin said.

Saeric let out a sigh. 'We'll have to ask Gerard.'

The two young men made their way back to the travelling party. Gerard stood with his arms crossed, waiting for an explanation. Selwin said that he remained deeply grateful to Saeric for all that the Briton had suffered on his account and wished to repay that debt, and he also wanted to apologise for bringing trouble to Lord Heremund. Gerard warned Selwin that Heremund was unlikely to be pleased to see him, but Selwin said that it was the right thing to do and that he would accept whatever punishment Lord Heremund commanded. He only wanted the opportunity to defend himself. Gerard remained unconvinced, but he said he would do whatever he could to deter the smith from chopping off his head, a guaranteed fate should Eadwald find him there. Selwin said that he would take that chance.

'Problem is,' Gerard said, 'with you tagging along, Selwin, we have too few mounts.'

'No trouble,' Saeric said quickly. 'I'll walk.'

'What?' Hildelith said, incredulous. 'I've picked a reliable mount for you.' She looked down at him, annoyed.

'In God's name, Saeric,' Gerard protested, 'it's too far to walk, and you aren't helping matters, Hildelith.'

'I know how to ride,' Saeric said defensively. 'I just don't like horses.'

Hildelith rolled her eyes and turned to Selwin. 'What about

you? Can you ride? If so, you may escort me.'

'Of course, my lady,' Selwin said, far too enthusiastically for Saeric's liking. The young man deftly climbed aboard the chestnut gelding, then reached around behind him and strapped his small bundle to the back of the saddle.

Hildelith shook her head at Saeric. 'I have no intention of dawdling along with you,' she said and trotted off. 'Enjoy your walk.'

'Is it safe for her to ride alone?' Saeric wondered.

Gerard smiled. 'Are you really asking that question?'

'She's not alone,' Selwin said, looking hurt, then he took off after her.

'You'll have to watch that bright-eyed boy,' Gerard warned. 'I think he quite fancies my daughter, poor lad. He's younger than you and has a fine body, fresh and mostly unmarked. He is also far less complicated. Women prefer uncomplicated men, you know.'

'Well, he's certainly that,' Saeric grumbled. 'He's barely been weaned. I doubt he'll have any idea where to put it.'

'I hope you're not suggesting that my daughter has loose morals?' Gerard said, but he was smiling. 'I think you know she can look after herself.' He tilted his head in thought for a moment. 'Perhaps she'll make you both fight to the death for her hand. That would be more her way.'

Saeric let out an annoyed grunt and hefted his travel sack over his shoulder. 'Selwin can have her. She hates me anyway.'

'No, she doesn't. Quite the opposite. Would it be so hard for you to let her care for you?'

'We've been through this. I've already been in the care of a Saxon woman, and I didn't much enjoy it.'

'And I have also said that Hildelith is nothing like that woman,' Gerard objected.

Saeric looked up at his mentor and saw that he had genuinely upset Gerard. 'I'm sorry,' he said. 'It's just that... she makes me feel....' He stopped, unable to admit that he felt helpless and inadequate in her presence, which frightened him.

Gerard grinned down at Saeric from his horse. 'So, you *do* fancy her,' he said, 'but you have no idea what to do about it? Was it the swordplay that sealed it for you?'

Saeric scowled up at Gerard, annoyed that the Saxon was right. In part, at least, although truth be told, Saeric had felt attracted to Hildelith from the first time he'd met her. He felt that same little tingle in his heart now as he remembered the moment.

'My advice is to let down some of those walls and see what happens. Hildelith has a good heart Saeric, and so do you. Now, at least let me take that,' Gerard added, nodding at Saeric's sack, but the Briton stubbornly refused and started down the road. Gerard let out a sigh and followed on horseback; his mount delighted that they were travelling at such a leisurely pace.

Eadwald frowned at the slim, well-dressed Dumnonian, who stood respectfully with his hands behind his back, awaiting his master's response. They stood in Eadwald's anteroom in Wintanceaster burh. 'Are you sure that's what Earl Talec said?' Eadwald asked, confounded by the spy's report.

The Dumnonian nodded. 'Yes, my Lord. He is definitely not the source of that summons. He also said that he believes Saeric is your son now, but before the incident with the summons, he was convinced that Saeric was the rebel who appeared in Escanceaster this summer past.'

'Tell me more about this rebel.'

'Reports from witnesses are that the young man was clearly from a wealthy background. They spoke of a standard woven in gold.'

'Gold?'

The spy nodded, his eyes fixed on Eadwald's.

Eadwald raised his eyebrows. 'But Talec has given up on his hunt now?'

'No, my Lord. If anything, he is keener than ever.'

'Remind me,' Eadwald said. 'When is all this meant to have happened?'

'Just after St Bartholemew's Day.'

'And nothing's been heard of this rebel since?'

The Dumnonian shook his head. 'Earl Talec has committed considerable resources to find him, but the rebel has vanished completely. That is why he was so excited when Saeric's letter arrived in court. He thought he had been looking in the wrong direction and that the rebel had come to you, perhaps to seek redress.'

Eadwald raised his eyebrows.

'You will be amused to hear that our king was more concerned about you betraying him by siding with the rebel, than any possible risk that the same rebel may have posed to your own life.'

'Why am I not surprised?' Eadwald said. 'Mael must have been very disappointed to hear that I remain in good health and that he was barking up the wrong tree.'

'Indeed, my Lord. But now Earl Talec is back where he started.'

'What happened to the young man you say was seen with the rebel?'

'He got away too and has vanished.'

'Back into the west whence he came, no doubt. I don't understand why Earl Talec should be so interested in these two? What's so special about them that deserves all this attention? Even a gold standard, if it is true, doesn't justify it.'

The spy took a sip of his wine and placed his goblet back on the table, his movements careful and measured, like a cat considering his prey. Eadwald felt a tingle in his spine as he looked into the dark, unsettling eyes of the Briton.

'More than one witness swore that the rebel who wore the golden wolves could neither speak nor understand a word of Dumnonian.'

Eadwald let out an involuntary expletive. He stared at the other man, stunned. *No. That's impossible. After all this time, they both appear within months of each other? What manner of enchantment is at work here?*

There was a knock on the door. Eadwald did not hear it, so a more strident thump followed it. 'What?' Eadwald snapped, coming to his senses.

The door swung open, and his adjunct leaned in and winced in apology. 'I'm very sorry, sir, but we've just received the information you sought about that recruit named Selwin. We need to make for Sceaptesburh immediately.'

'Why?'

'Selwin has never been to Escanceaster, was not on that ambushed wergild transport, nor can anyone find any evidence he was ordered to join Sceaptesburh garrison.'

'Then who is he? Is he a fyrdsman at all?'

'Oh yes, my Lord. It is to whom he is vowed that will concern you.'

'Jesus Christ!' Eadwald swore, the answer arriving immediately. 'Baldwyn?'

Saeric and Gerard spent the night in a cramped and filthy guard post halfway between Sceaptesburh and Scirburne, neither getting much sleep in the draughty building. They arrived at Heremund's the following afternoon, tired and irritable. Carwyn was delighted to see them and greeted them warmly. Heremund, however, was considerably less welcoming.

'Was that letter your idea or his?' Heremund demanded, nodding in Gerard's direction.

Saeric had barely set his travel sack on the ground. 'It was mine,' he said before Gerard could answer, 'but I don't need you to lecture me about it.'

'Saeric,' Gerard warned.

'Can we perhaps eat before you descend into an argument?'

Carwyn suggested. 'You must both be famished. From where did you set out this morning?'

'Ealdorman Talec's reeve stood right where you are now, Saeric,' Heremund growled, ignoring his wife, 'demanding that I hand you over to explain yourself. When he showed me your disgraceful letter, I was sorely tempted to do so. What in God's name possessed you to write it, and what part of "stay out of sight" do you not understand?' His voice rose in volume and pitch as he spoke.

'He was provoking me,' Saeric countered.

'And you snatched his bait and swallowed it whole,' Heremund roared, 'without even a second thought! You are beyond stupid, Saeric.'

'Heremund!' Carwyn cried, frowning at her husband. 'That's enough shouting, and stop treating him like a child.'

'I will gladly do so when he stops acting like one. What happened to all your fears of being found out by Talec's spies?' he demanded, shaking his head at his apprentice. 'I don't understand you at all!'

'Let them come!' Saeric snapped. 'I'm sick of all this waiting, and I'm sick of being told by everyone that I'm useless, can't spell, can't handle a sword, and don't know anything about my homeland! I was enslaved for most of my sarding life. What was I meant to do? I'm never going to be good enough for any of you, so I might as well just go back to my original plan and get my revenge.'

'You can't expect change to happen overnight, for God's sake!' Heremund said, exasperated, 'and you know what will happen if you try to assassinate King Mael!'

'I made a vow, and I should have stuck to it.'

'Saeric, you don't mean that,' Carwyn said in an attempt to calm tempers. 'You are still a young man with good prospects ahead of you, especially with my husband's support.' She took his hand in her own and switched to the Dumnonian tongue. 'I know you are suffering a great deal of pain and hurt for what was done to you, and they are very great hurts indeed, but that means you need to give yourself more time to heal and forgive.'

'They killed my sister in front of me, laughing while they raped her, one soldier after another. Then when they were done, they chopped off her head and threw it in my lap. I was nine years old, cowering in the corner, crying while she died trying to protect me. I only survived because my older brother found me, but then he got himself killed so that I could run away.'

Carwyn closed her eyes and took a long breath, then she opened them and said, 'and my husband and Lords Gerard and Eadwald will help you avenge them, Saeric, but you owe it to your kin to live and become the man you were destined to be.'

'And who is that, exactly?' Saeric said, feeling powerless and hating it.

Carwyn raised her hand and gently rubbed his cheeks. 'Only our Lord God knows your ultimate fate, Saeric, so you must trust in Him to guide you. He brought you here, did he not? I know you're more than you let on; I have seen your face in another man. It was many years ago, but the resemblance is unmistakeable.'

Saeric blinked at her, astounded. 'What? Who?'

Carwyn smiled but did not answer the question. Instead, she smiled and said, 'will you promise to stop all this nonsense about throwing your life away and instead return to your studies? While I know they are Westseaxna, the men who stand before you are genuine in their desire to help you, and you would be hard-pressed to find anyone better as instructors. Your rage is justified, but you need to find someone or something else to take out your anger on.'

Saeric glanced up at the smithy, took a long breath, and nodded at her. 'I am not ready to forgive,' he said.

'I know,' Carwyn replied.

'I think I'll go and bash some metal for a while,' Saeric said. He turned to Heremund, his anger having dissipated thanks to

Carwyn's intervention. 'What I did was stupid and wrong,' he said to the nobleman, 'and I should not have used your sigil. I'm sorry I did it without thinking of the trouble it might cause you.' He let out a sigh. 'And you don't need to punish me because Eadwald has already helped me atone for my sin.' He tugged off his tunic and turned so that they could see the fresh welts on his back, still raw and scabbed. He left them without waiting for their reactions and walked across to the smithy.

'God in Heaven,' Carwyn said, turning to Gerard. 'Lord Eadwald didn't do that, did he?'

Gerard nodded.

'Justifiably,' Heremund grumbled. 'Saeric should not have made such a threat in my name. I would have whipped him too.'

'What is the matter with you all?' Carwyn protested. 'Don't you know that it only makes things worse?'

'Eadwald would disagree, my Lady,' Gerard said, his tone one of regret. 'He believes that violence is the only way to get through to Saeric.'

'But you do not, surely?'

'No,' Gerard said, throwing a pointed look at Heremund.

'What passed between you two just now?' Heremund asked his wife, deflecting Gerard's censure.

'We can all see how deeply wounded he is thanks to the horrendous suffering he has endured. I reminded him that he is safe here and that he needs to trust that we have his best interests at heart.' She patted her husband on the arm, then added, 'so you need to be less hard on him, dear. Now, where have our boys got to?' She turned and strode over to the house, calling the twins' names.

There was a crash from up at the smithy, followed by the harsh whooshing of the bellows as Saeric began working them to bring the forge up to heat.

'What are we to do with him?' Heremund muttered. 'Dare I ask how his studies have progressed?'

'Ah,' Gerard said, wincing. 'I'm afraid not so well.'

Heremund frowned. 'Meaning?'

'He didn't get on with Brother Sigebert.'

'And?' Heremund growled.

'Saeric hit Sigebert with his staff.'

Heremund stared at the soldier, shocked by the news. 'Why in God's name did he do *that?* Is Sigebert all right?'

Gerard let out a long sigh, unsure what to say. 'Saeric broke Sigebert's arm.'

'Christ on a cross!' Heremund exclaimed, then his eyes narrowed. 'Where were you in all this? You've been trying to get rid of Sigebert for years.'

'He is old and senile, and it's no loss to either church or kingdom, in my opinion.'

'You should take care what you say, Gerard,' Heremund growled.

'You know perfectly well why I hate that odious weasel,' Gerard countered.

Heremund shook his head with disapproval. 'Why would Saeric do such a thing? Did he have another turn?' He looked up at the Briton working away at the bellows. 'Perhaps he is possessed by a demon after all.'

'No. It's simpler than that,' Gerard said. 'Carwyn has the nub of it. He is suffering deep hurts, and it takes nothing to send Saeric into a fit of rage. Sigebert made no attempt to hide his contempt for his British pupil, and he provoked and needled until Saeric could take no more.' Gerard let out a sigh. 'The old fool struck Saeric with his staff. Saeric took exception and hit him back with it.'

'Christ almighty,' Heremund said, letting out an explosive breath. 'Ealhstan is going to demand retribution, and rightly so.' He frowned at Gerard. 'I'm surprised he's not come here already, demanding wergild or a more severe punishment.'

'It's only just happened. That's why we left.'

'So you came running back here to hide?' Heremund said, disgusted. 'He'll have to face the consequences, and so will you.' The smith swore roundly at the fyrdsman. 'You were meant to keep an eye on him. If there's to be any compensation paid, it will damn-well come from you.'

'It's already done,' Gerard replied, struggling to keep his own temper in check. 'And there is only so much I can do, Heremund. Saeric is at his limit. We are pushing him too hard. You heard him: every day he spends with us, the more he realises how deficient he is. Saeric was born expecting to be a well-educated, carefree prince living a life of luxury and ease. Instead, he's an ignorant, horribly abused villein, furious at the world for all he has lost. We need to get him onto a battlefield somewhere, and soon. He needs to let out all that rage, or he'll burn himself up with it and us with him.'

As if to prove the point, Saeric began hammering ferociously at a rod of iron, whacking it with immense force, his teeth bared like a dog's as he snarled at the metal.

'He'd get himself killed on the first outing,' Heremund disagreed. 'He has nowhere near the skills required to survive. He'd just barge into the middle of the fray until he got cut down, which he would, eventually. It's one thing to fend off a few brigands, but faced with hundreds, if not thousands, of well-armed and armoured soldiers?'

'Well, we have to do something,' Gerard said. 'It seems the more we help him, the angrier he gets, which is somewhat insulting and greatly troubling. You and I both have family to think about.' Gerard frowned. 'Speaking of family, where's Hildelith?'

Gerard's frown deepened when he saw the confusion on Heremund's broad face.

'What are you talking about?' said the smith. 'Hildelith is with your mother, is she not?'

A stab of fear struck Gerard. He took a breath to calm himself. *She's probably gone to one of her friends, but then what of Selwin?*

'Gerard?' Heremund asked, seeing the alarm on the soldier's face.

'They left Sceaptesburh together yesterday afternoon on horseback,' Gerard explained. 'They intended to ride straight here. The weather was fair, and they left in plenty of time.'

'They?'

'Hildelith and Selwin.'

Heremund frowned at his friend. 'Who *is* this Selwin fellow?'

'An all-too-attractive young recruit who has taken a fancy to my daughter, and for his sins is also the subject of the summons that has caused us all this bother.'

Heremund frowned at his friend. 'And they rode out alone?'

'Saeric wouldn't ride, so he and I walked.'

'Gerard, how well do you know this Selwin?'

For a moment, Gerard didn't follow, and then he realised what the smith was suggesting. He suppressed another pang of worry. 'Not so terribly well, to be honest,' he said, 'but if you imagine some kind of conspiracy here, I just can't see Selwin being a part of it. He's not the type. He's a popular, good-looking recruit who, incidentally, was even more severely punished by Eadwald for his part in all this. And until he's proven innocent, Selwin remains accused of treason.'

'You think him blameless?'

'I didn't say that. If the summons was sent by Talec, then it's likely to have some basis of truth, don't you think? Talec is too canny to fabricate something that could be too easily disproved.'

'Yet you let that boy ride out alone with your daughter? What if he *is* part of Talec's plan? Or, worse, he's not, and instead, he's a desperate young man trying to save his skin.'

Gerard laughed. 'Whilst I don't know Selwin all that well, I know my daughter, and she is more than capable of fending off the likes of that boy.' Gerard shook his head, unable to see Selwin in the role of a kidnapper. 'I think it more likely that he hopes to win her heart, delusional though that may be. He's a villein's lad after all.'

Heremund smiled. 'Well, it's no mystery then, is it?' He tapped the side of his nose. 'Perhaps he's succeeded in his quest, and they've found a snug little bothy somewhere along the road to spend the night.' He winked at the soldier. 'That would surely attract Saeric's attention, would it not?'

'She scarcely knows the boy, and he's barely old enough to sprout whiskers,' Gerard said, mirroring Saeric, 'and you know as well as I do that she is too well-bred to succumb to such carnal desires, no matter how tempting. For all her protestations, she is a discerning woman who has, for whatever reason, chosen Saeric as her objective in love.'

'Well, she could do worse, and it would be a convenient match.' Heremund rubbed his stubbled chin and looked up at Saeric, who was busy pounding his rod of iron into oblivion. 'What do you think prompted Talec to send that summons? I still struggle to believe it is a coincidence that Selwin happened to be stationed at Sceaptesburh.'

Gerard took a sip of his ale, pondering that prospect. 'Do you think Talec has caught Saeric's scent?'

'I'm not sure,' Heremund said. 'Something is going on, certainly. You are right that the story behind the summons is true. There was an attack on an escort, presumably by rebels, and the wergild was stolen. Dumnonia has yet to send a replacement and is thus still owing our king a goodly sum.' He poured himself another ale and topped up Gerard's.

'So, what are you unsure about?' Gerard asked.

'Talec's reeve's line of questioning was odd, and he seemed frustrated with the answers I was giving him, as though they didn't meet his expectations. I'm not sure what he was after, but he left here disappointed.' He turned from the smithy and looked at Gerard. 'He let something slip that has left me feeling troubled.'

Gerard waited for more.

'He said something about a rebel appearing in Escanceaster during that last hot spell before autumn set in. I think he believed

Saeric was that rebel. But the timing didn't work, and as soon as he satisfied himself that Saeric wasn't his man, he took his leave.'

'Rebels appear from time to time, although not so often now, it is true. What's so special about this one?'

'I don't know. He shut up when I started asking about it. I think the letter was aimed to draw Saeric out, but for a different reason.' He shrugged. 'I've sent word to my contacts in the city to find out more. We'll have to wait and see, but I think Saeric's secret remains safe for the time being.'

'Well, I have a way we can throw Talec right off the scent,' Gerard said.

Heremund raised his eyebrows.

'Saeric and Eadwald have convinced the men of Sceaptesburh that Saeric is his bastard son.'

Heremund's eyebrows arched in surprise. 'Really? That *is* a grand tale and quite plausible too. Whose idea was it?'

'Saeric's. It happened after one of the many all-too-public arguments he was having with Eadwald. He called him 'father.' What made it so believable was how Saeric said it. He really meant it. Saeric does see Eadwald as a father figure, and dare I say it, old Eadwald does seem to have taken a less than impartial interest in Saeric's welfare, despite what he says otherwise.'

Heremund smiled at that. 'For all his stiff-necked aloofness, our master-at-arms has a heart after all, eh? I think we should blow on those coals and fan the flames. Let's begin in the mynster on Sunday. We can argue about Saeric, and you can blurt it out. In the meantime, I will send another man to Escanceaster to spread the rumour there.' He nodded to himself. 'Yes, this is a fine plan.'

He looked into his empty mug and then up at the sky. 'Your girl had better hurry along if she wants to avoid the bad weather,' he said. 'You are worrying needlessly, my friend. Hildelith is off having a lovely time tormenting that boy. She'll be here tonight with the poor fellow panting at her heels so she can rub Saeric's nose in it. I'll wager a purseful of pennings on it.'

It had been easy to say, but as the sun began to set three hours later, Gerard was no longer so sure. He stood beside Heremund, frowning along the road to Sceaptesburh. The weather had turned blustery and cold, with sporadic rain squalls sweeping across the town—hardly ideal conditions for a romantic interlude.

'Are you sure you're not over-thinking this?' Heremund asked, frowning at the lead-grey sky. 'God knows Hildelith takes after you when it comes to lacking common sense, but are you certain she was coming here to us?'

Gerard made a face. 'Well, not exactly. She was too busy telling Saeric off for choosing to walk that we didn't discuss their destination, but the intention was always to return to Scirburne.' He squinted through the rain into the distance. He could just make out another traveller in the deepening gloom, leading a horse. He and Heremund had been standing on the road for the past hour and were soaked through. They had questioned all passing travellers, but none had any word of Hildelith or Selwin.

'Is he waving to us?' Heremund asked, peering into the rain.

'I think he is,' Gerard said, the knot of panic returning. He uttered an expletive when he recognised the horse. 'That's Hildelith's mare!'

He set off running down the road. The distant horseman picked up his pace too, and Gerard saw that the beast was lame, favouring its front left leg. A man was definitely leading it – Gerard knew his daughter's gait as well any father would – but in the worsening conditions, he couldn't see whether or not it was Selwin. Gerard turned to Heremund. 'Raise the alarm,' he said. 'Round up the men and horses. I'll meet you back at the burh.'

He continued running, and then his heart froze. The man leading the horse was not Selwin; in fact, he didn't recognise him at all. 'Christ in Heaven, Hildelith,' Gerard muttered in despair. 'What have you gone and done now?'

6
Mine Alone

Scirburne, Wessex

As Gerard approached the horse, he saw that her shoulder had been slashed, and a trail of blood ran down her leg from the wound.

The other man let go of the reins and raised his hands in entreaty on seeing Gerard's wrathful expression. 'M'Lord, I came upon this horse in the woods near my 'ouse. It was frightened and 'urt, as you can see. I saw the brand on its rump and knew that it belonged to a Lord. So I brought it 'ere, fearing bandits 'ad attacked its rider.'

'You did well,' Gerard reassured the man, who was, like Gerard, soaked to the skin, but unlike Gerard, dressed in the plain clothes of a ceorl. Gerard quietly swore as he inspected the horse and saddle. The cut in the animal's shoulder was deep, caused by a sword or perhaps a glancing blow from a spear or lance. Hildelith's travel pack was still tied to the backrest. 'How and where did you come upon her?'

'Not so far up the road, me Lord. Me 'olding is near Thorent. I'm tithed to Lord Dunstan. I was feeding me 'ogs when I 'eard the 'orse whinnying in the wood. It seemed to be looking for 'elp. It didn't run from me when I took its bridle.'

In the town behind them, the mynster bell began pealing the alarm. The call to arms had been raised, and those men of the fyrd who were in town this night would soon be gathering in the burh.

'Do you know whose horse this was, me Lord?' The man asked.

'Yes,' Gerard said. 'Come with me. You must tell us everything you know. And you need to get dry.' He took the bridle, and they made their way straight to the burh, although progress was slow thanks to the mare's injury.

Dunstan was still abroad with most of the fyrd, but by the time Gerard and the ceorl passed under the gatehouse, at least two score men had gathered in the inner courtyard. Not the best fighters, but men-at-arms nonetheless. Heremund was shouting orders at the slaves and servants, sending them on various errands to prepare for an expedition. He spotted Gerard and called him over. Gerard handed the horse to a manservant, then led the ceorl over to Heremund.

'Damn this rain!' the ealdorman shouted over the uproar. 'How will we see anything without torches? All clues to their whereabouts will be washed away, sard it. Is this the man who found the horse?'

Heremund fired a stream of questions at the poor ceorl, who tried his best to answer with as much detail as he could recall. When the ceorl had provided sufficient information to meet Heremund's satisfaction, the ealdorman dismissed him, instructing him to go into the hall and dry himself by the fire.

'Regardless of the outcome, we must remember to reward that man for his honesty and wit,' Heremund said. 'Ah, there he is,' he added, waving at Saeric. His apprentice was hurrying through the gates bearing an armload of swords. He also had his bow over his shoulder, and a quiver of the heavy arrows slung across his back.

'Take it all into the hall,' Heremund said. 'And leave the bow and arrows behind. You must know the rain will wreck them?'

An unburdened Saeric reappeared shortly afterwards and made his way towards the gate.

'Where are you going?'

'To get the ploughshare.'

'For Christ's sake, Saeric. You have a sword. Use it!'

'Well, I need to get it then,' the Briton said coldly and hurried back down the hill.

'Is it a good idea to bring him along?' Gerard asked. 'He hadn't even noticed that Hildelith was missing.'

'He was too busy chafing over my rebuke,' Heremund answered, 'but he's come to his senses now, so I don't think we have a choice, do you? Thank Christ,' he added, as the rain shower ended as suddenly as it began. 'Our main problem is that we have only a few horses. Dunstan took most of them with him on his campaign. I've sent word to Sceaptesburh, for what good it will do us now.'

'We're better off without them,' Gerard said. 'It's dark, and Thorent is not so far away. If we take oil-soaked torches, we can light them between squalls. Maybe bring one or two horses to carry the gear and return the injured?'

'If they're alive,' Heremund said, 'and if they're anywhere near there. We've no idea where they were attacked, if indeed they were attacked, whether they've been taken hostage or slain by the roadside, or even how long that horse was wandering the road. You and Saeric were following along behind them. Did you not see anything out of place?'

Gerard shook his head. 'Nothing at all,' he murmured.

The ealdorman rested his hand on Gerard's shoulder. 'I'm sorry old friend. I should have listened to your concerns earlier. She's a feisty lass, well able to look after herself. You taught her that, so if anyone has a hope of fighting them off, she does.'

'If that's so, then where is she?' he demanded.

'Sheltering somewhere? Tending to Selwin perhaps, afraid to leave his side?'

Gerard knew both were unlikely, but he appreciated that Heremund was maintaining an optimistic front. 'We'd better get this rabble organised, or we'll have no hope of finding anyone.'

It took a further hour or more – it was impossible to tell, for the bellringer at the mynster seemed to have forgotten to toll the liturgical hour in all the excitement – but at last, the search party set off towards Thorent. Heremund, Gerard and Saeric led the way, alongside a freshly re-clothed ceorl, who bore a fine new cloak in thanks for his duty to his Lord.

More rain came through, and a breeze picked up, making for miserable progress. It was deep into the night by the time they arrived at the village of Thorent. All the windows were shuttered, and Gerard heard the clack and clunk of bolts being rammed to as the frightened villagers locked their doors upon the arrival of the small war host. Heremund ordered some of the men to search the houses in case the pair were sheltering or being held in one. He asked the ceorl to take them to his house and show them where he had found Hildelith's mare. They lit their torches and began combing the woodland on either side of the town. They called the names of both the missing, but the only replies they heard were cries of startled birds and the rustlings of the animals of the night as they scurried to safety ahead of the search party. After a fruitless hour, the men fanned out, widening their hunt, always moving eastwards towards Sceaptesburh.

Then, suddenly, there was a shout from further up the road. The searchers converged on the voice, which came from somewhere deep in the woods north of the main party.

'What is it?' Gerard demanded, his words edged with desperation as he bashed his way through the thick undergrowth to the serf who stood pointing down into a gully.

'A horse, my lord.'

Gerard snatched the torch from the fyrdsman and scrambled down the muddy slope, stumbling on the roots and brambles that clogged the ditch. It was Selwin's gelding, no doubt at all. The animal's throat had been cut, and he had bled to death where he lay. Of Selwin, there was no sign. More men were arriving with torches, and soon the forest was alive with bright flame and dancing shadows as they spread out in search of Hildelith and Selwin. Heremund made his way over to Gerard, whose face was drawn and pale.

'Neither of them is here. I don't know whether that is a blessing or not. Someone led this gelding here and slew him, Heremund. This was no accident.'

'No, it wasn't,' the big man said, struggling to gather his wits. 'They were ambushed, that is certain.'

'Who would do this? And how did Saeric and I miss it?'

'I'm not sure,' Heremund answered, uncharacteristically indecisive. 'They certainly went out of their way to hide this horse. I–'

He was interrupted by a long, anguished cry that came from somewhere behind them. Heremund's heart froze. Both men looked at one another, then spoke the name together. 'Saeric!'

The sky had just begun to lighten to a steely grey pre-dawn when Saeric's torch sputtered out. He muttered a curse and closed his eyes, waiting for his vision to reset. He stood unmoving in the woodland, listening to the juxtaposed sounds of water dripping from leaves interspersed with the urgent shouts and calls from the men around him in their frantic search. The musty smell of damp earth and rotting leaves filled his senses, and there was something else. Blood? Saeric opened his eyes, but he could see little in the gloom. Every so often, there would be a burst of orange as one of the searchers' torches came into view, vanishing again as they passed back into the thick underbrush. He closed his eyes and sniffed again, then, following his nose, turned to his right and took a few steps.

There was a shout from somewhere ahead and to his left, and while he couldn't make out what was being said, he knew that it was different to the other calls. He saw that the torch-bearers nearest to the road were turning towards the shouts.

They've found something!

He dumped the expired torch and turned to follow. Almost immediately, he stepped on something that was neither hard nor soft, and he tripped over whatever lay in his path. Startled, he scrambled to his feet and looked down to see that it was a person lying on their back. They lay unmoving, their eyes wide open but unblinking. He could just make out the pale skin of a hand clutching a grievous stomach wound. Blood had spread from the deep gash to soak the tunic and pool beneath the body. Although diluted by the rain, the air still carried the unmistakable smell of death.

Saeric opened his mouth to call for help, but he was far too late.

'No,' he murmured instead, shaking his head, shocked and angry. 'How can it happen again? Why? WHY?'

Saeric's cries of fury and despair rang through the rain-soaked forest as another squall swept over the breaking day.

Gerard arrived first, having taken as straight a line as possible across the road and through the forest to where Saeric crouched beside the body. The soldier came to a hard stop, panting, then he let out a sob of relief when he saw who Saeric had found.

'Selwin?' he asked, rain-mingled tears dripping from his nose.

Saeric didn't hear Gerard at first, and the soldier had to repeat himself. Saeric came to his senses, looked up at Gerard, and then nodded silently.

'Requiem æternam dona eis Domine,' Gerard murmured the last rites, crouching down opposite Saeric and making the sign of the cross over Selwin's forehead. 'Et lux perpetua luceat eis.' Selwin's face was frozen in death with an expression of shock and surprise. Gerard closed the dead soldier's eyes and muttered a further private word for him. Around them, the woodland flared with flickering light and shadow as the men converged on Saeric and Gerard.

Heremund pushed his way through the gathering. He took one look at the tableau before him then he began issuing orders. 'Spread out. Look for signs. Footprints, hoofprints, blood, broken undergrowth, torn clothing, lost arrows, anything! Go!' Saeric rose to join the search, but Heremund grabbed his arm and nodded at the body. 'I take it this is Selwin?'

Saeric nodded.

'Hopefully, the men will find something that tells us what has befallen Hildelith, but I am more certain now that she is alive.'

'How can you know that?' Gerard growled. 'We've only just found Selwin, whose horse was slain too. My daughter could be lying anywhere in this wretched forest, dead or dying, so I'm damned if I will stand around waiting for news!'

'Two score men are looking, Gerard, and light is coming. She is not here. We need to start thinking about where she might have gone or been taken, most likely the latter.' He looked down at Selwin. 'What is he doing here, so far off the road?' he said. 'Were you running away from or towards someone, I wonder?'

'What do you see?' Saeric asked his mentor.

Another burst of rain arrived, and Heremund let out a curse as he rolled the stiffening body on its side. He pointed at the hole in Selwin's back. 'A spear did this. Went right through him. Close-range thrust from the front; not thrown. Was he chased in here to be ambushed? He didn't receive that wound on the road. It put him down where he stood.'

'Maybe he was taking a piss?' Saeric suggested.

'This far in? And if someone was waiting to ambush him, how could they know he'd stop at this very spot to relieve himself?' He dropped Selwin back down onto the ground.

'Because it was planned,' came Gerard's voice, hard with anger.

'What?' Saeric said.

'We don't know that,' Heremund cautioned, looking back down at Selwin. 'What have I missed?' He saw it as soon as he said it. 'Sarding Christ. He's still wearing his sword.'

Saeric blinked at Heremund in surprise, and then he too looked down to see that the fyrdsman's sword was sheathed in its scabbard. *How did I miss that?* He wondered. *Had it been obscured by the way the body had been lying? Surely he would have drawn it at the first sign of trouble?*

'It was dark and raining,' Heremund said. 'He must have been taken by surprise.'

'It wasn't raining last night,' Gerard countered, 'and you said yourself, he is too far in. There are no signs he was dragged from the road. I think he was killed right here, and he knew his attacker. Why else would he be unprepared? This has to be Talec's work, and that little shit betrayed us!'

'Let's not jump to conclusions,' Heremund warned again. 'I agree it is likely Hildelith has been kidnapped. The question is, by whom, and why?'

'Because Talec didn't get what he wanted, Heremund, and now my daughter is paying the price.' He turned his gaze onto Saeric, and the Briton felt a chill when he saw Gerard's cold glare. 'I expect he will soon be offering a trade.'

'Perhaps, but you do have one or two other enemies,' Heremund said, deep in thought. The forest around them was lightening as the day brightened. They heard the occasional calls from the men as they conducted their search for clues to Hildelith's whereabouts.

'And that's if they did take her,' Saeric said. 'What if it was brigands and she's waylaid or wandering about somewhere, carrying an injury? Maybe she has been found already and is in someone's care?'

'True, but unlikely,' Heremund said. 'Nevertheless, we mustn't leave any stone unturned.'

He shouted to one of the nearest fyrdsmen and issued new instructions. 'Split up. Some of you continue searching the forest. The rest of you spread out and go to every house and knock on every door again, in my name. Knock them down if need be. Hildelith may well be hiding or being tended by someone, and if not, someone must have seen or heard something.' He turned to Saeric. 'Pick him up. We need to take him back to Scirburne. He'll be a pig to strap onto a horse in that condition, but we'll have to do our best.'

'I'm not leaving here until I have my daughter,' Gerard said.

Heremund let out a sigh. 'You must do what you feel is right,' Heremund said, 'but I think we are best off returning to Scirburne. If Hildelith has been taken for ransom, as is most likely, they will send word there. Come, Saeric.'

Heremund was right about Selwin's body. While they did manage to get the awkward corpse up on a horse, Selwin in rigor mortis made for a macabre scene. 'He'll soften up again in time,' Heremund said. The old general frowned, then touched Saeric's forearm. 'Listen to me, Saeric. Gerard is not thinking straight. I think it's best you avoid him for the time being.'

Saeric nodded dumbly, still shocked by the terrible turn of events. There was no avoiding the fact that this was a direct result of his own foolish actions, and Gerard must be thinking the same. He made a final adjustment to one of the knots tying Selwin to the horse and gave it a good tug to test his handiwork. It wasn't as solid as one of Gerard's knots, but it held. He looked into Selwin's handsome face, marred by death, and suppressed a surge of self-hatred. *This is all my fault*, he thought. *None of this would have happened if I'd not been so desperate to lash out at Talec.*

Heremund clamped a fatherly hand on Saeric's shoulder. 'Don't be too hard on yourself, Aneurin,' he said, breaking his promise and using Saeric's birthname. 'If the evidence is to be believed, then Selwin betrayed you. Perhaps this was Talec's plan all along?'

'Selwin can't have been involved,' Saeric protested. The Saxon recruit had been such a bright, carefree young man; there had been no hint of treachery in the admittedly brief time he'd known him. Yet here he was, his dead face right there before Saeric. *A victim, surely?*

Heremund shook his head. 'It is just too coincidental that a fresh recruit should arrive in Sceaptesburh, befriend you, then receive a summons from one of your greatest enemies; second on your vengeance list, no less.'

Saeric let out a long breath, wishing he could somehow reach back in time and tell his impetuous self not to rise to Talec's bait, as Heremund had warned.

'If you want to put things right,' Heremund offered, 'then find Hildelith.'

'Oh, don't worry,' Saeric said. 'I'm going to find her, save her, then when I know she is out of harm's way, I will go after those who did this, no matter who they are.'

Heremund was about to reply when a shout rang from the forest. 'We've found another one!'

&

'What have you done?' Eanswith cried in dismay, staring at the woman trussed like a stag over the back of the horse. She was almost certainly Sugu's woman, and she looked to be in poor health.

'She's alive, m'lady,' said the man leading the horse. 'See?' He poked the woman, who frowned and muttered something, then fell still again.

'You dumb-witted fool!' Eanswith shrieked. 'I gave you clear instructions. Lure Selwin away from the burh, kill him and dispose of his body. Simple. So what the Hell is *she* doing here? And where is Selwin?'

'I thought you'd be pleased, mistress,' the man said defensively. 'We had to act quick, 'cause they decided to go back to Scirburne. She rode with fyrdsman Selwin, so we didn't have no choice. She came after us because the weasel screamed when we skewered him.' His mouth twisted into a sneer at the memory of it. 'She killed me bruvver, m'lady, and nearly got me.' He turned and punched the prisoner to emphasise his point. She barely reacted.

'And where is your 'bruvver' now,' Eanswith demanded icily, looking at the other horses beyond him.

'We 'ad to leave 'im, m'lady. What with 'er an' 'er horse kicking up such a racket, we got out of there wit' haste.'

'Jesus, son of a whore,' Eanswith swore. 'You left him and Selwin *behind?*'

The villein nodded, his scowl deepening. 'We did what you told us, miss.'

Eanswith sprang at him, tugging her dagger from its sheath and plunging it into his chest with both hands. She fell with him, kneeling on his stomach as she wrenched out the blade. She slammed it into him a second time, just to be sure. He croaked and coughed blood. 'No, you did none of what I asked.'

'Bitch!' cried one of the men, and she heard the tell-tale hiss of a sword being drawn from its scabbard. She turned to see a flash of steel. There was an odd splocking sound, and then the fyrdsman flopped forwards onto the ground, headless. Bright red blood spurted from the stump of his neck, and Eanswith sprang up out of the way, dagger in hand.

A second fyrdsman's cry came to a gurgling end as a sword burst through his right lung. He slid off the blade to reveal Eanswith's brother standing behind him. The third man turned to run, but Edward cut him down, hacking off his arm at the shoulder and then plunging his blade into the man's chest.

Blood was everywhere, spattered all over Edward and the yard, and a goodly amount had made it onto Eanswith's skirt. Edward stood amidst it, his face dark with rage. He stepped over the body of the first fyrdsman to stand before his sister, who blinked at him, shocked but grateful for his violent intervention. Edward punched her in the face; a forceful blow that sent her reeling backwards. She screamed in shock and pain. Blood streamed from her nose, and she fell onto her bottom in the bloodied dirt, gasping.

'How many more people must I kill to protect our family because of *you?*' Edward yelled at her. 'You have gone too far, sister. This will bring the full force of the king upon us. He will slaughter us all, thanks to you. I told you to forget Sugu; I even found that young fyrdsman for you. But no, you had to keep chasing Sugu, biting at his ankles like the mange-ridden bitch you are.' He stood over her, his mouth an ugly sneer. 'Well, I've got a new plan. We do have a hostage, but it isn't her.'

Eanswith scowled up at him, wondering what he was talking about.

'It's you, stupid bitch,' he snapped. 'In return for a promise of immunity, I will hand you over to Ealdorman Heremund, who can do whatever he wants with you. I expect Sugu will be very pleased with my gift. I'll be the hero who rescued Sugu's betrothed and handed over her kidnapper.' He stood back, his sneer turning to a bitter smile. 'Who knows, I may even be gifted my own burh in thanks for my service to the kingdom.'

Eanswith glared up at her treacherous brother, eyes streaming with tears of pain and indignation. Her siblings appeared from the hall, staring in shock at the scene of the slaughter. 'You imbecile,' she muttered, her voice muffled by her swelling nose. 'After everything that you did to Sugu, he'll cut you down before you can speak. It's my attention he craves, not yours.'

'I treated him well; you're the one who sliced, beat and strangled him in your foul games.'

'So says the sodomist,' she snarled. 'He hates you, brother. He'll kill you the moment he sees you, and believe me, you're no match for him.'

'Pah,' he scoffed, moving over to the horse and their prisoner. He began loosening the ropes and called to his younger brother to come and help him. His pet slave attended instead, and the dark-skinned boy deftly released the knots and bindings. He and

Edward then eased the woman to the ground, and she flopped over them, barely conscious.

Easy for you to tell me to leave Sugu alone, she thought, glaring at her brother, *now that you've got your own plaything*. 'Shove a sword through her and feed her to the hogs,' Eanswith said, then she let out a whimper and stopped talking, for the pain in her face was becoming unbearable.

Edward ignored her, and with his scortum's help, he half carried, half led their captive into the hall. Eanswith was left sitting alone on the bloodied ground, surrounded by the bodies of her father's fyrdsmen. Edward reappeared in the doorway moments later and called out to her. 'You can sort out that mess since you made it, and you can explain to father why more of his men are dead.'

Eanswith let out a sob, and then she scolded herself for succumbing to her distress. *No*, she thought angrily. *I will not become a bargaining piece for you, brother. If I am to go down, I will do so fighting, and I will take Sugu, his bitch, and you to join Satan in Hell. A fitting end, don't you think, for there we will be free to play our sinful games for eternity.*

❧

'Selwin was up to his neck in this,' Gerard said. 'It can be the only explanation. How else would they have known when and where to attack?' The retired fyrdsman's voice was strained, and Saeric knew his friend was close to breaking point. Hildelith was his first and only surviving child. Gerard's wife had died in childbirth when Hildelith had been just six years old. The boy had been stillborn, trapped in the passage to light and life, taking his mother with him as she bled until she was drained white.

Heremund rubbed his temples, deep in thought. He and Gerard, as well as Saeric and several others from the search party, stood around two bodies, which lay in the forecourt of Scirburne burh. This morning there was no sun, just heavy grey clouds threatening more rain. No one in Dunstan's burh recognised the second man, who had been found in a thicket between Selwin and the road. He wore the plain, unidentifiable clothing of a villein or ceorl. A long blade had killed him; not Selwin's, because his sword was clean, so possibly Hildelith? Or someone else? Most of the men of the town were still out in search of Hildelith or a clue to her whereabouts, but few now believed she would be found. Most agreed this was a good thing because the absence of a body – considering that the assailants had not been concerned to leave two behind – likely meant she had been taken alive after all.

'I agree,' Heremund said at last. 'This is not the work of bandits, and Selwin was a part of it. We just don't know whether his death was a betrayal or bad luck, or perhaps even Hildelith defending herself.'

'I know it has to be true,' Saeric said, 'but I still can't quite believe it.'

'Why, because you don't want to admit he duped you too?' Gerard said angrily. 'He wanted to come with us to Scirburne, and he leapt at the chance to ride alone with Hildelith. I think he played his part, then was executed when his job was done. Damn you, Saeric, if you weren't so frightened of bloody horses and had ridden with us, Hildelith would not have been taken! There would have been four of us, not two.'

'Gerard, this is not helpful,' Heremund said. 'The last thing we need is to start tearing at each other's throats. For what it's worth, I believe this has the marks of Talec all over it. Hildelith was present when Earl Talec's man paid us his visit. She was not especially polite to him. You might say she defended you and your honour quite strongly, Saeric.'

'Oh,' Saeric said, somewhat humbled by that revelation. Then a worrying thought occurred to him. 'What did she say…?'

'Did she give you away, do you mean?' Heremund knew exactly what Saeric was thinking, and he shook his head at him, unimpressed. 'She told the Dumnonian the truth as she knows it, which is that you are a recently-freed British slave who hates most everyone around you, Westseaxna and Dumnonian alike. He asked whether you were a rebel. She answered, not yet.'

'Christ Almighty,' Saeric muttered.

'You should be grateful she spoke up for you. She also told him that I was high on your retaliation list, as was Talec himself, but that Carwyn had convinced you not to slash my throat, and instead, you have set the past behind you to start a new life as my apprentice.'

'Christ on a cross. She did everything she could to get me arrested!'

'It's the opposite, you addlepate, and is it not the truth? Her words, not mine, convinced Earl Talec's reeve that you were no danger to him. Her frank answers painted you for what you are: one of the many aggrieved and deluded Dumnonians who dream of returning to a time long past, and that the letter was a misguided attempt to relieve yourself of some of your guilt and frustration. I only wish I had learned of your status as Eadwald's son before the reeve came so that I could have planted that seed too.'

'So he kidnapped Hildelith for being rude to him?' Saeric asked.

Heremund shook his head. 'While I can understand why the reeve might want to teach Hildelith a lesson for her lack of diplomacy, what good would it serve? Why invite retaliation from Westseaxna Ríce, which in this case would be considerable? It makes no sense.' He paused, then shifted his gaze to Gerard. 'There is one other thing I cannot reconcile... get right in my head,' he added, seeing Saeric's querying frown at the big word. 'The Dumnonian envoy didn't seem to know who Selwin was.'

Both Gerard and Saeric made expressions of surprise.

'But the summons was all about him,' Gerard protested.

'Yes it was. The reeve very much wanted to see that summons and was unable to hide his frustration when I told him that both it and Saeric were in Sceaptesburh. Remember that I have never seen it; only Saeric's response to it. The reeve shut up when I started to ask him questions about it. It was almost as if he didn't know what was in it.'

'So, what are you saying?' Gerard demanded.

'I think the summons was a fake.'

'What? Then who…?' Gerard said.

'It isn't beyond the realms of possibility that this has nothing to do with Saeric at all,' Heremund said, 'but the people who could answer our questions lie dead before us. We have no clue about one of them, but the other, we do know. We need to look into Selwin's past, if indeed that is even his real name. Who is he, and from where did he hail? For what reason did he come to Sceaptesburh? That may give us some clues.' He took a swig of his ale. 'We need to send word to Sceaptesburh garrison, but who can we trust there? Was Selwin working alone? You knew him. What do you think?'

'He was intelligent and self-interested,' Gerard said, 'but he was too young and inexperienced to have devised such a plot. That summons looked genuine to me and would have been expensive to prepare, fake or not. Someone else is behind this, and I don't think you should be so quick to discount Talec. Saeric's letter was deeply offensive, after all.'

'And so have your actions been in the past, Gerard, which is why you shelter here under me and my brother's protection. Do not be so quick to discount *your* enemies, my friend.'

Saeric looked at Gerard, intrigued.

'They wouldn't dare,' the old soldier growled. 'I made my peace with them, and in any case, they would have to answer to my mother, and no one is that foolish.'

'Regardless, we may need to bring Eadwald's influence to bear. If it is your enemies, which I think is increasingly likely, you will need his support.'

'I promised never to put Eadwald in that position again,'

Gerard said. 'It was a condition of my reprieve, remember?' He glanced at Saeric and the other onlookers awkwardly. 'Why wait until now to act? It makes no sense.'

Saeric stared at the soldier. *Reprieve? What in God's name have you done?* he wondered.

'Where is Eadwald now?' Heremund asked. 'He said he was going to make his way back to Wintanceaster after dropping in to talk to you both. I know there is some concern over the rise of this new king in Mercia – Beornwulf, is it? I don't fancy a tussle with that kingdom, but I hear he has his eyes on Wessex.'

'He'd be a fool to try it,' Gerard said, 'but a man who deposes his own king is not to be trusted, is he? Eadwald is in Wintanceaster, as you say.'

Heremund turned to Saeric. 'I need you to go to Eadwald.'

Saeric looked back at him, surprised. 'Me? I've never been to Wintanceaster before. I don't even know where it is.'

'It's the biggest town in the kingdom, for Christ's sake!' Gerard exploded. 'Ask anyone, and they'll point you in the right direction. And you will damn well ride a sarding horse!'

'But what about Hildelith? Shouldn't we be looking for her?'

'We've men aplenty doing that,' Heremund said, 'and you're the only person other than Gerard who I trust right now.'

'How do you know it wasn't him?' one of the onlookers said, pointing at Saeric.

Saeric, Gerard and Heremund all turned in unison to the fyrdsman, who flushed and muttered an apology. Saeric, having spent so much time getting to know the men of Sceaptesburh, had forgotten that he was somewhat less popular at Dunstan's burh.

'Go to Wintanceaster, find Eadwald, and tell him what has happened,' Heremund said. 'Follow whatever instructions he gives you. Gerard will stay here to await the ransom demand, and I will ride to Sceaptesburh. Someone has to tell Lady Ethelfleda the bad news.'

'Why don't I visit her on the way?' Saeric said.

'Because she won't take the news well from you,' Heremund said, 'and I don't need her declaring war on Ecgberht.'

'What? Why would she–?'

'You think Ecgberht is behind this?' Gerard snarled.

'We can't be sure of anything yet,' Heremund warned. 'Someone also needs to go to Escanceaster.'

'Why Escanceaster?' Saeric asked.

'We still need to rule out Talec.'

A new voice entered the conversation. 'None of that will be necessary.'

They all turned to see a sweaty, dusty ealdorman striding through the gates, followed by a small group of equally saddle-worn soldiers. Rodor was among them. Given the state of the men, they had clearly ridden fast and hard.

'Eadwald! We were just about to send word,' Heremund said.

'I have news,' Eadwald said, 'but first, a drink for my men and me if you please. He held out his hand to receive the mug of ale thrust at him by one of Dunstan's ceorls. He gulped it down thirstily and asked for another. He and his fyrdsmen stood stretching their aching muscles, glad to be off their horses. 'I'm getting too old for hard riding,' Eadwald said, gratefully taking a second mug of ale. Once he had finished it, he began to explain. 'Following my first visit to Saeric and his new friend over the summons, I made some enquiries about Selwin. I came as soon as I received my answer, but I see I am too late.'

'What answer?' Gerard and Saeric said in unison.

'Firstly, you can rule out Ecgberht. This has nothing to do with Gerard's past misdemeanours.'

'Thank Christ,' Heremund muttered.

'Would it surprise you to learn that Earl Talec had nothing to do with that summons either?' Eadwald said. 'He doesn't know who Selwin is because Selwin was not on that robbed wergild shipment. The lad's never been anywhere near Escanceaster, nor is he a rebel sympathiser. We have, however, been able to establish to which fyrd he is tithed. Can you guess?'

Saeric swallowed and felt a cold hand of dread grip his heart. 'Baldwyn?' he said, his voice a hoarse whisper. *Now why did I know that?*

Eadwald nodded.

'But why?' Saeric felt as though someone had punched a hole in his stomach and was stirring his insides with a laundry paddle.

'I was hoping you might be able to answer that,' Eadwald said.

'Is it because I escaped? It's nearly a year past. Why wait until now? I don't understand.'

Eadwald shrugged. 'You know the family better than any. Perhaps they've been planning it for a while, and perhaps this isn't their first attempt.'

Saeric frowned, and then he came to the realisation at the same time as Gerard.

'Leofwynn?' Gerard asked. 'But I thought–'

'I've no proof, but I would not be surprised if we learned this was the work of the same person behind the assault on you and Leo.'

Gerard's attack on Saeric came so suddenly and violently that it caught everyone by surprise. The old soldier grabbed Saeric by the neck and crushed his throat with his hands, screaming an incomprehensible tirade at the Dumnonian. 'I told you we needed to deal with her, but you were too frightened, too enthralled by her spell. This is your doing, Saeric, and I will gladly hand you over to her, and she can do her worst to you!'

It was then that Saeric appreciated why Eadwald had brought along Rodor. The thick-necked sergeant took the enraged Gerard down with a single, carefully aimed blow to the temple. Saeric sank to his knees, gasping and coughing, holding his hands to his throat, stunned by the viciousness of Gerard's assault and the realisation that the unhinged Saxon would have killed him were it not for Rodor's intervention. Heremund came to Saeric's aide, easing him to the ground and holding him upright with a hand to his back.

'Don't try to talk,' Heremund said. 'Can you breathe?'

Saeric nodded, although in truth, it was an effort to do so, and his throat felt like he had swallowed molten iron.

'Saeric,' Eadwald said, 'Gerard is right. You have indulged your fear of that woman for long enough. We are riding there to resolve this matter, once and for all.' He turned to Rodor. 'Wake that idiot up. I assume you didn't kill him?'

Rodor replied with a grim smile, then he took up a bucket of water and dumped it over Gerard.

The Saxon fyrdsman spluttered in protest, anger returning when he remembered what had happened.

'I've ordered Rodor to knock you out again if you don't calm down, Gerard,' Eadwald warned. 'I agree that Saeric is indirectly responsible for what has happened here, but we need to focus our attention on the real villain: Baldwyn and his daughter. And more importantly, we need to get your own daughter back alive, and preferably unharmed. Can I trust you not to attack Saeric again?'

Gerard looked at Saeric coldly, and again the Briton was shocked by the change that had come over the Saxon. He was like a friend's hunting dog, who on most occasions might lick your hand and nuzzle you, but if you are foolish enough to stand between him and his pups... 'I make no such promise if my daughter is dead,' Gerard said.

'Then we'd best get moving,' Eadwald said. 'Heremund, you stay here in case a ransom is delivered or, God forbid, worse news arrives. Bring Carwyn and the twins into the burh and shut the gates. I've mobilised the Sceaptesburh garrison, who are on their way here now. Gerard, I want you to wait for them, leave a cohort behind to guard this burh, and then bring the main host to Baldwyn's. We will go on ahead and scout the way.'

'I will ride with you,' Gerard growled.

'No. I want you at the head of that host. I promise not to take any action until you arrive.'

'Is all this necessary?' Heremund asked.

'Baldwyn has a large fyrd, and whilst I've taken measures to mitigate that, if he is wise to us or we fail for some reason, and he comes after you, you need to be prepared.'

'He wouldn't dare strike us!'

He waved at the two dead men at their feet. 'He already has.'

7

Burn it down

Baldwyn's Burh, Wilcote, Wessex

Hildelith allowed the men to jostle her, moaning and unhelpfully flopping as they tied her to one of the posts in the hall. The man named Edward was explaining that this was Eanswith's fault. Nothing to do with him or his father. She is a stupid bitch and will pay for this crime. Hildelith wanted to say to him, 'then why tie me up?' but her instincts told her to continue to feign her swoon until she understood the full magnitude of her situation. That this man would pay for his part in her kidnapping was never in doubt, but Gerard had taught Hildelith that impetuousness and panic in the face of peril were the mark of a poor fyrdsman and would just as likely get her killed. *Best bide my time*, she decided, taking the opportunity as she lolled her head to survey her surroundings.

She could see that they were in a sizeable hall similar to Dunstan's, with a two-storey section at one end where the family's private chambers would be located. There was one main entrance into the hall through which she had been led, but if the layout were similar to Dunstan's, there would be another smaller door in the room underneath the family chambers. The whole place had a distinctly fetid air; the rushes on the floor were severely in need of changing, sections of the limewash were flaking off the wall, and the roof timbers were cloaked in a brooding coat of dark soot.

'I'll hand you back, don't worry. I just need to deal with my sister first,' came Edward's voice. He let out a sigh as he tested the ropes for tightness. 'Are you hearing anything I'm saying?'

'What in Hell's Damnation is going on here, boy?' came a loud, ale-slurred roar from behind her. 'Who is that, and why is there a pile of slaughtered villeins in my forecourt?'

'Father!' Edward said, his tone defensive.

Interesting, Hildelith thought.

'It's Eanswith's doing, my Lord. This is Sugu's woman.'

Sugu? A sow? Hildelith thought, surprised. *That can't be what they call Saeric? Why on Earth did they give him that nickname?*

'I will hand her back just as soon as I've dealt with my sister.'

The father appeared in view: a large, overweight but broad-shouldered and well-muscled man, similar in age to her own father, but with worse teeth and an unpleasant face. He obviously held personal hygiene in contempt, if his foul breath and unshaven chin were any indication. It certainly explained the state of his hall.

'What's she doing here?'

'I told you. Eanswith had her kidnapped–'

That was as far as he got. His father punched his son hard in the stomach, and Edward doubled over, gasping for breath.

'Useless faggot,' Baldwyn growled. 'It's your job to keep her in check.'

'I had no idea!' Edward said between breaths.

'And that makes it better, does it?' Baldwyn roared. He hit his son again, twice. 'What did I do to deserve such a waste of air as you, baedling? If you weren't my first-born….'

'It's not my doing,' Edward repeated, his face reddening with anger, 'and I have no choice in what I am because I *am* your firstborn. *You* gave me my gift of depravity, father, and *you* are the one who named him Sugu, remember? Your little joke. "Bend over Sugu so that I can rut you like a boar." You and Eanswith forgot that he belonged to me. I should have known that I'd have to share him with you two. You're just angry because you can't get it up anymore. And hit me again, and I'll add you to the pile

I've already left on the forecourt.'

Hildelith waited for the inevitable violent response from Baldwyn, but it did not come. She risked a peep through half-closed eyes and saw father and son staring each other down, the younger's face a mirror of the elder's. She uttered a silent prayer of salvation. *What manner of a family is this?* she wondered, horrified. *Did Baldwyn really give Saeric to his son for… that? No wonder Saeric is so frightened of them.*

'What is her name?' Baldwyn growled.

'I don't know.'

Baldwyn crouched down and peered into Hildelith's face. The stench of his ale-laden breath was overpowering, and it was all Hildelith could do to prevent herself from flinching. She maintained her pretence of faint as she furiously wondered how best to play this situation. Baldwyn let out a sigh that sounded more like a growl, and he turned again to his son.

'You do know that your precious deorling Sugu is apprenticed to Heremund, former master-at-arms to the King?'

Edward nodded.

'Then why have you kicked that hornet's nest, you imbecile?' he roared. 'Go and fetch Giffre. We must recall the fyrd.'

'But didn't you just send them to Wintanceaster? You can't ignore the orders of the king.'

Baldwyn punched his son again, sending Edward stumbling backwards into Hildelith. Edward grabbed the post to steady himself as Baldwyn stepped up to him, eyes narrowed and teeth bared in anger. 'Why do you think he has ordered our force away from here, idiot? They'll be marching upon us shortly, if not already. They've probably been planning this for months, only you've gone and made it a thousand times worse. Before you brought her here, I may have had some hope of negotiating a settlement, but now?'

Edward began to speak, but Baldwyn silenced him. 'I don't want to hear another word. You are as equal in blame as my daughter. You will put this woman to the sword and get rid of the body. Then you will find your sister and bring her to me.'

'I left her outside to clean up her mess.'

'Well, she isn't there.'

'What will we do?'

'Hand Eanswith over, of course. Let Sugu do whatever he wants with her. But there will be no mention of this kidnapping.'

'But what about me? He was my slave, not Eanswith's.'

'Then that should be an interesting exchange.'

'You bought him for me, father, to celebrate my coming of age,' Edward reminded him. 'He'll have all our heads on stakes.'

'Then I suggest you grow a pair of balls and deal with him before he gets here with the king's fyrd at his back. But first, get rid of this one, then go and fetch your sister. I will begin preparations to receive the king's war host.' Baldwyn turned and went outside.

Moments later, Hildelith heard the hiss of a sword being drawn. She opened her eyes and glared at the Saxon. 'You know they'll kill you,' she said. 'They'll raze this place to the ground and gut you all for what you have done.'

Edward blinked at her, surprised. He held his blade loosely in his hand.

'Yes, I heard everything,' she went on, then immediately regretted saying it. *Fool!* she scolded herself. *Why not just say, kill me now?*

'I treated Sugu well,' Edward said. 'It was my sister who tortured him. Father occasionally had his fill, just as he did with all of us, but that was to remind us of who was master in this burh.'

'What you have done is wrong,' Hildelith said, appalled at these debased people. 'God will strike you down, and you will all burn in eternal damnation for what you've done.'

Edward nodded. 'I know,' he said simply, 'but so will your boyfriend – and so will you, now that he's bedded you too.'

'His name is Saeric, and he has not bedded me.'

He smiled at her, clearly not believing her denial. 'He enjoyed our games, you know,' he went on. 'He wanted my sister to hurt him. He needed her to hurt him.'

'You are truly evil,' Hildelith said, horrified by this man's dreadful revelations.

Edward shrugged. 'The funny thing is, I've been doing heinous and corrupt things since I was ten.' He frowned in thought. 'Perhaps even younger. Yet here I am, a man now, still committing mortal sin every day, and I have not been struck down. Your Saeric – my Sugu – is marked by the same sin, yet he still walks this Earth just as I do. God doesn't seem to care one way or another.'

'Saeric did not have a choice,' she snarled. 'He is tormented by what you did to him.'

'Really? Or is it that he misses us?' He swung his sword in a figure of eight, contemplating her. 'Eanswith knows he does. She's been watching him and you. Yes, that's right, down there in your lovely little nest in Scirburne. She has made me very angry, my sister, because while I've been seeing to my duties here, she has been sneaking off with Sugu, right in front of our eyes. They've been stealing away at night, playing their disgusting little games. Have you not wondered why he has never come here to get his revenge? He needs my sister as much as she does him. They are monsters conjoined by their depravity.'

'That is a lie,' she hissed.

'I can see the doubt in your eyes, my dear. You know it to be true.' He swung his sword again, then held the point to Hildelith's left breast. 'You're better off dead because your association with him has stained you already. He is a demon, my lady, a servant of the Devil. You are attracted to the brutality and strength of Satan's spawn. I'll wager you fantasise about him gritting his teeth and growling like a beast when he thrusts into you, no?' His eyes glazed for a moment. He let out a small sigh and smiled at her. 'Your lust for him is warranted, for it is quite something else to feel that powerful demon inside you, or better still, to throw him on his back and rut him until he has drained you.' He ran the point of the blade in a smaller figure of eight over her chest, but he was careful not to cut the skin.

'No,' Hildelith said, hating this vile man and his equally despicable words. Saeric had been the victim in this place, not the instigator.

Edward's wicked smile broadened. 'No?'

'Your father is wrong,' Hildelith said, desperately wanting to change the course of this conversation and wondering whether she should reveal her identity. 'You have to keep me alive as a bargaining piece. My life in return for yours. Saeric is a man of honour. I think you know that too. I will say you protected me and that Saeric must let you go. But know that I will not give the same undertaking for your sister,' she added coldly.

Edward's lips curled into a wry smile. 'Nor would I,' he said. 'How do I know you will keep your word?'

'What have I to lose?' she countered. 'My life is in your hands.'

'Indeed it is,' he said. He withdrew and sheathed his blade, then he unbuckled his swordbelt and let it fall to the ground. 'However, I think I require a little more than your word,' he said, letting his pants drop to the floor. 'And although I do not possess the power of our mutual paramour Sugu, I can growl if you like.' He stepped out of his pants and moved over to her. 'Stand up,' he said quietly. Then, once she had done as he had bidden, he reached forward, grabbed her tunic by the hem and tore it roughly up out of the way.

❧

'I can't wear that!' Saeric said, frowning at the tabard that Eadwald held out for him. It bore the crest of Ecgberht.

'Why not? You're my acolyte. You train with my men, eat with my men, you are one of my men.' He held his hand up when he saw Saeric's darkening expression.

'Humour me. Just put it over your chainmail. Hopefully, it's big enough with all those layers of armour you've got on. I had to borrow it from one of the…, er…, broader men.'

It did fit, quite well in fact, and the gathering all agreed it suited him.

Saeric frowned at them, not at all keen to be wearing the standard of his enemy and feeling like a fraud and a traitor himself. It was one thing to wear Heremund's Gryphon, but the Wyvern of Westseaxna Ríce? *But if this is what I must do for Hildelith*, he thought, *then it is a small price to pay.*

The men, excluding Gerard and Eadwald, saluted him.

'What are they doing that for?'

'You outrank them.'

The men smiled at one another, delighting in Saeric's confusion. 'It's okay, Lord Saeric,' one of the fyrdsman said, 'we know who you are.'

'What? How?'

'As my son, it is my prerogative to bestow upon you whatever title I feel is appropriate. I am an ealdorman, and thus so are you.'

'Prerogative?'

'Choice.'

'Oh,' Saeric said. *So, you've not told them who I am after all.*

'Now, we need to get going. It will be a hard ride, and I want to get to Baldwyn's before sundown tomorrow. You may bring your ploughshare if you like.' He snapped his fingers, and one of the men presented the weapon to Saeric. 'I took the trouble of having a sheath made for it,' Eadwald said. 'Mount up.'

Saeric climbed onto the impossibly high horse with the help of two of the fyrdsmen. The stallion took a sideways step at the weight on its back.

'You could be sensible like the rest of us and put your chainmail on once we get there. Hercules is the biggest horse I could find, and even he is struggling to carry you.'

'The horse has to carry it whether it's on me or in a saddle pack,'

Saeric said, still coming to terms with just how large this animal was now that he was perched atop it. 'What does Hercules mean?'

'It is from Greek legend, according to Gerard. He could tell you the story better than me, but I believe he was a hero of very great strength.'

Hercules was aptly named then, for although he stood as high as Eadwald's magnificent stallion, he was far stockier. Saeric had seen animals this shape and size hauling large wagons, but this mount was subtly different in the way he held himself. Most evident was his powerful build, with a thick neck, exceptionally sturdy chest and legs, and hooves covered by thick feathering.

'He's a Frankish warhorse,' Eadwald said, seeing Saeric contemplating his ride, 'on loan from a friend, so please don't scratch or dent him. A packhorse would normally carry your armour, and in any case, normal men can't ride all day in chainmail, and I doubt you can, either. You're top-heavy wearing all that iron.'

Saeric smiled at his proxy sire. 'I'll be alright, father,' he said, quite enjoying playing up his new role with Eadwald. He noticed a couple of the men smirk at Saeric's cheeky disobedience. 'And I think this brute you've chosen for me will be fine too.'

'Then let's go before he collapses under you,' Eadwald said, 'and for God's sake, don't fall off. The whole fort has money on it, and I'll owe them a fortune if you do.'

❧

Hildelith sat upright against the post, listening to the frantic sounds of the burh preparing to defend itself. Her cheeks were moist with tears of fury and disgust, but she was still alive, which was what mattered. Many women before her had suffered far greater injustices and lived to exact their revenge. *And I shall get mine*, she vowed to herself. Her foremost concern was the father. *Where is he? What will he say or do if he finds me still bound to this post, alive?* She tested her bonds again, but they remained as tight as ever.

There was a sound by the doorway, and the dark-skinned youth who had earlier helped Edward entered the hall, bearing a mail shirt slung over his shoulder, presumably for his master. He wore a collar and ankle irons, which were connected by a chain long enough to allow him to walk freely. He saw her and frowned. He was strikingly beautiful, with golden-brown eyes and a mop of wild, dark hair framing an impish face. Hildelith had thought him a young boy when he had helped carry her, but now she saw that while his lithe, attractively muscled body was as smooth as a child's, he was clearly an older teenager, which made more sense if he was to serve his master in the way she understood. She shuddered at the thought of it and muttered another prayer of salvation for both herself and this poor boy.

He started towards the door to the family chambers.

'Boy?' she whispered hoarsely. 'Untie me. Please.'

His frown deepened, and he looked around, then moved closer to her.

'My friends are coming for me,' she said. 'I am the daughter of an important nobleman, and my Godfather is master-at-arms to the king. Free me, and I promise you will come to no harm.'

He shook his head, and for a moment, she wondered whether he could understand her. He was definitely foreign, for she had seen the occasional trader from across the seas with skin of this same rich complexion.

'If they find me dead, you will all be killed,' she urged. 'They will show no mercy for any of you, slave or no.'

He looked down at her bonds, then glanced upstairs, uncertain.

'Just loosen the rope. That's all you need to do. Your master need never know you helped me.'

As though he'd been listening, Edward shouted from upstairs. 'Asaf? Where the Hell are you?'

The boy tilted his head in apology, and then he darted off to tend to his master.

Hildelith cursed him roundly, wrenching at her bonds and

wishing eternal pain and damnation on the wretched little slave and his master.

'Now then, my lady,' came a female voice from the hall's entrance to Hildelith's left. It was impossible to see who it was against the bright light of the doorway, but Hildelith knew by the cold malice in the woman's voice who it must be. 'That's no way to talk about my brother.'

❧

It was midway through the second day that Saeric and his entourage entered Baldwyn's territory. They had ridden hard, and Eadwald had been right about the armour. Saeric had peeled all of it off just shy of two hours into the first day. His legs and arse ached painfully, and he silently cursed Eadwald for making him ride this giant beast. He knew he had to do it, but it was hard work, especially as this musclebound monster was twice as wide as any other horse.

Eadwald noticed Saeric's discomfort and smiled. 'You've done very well, my son,' he said, 'for someone who claims he can't ride. You and Hercules have taken to one another quite nicely. I thought him a good match when the equerry brought him out to me.'

'I said I didn't like horses, not that I can't ride them.'

Eadwald frowned at him. 'You aren't afraid of anything. Why horses?'

Saeric let out a long breath, his mind flying back to the time before the routing of his family and the vicious stablemaster who had thrown the unprepared eight-year-old Aneurin into the lunging ring with a young, unbroken colt. This was one of Cadwyr's little tests for his sons to determine whether they had the courage and wit to tame a beast that was ten times their size. Aneurin had failed spectacularly and had to be dragged from the ring with a broken arm and cracked ribs, having been trampled by the nasty young horse. As a reward for his failure, his father had ordered him thrown back in, broken arm and all, to try again. He'd been knocked out the second time with a crack to his head. From that day onwards, Aneurin had held a justified fear of horses and had steadfastly refused to have anything to do with them. He let out a little grunt of surprise, for this was the first time he had reflected on his father's cruelty to both horse and child.

'Saeric?'

'When I was young, my fa… I was made to break in a colt as a trial. It won.'

'Ah,' Eadwald said. 'Well, I think you'll find Hercules won't let you down. He'd have thrown you off by now if he'd disapproved of you.'

'How reassuring,' Saeric said. 'But it doesn't matter, anyway. I can't afford a horse. Especially one this majestic.'

'Well, in time, you will. Is this area familiar to you?' Eadwald asked, changing the subject.

'It all looks the same to me,' Saeric said, looking around. 'Filled with Saxon squatters.'

'Yes, but this hundred,' Eadwald observed, ignoring Saeric's complaint, 'belongs to a very particular Saxon.'

Saeric pulled his horse up, his heart growing cold.

'We'll be there shortly. You may want to put on your armour now.'

Eadwald gave the order to halt and slipped down from his horse, then helped Saeric off Hercules.

'I don't know who or what we will find there, Saeric, but you are free to do whatever your heart tells you. This is your chance to expiate yourself, so I won't stand in your way, but know that Baldwyn is a powerful thegn in his own right.'

'Expiate?'

'Get revenge,' Eadwald said.

'I'm not afraid of Baldwyn or his kin.'

'Quite. Even so, don't underestimate him. Ah, we're too late. We have company.'

Saeric turned and looked up the road ahead to see three riders approaching. It wasn't Baldwyn himself; perhaps Edward and a couple of retainers? Whatever the case, there was no time to don his armour.

'Arrows at the ready,' Eadwald ordered, and the four escorts quickly armed their short bows. Rodor remained on his horse, pulled out his sword and rested it on his lap.

The lead rider pulled his horse up and, somewhat breathlessly, welcomed Eadwald to Baldwyn's estate, and wondered how he might be able to help, all the while noting the alarmingly high rank of the leader and the similarly high rank of the man standing beside him. Saeric frowned back at the rider, knowing that he was a household member, but struggling to place him.

'We wish to speak with your Lord,' Eadwald said.

'Of course, your excellency,' the man said, eyeing the bowmen nervously. 'I assure you, there is no need for concern. I would be glad to escort you if you would like to follow us.'

Saeric noted that none of the three had dismounted, as courtesy demanded. Hardly surprising, he supposed, with four arrows pointed at them.

'That won't be necessary,' Saeric said. 'We know the way.'

The fyrdsman let out a tense cough. 'Truly, it would be an honour to do so, my….' His voice trailed off as he addressed Saeric, his eyes widening as he took in the uniform, the weapon, and finally, the face. A face that couldn't possibly be wearing the arms of the king. Saeric smiled back, finally recognising him as one of the sergeants of the fyrd; not a particularly bad person from what he could recall of him, but Saeric felt a powerful rush of exhilaration on seeing the fyrdsman's expression change to astonishment, then fear.

Saeric took three steps, grabbed the fyrdsman's bridle, and then hauled as hard as he could on the bit. The horse shrieked in pain and fell in the direction of Saeric, bringing both horse and rider crashing to the ground, trapping the fyrdsman beneath it.

The other two men cried out in protest and moved to draw their swords, but each had two arrows pointing at them, and from this range, the king's soldiers could not possibly miss.

The fallen horse clambered to its feet, angrily nickering as it pranced out of the way of its rider and Saeric.

The soldier remained on the ground, looking up in shock at the Saxon nobleman who was once a slave standing over him.

Eadwald addressed the fyrdsmen. 'May I introduce you to Lord Saeric. I believe he has enjoyed your hospitality in the past. You may have known him by a different name, perhaps?'

'My Liege,' one of the two mounted fyrdsmen said in a panic. 'We had no part in this.'

'You are all guilty,' Saeric snarled at him. He drew his sword and held the point to the man's throat. 'Now, where is Lady Hildelith?'

The soldier swallowed. 'She is Hildelith? I… I had no idea. Lady Eanswith did not tell us her name.' He turned his head and looked at Eadwald, his expression panicked.

'So, she is here then?' Eadwald said.

The fyrdsman nodded.

'Dismount and drop your weapons,' Eadwald barked at the two fyrdsmen. 'Rodor, tie them all up. And tether the horses to that tree over there. We might need them later.'

'Who… who are you?' the sergeant asked Saeric, his gaze falling again to the royal standard of Ecgberht.

'He is my son,' Eadwald said.

The sergeant paled at that revelation. He looked from Saeric to Eadwald and back again, speechless.

Suddenly one of the two riders spurred his horse back in the direction of the hall. There was a whoosh and a thud as an arrow struck him between the shoulders, and he tumbled forward, tripping up his horse as he fell over its neck. He twitched for a moment, and then he died.

Eadwald looked at the last rider, his eyebrows raised in

challenge, but the fyrdsman threw aside his weapons, hastily dismounted, and stood ready to be bound.

Our time has come, the Devil said, his voice trembling with excitement.

'Get me my armour,' Saeric said.

'Stop!' Rodor barked, holding up his hand.

Ahead of them stood Baldwyn's burh, exactly as Saeric remembered it.

Of course you do, said the Devil. *You grew up here*.

Built atop a low rise, the burh comprised a large hall and various ancillary buildings surrounded by a solid wall of oak and earth. Bolstering the defences was a steep-sided ditch in front of the wall. The wall itself was topped with a crenellated palisade of oak. Towers stood at all four corners, and there was a sturdy gatehouse protecting the single entrance. A township sprawled untidily around the burh, with a small church sitting to one side, outside the protection of the burh. The road led straight to the gate. One of the leaves was closed, but the other hung partway open, wide enough to let a man pass through.

Rodor pointed to a small white mark on a tree closer to the burh. 'That indicates arrow range,' he said, then nodded up at the palisade. 'I count six archers.'

Saeric looked at the soldier, impressed. He could see only two.

'I daresay you could easily dispatch them with your Frankish bow,' Eadwald said to Saeric, 'but we should perhaps offer a less threatening face in the first instance. We don't want to put Hildelith in any more danger than she already is. You and I will approach the gate. The rest of you come up behind us. Be prepared to defend us, especially from those archers.'

'Sir?' Rodor said, clearly unhappy with the arrangements.

'Saeric can go out in front and draw their fire. He's got enough armour on for two men.'

'Thank you, father,' Saeric said sarcastically.

'They will not parley,' Rodor warned.

'I don't wish to appear contrary, but it would seem they may,' Eadwald said, nodding at the gateway. Someone was coming out, flanked by two guardsmen.

'Edward?' Saeric said, surprised.

'Which one is he?' Eadwald asked.

'The first one to die,' Saeric replied, unhitching his bow and slinging his ploughshare and a quiver of arrows over his shoulder. He checked his sword and dagger and started his horse towards the gate.

'Let's not forget about Hildelith before you start chopping off heads,' Eadwald suggested, hurrying to catch up.

'Don't worry, Eanswith will have her tied up in there somewhere. She's sent out her brother to test our mood.'

'Then you need to calm down, or this excursion will be for nothing. I'll do the talking.'

Edward greeted the men with a deep bow. The two guardsmen did not respond in kind but instead stood on guard, their spears pointed upwards but nevertheless at the ready.

'My Lords,' Edward said. 'Welcome to Burh Baldwyn. To what do we owe this visit from such an esteemed delegation?' He looked beyond Saeric and Eadwald to Rodor and the rest of the escort. 'Did you not come across my fyrdsmen?'

'We did,' Eadwald said.

'Oh,' Edward replied, confused, still looking past the visitors and wondering where they were.

'They stayed behind,' Saeric said coldly.

The two guardsmen dropped their spears into a defensive position. Edward held up his hand. 'My father is an ally to the king. Why would you attack his men?'

'Where is Lady Hildelith?' Saeric said.

'Who?'

Saeric dismounted, landing with a firm thud on the ground,

then he calmly shrugged off the heavy bow.

'What are you doing?' Edward demanded.

Saeric turned to him and smiled. It was obvious that Edward, like his fyrdsman before him, had not recognised Sugu.

'Never mind him,' Eadwald snapped. 'Answer my question. Where is Lady Hildelith? We know you kidnapped her. The Sceaptesburh Fyrd is behind us. We come in advance of the war host to offer you one chance of redemption for your house, but that opportunity is fast diminishing.'

Edward appeared shocked. 'We have done no such thing, my Lord,' he protested, 'and please tell your retainer to put down that weapon.'

Saeric ignored him, selecting a bodkin arrow and nocking it. He drew back the thick string, the wood creaking as he did so. He pointed it at Edward and looked him in the eye.

'My Lord,' Edward objected, but Saeric saw that his enemy was faltering in the face of the powerful archer with the huge bow pointing an equally large arrow at him from an uncomfortably short distance away. Saeric could see Edward's thoughts written on his face: "He wouldn't dare. I am wearing chainmail. I should be alright. I have archers on the wall above me. I am the first-born son of Baldwyn, Lord of this hundred. He wouldn't dare."

'You are welcome to search this burh and surrounds,' Edward said, although his voice lacked its earlier conviction. 'You will find nothing here.'

'He has no idea who you are,' Eadwald observed, glancing at Saeric. 'Amazing the difference that a wash and a change of clothes will do for a man.' He turned back to Edward. 'I believe you have met my son, although I think you called him by a different name.'

'Hello Edward,' Saeric said.

Edward's eyes widened with astonishment and horror when he finally recognised the archer. His mouth moved as he soundlessly spoke Sugu's name.

Saeric loosed the arrow, and it slammed into Edward's chest with a loud and satisfying thunk. It cut right through Edward's chainmail, as it was designed to. Edward stumbled backwards under the impact, but he stayed on his feet, coughing blood. He stared in shock at Saeric and at the arrow that had pierced his armour. Saeric reached into the quiver and calmly nocked another arrow.

One of the spearmen came to his senses and launched himself at Saeric. Saeric shot him without hesitation. Unlike Edward, the guardsman was thrown backwards by the force of the impact, as he wore little more than a leather jerkin for protection. The other guardsman hesitated, unsure what to do now that his comrade and their master had been shot.

Something struck Saeric in the shoulder and bounced off his hauberk. He looked up to see an archer duck below the wall. Saeric nocked another arrow, pulled back the string and took aim. The archer stood up in a smooth action to fire again at Saeric. Saeric had anticipated the move and loosed his own arrow as soon as he saw the brown peak of the archer's leather cap rise above the parapet. His arrow caught the archer in the mouth and burst out the back of his head. The archer's arrow, in turn, slammed into Saeric – a better shot to the middle of his chest this time – but again, the chainmail and gambeson did their job, and the arrow fell away harmlessly. Saeric drew another arrow from his quiver.

'For Christ's sake, Saeric, you could at least have the decency to duck or stagger or something,' Eadwald said, astounded that Saeric hadn't even flinched, despite that last arrow hitting him with some force. Saeric was vaguely aware of the hiss of more arrows in flight, but these came from behind him, so presented no danger.

'Goodbye, Edward,' Saeric said and fired another arrow. It slammed in hard at the base of Edward's neck, and Baldwyn's son fell backwards and hit the ground heavily, choking on his own blood.

'Christ Almighty,' Eadwald swore again. 'You didn't give him a chance to tell us where Hildelith is.' He glanced at Saeric's bow. 'And we need to get more of those.'

Saeric put away the bow and quiver and unsheathed the ploughshare. 'Shall we?' he said.

'We need to take control of the burh first,' Eadwald said. He turned to Rodor and the others, who had hurried to join them. 'Check the outbuildings and secure anyone you find. You can start with him.' Eadwald jabbed his thumb at the remaining guardsman, who had abandoned his spear and dropped to his knees, pleading for mercy.

Saeric didn't wait for Rodor. He swung the ploughshare and took off the man's head in one blow. Saeric looked down at it, frowning in surprise.

'For Christ's sake, Saeric!' Eadwald snapped.

'Someone sharpened it,' Saeric said, surprised. He noticed Rodor shaking his head with disgust in the background.

Eadwald gripped Saeric's arm. 'I know that killing Baldwyn's son must have felt satisfying but remember why we are here. You can do whatever you like once we've freed Hildelith, but she comes first, do you understand? Saeric, do you hear me?'

'I intend to free Hildelith, father, but do not expect me to show mercy to this filth.' Saeric pulled his arm free and walked through the gate. He saw two archers lying on the ground at the base of the palisade walkway, both with arrows protruding from their bodies. No one came at him as he walked the short distance to the hall, but someone did burst out just as Saeric arrived at the door. He swung the ploughshare in a powerful uppercut without waiting to see who it was. It struck his victim's jaw, and their head snapped back with a loud crack. The man crumpled at the threshold, his neck broken. Saeric stepped over him and received a powerful thrust to his chest with a spear. The attack breached the chainmail, and Saeric staggered backwards, feeling a sharp sting as the point cut through the underlying gambeson and into his skin beneath. He danced out of the way, cursing his recklessness. The fyrdsman came straight after him, the spear held in both hands as he charged. Saeric barely managed to knock it aside with the ploughshare, and the blade caught him with a glancing strike on the shoulder. This time the mail protected him, and Saeric lunged at his attacker, allowing the man's momentum to deliver him into the path of Saeric's heavy iron weapon. He rammed it into the fyrdsman's chest to knock him off balance, and then he delivered a blow to the top of the head. The huscarl dropped like a stone, his skull split. Saeric felt a sharp prick in his back as yet another arrow struck him from above, and he angrily turned on his hip to see an archer on the wall hastily nocking another arrow. Ignoring him, Saeric stepped inside, leaving the archer for Rodor.

Saeric came face to face with none other than Baldwyn himself. The master of the house stood ready with his sword drawn and held en garde before him. Oddly, there were no other guardsmen inside, and neither did Baldwyn wear armour. The latter came as no surprise to Saeric, for that was typical of Baldwyn's towering arrogance.

'What is the meaning of this?' Baldwyn growled, clearly not recognising Saeric. 'How dare you attack my fyrdsmen! If the king has an issue with my house, he should behave with honour and within the law.'

'Honour? What do you know of honour? You screw your own children.'

'What?' Baldwyn blustered. 'You can go to hell.'

'Oh, I will,' Saeric agreed, 'thanks to you and your spawn, but I'm sending you there first.' Saeric sprang sideways and forwards and slammed the ploughshare down on Baldwyn's sword arm as he passed. It wasn't the best-aimed strike, but he heard the snap of bone breaking, and Baldwyn roared with shock and pain. The thegn dropped the sword and gripped his forearm, cursing his attacker. Saeric let go of the ploughshare and retrieved Baldwyn's very fine weapon from the floor. Baldwyn backed away, shouting for the guards. Saeric followed him until the thegn was up against the wall.

'They won't help you, Baldwyn,' Saeric said. He smiled. 'Like your son, you don't recognise me, do you? Did they tell you who I am? Who you kept in slavery all that time? Who you beat, abused and sodomised? See this standard? My guardsmen wait outside, and the rest of my war-host rides towards this burh as we speak. They will meet your pitiful fyrd along the road and slay every one of them for what you did to me.'

'Sugu?' he stammered, knowing that it could be no other, but still unable to reconcile the slave he once knew with the man standing before him who wore an ealdorman's tunic with the king's standard on his chest.

'Where is Eanswith?' Saeric demanded.

Like his son, Baldwyn shook his head and mouthed something Saeric could not hear or understand.

Saeric didn't bother to ask again. He knew where she would be: upstairs in her bed-chamber waiting for him, Hildelith no doubt stripped naked and strapped to the bed. Saeric ran Baldwyn through – stabbing him in the stomach, all the way to the hilt. Then, using all his strength, he dragged the blade upwards until it struck the thegn's sternum. Baldwyn's guts spilt out, and he collapsed, making strange gurgling sounds while he tried to hold his intestines in with bloodied hands.

Suddenly a boy, aged twelve years old, burst out from the family chambers, saw what Saeric had done, screamed and then ran back upstairs, calling for help. Saeric knew the house well. There was no other way out from up there. They couldn't even escape through the windows because they were intentionally made too small to allow passage. He left the sword buried in its owner, recovered the bloodied ploughshare, and then walked up the stairs after the boy. Saeric stepped into the antechamber from which the bedrooms opened and came upon more resistance. Two huscarls guarded the bed-chambers. Both were well armed and armoured, but neither was prepared for Saeric.

'Is the witch Eanswith here?' Saeric growled, 'and Lady Hildelith? Step aside.'

The men, who each guarded a doorway, hesitated, confused by their opponent's choice of weapon. The man standing before them in the king's insignia wore a sword, but instead, he held what looked to be an oversized iron axe head, which might have been a ploughshare in other circumstances. Both had heard the rumours of an immortal demon who had slaughtered Eanswith's entire band of brigands with just such an implement.

'I'll ask one more time,' Saeric said, 'or do you refuse the will of your king?'

One of the men put up his hand and laid down his sword, and stammered, 'Lady Eanswith took the prisoner away–'

'Shut up, idiot!' snapped the other fyrdsman,

'Where?' Saeric growled.

'We answer only to Lord Baldwyn,' the belligerent guardsman said.

'No, you will answer to God,' Saeric said coldly, then he sprang at the disarmed fyrdsman. This took both soldiers by surprise. The defenceless guard realised his peril too late and tried to get out of the way, but Saeric was too fast and strong. He brought the heavy iron blade down on the nape of the man's neck; something he had learned from his previous outing was the most effective attack. The man fell backwards into the room he was defending, spattering blood on the wall as he fell. There was a terrified scream from within the room beyond, but Saeric found himself with a new problem. The ploughshare had jammed in his victim's shoulder, and for a moment, Saeric was himself defenceless. The other fyrdsman took advantage and, shouting a loud expletive, swung his sword and slammed it into Saeric's midriff. The blow was surprisingly powerful, and Saeric staggered sideways, bouncing off the opposite wall. The blade made no mark thanks to his mail armour, but it left Saeric still on the defensive, and he wrenched out his own sword as his opponent swung again. The guardsman caught Saeric across the chest, but again the slashing blow was ineffective. The fyrdsman was panicking, forgetting that a thrust is the most effective attack against a mail hauberk. Shouting his own warcry, Saeric ran at the man and demonstrated how it should be done. He shoved his sword as hard as possible into his opponent's chest, using his own body behind the hilt to drive the blade through the man's armour. The fyrdsman blinked in shock at Saeric, then he coughed up blood and slid down the wall, muttering something unintelligible as he died.

Well, that was stupid, offered the Devil. *Now you don't know where Hildelith has been taken.*

'Sard off,' Saeric muttered, convinced that Eanswith was in the room, waiting for him. He heard whimpering from inside, so he pulled his sword free and looked into the darkened bed-chamber. They'd closed the shutters and doused the lamps, but Saeric could see a shape cowering against the far wall, its eyes glinting in the reflected light. Could it be Hildelith? Saeric lifted one of the oil lamps from its bracket and stepped into the room, his sword held firmly in his other hand.

'Please, Lord,' came a young male voice from the opposite wall. 'We had nothing to do with this. Please!' Baldwyn's son, Aelfwig, stared wide-eyed at the blood-spattered warrior facing him, his body quivering with fear. He held a small dagger out in front of him, but his hand shook violently.

'Where did your witch of a sister take Lady Hildelith?' Saeric demanded.

'I don't know,' the boy said, crying. 'She… she snuck her away without our father's leave. Lord Edward, my brother, was about to go off to find her when you came.'

'So, she was here then?' Saeric moved towards the boy.

'Yes, Lord. They brought the Lady to my sister, but Eanswith was angry they'd kidnapped her. They weren't meant to. She killed the man who did it, Lord, I swear. They were all executed for it. My brother made sure of that. Ask him, Lord. He will tell you.'

Saeric let out a sigh, then set the lamp down on the oak chest beside him. 'I'm afraid I can't because I killed him. As I did your father and all the guards in this house.'

'Please, Lord. My brother and I are innocent,' Aelfwig said, tears in his eyes. He glanced to his right, and Saeric saw a younger boy pressed into the corner by the bed.

Saeric frowned down at Aelfwig. 'Whose standard am I wearing, Aelfwig?'

The twelve-year-old swallowed. 'K... King Ecgberht?'

Saeric nodded. He pointed to his face. 'And who am I, Aelfwig?'

The boy was breathing rapidly now, barely able to manage his terror. 'S... S... Sugu?'

'No, that's the name your Godless family gave me. My true name is Aneurin, Crown Prince of Dumnonia, although most know me by my Saxon name, Saeric. I wear this standard because the King of Wessex stands in support of me. What hope, therefore, do you think you and your family have of salvation?'

'P... Please, Lord An... Aneurin. We didn't know. We–'

Kill the little rat, the Devil said. *He is the spawn of Baldwyn.*

Saeric looked beyond Aelfwig to his brother. Osgar, seven or eight years old – Saeric couldn't remember – shivered in terror like his brother, his eyes following the bloodied point of Saeric's sword as the demon they had called Sugu turned his gaze upon him. He tried to jam himself further into the corner, hunching into as small a shape as possible. Saeric was struck by the disturbing similarity to his own experience sixteen years ago, at nearly the same age, when he had watched his own brother butchered in front of him. However, young Aneurin had managed to get away because, unlike Aelfwig, Owain had fought like a wildcat and had drawn the swordsmen away from his little brother, enabling

Aneurin to flee.

Kill them! urged the Devil.

Saeric looked down at the terrified twelve-year-old and smelled the reek of urine as the boy peed himself. He stepped forward and held his sword to the boy's chest.

Do it! shrieked the Devil. *Run him through and send him to me.*

'Please?' whimpered Osgar from the corner. 'My sister took the Lady away with her this morning when she heard you were coming.'

'Where has she gone?' Saeric asked Aelfwig, but the boy was past speaking. Saeric turned to the youngest brother. Osgar shook his head vigorously. 'We don't know, my Lord. She didn't say. She took many of the huscarls with her. It made father very angry. Edward was supposed to bring her back.'

Kill them! pleaded the Devil.

Saeric let out a long breath, fighting the overpowering urge to shove his sword into Aelfwig and be done with it, but his mind kept returning to the near-identical circumstances of his own family's slaughter by Mael and his men. *If I kill these boys, I am no different to Mael,* he thought. *Aelfwig lacks Owain's courage, but he still has enough honour to know that he must try to defend his little brother, no matter the price.*

Saeric turned and walked out of the room and across the landing to check the bed-chamber opposite, in the event the boys had been lying. The room was empty. Cursing, Saeric wiped his sword clean on the bedding, sheathed the blade, and then retrieved his ploughshare from the dead huscarl. He thumped back down the stairs and walked across the hall to Baldwyn, who lay slumped against the wall, his hands still trying to contain his entrails. Incredibly, he was still alive. His eyes followed Saeric as he came up to him.

'I told you I would come back for you one day,' Saeric said. 'My time for vengeance has come, and it starts with you. Here, in this hall, I vow before you that I will not stop until every last one of you Saxons responsible for the slaughtering of my family and the theft of my kingdom is dead. Know that Dumnonia is far from vanquished. It will be Wessex that lies a smouldering wreck when I am done, and know that you have played your small part in bringing about the destruction of your kingdom.'

He turned and walked out the door.

'Burn it down,' Saeric said to Rodor, who stood near the entrance. 'But let the boys go free if they come out.'

Eadwald raised his eyebrows at Saeric.

'They weren't a part of this,' Saeric said. *And I need to be better than them.*

Pitiful, said the Devil.

'Did you mean what you said in there?' Eadwald asked. 'Do I need to be concerned?'

Saeric smiled back at the ealdorman. 'That depends on what comes to pass, doesn't it?' he replied.

Rodor went to his horse and unwrapped two firebrands. He took one of two pots of oil from his saddle pack and primed both torches. He handed one of them to Saeric, who took it and the other pot of oil. Without a word, Saeric went back into the hall and emptied the oil over Baldwyn and dropped the empty pot into his lap. Whether he was still alive, Saeric had no idea, and nor did he care. He walked over to the hearth and shoved the oil-soaked cloth into it. It threw off a cloud of thick black smoke and then burst into flame. Saeric went back and tossed it onto Baldwyn. The oil flashed alight, and soon the wall behind him licked with flames, which hungrily clawed at the banners hanging above.

Rodor rammed his torch into a pile of wood stacked under the low eaves. The wood caught alight quickly and, within moments, had begun to eat away at the shingled roof. Rodor and his men moved to a safe distance as the hall caught alight from within and without. Soon the place was ablaze, the heat too intense to stand within fifty yards. Saeric stood watching the door, surprised that the boys had not emerged. He was about to go in when Osgar burst out the door, leading his older brother. The two of them fell to their knees in front of Saeric, coughing and crying, their faces and clothes covered in soot. Osgar let go of his brother and turned to go back in.

Saeric grabbed him and held him back. 'Your father's gone,' he said. 'There's nothing in there for you but death.'

Osgar let out a sob and returned to his older brother, and they kneeled hand in hand, tears in their eyes as they watched their home burn.

'Take them somewhere safe and tie them up,' Eadwald instructed Rodor. 'We'll work out what to do with them later.' He turned back to Saeric. 'Did you find out where Hildelith is?'

'They didn't seem to know,' Saeric answered, 'but Eanswith has her; that they did say.'

'Christ Almighty,' Eadwald swore. 'She could be anywhere. We need to go. Baldwyn's fyrd have turned around.'

'I'm not leaving without Hildelith.'

'We've checked everywhere,' Rodor said.

'What about the byre?' Saeric asked. It would be just like her to hide in the place that had been his home for so many years and the place where she, Edward and Saeric had enjoyed their carnal experiments.

'Saeric, there's no one in there, save a few cows and a slave,' Eadwald said. 'We need to go. Even you with your ploughshare will be no match for a hundred or more enraged fyrdsmen, hungry for your blood.'

Saeric started towards the long building beside the hall, but Rodor grabbed his arm. 'It's empty,' he said firmly.

'No, it isn't,' Saeric growled back. He shoved the bloodied ploughshare into Rodor's hands, then strode to the entrance.

'Saeric!' Eadwald called. 'What are you doing?'

Saeric ignored the ealdorman and stepped inside. It took a moment for his eyes to adjust to the dark as he stood in the doorway, peering into the gloom of that horrible, familiar place. There was no possibility that Edward would have accepted the loss of his plaything, and, sure enough, Saeric saw a slave pressed into the darkest recess of the building. They'd made a new collar and chain for him, with brutal spikes on the outside such as a fighting dog might wear. His posture was exactly like that of the boys in the house, and he shook with fear as Saeric approached him, no doubt terrified by the sight of the demon with his blood-spattered arms and tunic emerging from the fires of Hell to claim his soul.

Saeric held out his hand. 'I've come to set you free,' he said.

8

Into the flames

Baldwyn's burh, Wilcote, Wessex

The boy was naked, save for a ragged pair of short trousers. He had a fine physique, no doubt pleasing to both son and daughter. Saeric blinked, suddenly remembering one of the times they had both had their way with him, forcing him onto Edward whilst she, in turn, had sat upon him. That was one of their favourite games, and Edward had become increasingly demanding as time went on, forcing Saeric to do ever more terrible things, things that should not be asked of anyone. He let out an oath and pushed the memory from his consciousness, trying to focus on the here and now.

The boy let out a whimper when Saeric picked up the chain. It was much like Saeric's had been, long enough to get on with his chores in the byre but not so long that he could ever go out into the fresh air. Saeric was conscious of the roaring fire nearby, and the animals bayed with panic in their stalls. Smoke was already filling the space and stinging his eyes and making him sneeze. There was little question that this building would soon catch alight and burn down with the hall, and for a moment, Saeric contemplated leaving the boy in there, for what life could he lead now, after what they'd done to him? He was marked by mortal sin, a pariah in the eyes of God and his flock. *As am I*, he thought. *Yet here I am, a free man, a Saxon earl no less, so who am I to decide this boy's fate?*

He picked up the chain, following it to its source. Like his had been, it was pinned to one of the thick oak columns that supported the roof. There was a sudden whoomph above his head, and he ducked instinctively as the thatch above him caught fire. The animals started bawling in terror. There was no time. Saeric looked over at the boy, who stared back at him, terrified, knowing he would die.

Cursing, Saeric took up the chain and wrenched at the fastening as hard as he could, but it didn't budge. The flames were taking hold now, and he felt their heat on his head and arms. He could barely hear Eadwald yelling at him from outside, and he yanked again. Nothing. Suddenly it mattered to him that the boy lived, so he drew his sword and started hacking at the timber with it. Sparks flew when the blade struck the iron ring that held the chain. A clump of burning thatch fell into one of the stalls, and the hay there caught fire. He couldn't hear himself above the roaring of the flames and the screaming of the animals. In desperation, he wedged the sword between the wood and the iron ring encircling the post and tried to prise it apart. The fine blade snapped near the hilt with a high-pitched ping. Saeric swore roundly, abandoning it. Instead, he grabbed the boy and dragged him over to the post, then he took the end of the chain nearest the boy and wrapped it first around his left arm, across his chest and then around his right arm. Then he took up the slack, scooped the boy up in his arms, and turned and ran hard toward the door, unravelling the length of chain attached to the post.

He was thrown off his feet and onto his back the first time when it failed to give, the fall winding him. A piece of burning thatch hit him on the shoulder, but he swept it off and struggled to his feet, gasping for breath, his eyes streaming from the smoke and heat. He tried again, just as Rodor ran into the byre, his head wrapped in a wet cloth. Saeric got a better grip on the boy, then he ran back to the post, turned and charged at the doorway, roaring at the Devil to lend him strength and show him one small piece of mercy, if not for him, then for the boy. The chain snapped taught, but this time it gave way, and Saeric stumbled forwards, dropped the boy, and fell out of the doorway, tumbling head over heels. He sprang up and turned to run back inside, but Rodor surged out of the burning building and shoved Saeric away from the entrance, shouting at him.

'It's too late, you fool!' he yelled at him over the roaring of the flames.

Saeric still had the chain wrapped around his body, so he grabbed the trailing end and hauled it with all his might. Rodor quickly realised what he was doing, and between them, they pulled on the chain together. The poor boy popped out of the flaming doorway, bouncing along on his back with his hands clamped on the collar to prevent himself from being decapitated by it. His trousers were alight, and his hair was crackling. Saeric scooped him up, chain and all, and ran for the river. He threw himself in with the boy without a second thought. They sank straight to the bottom under the weight of all the iron that he and the slave wore between them. Saeric panicked as he stumbled downstream underwater, tripping and slipping on the stones underfoot as he tried to find purchase before his breath ran out.

Whether by luck or fate, they came to shallow water, and Saeric burst to the surface and drew in a great, ragged breath. The boy, who was clutching onto Saeric's powerful shoulders, coughed up water, and he too gasped for air. They stood there for a while, buffeted by the river, Saeric panting from exertion, the boy pressing his face into Saeric's neck, sobbing. He was completely unaware that the metal spikes on his collar were driving into Saeric's skin, but the smith's apprentice bore the pain, for he knew that it was nothing compared to what this poor boy must have endured.

Eadwald and the others arrived moments later, having run hard along the bank after Saeric. Saeric saw that Rodor had stripped off his armour, sword, and shirt, presumably preparing to come in after them. It had felt like he'd been underwater for a goodly time, but most likely, it had been only as long as it had taken Rodor to tear off his clothes.

'Are you mad?' the ealdorman yelled at him. 'What the Hell are you doing? That's a full coat of mail you're wearing, and I haven't put all this effort into you to have you burn to death or drown saving a bloody slave!'

Saeric's eyes narrowed in anger, but Eadwald quickly raised his hands in apology, realising he had been insensitive.

'You're sarding insane,' Eadwald repeated, then he turned to the boy, who still clung onto Saeric like a limpet. 'And you're very bloody lucky.'

Saeric started for the shore, but Eadwald shook his head. 'You're better off staying in the water because you've both been burned. For God's sake, Saeric. You're beyond help, do you know that?'

'He was my replacement,' Saeric said angrily.

Eadwald wisely said nothing. For his part, Rodor shook his head at Saeric, then began walking back upstream, collecting his discarded clothing and armour. Behind them, the flames reached far into the sky as the whole place caught alight and burned unchecked. A pillar of thick brown and white smoke rose above the fire, signalling the destruction to the villagers and farmsteaders for miles around, and also to Baldwyn's fyrd.

Saeric – still bearing his young passenger – sank into the river up to his neck, allowing the freezing water to take away the sting of the burns. With some effort, Saeric prized the boy off him. 'I just want to see where you're hurt,' he said. *And I need to pull those sarding spikes out of my neck.* He looked into the boy's exotic face. 'You're not from anywhere around here, are you?' Saeric said, more a statement than a question. 'What's your name?'

The boy looked back at him, confused. Saeric tried British but still got nothing.

Suddenly the boy started speaking in a completely incomprehensible tongue.

'He's foreign,' said Eadwald.

'Definitely a wealh,' Rodor said, 'with filthy brown skin like that.'

'No,' Saeric said, scowling at the fyrdsman for that insult. 'He'd understand me if he was Dumnonian. Maybe he's from over the seas somewhere?

Rodor crossed himself. 'A heathen?'

'No,' Eadwald said. 'I think Saeric is right. I think he may be from one of the Caliphates. Asturian perhaps? Certainly a very long way from home.'

'Where's Asturia?' Saeric asked.

'Somewhere he's never likely to get back to,' Eadwald said. 'Now, how are those burns?'

Saeric had come off lightly, with only the slightest burn on his neck, as this was the only part of him unprotected by armour. The slave, on the other hand, had been chiefly naked, so he fared far worse, with a nasty burn on his shoulder, another further down on his torso, and some patches on the backs of his legs. Some of his hair had also fizzled in the flames, but his face was untouched. His back also bore score marks where he had been dragged along the earthen floor on his way out. He would be in terrible pain before long, but as Eadwald said, they had to get moving and find Hildelith. *Have I done the right thing by saving you?* Saeric wondered, looking into the boy's elven face.

Saving him will not atone you for your sins, the Devil warned.

I'm not trying to atone for them. I can't. You know that.

Perhaps you should kill him then? That might make you feel better.

But the Devil was wrong. Killing Baldwyn had made no difference at all to how Saeric felt. It hadn't even brushed the edges of the gaping hole in his heart. Or was it his soul? Saeric didn't know what this emptiness was that he felt within him anymore. He looked into the face of the boy in front of him. *Saving you, on the other hand....* That had made a difference.

The boy was still in shock, and he looked around him, then

back at Saeric, evidently still confused about what had just happened.

'You're safe,' Saeric said to him. 'No one will hurt you.'

The boy's lip quivered, and he burst into tears again. He moved to hug Saeric, but the Briton held his hand on the boy's chest to stop him. The boy frowned, confused even more, so Saeric tapped the spikes on the slave's collar.

This brought a gasp of understanding to the boy's face, and his eyes flew to Saeric's neck and the row of bleeding marks the collar had left there.

'I sorry, sir Lord,' the boy sputtered in the Seaxna tongue, surprising Saeric.

Saeric managed a smile. *So, you can speak then.* 'What's your name?'

'Asaf,' the boy said.

'I'm Saeric.'

'Thank,' the boy said. 'For save me.' He looked up at Eadwald, who was anxiously watching the burning burh. 'Who that...?' He was pointing at Eadwald, trying to find the word. Then he realised Seric also wore the same tunic. He touched the emblem on Saeric's chest. 'Who this? You?'

'That man is my... father. He is an ealdorman to King Ecgberht.'

'He king?!'

Saeric shook his head. 'No. No, he is a servant of the king.'

'I pleased meet you, sir Lord,' Asaf said awkwardly.

Saeric let out a sigh. 'I'm sorry, Asaf, but we have to go. I must find Hildelith.'

He rose, but Asaf grabbed his arm and held on. 'You not leave me here,' he said, in a voice that was both determined and hesitant.

'Don't worry, you're coming with us,' Saeric said, holding out his hand to help the boy out of the river. He nearly tripped over Asaf's chain on his way up the bank, and he swore at the trailing obstruction still wrapped around his body. 'We need to get this off you,' he said, 'and me.'

Saeric untangled himself from the long chain, bundling up the iron links and handing them to Asaf to hold while Saeric rubbed his arms to restore circulation. Saeric felt sore all over, and his lower back ached thanks to his wrenching stops in the byre. *I'm going to pay for this in days to come*, he thought.

'Where's your sword?' Eadwald said.

Saeric instinctively put his hand where the hilt should be, and then his shoulders slumped when he remembered he'd snapped it. 'Wasn't as strong as I thought,' he said. 'I broke it.'

'It's not the only thing you broke,' Eadwald said reflectively, inspecting the shattered piece of iron ring that remained attached to the other end of the boy's chain. 'Just how in the name of God did you do *that*?'

Saeric peered at it. He'd assumed he'd torn the whole thing from the mountings, not broken the actual band of iron that held it to the post. 'Poor workmanship?' he offered, somewhat shocked himself. 'Heremund says that badly forged iron can be brittle.'

Eadwald shook his head at him. 'Well, happily, you're a blacksmith, so you can make yourself another sword. Pity, though, it was a decent blade. In the meantime, what are we going to do with all this chain?'

Saeric inspected the collar around the boy's neck, but it was tightly fastened. Unlike Saeric's, this one was not designed to be removed so readily. Saeric recoiled at that realisation. He shuddered because being so close to it frightened him inexplicably. *They're gone now*, he thought, *yet why am I still afraid?*

Because the witch is alive and waiting for you, the Devil reminded him.

The boy's neck and chin were bleeding thanks to being dragged out of the byre by that same collar, but he didn't seem to mind. *You're just glad to be out of there*, Saeric thought, knowing exactly how that felt. There was also the matter of Asaf's ankle irons, which would hinder his ability to run or ride.

'We need to find a blacksmith,' Saeric said, then, aware of the irony, explained, 'I need the right tools.'

'Well, it will have to wait,' Eadwald said. 'Baldwyn's fyrd will have seen the smoke, and they'll be making all haste in this direction.'

'Not before we find Hildelith,' Saeric argued.

'Then where is she?' Rodor demanded angrily. He was fully clothed and armoured again. 'You slaughtered everyone before we could ask them, you idiot.'

'Rodor,' Eadwald warned.

'Sir Lord?'

'They wouldn't say or didn't know,' Saeric responded. 'And remember who you're talking to.'

'And who would that be, exactly, wealh?' Rodor snarled.

'Sir Lord?'

'Enough! Both of you,' Eadwald snapped. 'We can't loiter around here. They'll be upon us any moment.'

'Sir LORD!' Asaf shouted, pulling so hard on Saeric's tunic that it nearly toppled the Briton. 'I think I know where she gone!'

They all looked at the slave. 'What?' Saeric said.

'I hear fyrdsmen talk. They say about hunting lodge.'

'Where is that, boy?' Rodor asked. 'Is it far? Will we get there before nightfall? Speak up now.'

Asaf frowned at the bossy fyrdsman. 'Not far on horse.'

Rodor immediately gave instructions to the other soldiers to bring the horses. He turned to Eadwald. 'We can't take the slave. We haven't a spare mount.'

'He can ride with me,' Saeric said, casting Rodor a dark glare.

'You're already too heavy for your horse,' Eadwald warned him.

'He comes with me,' Saeric repeated firmly, 'and I'll walk if the horse can't manage.'

They quickly gathered themselves, Saeric wishing he had something else to wear, for he was feeling the cold now, dressed in his sodden and bloodied gambeson and chainmail. He climbed aboard his horse, and the others helped the boy up behind him. Then they bundled the chain up as best they could and placed it in the boy's lap. The boy wrapped his arms around Saeric's waist and rested his head on the nape of Saeric's shoulders, and Eadwald wrapped a wet blanket around the slave's shoulders and body. 'It will make you cold, but with those burns, you will thank me.' He looked up at Saeric, a wry smile on his face. 'You've found yourself a loyal servant, methinks.'

Saeric shrugged back. He could think of worse things.

Eadwald sent two men to warn Gerard that Baldwyn's fyrd had turned about and to make his way towards the burh and be ready to escort them back. 'If he asks, tell him that Hildelith is safe.'

The men saluted and rode off.

'Before you ask,' Eadwald said to Saeric, 'I need Gerard to stay at the head of our fyrd.' He looked down at Asaf. 'Now then, lead us to this lodge. It'll be dark soon.'

They rode as fast as they dared, but the path soon became rough as it wound its way into a thickly wooded valley, through which the river rushed noisily in autumn spate. It was the same wood into which Saeric had fled when he had escaped last winter and the same torrid river into which he had leapt. He shuddered at the memory of it.

'Sir Lord?' came a concerned voice from behind him.

'Bad memories,' Saeric said. He turned to Eadwald, who was behind them. 'I don't like this.'

'Not far now,' Asaf said quietly.

'We need to get off this path,' Saeric decided. He stopped and dismounted, and then he helped Asaf down. 'You two,' he said to Rodor and the other soldier. 'Take the horses back somewhere safe, then follow us in.'

'I don't take orders from you, wealh,' Rodor reminded him.

Eadwald closed his eyes, and then he slowly turned to his subordinate. 'Speak like that to my son again, and you won't be taking orders from anyone. Am I clear?'

'Yes, Lord,' Rodor ground out between gritted teeth.

'Good. Now do as he says.' The ealdorman dropped down from his horse. 'But don't be too long about it. This feels like a trap to me.' He looked at Asaf, suspicion in his eyes. 'Saeric, you need a sword.'

Saeric shook his head. 'I have what I need,' he said, pulling out his bow and the depleted quiver of arrows and slinging them over his shoulder. He then took his now-favourite weapon from the saddlebag and waited for Eadwald to arm himself.

'For Christ's sake Saeric. Next, you'll be insisting on riding into battle with that thing.'

Saeric smiled. 'Why not? Anyway, you told me I could bring it.' He nodded at Asaf, who stood shivering beside him, bare-footed with the blanket wrapped around his shoulders. 'Shouldn't we give him a dagger or something?'

'Absolutely not,' Eadwald said. 'Lead on, boy,' he added, waving down the path.

It had been a sound decision to abandon the horses, for their passage on foot soon became difficult through the thickets of brambles and underbrush that overgrew the path. Asaf stumbled many times, and his chains clinked noisily, leading Saeric to question the wisdom of bringing him. It would hardly be a surprise attack with all the noise they were making.

'Are you sure this is the right way?' Saeric asked.

'It is best way,' Asaf whispered, then he pointed through the trees ahead.

Saeric could just make out the shape of a low, shingle-roofed building through the trees. At first glance, it appeared to be deserted, but then Saeric caught sight of movement in the small clearing beside the lodge. Saeric shouldered off his bow, then quietly took out an arrow and nocked it loosely. It was a standard leaf point; not much use against mail armour, but he'd noticed that the fyrdsmen wore little protection. T*ypical of Baldwyn to rook his men*, he thought, *but helpful right now*.

Asaf abandoned his cloak and led the way through the underbrush, giving the building a wide berth. Saeric noted that the boy was careful about where he put his feet, and Asaf rarely brushed against the branches around him. And all the jingling of chains Saeric had heard earlier seemed to have vanished. Just how Asaf was managing it, Saeric couldn't fathom, but moving with stealth – even hindered though he was – appeared to be one of Asaf's skills. Saeric was less successful if for no other reason than his considerable bulk. His other problem was his chainmail, which clinked and jingled no matter how delicately he trod. He felt an odd tingling in his chest that grew stronger as they approached the building.

She is here, agreed the Devil, *and she knows you are close by too.*

Asaf came to a stop and pointed through the trees and undergrowth. They were now end-on to the building, with a good view of either side of the lodge. On the far side of the large clearing to the right of the lodge were four horses, hitched to a rail. Closer to the building stood a tall beech tree, and tied to the trunk of that tree was Hildelith. Gerard's daughter was stripped to the waist, and her arms were pulled back on either side around the tree trunk, presumably tied at the back. Saeric saw that a star was drawn in black on Hildelith's breast, in exactly the same place as Saeric's. From his hiding place, Saeric could not be sure how the mark had been made, and he clenched his teeth, biting back the roar of fury and anguish that rushed to his lips. He felt Asaf's hand on his forearm, and he glanced down to see the boy frowning up at him.

Yes, that's her, Saeric confirmed in his thoughts, nodding.

He turned back to Hildelith. She stood stiff-legged, and her face bore a dark glare. Saeric followed her gaze and his breath caught in his throat. Eanswith sat on a bench against the lodge wall, a vicious smile twisting her face. Her sword lay unsheathed across her knees. Two guardsmen stood on either side of Eanswith, armed with spears and swords, looking outward into the surrounding forest.

'So, what now?' came Eadwald's whisper in Saeric's ear.

It was clearly a setup, but Saeric could see no other alternative than to rush them. He and Rodor could each take down the two men with their bows, but there would surely be more men hidden somewhere, potentially in the lodge and surrounding trees, but as to how many was anyone's guess. There had been so few defending the burh that it would not surprise Saeric if Eanswith had brought the majority of them here to protect her. What would she care for her family? Saeric had an escort of just five men, including Eadwald and Rodor, in unfamiliar territory against a ruthless monster who had undoubtedly planned this ambush for months. Should they wait for Gerard to arrive with the fyrd and take this place by force with superior numbers? Did Eanswith know that the burh had been razed? Saeric fancied he could smell the smoke.

'I know you're there, Sugu, or should I call you Saeric?'

Eanswith's voice startled him, and he swallowed as she looked straight at him. He knew he was well-screened by the thick grove of holly, but as she had always done, she had sensed him long before he came into sight.

Eanswith stood and walked casually over to Hildelith, who was also looking into the forest, but unlike Eanswith, her face showed confusion, for she could see nothing.

Eanswith held her sword point to Hildelith's breast and traced the star. 'Do you like it?' Eanswith asked. 'I made it especially for you.' She moved the point of the blade into the middle of the star and held it there. 'Come out now, my darling, so that we can play. I know you want to.'

'Stay here,' Saeric whispered to Eadwald.

'Don't be a fool,' Eadwald whispered back. 'You'll be cut down the instant you step out there. We must withdraw.'

'And let her kill Hildelith?' Saeric said. His bow drawn tight, Saeric stood up and stepped past the holly screen and out into the clearing. He aimed his arrow at Eanswith's chest.

As Saeric expected, four men appeared from the undergrowth on the other side of the clearing, each armed with a bow, and all of them trained on him. Three more men appeared from within the lodge, all armed with swords. One of the men took up position just outside Saeric's sword reach. Saeric had no doubt there were still more hidden among the trees.

'Well, look who it is,' Eanswith said in mock surprise. 'My faithful little dog led you straight to me, just as instructed. Good boy, Asaf. You can come to me now.'

There was a blurted expletive, and Asaf burst from the undergrowth, running up to Saeric.

'I not do that!' Asaf said. 'She lie, Sir Lord!'

The man nearest Saeric struck the boy with the hilt of his sword and knocked Asaf flying, his chain trailing behind him. The boy fell to the ground, dead or unconscious; Saeric didn't know. All the while, he kept his weapon trained on Eanswith.

'My, what a big bow you have,' Eanswith said, moving a little to the side, so Hildelith was better exposed to the men. 'Normally, that would hint at inadequacies elsewhere,' she smiled, 'but in your case, the bow befits the arrow.' She looked at Hildelith. 'Have you felt the thrust of his arrow yet, my dear?'

Hildelith stared coldly at her attacker but remained tight-lipped.

Suddenly Eanswith slapped Hildelith. 'That is for daring to sample my Sugu without my permission.' She considered Hildelith a moment. 'How does he compare to my brother? Edward said he enjoyed his time with you. How did you find him? He is quite skilled, don't you think? In my experience, Edward is the lesser of the two men, but for all his size, Sugu's stamina was always a little wanting. I wonder if his newfound muscle brings a greater vigour?'

'That's enough, Eanswith,' Saeric growled. 'Get away from her.'

Eanswith tilted her head and smiled at Saeric. 'My dear Sugu, there is nothing you can do that will hurt me. You know that. You and I are beyond hurting. But I know you want me right now, just as you have ever since you ran away. I've been watching you, in your hot little smithy in Scirburne, banging away at your iron, growing ever stronger before my eyes. Ah, how I've yearned to try that lovely new body of yours. Such raw power! I nearly came to you at the ford, did you know that? What would you have done, I wonder? You were a delight to watch with that brutal weapon. They tell me it was a ploughshare. Do you still use it? Perhaps you have it with you now?' She smiled at Saeric's horrified reaction as she confirmed Eadwald's claim that it had been Eanswith behind the attack on Leo.

'You know that this woman can never sate your need. Only I can do that. Come back to me, Sugu, and I may even let her live. She can be our serving wench. What do you think?' Eanswith moved her sword down in little swirls over Hildelith's belly, but she was careful not to cut her.

'Get away from her,' Saeric ground out between clenched teeth.

You know she's right, the Devil said. *Your place is with her, in her.*

Shut up, Saeric said, his mind working furiously. *What am I to do? We're hopelessly outnumbered. Why hasn't Eadwald done anything?*

Eanswith was watching him, her smile malicious. 'No, Saeric, even you aren't strong enough to fight this many men. You could shoot me, of course, and you might even put down one or more of my men before they overcome you. They won't kill you straight away. They will tie you up so that you can watch while they each have their way with your precious filly. Perhaps they have already had a taste? Unfortunately, they will likely be a little rougher with me gone, and I expect she will eventually die. My men will then cut a vein or two in your arms and string you up by this branch here, leaving you to bleed to death beside your newfound love. That's if they don't just kill you outright since I will not be there to protect you.'

Saeric glowered at her, rendered impotent by her words and his impossible situation. His arms were beginning to shake under the strain of holding the tightly strung bow. He would be unable to hold it for much longer.

'What do you want, bitch?' Hildelith hissed. 'You know this cannot end well for you.'

'I told you. Your beau will kill me, and then my men will rape and kill you while he watches on. Then he will either kill himself or be killed so that he can join me in Hell, where we can be reunited in eternal sin.'

'Release her in the name of the king,' came a deep, commanding voice from the trees. Eadwald stepped into the clearing, his sword sheathed. 'You've nothing to gain here.'

Eanswith raised her eyebrows, evidently impressed that she had drawn out none other than Eadwald. 'Oh, I've everything to gain, my Lord. I offer you a trade: this wench for your illegitimate son.'

'Release her,' Eadwald repeated, 'and I might be persuaded to consider saving the rest of your family from execution for your crimes.'

'Come now, my Lord, Sugu can't mean as much to you as your precious Goddaughter. You abandoned your boy to a life of deprivation and humiliation. Were you even aware of his existence before he came to you? What lies have you told him to dupe him into believing you actually care about him?' Eanswith turned her gaze to Saeric. 'You know that only I can care for you in the way you need.'

'I will not ask again,' Eadwald growled.

'Or what?' Eanswith hissed. She moved the point of her sword to the star above Hildelith's heart. 'What will His Grace Prince Ethelheard do to you when he hears that you refused to trade a half-blood slave for his pure-blood daughter, Princess Hildelith, the last of his line.'

Saeric let out a startled expletive.

'She hasn't told you?' Eanswith said, her tone derisive. 'Had the fates taken a different turn, this girl's father might have been the king of Wessex, but alas, things did not go so well for Prince Ethelheard. In fact, they went so badly that he was stripped of his name and title. But killing a king does tend to mark a man, doesn't it, Lord Eadwald?'

'Be silent!' Eadwald snapped.

'Or what?' Eanswith said, revelling in the ealdorman's powerlessness. She turned back to Saeric. 'It's only thanks to Ealdorman Eadwald here that King Ecgberht didn't execute the ætheling; your father convinced the king that he wouldn't be sitting on his throne were it not for Prince Ethelheard's actions, even if Ethelheard had been planning a different outcome. Word is that Ethelheard's mother – who is sister to the murdered king Beorhtric – still plots to return her son to the throne, with the help of Earls Heremund and Eadwald, of course.'

Saeric stared at Eanswith, astounded. He desperately wanted to look at Eadwald's face, but he dared not move his eyes from Eanswith. He eased the pressure on the bowstring. 'Is any of this true?' he said, directing his question at the ealdorman, but it was Hildelith who answered.

'Yes,' she said simply.

'Saeric,' Eadwald began, his voice betraying his fear that his unpredictable acolyte might turn on him. 'I will explain–'

'Don't worry, father,' Saeric interrupted, his voice hard. 'You can fill me in once we've dealt with her.' He drew back the bowstring. 'Move away from the princess,' he growled at Eanswith.

'Come now, Sugu,' Eanswith said, frowning at him, 'you don't–'

A wild shriek cut her off from their right, and suddenly Asaf appeared from the underbrush and threw himself at one of the archers and knocked him down. The others turned towards the commotion as Asaf grabbed the shaft of a spear and shoved it at the man holding it. He then used the chain still attached to his collar as a weapon and swung it above his head as he rushed the three men by the lodge.

Saeric instinctively loosed his arrow at the other archer who was swinging around to take a shot at the boy. He then sprang sideways, ducking out of the way of a spearman just in time. He stumbled backwards and scrabbled for another arrow. There was a shriek from either Eanswith or Hildelith, but he couldn't look because the fyrdsman in front of him had abandoned his spear and had wrenched out his sword. His wild swipe caught Saeric on the side, but Saeric's mail armour saved him. Saeric got off a shot that hit the soldier in the right shoulder–enough to slow him down. Saeric dumped the bow and quiver and hoisted his ploughshare in time to fend off another blow from one of the other men. He saw Asaf flying through the air in the background, his chain trailing him as he tumbled into the bushes at the edge of the clearing.

Three men were coming at him, and then suddenly, the one nearest Saeric lost his head. Rodor's face appeared momentarily, and then he was gone, defending himself from another attacker. Saeric threw himself at the swordsman in front of him, ramming his ploughshare into the soldier's body. Like in the burh earlier, the heavy implement jammed in the man's chest, and the soldier stumbled away, trying to pull the blade out of himself. The remaining fyrdsman seized the advantage and swung at Saeric, slamming his sword down onto Saeric's shoulder. Saeric felt his knees buckle with the force of the blow, but the blade lost its potency when it sliced through the mail, snagging briefly on the gambeson. That was enough to save Saeric, who stumbled backwards, frantically searching for a weapon. His hand found the shaft of a spear, and he snatched it up, using it for batting away an attack from his assailant. Over the man's shoulder, Saeric saw to his horror that Eanswith had cut her prisoner free and was bringing her sword up to Hildelith's throat. Saeric was helpless to prevent Eanswith from carrying out her promise.

But none of them had counted on Asaf, who suddenly appeared behind Eanswith, his mouth twisted into a snarl. He yelled at her in his unintelligible foreign tongue and sprang towards her, slinging his chain around Eanswith's neck. Eanswith shrieked and swung her sword at the boy as he leapt up at her. Halfway through her attack, she dropped her sword and pirouetted on her ankle, then she fell to the ground, a dagger sticking out of her back, high up near the left shoulder blade. Asaf tumbled to the ground beside her, his chain still wrapped around Eanswith's neck.

Eanswith let out an enraged scream and staggered to her feet, looking around for her sword. Her eyes found Saeric, and she came for him, her teeth bared, oblivious to the chain. It did not surprise Saeric that she was still alive; she was, after all, a demon.

'You will join me in Hell, thrall!' she yelled, reaching behind her and wrenching the dagger from her shoulder.

She leapt at Saeric, the weapon held high, intent on plunging it into his chest. Then miraculously, she jerked to an abrupt stop as she came to the end of Asaf's chain. Eanswith staggered backwards, grabbing at her throat as she choked. Asaf yanked hard on his chain again, pulling her away from Saeric. Saeric's spear shuddered as she slid off it, but the tanged iron head caught in her back, and she came to a stop, her weight being borne now by Saeric. She frowned down at the bloodied shaft protruding from her stomach, astonished. She hadn't even seen the weapon in her scortum's hands, and neither she nor Saeric knew that she had run onto it in her rage. Her eyes lifted to meet Saeric's, and her mouth twisted into a sneer. She opened her mouth to speak, then suddenly it was gone. Her head disappeared in a flash of steel and a spray of blood, and Saeric found himself looking instead at Hildelith's grim face as she held Eanswith's sword in a two-handed grip, blood running in little rivulets down the blade.

'Do I need to cut out its heart too?' Hildelith asked, breathing heavily.

Saeric looked down at the decapitated head at his feet, the face still twisted into a snarl. 'No,' he muttered. 'She's dead.'

He let go of the spear and looked around, realising that the sounds of fighting had stopped. Eadwald and Rodor were both bloodied but still standing, and beyond them, just out of reach, stood the last remaining fyrdsmen, their weapons abandoned and their hands in the air. In the background, Asaf swayed on his feet, then his eyes rolled up, and he sank to the ground.

Saeric met Hildelith's eyes, and he shook his head, reeling at the realisation that he was at last freed of Eanswith. He found himself unable to find words to express himself, so he simply said, 'thank you.'

'What for?' she asked. 'We each played our part in putting away that demon.' She managed a grim smile, despite the circumstances. 'You chose me. That tells me everything I need to know.' She stepped past him and hurried over to Asaf.

The Asturian appeared to have no apparent injury other than his burns, and the boy was still breathing, so perhaps he had simply fainted. *God knows he must be suffering horrendous pain*, Saeric thought, *so perhaps it's best he is unconscious.*

'I owe my life to that little one,' Hildelith said, standing back up. 'I wonder who he got that dagger from?'

'Aye,' Saeric said, then, on realising that Hildelith's torso remained exposed, tugged his tabard off and offered it to Hildelith. 'Sorry, I know it's filthy, but I thought you might want to… We'll have a spare tunic somewhere.'

Hildelith nodded in thanks and drew it over her head and

shoulders. It was disgusting, but it was better than nothing. Saeric bent down and picked up Asaf's chain, then wrenched the other end of it roughly away from Eanswith's body. He hoisted the boy and his chain into his arms. 'Let's get away from here,' he said.

Around them, Eadwald and his men tidied up, tying those huscarls who were still alive together and collecting all the weapons and items for confiscation. They left Eanswith and her slain men where they lay for the wolves and ravens.

Saeric and Hildelith left the scene of the slaughter and went back to where Rodor had tied up the horses. Saeric carefully put Asaf down and propped him against a tree. He checked that the boy was still breathing, and then he turned back to Hildelith, taking advantage of this brief moment of privacy.

'Are you hurt?' he said awkwardly, knowing it was a stupid question and wondering whether he should have asked it.

Hildelith gave him a long look, then said, 'I am alive, and that's what matters.'

Saeric closed his eyes, knowing what they must have done to her and feeling anger and guilt for the terrible cost of his weakness. 'I'm sorry,' he said again.

'Oh Saeric, what I have endured gives me a small glimpse of what you must have suffered day after day, year after year, at the hands of these abominable people. I cannot imagine what it must have been like for you. You do not need to keep apologising.'

'But all of this is my fault. I should have dealt with her long before now but was too afraid and didn't, and now you've been....' He stopped, having no idea what to say.

Hildelith looked back at the forest behind them. 'Well, you are free of her now.'

Saeric felt a prickling in his spine when she said that. A great weight seemed to have lifted from his shoulders, and again he felt light-headed with relief. Tears sprang to his eyes, and he roughly wiped them away, knowing that if he started now, there would be no stopping them.

'Saeric, it's alright,' Hildelith said, resting a gentle hand on his arm.

'No,' he said gruffly. 'I should be consoling you, not the other way around.' Tears came again, and he wiped them away angrily. He turned from her and rifled through the various saddle packs and travel rolls to find something better for Hildelith to wear. He came up with a pair of breeches, an undershirt and a tunic and offered them to Hildelith.

'I don't know if any of these will fit...' he said. He stopped on seeing her staring at him, tears running freely down her face as her body shook violently. Saeric instinctively took her in his arms and pulled her tight. 'It's over,' he said, having no clue what words might console her. At first, she stood rigidly, her arms by her sides, but then she lifted her hands and hugged him tightly while she sobbed into his chest, her face pressed into the cold rings of his chainmail. Saeric, too, succumbed and allowed his tears to come as he held her in his arms.

'Saeric?' Hildelith asked eventually, her voice muffled by his chest. 'Will you forgive me?'

'For what?' he said.

She lifted her face from his chest and looked into his eyes. Hers were red from crying. 'For keeping the truth from you. I thought that if you knew who I was, you'd want nothing to do with me.'

Saeric frowned at her, bemused. He remained astonished that she was attracted to him at all.

'My family and I are pariahs in court,' she said. 'I am unmarried because no one will have anything to do with me or my father. You talk of being stained by sin. You are not alone in that.'

Saeric let out a little laugh. 'Ah Hildelith,' he said. 'You and I are a perfect match then.'

She frowned at him. 'You're the opposite of me. Everyone admires you. You're strong and brave and honourable. Eadwald is lucky to have found you. But I've already told you all this.'

Saeric let out a long breath and pulled away from her. He thought about whether he should go on, but what could he lose after today's momentous events? 'Hildelith, you aren't the only one keeping secrets.'

'But you have been acknowledged publicly by your father. I am pleased you are his son.'

He shook his head. 'He's not my father, Hildelith. That's just a story I made up to hide who I really am.'

Her frown deepened.

'I didn't want to tell you because it isn't safe for you to know. Earl Talec is even more zealous than Baldwyn. He is hunting for me right now. That's why we made up the story about me being Eadwald's son. We are trying to throw him off my scent.'

'Earl Talec? Why does he care about you?'

'I tried to tell you on the night of that storm,' Saeric said, then he paused, wondering how to say it. In the end, he decided on the plain and simple fact. 'My name's not Saeric, and I'm not Eadwald's bastard son. I'm Aneurin ap Cadwyr, and my real father was king of Dumnonia.' It sounded strange to say it so matter-of-factly in this West Saxon forest, surrounded by the smell of blood and smoke mingling with the damp woodland air.

Hildelith stared at him, open-mouthed. 'You're *who?*' she whispered, then after a speechless pause, 'who else knows? Does my father? What about Lord Heremund?'

'Of course we know,' came Eadwald's voice from behind them. Hildelith and Saeric both turned, but the ealdorman raised his hand. 'Don't worry; it's just me. The others are still tidying up.'

'But the lost princes are supposed to be a myth,' Hildelith said to Eadwald, 'and how in all of sarding creation did he come to be her slave? And why are you and Heremund, of all people, helping him?' She turned to Saeric. 'And why are you accepting it? I don't understand.'

'I'm afraid it's a tale that will have to wait,' Eadwald said. 'Remember, he is a prince with neither crown nor kingdom, just like your father.' The nobleman's face bore a grim expression. 'As far as everyone is concerned, Saeric is my bastard son. Do you understand? Not even Carwyn knows the truth, Hildelith.'

'Ah, actually–' Saeric began, but he was cut off when Hildelith slapped Saeric hard across his cheek.

The Briton staggered sideways, taken by surprise.

'That's for not telling me sooner,' Hildelith said, then she slapped him again. 'And *that's* for telling me.'

Saeric raised his hands, confused.

'I knew you were noble-born, but the Dumnonian *ætheling*, for God's sake? Do you know how much more complicated this makes things for me?'

'I'm sorry,' Saeric muttered, unsure what to say to that. He handed Hildelith her clothes, and the two men turned their backs while she dressed. The outfit was far from a perfect fit, but at least they were clean and unsullied. She returned Saeric's tabard but left her tattered dress on the ground.

'Now we really must leave,' Eadwald said. 'Will you be able to ride?' he asked Hildelith.

She nodded.

Saeric bent down to pick up Asaf. The boy came to and let out a snarl when he realised that he was being manhandled. When he saw who it was, he let out a yelp of delight and hugged Saeric tightly, crying with joy that they were all still alive.

'Whoa there, polecat,' Saeric said. 'You're alright then?'

Asaf shook his head, turned grey, and threw up. He blinked, wiped his hand over his mouth, and fainted again.

'It's all those bangs to his head,' Eadwald said. 'He seemed to get thrown about quite a lot, but he'll come good. Better he's unconscious anyway. Those burns must be Hell for him.' He looked at Saeric's neck. 'And we have to get rid of that collar of his. He'll pierce your jugular next time he hugs you.'

Saeric put his hand up and felt blood on his throat. This time he hadn't noticed the spikes puncturing his skin.

'Time to mount up, you two,' Eadwald said, holding his hand out to the horses. 'You can continue your marital negotiations on the way to Worgemynster.'

9

Saeric Iron-cleaver

Worgemynster, Wessex

Rodor appeared shortly afterwards with two more horses. Saeric recognised the finest of them as Eanswith's mount. 'I thought we might need one or two spares. We've put all the gathered weapons on another one and left the three survivors tied up by the lodge.' His mouth twisted into a sneer. 'We stripped the witch and strung her up by her ankles for her fyrdsmen to find.'

'For Christ's sake Rodor,' Eadwald said. 'Just because she was a monster does not mean we should be.'

'I'll have that one,' Hildelith said, taking the stallion's reins from Rodor.

'Is that a good idea?' Saeric began, but he received a questioning glare from Hildelith.

'If that horse was hers, then I want him,' she said, then deftly mounted the stallion and tugged on the reins, letting him know she was now his master. 'And give me her sword. I want that too.'

Saeric mounted up, and this time they placed Asaf in front of Saeric so that he could cradle the boy in his arms. Both he and Asaf were shivering with cold, so Eadwald wrapped a riding cloak around them.

'Straight to Worgemynster,' said Eadwald. 'There's no telling what Baldwyn's fyrd will do now that it is leaderless.' He frowned. 'Matter of fact, why wasn't Edward leading it? I wonder if that means most of his men are still nearby. That is not good. Baldwyn always was a canny bastard.'

'What happened at the burh?' Hildelith asked.

'Saeric dealt with Edward and Baldwyn, and then we set fire to it all.'

'And the children?' she asked, staring at Saeric.

'He let them out,' Rodor said derisively. 'Should have left them to burn because they'll come after him now to avenge their kin. Still, that would be fair justice if you ask me.'

'That's enough, Rodor,' Eadwald snapped. 'I want you to ride ahead to Gerard and tell him to make straight for Worgemynster. I don't want him engaging Baldwyn's fyrd unless he has no choice. In the meantime, we will take a more westward route to put his force between us and Baldwyn's. We will meet you in Worgemynster. We're unlikely to make it before dawn tomorrow, possibly even later, depending upon who we encounter along the way.' He turned to the other fyrdsmen. 'Go with him.'

'My Lord!' Rodor protested. 'You must take an escort! This is Baldwyn's country. Word will spread.'

'Faster than we can ride? We will be fine,' Eadwald said. 'I have my ploughshare-wielding son here to protect us.'

'Who will just as likely hack off your head as soon as you turn your back,' Rodor growled.

Saeric let out a snort. 'There's only one head in danger here, arsehole, and my father is sending you away to ensure it stays on your shoulders.'

'That tale is wearing thin, wealh. I know who you are.'

'And you will keep that information to yourself,' Eadwald warned, catching the eyes of all his men. 'Saeric had nothing to do with the deaths of your kin,' Eadwald added for Rodor's benefit, 'so I would appreciate it if you'd stop taking it out on him.'

Rodor's eyes narrowed, but he saw his superior's warning glare and reluctantly spurred his horse southward, leaving just Eadwald, Saeric and Hildelith to ride hard into the west to take them out of harm's way.

Some while after leaving the hunting lodge, Asaf came around again, this time to searing agony thanks to his torn blisters. He tried to be brave, but eventually, he succumbed to the pain and broke down, pleading with Saeric to stop and let him down.

'We can't, Asaf,' Saeric said. 'It's not safe.'

'Then leave me,' he said. 'I make own safe.'

'You won't last a day,' Saeric said. 'They'll know who you are the moment they set eyes on you.' He turned to Eadwald. 'How far away are we?' He could barely see in the gloom, but the roadway was a lighter shade of grey, and Eadwald rode ahead with confidence. *It would be just our luck to encounter bandits*, Saeric thought.

'Just keep riding,' Eadwald said. 'We'll be there soon enough.'

The ealdorman had used the term very loosely, and it was much later in the night when Saeric heard a bell tolling somewhere in the distance ahead of them. He let out a croak of dismay, knowing that it could not signal good tidings.

'It's the burh's call to arms, Saeric,' Eadwald reassured him. 'It means they've been alerted to the danger. Don't worry, there is no possibility that Baldwyn's fyrd has got here before us.'

Shortly afterwards, they turned a bend and saw the bulk of Worgemynster burh and the mynster church looming out of the darkness. Torches blazed reassuringly at regular intervals along the palisade, and Saeric saw the shapes of fyrdsmen lining the battlements. He heard the challenge from the gatehouse, Eadwald shouting his name and rank, and soon afterwards, the gate ground open. Two men with torches emerged, backed up by more men with spears, to confirm the travellers' identities. They snapped to attention and saluted when they saw the high rank of the riders. The camp's commander hurried out to meet their visitors.

'Has my fyrd not arrived?' Saeric heard Eadwald ask.

'No, Lord, but we have news that they approach in haste. They will not be far behind you, I am sure. We have been readying the burh for battle.' The commander hesitated, then said, 'Lord, a runner arrived not long ago to report that Thegn Baldwyn's house has been razed. They were burned alive, including the children.'

'While it is true that I burned the hall, the children were spared,' Eadwald said. He raised his voice so that all around could hear him. 'The King wishes to remind the people of that hundred, indeed all the peoples of Westseaxna Ríce, that there are certain standards we are expected to uphold, particularly the leaders amongst us. That family were little better than depraved monsters, and the King decreed that it was time they were brought to justice for their many crimes; not least the murder of Thegn Dunstan's daughter, Leofwynn, and most recently, the kidnap and maltreatment of Lady Hildelith. As a result of these crimes, Thegn Baldwyn, his son Edward, and his daughter Eanswith have been executed.'

The commander blinked in shock. 'My Lord, I would never presume to question our King's orders, and I know that Lord Baldwyn was not the best of men, but to execute all of them? Will this not give rise to more dissent here in the west? Lord Baldwyn has many allies.'

Eadwald raised his eyebrows at the commander's impertinence, and then he turned to Saeric. 'What do you think, Saeric? Did Baldwyn deserve his execution?'

'He most certainly did, father,' Saeric said coldly. 'Let his allies come. I am not afraid of them.'

'My son here has a particular dislike of that house, thanks to their poor treatment of him whilst confining him to slavery for a goodly part of his life. Now, Lady Hildelith needs a hot bath if you would be kind enough to oblige.'

The commander glanced at Hildelith. 'Very good, my Lord,' he said. His gaze slid back to Saeric, his frown deepening when he realised that Saeric held a boy in his arms, a boy who wore a slave's collar.

'My advice is to keep your opinions to yourself,' Eadwald warned, 'especially as Lord Saeric is very tired and can be prone to acts of violence at the merest provocation. Such long captivity has left him in an unpredictable mental state. Now show us to your quarters.'

Saeric barely noticed the clamour around him as they rode up to the commander's small hut beside the main barracks hall. Someone took the reins of his horse, and others took Asaf. Saeric half fell, half climbed down, shattered and exhausted. He managed to pull himself back to his feet, and then he held out his hand to help Hildelith dismount. She dropped down, grateful to be off the horse and somewhere safe.

'Are you alright, Saeric?' she asked, feeling him swaying on his feet.

'I'm fine,' muttered. 'We need to get you to your bath.'

She was about to answer him when he let out a little sigh and sank to his knees.

'Help him out of that armour, now!' Eadwald ordered, and before long, someone was deferentially asking Saeric to lift his arms. Saeric willingly followed the armourer's instructions as he was stripped of his chainmail, gambeson, and undershirt.

'I trust you've got a fire burning in there,' Eadwald said to the commander, then he told one of the men to help Saeric and Asaf inside. 'And fetch me the physician,' he added.

With great relief, Saeric sank down in front of the hearth in the commander's hut. He could barely hold his eyes open, and he curled up on the floor by the fire, feeling slightly troubled that he should instead be tending to Hildelith, who had, after all, suffered the most through all of this. An equally exhausted Asaf settled in beside him. They were both fast asleep by the time the physician arrived, so Eadwald waved him away, deciding that rest was what they needed most. The ealdorman found a blanket and carefully laid it over them.

'What is wrong with him?' Hildelith asked from the doorway, equally tired but surprised by Saeric's unexpected fragility in the face of his otherwise formidable strength and endurance. 'Has he been wounded?'

Eadwald considered his surrogate son and tilted his head in thought. 'I think he is overcome by the realisation that he is finally free. He was enthralled by that dreadful woman for most of his life, but now she is dead, and he is released. That is no small thing, Hildelith.'

'But he knows who I am now, Lord Eadwald. He won't want anything to do with me.'

Eadwald turned his gaze from Saeric to his Goddaughter and smiled. 'I think it will be quite the opposite, my dear.'

Saeric slept through the noisy arrival of the Scirburne war host and the joyous reunion of father and daughter. Gerard had ridden on ahead of the fyrd as soon as the runner had arrived from Worgemynster bearing the good news. Gerard left command of the force to Rodor and rode straight to his daughter. She was not in the garrison when he arrived, Eadwald having taken her to the Thegn of Worgemynster's hall to receive proper care after her ordeal. Despite the ungodly hour, the lady of the house had swept into action the moment she saw the identity of her guests. Within a short time, the household staff had the fire roaring, mead, wine and food warming, and a bath prepared in what appeared to be a drinking trough for the horses. No matter; it was long and deep enough to immerse herself completely.

Hildelith's first act had been to strip off the clothes Saeric had given her and throw them into the fire. She needed to start afresh, to clean away everything that bore any marks of her ordeal – the physical ones at least – so that she might feel a little less dirty. There was little she could do about her violation, but Eadwald must have spoken to the lady of the house because she gave Hildelith a disgusting infusion before helping her into the bath. Neither had said anything about it, for nothing needed saying. Hildelith prayed that the potion would do its job if, in fact, it was required. Thankfully, despite what the witch Eanswith had boasted to Saeric, Hildelith had only been violated the once by Edward, and Saeric had dealt with him.

She was still soaking in the bath when Gerard arrived. The veteran sank to his knees and cried tears of joy and relief, thanking God for saving his precious daughter.

'She is not unscathed,' Eadwald warned him.

'I am perfectly fine, Lord Eadwald,' she said from the other side of the woollen curtain.

'If any of those bastards have seeded her….' Gerard growled.

'They're all dead, my friend. Saeric and Hildelith saw to that. There's nothing you can do even if you wanted to.'

'I'll start by taking his lands,' Gerard snarled, 'and I want his family's name scrubbed from the annals.'

'I think our king will be ill inclined to grant you that wish, given that Baldwyn supported Ecgberht in his return from exile. Would it not be more fitting for Saeric to be bestowed Baldwyn's hundred after all hc has suffered?'

'That filth defiled my daughter. I do not intend to let it go unpunished.'

'You do know that I can hear you both,' Hildelith said. 'Saeric slew those responsible, father. It is done. I want no more talk of this.' Splashing sounds came from behind the curtain as Hildelith stepped out of the bath. 'What I wish to know is what plans you have for Saeric – Aneurin,' she corrected herself. 'Prince Aneurin. You know that it will only be a matter of time before Rodor or one of the others realise Saeric's true identity and blab about it? Now leave me be so that I may get dressed. I will join you in the commander's quarters shortly.'

The men left her be, and when she was sure they were gone, she sank to the floor and wept.

❧

Saeric came awake slowly, aware that someone was cradled in his arms, breathing softly, still asleep. He felt the weight of a blanket on his shoulders, the softness of a pillow under his head and the warmth of a fire on his face. He heard the unmistakable sounds of a busy burh around him and the soft murmur of a man and woman's voices nearby. For a moment, he wondered where he was and how he'd got here, then a few disjointed fragments of their arrival in the night flashed into his mind, and then he saw the terrified faces of Baldwyn's children amid flames and smoke. He let out a cry and opened his eyes, breathing heavily. *No*, he thought. *I'm sure they did not burn.* In front of him, he saw the crackling flames of a hearth fire and, through the fire, Hildelith and Gerard sitting side by side. He let out a sigh of relief. *It wasn't a dream*, he thought, still not quite believing it could be possible. *She's gone!*

'Morning, Saeric!' Gerard said lightly, all hint of his previous hostility gone. He peered at the Briton, frowning slightly. 'Are you alright? You look unwell. Not unexpected, I suppose, what with slaying hordes of Saxons and jumping in and out of rivers fully armoured. And even I, who have slept on my horse, can't lie on a hard floor all night and not even turn over once. You snored all night, by the way.'

Saeric was surprised to learn that he'd slept through all the commotion without stirring. *So, slaughtering your foes is good for sleep*, he thought. *Perhaps I have atoned for my sins by sending those wretches to the Devil. Could it be as easy as that?*

The Devil laughed at him for his naivety.

Saeric tried to lift himself up, but he was hindered by Asaf, who had wrapped himself tightly around his saviour. The boy awoke at the disturbance, muttered something unintelligible, blinked, and looked into Saeric's face. He burst into tears of joy and relief.

Saeric knew precisely how he felt. 'Yes, we're safe now,' he said, prising Asaf off him, careful to avoid the spikes on the boy's collar. He sat up and stretched his aching body. He was stiff down one side, and bruises had started to appear where he had wrapped Asaf's chain around his arms and torso in the byre. Asaf sat up, too, rubbing his eyes and frowning at their surroundings.

'Hildelith told me what you did, going into that burning building for him,' Gerard said. 'You're crazy, do you know that?' His voice held no sanction in it at all; instead, admiration. The old soldier looked down at the olive-skinned boy. 'And you? Asaf is it?' Gerard rose and came over to crouch in front of the boy. 'I believe I owe you a debt because you led Saeric to my daughter and then helped overcome her bastard abductors. Took them on single-handedly, if the accounts are true.'

It was clear that Asaf only partly understood what was being said. Still, Asaf took from Gerard's beaming smile and outstretched hand that he was receiving a compliment, so he nodded in acknowledgement, bowed, and clasped Gerard's wrist.

Saeric glanced over at Hildelith, who was watching silently from the bench on the other side of the fire. She had bathed and was now dressed in fine new clothes. She seemed anxious, and her silence was unsettling him. 'Are you feeling better?' he asked. It was a stupid question. *Of course she's not, you dalcop.*

Hildelith made it easy for him and smiled. 'As well as can be expected,' she said. 'What matters is that we are safe, and she is gone.'

Gerard stood and opened the door, leaned out and called for food and drink, and then he turned back to Saeric. 'In case you were wondering, we came upon Baldwyn's fyrd just after Rodor caught up with us. They surrendered without a fight.' Saeric could hear the disappointment in Gerard's voice. 'We saw the column of smoke from miles away. Thank you for that; it was quite helpful in our negotiations with the fyrdsmen. I hear your ploughshare came in handy again too?'

Saeric nodded, then he frowned as he considered Gerard, the would-be king of Wessex. *Is it true?* he wondered *Or did I dream all of that?* Looking upon Gerard now, it seemed impossible.

As though he had read Saeric's mind, Gerard smiled in

apology. 'I believe you learned a little about my distant past from the witch.'

So, it is true? Saeric thought, surprised. He nodded again. 'You should have told me,' he said.

Gerard let out a snort. 'Why? What difference would it have made?'

'A lot!' Saeric said, exasperated.

Gerard raised his eyebrows. 'Which is precisely why I said nothing.'

'Is it why you help me?' Saeric asked.

Gerard let out a sigh. 'I help you because I like you, pure and simple. I suppose I feel some affinity with you and a little bit sorry for you too, but you're a good man, Saeric. I don't have a lot of friends, and I was glad you came to like me as Gerard the humble fyrdsman, not the disgraced prince.'

'What did you do?'

'Nothing that warrants his punishment,' Hildelith said, leaping to her father's defence. 'Queen Eadburh poisoned her husband, king Beorhtric – my father's uncle – then she fled to Francia to seek protection from Ecgberht, who has no claim to Westseaxna Ríce at all, yet now he sits in Wintanceaster on my father's throne!'

'Steady on, Hildelith,' Gerard said. 'It was never my throne. I was but one of several contenders.'

'You have far more claim than anyone else, especially that Kentish usurper,' Hildelith spat.

'You've been spending too much time with your grandmother,' Gerard countered.

'But what did you do?' Saeric persisted. 'Eanswith said you killed the king!'

'She was lying,' Gerard said irritably, 'but I don't want to talk about it.'

'Father was bishop of Wintanceaster,' Hildelith explained. 'He excommunicated the murderer Eadburh for her crime, but

Ecgberht had her punishment overruled by the Frankish king, and she was granted a position in a Frankish nunnery. They then claimed the murderer was not Queen Eadburh but, in fact, my father. They said that he poisoned his uncle to gain the throne for himself and then made up the whole story about Queen Eadburh to hide his crime.'

Saeric stared at them both, shocked.

'Obviously, it was all lies made up by Ecgberht to discredit my father so that he could claim the throne for himself.'

'But how come you weren't executed?'

'In return for keeping my head, I agreed to relinquish my claim, title, and even my name,' Gerard explained. 'And I was excommunicated too.'

'But that's terrible,' Saeric said.

'Indeed it is,' Gerard said. 'My mother was furious with me for acceding to his demands. She wanted him to execute me to give her an excuse to go to war, but Ecgberht was no fool. He knew my family had too many allies to risk cutting off my head. I still do, fortunately.' He shrugged. 'It suited me because I never wanted to be king, despite what my family might say.'

'So, you didn't kill the king?' Saeric asked.

'No,' Gerard said, hurt. 'It really was Eadburh, as far as I know. I presume she was acting on behalf of Ecgberht, just like Hildelith says. Now, I wish to end this conversation because we have other, more important matters to discuss.'

Saeric rose and moved toward the door. Asaf immediately rose too, anxious that Saeric was leaving him, prompting Saeric to explain, 'I need to pee.'

That earned him a chuckle from Gerard, and Saeric smiled back at him, feeling a sudden wave of relief and gratitude. Instinctively he grabbed the older soldier and crushed him in a hug, then, embarrassed when he felt himself welling up, hurried out of the hut. He didn't bother looking for the latrine and relieved himself against the wall instead, aware that it was a punishable offence but not caring at all. *It's over*, he thought. *I'm free, and there's nothing any of you can do that will hurt me, including you, Rodor.* On cue, the subject of his thoughts appeared, took one look at the bare-chested Briton pissing on the wall, and then shook his head with disapproval. However, he said nothing and instead knocked on the door to the hut.

The door flew open, and Rodor was all but bowled over by Asaf, who bounded out in search of Saeric. The slave found Saeric and said, delighted, 'look, someone take chain away.' He pointed at his collar and then his ankle irons and did a little dance to celebrate his newfound freedom of movement. Then he stood next to Saeric and joined him in relieving himself.

'For Christ's sake, you disgusting wealas, there is a latrine for that,' Rodor growled.

Saeric and Asaf swapped grins, then they returned to the hut.

'We need to get that collar off you,' Saeric said as they went inside, frowning at the troubling reminder of their enthrallment.

'I took the liberty of asking the armourer to remove the chains last night,' came Eadwald's voice from behind them. 'You slept through it all. He wasn't keen to do the finer work, so I've asked for the town smith to come and look at the collar and shackles.' He looked down at the slave and frowned at the blisters and sores on his shoulder. 'Do they hurt?'

Asaf nodded.

'Well, we'll see what we can do about it once we get back to Sceaptesburh. In the meantime, here comes someone with food.'

The commander's attendant arrived with steaming bowls of porridge and offered them to Saeric and the Asturian. Asaf dug in hungrily and gobbled his bowl up in a flash. Amused, Eadwald called for more. The attendant returned with two more bowls, larger and laced with milk and honey. Saeric sat on a stool by the fire to eat while Asaf settled in between his legs.

'Can you not do that?' Saeric asked self-consciously. 'You aren't my dog.'

It had no effect whatsoever, as Asaf stayed where he was and wolfed down his second bowl.

'Well, he certainly has a big appetite for a little fellow,' Gerard said.

'It's probably the first meal he's had in weeks,' Hildelith said.

'Perhaps,' Saeric said. 'Although they never denied me food,' he added.

'What are you going to do with him?' Gerard asked.

Saeric looked down at Asaf's expectant face and let out a sigh. 'No idea. I wasn't thinking that far ahead when I went in there.'

'You weren't thinking at all, I take it.'

Saeric looked at the Saxon and said, 'Oh, I was, Gerard. I knew exactly what I was doing.'

The Saxon was unfazed by Saeric's intensity. 'Rodor tells me you slaughtered the whole lot of them with your ploughshare. Except for the witch, of course,' he added, patting his daughter on the arm. 'And your little pet here fights like a wildcat too, I hear.' He winked, grinning at Saeric.

He was saved from Saeric's exasperated response by the blacksmith, who entered the hut at that moment.

'Ah, you wish me to repair his shackles?' the smith said when he saw Asaf's ankle irons. 'How much movement do you wish the wealh to have?'

Saeric slowly stood, set aside his porridge, and turned to face the smith. They stood eye to eye for a moment, then Saeric snapped up his hand and clamped it on the smith's neck.

'Whoa, steady there, Saeric,' Eadwald said.

'I want all of it off, *especially* the collar,' Saeric snarled, releasing the smith, who rubbed his neck angrily. Saeric was unrepentant. 'Not nice, is it, having something wrapped tight around your throat like that? You wouldn't happen to know anything about this, would you?'

The smith paled and shook his head quickly, suddenly seeing the scars on Saeric's neck and realising his error. 'No, Lord. I will take it off this instant,' he said, his eyes still on Saeric's throat. He took a portable anvil from his tool bag and set it on the floor, then told the boy to kneel and rest his neck on it.

'You're not going to do it?' Eadwald asked his charge, clearly not expecting Saeric to entrust the task to this unproven guildsman.

The smith looked up at Saeric, surprised.

'My son is a blacksmith himself, apprenticed to Earl Heremund of Scirburne. You may have heard of him?' Eadwald said, permitting himself a tight smile as the smith swallowed and paled a little more.

'Your son?' the smith said nervously, his eyes darting from the ealdorman to Saeric. 'Of course, my Lord.' He moved to hand Saeric his tools, but the Briton shook his head.

'I'm not yet skilled enough,' he admitted.

'Of course,' the guildsman said again, returning to his preparations. 'I will be most careful, I assure you, my Lord.'

The boy stared with frightened eyes at the anvil.

Saeric smiled sympathetically. 'He's not going to cut off your head, just this.' Saeric tugged on the collar for emphasis.

The boy did as he was told, but he clenched his eyes shut. Saeric crouched down and put his arm around the boy's shoulders to reassure him, careful not to rub the raw skin of his burns.

'If you leave so much as a scratch on him, I'll cut off your hands,' Saeric warned the blacksmith.

The smith was good, and he broke the pin with a single blow. He even managed to do it without hurting the boy. He quickly moved to the ankle irons and had them off with a minimum of fuss. Relieved, he hastily packed his things, his job done.

As he was about to leave, Saeric gripped his forearm and squeezed it tight. The smith winced. 'If I hear that you have taken on any commission that involves the instruments of torture, I will put you in one of those myself, but with the spikes on the inside, nail you to your centre-post, then set your house alight and burn you alive, just as I did Baldwyn. Understand?'

The smith swallowed and nodded, his eyes tracing the various scars on Saeric's bare chest, inevitably halting on the star-shaped mark over his heart. 'I swear, Lord, this was not my work.'

'I hope you speak the truth for your sake,' Saeric said, 'for I *will* be making inquiries.' He released the smith, who hurried out of the door.

'Did you need to terrorise him like that?' Eadwald asked once the smith had gone. 'He was only trying to do his job.'

Saeric shrugged. 'I'm sorry, but there are some things that set me off. Slave collars especially.'

'Yes, but he was taking it off, not putting it on.'

'I know, alright?' Saeric said, frustrated with himself. 'I need to control my temper. I know that. It's just not so easy when you're constantly reminded of your torture.'

'We need to get you clothed,' Eadwald said, changing the subject. 'I've had your shirt and tunic washed. Let me see where it is. Oh, and let me get rid of that.' He reached out his hand to Asaf, who held the open collar in his hands, tears on his cheeks. Eadwald took it off him, and then he rested his hand on Asaf's uninjured shoulder. 'It will take time to adjust,' he said, 'but you're now a freeman, a member of our family now.' He paused in thought. 'Indeed, you will need articles of release. Let me sort that out too.' He left and closed the door behind him.

Asaf looked around the little room, tears flowing freely now. His eyes rested on Saeric, and he bowed.

'You don't have to do that,' Saeric said, shaking his head.

Asaf looked crestfallen. 'But I your scortum now?'

'No!' Saeric flared. 'You will *never* be that for me. Do you hear? You are free, Asaf.'

'But I don't want be free,' the boy objected, confused and distressed. 'You save me. I serve you now.'

'Oh, you poor thing,' Hildelith said, and she took him in her embrace, careful not to touch his burned skin. 'Are you worried we'll abandon you? Saeric is trying to say that he will be delighted to have your company as a friend. Not as a slave.' She released him but held his gaze. 'You saved my life, Asaf, so you will always have my protection, too, and that of my father and our family.'

Gerard nodded in agreement.

Saeric could see from the boy's face that he had not followed the conversation. He stepped up beside Hildelith. 'You don't have to do anything you don't want to anymore, Asaf,' he explained. He spoke slowly so that Asaf might understand. Asaf frowned back at Saeric through his large, brown eyes, clearly not understanding why they didn't want him. Saeric sighed and took one of Asaf's hands and pressed it to his broad chest, just as Hildelith had done during the storm, then he put Asaf's other hand on top of Hildelith's. 'You will stay with us,' he said, 'but as a friend and equal.'

Asaf nodded earnestly and said, 'I serve you as friend then.'

'I think you've lost this battle,' Hildelith observed.

'Will you forgive me?' Saeric asked her suddenly.

'That depends,' Hildelith said unhelpfully, smiling at his bewildered expression.

There was a knock on the door, and a soldier entered, saluted, and offered Saeric his freshly-cleaned clothes. 'Your gambeson is stitched but still drying, my Lord, and the armourer has repaired and oiled your chainmail. I also have a fresh pair of trousers for you. I will wait for you to change, and I will have your other clothes washed.' He looked to Asaf and added, 'Lord Eadwald also instructed me to find apparel for the boy. May I measure him?'

Saeric nodded, but Asaf snarled at the soldier when he approached.

'He just wants to fetch you new clothes,' Saeric explained, showing the boy his own fresh-cleaned shirt.

Asaf stood still while the soldier used his hands to quickly get a measure of the boy. He nodded to himself, then departed.

Saeric pulled on his clothes just as Eadwald returned. The ealdorman nodded with satisfaction. 'You do look good in that surcoat. You wouldn't consider joining my garrison?' Eadwald asked.

'What?'

'Royal blood or not, I know a good soldier when I see one. Moreover, I know a good leader. I'd be honoured to have your company. Men will fall over themselves to serve under you.'

The idea was so preposterous that Saeric rejected it out of hand. 'I like being a blacksmith,' he added, trying to find a non-offensive excuse.

'Who says you have to stop your trade? You can set up in the fort. It's part of who you are now. Bring grumpy old Heremund with you if you like, although I doubt he'd want to come.' He smiled at that thought.

'I can't,' he said again. 'I can't be a Saxon soldier.'

'Why, because you are Dumnonian?'

'Yes!'

'Dumnonia is Wessex's ally,' Eadwald continued, 'I don't see what's wrong with a Dumnonian joining Ecgberht's troop.'

'I do, when he orders me to take up arms against my own people.'

'You won't have to. Ecgberht's problems are elsewhere, and I don't mean forever, because you have a different destiny, as we all know. You are a bold fighter, but you need to learn the subtleties of military tactics. What better place than at my side?' When Saeric said nothing in reply, Eadwald added, 'I heard what you said to Baldwyn. That path is fraught and inadvisable. You stand at a fork in your journey. Impatience will almost certainly lead to disappointment and self-destruction. Nor can you take on the might of Wessex single-handedly. Mael is your enemy, not us. You did what you had to; you rid Wessex of a family of disgusting tyrants. Leave that past behind you now and look to the future. Who knows what glory awaits you on the path I offer you? Now, if everyone is happily fed and watered, I think we should continue to Sceaptesburh.'

❧

They set off to return home after an earlier-than-usual main meal so that they would arrive at the burh by nightfall. It was a cold but clear day, and the sun warmed their backs as they set out from Worgemynster. The men of the fort all saluted Saeric Iron-cleaver as he passed by on Hercules to take position at the fyrd's vanguard with Gerard, Hildelith and Eadwald.

'Iron-cleaver?' an incredulous Saeric asked Gerard when he heard them call out the title. Gerard shrugged back, grinning.

'I'm afraid that Gerard kept the shattered ring and has been showing it to all the men,' Eadwald said. 'You're quite the hero, you know. Inspiring is a word I heard during my inspection earlier. Just how strong *is* he? another asked. Saeric, the slave-saving soldier-smith. Has a ring to it, no?'

Saeric frowned at him, uncomfortable with the accolades and missing the pun entirely.

The story of the liberation of the slave from the burning building and subsequent gallant rescue of Lady Hildelith had swept through the camp, albeit in somewhat altered form, and it was this that had caught the men's imagination, not Saeric's cold-blooded execution of a thegn and his son and daughter. Apparently, he had scooped the boy up in his arms once he'd torn the chain free and had run through a wall of fire out of the building, clothes and hair ablaze. The men also learned that Saeric had once been a slave to that same household, which explained his fury at finding the boy in collar and chains, just as he himself had been bound before he had escaped. They had also been told of his desperate efforts to save Thegn Dunstan's daughter from a band of thugs months earlier – thugs sent by Baldwyn's daughter no less – and Saeric's saving of Gerard's own life and his vengeful butchering of every last one of the villeins for their crime. Several men made the sign of the cross as he passed, believing him blessed by the Lord with the strength and immortality that enabled His Soldier to perform good deeds and right wrongs. In just one evening, Ealdorman Baldwyn had been rebranded a monster who deserved his punishment, and it was Saeric, the hero, who had dispensed it.

It also transpired that the men of Sceaptesburh had spread the story of Saeric's heritage as the Ealdorman's bastard son and how he had been dissuaded from killing the two ealdormen out of revenge, instead to be acknowledged by Eadwald and brought into Heremund's household. The fyrdsmen had all agreed that their commanding officer was especially fortunate to have been delivered such a remarkable son from so wretched a beginning.

It was strange for Saeric to be surrounded by those he had once thought his enemies, complimenting him for his exceptional valour. Their respect was genuine, yet Saeric had not been trying to earn it from these men. He'd not even been thinking about them. Perhaps Eadwald was right. He hadn't been thinking at all.

He shifted in his saddle, wishing his new attachment would ride another horse, but predictably, the newly freed Asturian had no intention of being anywhere that Saeric wasn't. The young slave sat confidently behind Saeric, looking around at the scenery as they rode. Despite the frigid conditions, he rode bare-chested due to his burns.

Saeric glanced over at Gerard, who rode contentedly beside his daughter.

The old soldier threw him a smile. 'All's well that ends well, yes?' he said.

'You came up with that ridiculous name, didn't you?' Saeric realised. 'Why?'

'We both did,' Eadwald said from up in front. He and Rodor rode at the very head of the caravan of soldiers, followed by Saeric, Gerard and Hildelith. The bannerman rode behind them, the Scirburne gryphon pennant flapping at the top of the rider's spear. Then came the small troop of light cavalrymen, and snaking out behind them were the foot soldiers, marching to rowdy songs that kept them to time and pace. 'It's important that this lot grow to respect you if you're going to lead them into battle one day. By good fortune, you are a formidable warrior in your own right, and despite your prejudices, you can't seem to help yourself when it comes to keeping your enemies – and by that, I mean us Saxons – safe. We've just accelerated the process a little.'

Saeric let out a long breath. Once again, he had been thoroughly outfoxed and outmanoeuvred by his wardens. Gerard gave him a wink, then he peeled away to check on the foot-soldiers, and no doubt spread more tall tales about Eadwald's invincible smithing son. Saeric glanced over at Hildelith now that they were alone, as much as one could be when surrounded by a few hundred soldiers.

'Are you still annoyed at me?' Saeric asked.

She turned and frowned at him. 'Yes, especially as I'm the only one who has been kept in the dark about you being the ætheling,' she said testily, waving her hand in Eadwald's direction.

'So says the *princess*,' Saeric replied, equally annoyed.

'I'm *not* a princess,' Hildelith said, 'thanks to my family being stripped of our titles. I am but a simple lady of a once noble house. I might as well be invisible for all the hope I have of attracting any nobleman's attention now.'

'You've got mine,' Saeric said, feeling a little hurt by her careless dismissal of him.

She turned to him, frowning, and then she smiled. 'What a pair we are,' she said.

'None of this changes who I am,' Saeric said. 'I'm still the hopelessly ignorant wealh who can't even spell the name of his own kingdom. Or probably my own name, come to think of it. And all these soldiers will get a horrible shock when I collapse on the battlefield and curl up, wailing like a child in one of my hysterical fits. I'm not the great warrior they make me out to be.

You know that. You've seen what happens to me.'

She considered him a moment, then asked a completely unexpected question. 'Why don't you ride? You're a natural.'

He let out a snort. 'I've got someone propping me up.' He poked Asaf playfully in the side. The boy snapped out of his daydream and swore at Saeric in his mother tongue, causing Hildelith and Saeric to laugh. 'Sorry Asaf. You can go back to dreaming now.'

His pretty face twisted into a thoughtful frown. 'What is aethelink?'

When Saeric didn't answer, Hildelith said, 'heir to the throne.'

'Air?'

'A prince who will one day be king.'

That caused a change in Asaf's expression and demeanour. He sat up and leaned around so he could see Saeric's face. '*You* are king?!'

'No,' Saeric said, 'and don't do that. You'll fall off.'

'Pff,' Asaf said, then he sprang to his feet and stood with his arms crossed on Hercules' rump. The horse let out a snort and missed a step thanks to the unexpected antics of one of his riders.

'Jesus Christ, Asaf. Sit down,' Saeric said, startled.

In response, Asaf deftly turned around so that he was now facing backwards. Then he turned on his heel again to face the front, all the while with his arms crossed.

'Sarding Hell!' exclaimed the standard-bearer behind them. 'How does he do that?'

Eadwald and Rodor turned to look behind them, and both broke out in grins at the pugnacious expression on the boy's face.

'Now there's someone who can ride!' Eadwald said, impressed. 'What other tricks do you have up your sleeve?'

'Tell him to stop it,' Saeric grumbled. 'He's making me and my horse nervous.'

'You tell truth,' Asaf said. 'Who are you? You no lie. You say you slave like me, but they say–'

'Hush, for God's sake. And would you sit your sarding arse back down!'

Asaf swung past Saeric and sat himself in the Briton's lap, facing him. Hercules let out a snort and shook his head, but Asaf would not be dislodged.

'It would take the whole day to explain,' Saeric said, looking down at the boy, 'but I'm not going to do it now. Yes, I was Baldwyn's slave, but before that....' He trailed off, a powerful sadness welling up within him. 'Just... go back and be quiet, please.'

To his credit, Asaf could see that he had upset Saeric, so he returned to his place behind his new master. 'Sorry I upset you,' he said.

They rode in silence for a while as Saeric pondered the implications of all that had happened these past few days. Undoubtedly most surprising was the revelation that Gerard was a prince, a disgraced ætheling no less, accused of murdering a king! *I need to hear more of that tale*, he thought. And then, of course, was the fact that Hildelith was a princess of the Westseaxna royal line by her very birth. *And I have feelings for her*. Yet, whereas even a month ago, this fact would have troubled him, oddly, right here and now, it did not. Perhaps it was because it was destiny that had brought them together. He'd not intended to seek her, or indeed any of this party out, but fate had brought Saeric to Heremund, through whom he had met Gerard and thence Hildelith.

He looked over at her and smiled to himself. She was as lost in thought as he, and he caught himself admiring her strikingly beautiful face. She looked more herself today, clothed in a fine green dress hemmed in brown and white embroidery, and with her hair braided and bound with a ribbon. There was no hint of the haggard captive in the tattered skirt and bare feet he had rescued just a couple of days ago.

She felt his scrutiny and turned her head. He blushed as she offered him a smile, and then she turned her eyes back ahead, still smiling.

Are you thinking the same thing I am? he wondered. *Do you believe in fate, or do you think our meeting is a mere coincidence? What does me being crown prince of Dumnonia mean to you? Is it a good thing or bad?* He did know that he was pleased he had shared the truth with her. It was important to have offered her something that she could hold in trust. *Is that what love is?* he wondered, stealing another glance at her. *Is that what she was telling me on the night of that storm? Yet how can I trust them when they have kept so many truths from me, and they are, after all, my enemy?*

He turned to the front and his gaze settled on Eadwald's back. The ealdorman rode with the easiness of one born to the saddle, as did Rodor beside him. Neither was speaking, both probably in deep thought too. *What are you up to?* Saeric wondered. *You say you are not my adversary, but you and Heremund led the Saxons in alliance with the traitor Mael to overthrow my father. And where exactly does prince Gerard, or whatever his name is, fit into this puzzle? There is so much more to all of this than I understand.*

Foremost in his mind was Eanswith's question: why are they helping you? Eadwald and the others were obviously expecting something in return, but what was it? *I am entirely out of my depth*, he realised, wondering whether he may actually have slain the lesser of two demons back at Baldwyn's and that the actual devil rode in front of him in the guise of Eadwald, master-at-arms to King Ecgberht, Godfather to Hildelith, friend to a disgraced prince, and now mentor to the heir of a vanquished kingdom.

❧

Asaf winced and bit his lip when Carwyn applied more salve, but he was clearly determined not to cry in front of his hero. 'You poor thing,' Carwyn said, frowning at the extent of his injuries.

'This shoulder and arm may scar, I'm afraid, and likely your ankles from the shackles, but your lovely face is unmarked.'

Carwyn was administering her attentions to their new guest under the watchful eye of Brother Cuthbert from the mynster infirmary. The monk had refused to touch the dark-skinned slave, fearing the possibility of demonic infection from the infidel child, but had been coerced by Heremund to provide direction in his treatment. Saeric was sitting with Asaf, giving encouragement to the boy and receiving care himself for his own less substantial burns. Hildelith sat beside Saeric, tutting at the bruises on his arms and torso.

Carwyn placed a gentle hand on Asaf's neck, and the boy flinched and clenched his eyes shut. It was a reflex action that immediately upset Saeric, for it brought back memories of his own captivity. Carwyn apologised and made a reassuring cooing sound to Asaf, then gently rubbed a strong-smelling salve into the bruises and lacerations where the iron ring had cut him. 'This is lanolin, and it will help with the pain and healing,' she explained. She looked into the earthenware pot and shook her head. 'But you must both promise to stay out of trouble until we get some more. You've used it all up.'

'Well, don't waste any more on me,' Saeric said. 'Asaf needs it more than I do. He has more hope of healing.' He hadn't meant anything by it other than his already scarred body was past fixing, but Carwyn read more into it.

She looked up at Saeric. 'You will heal,' she said. 'It will take some time, but she is gone now.'

'Aye,' Saeric muttered, still unsure what that really meant to him.

'It will take time,' Carwyn repeated, 'and it will not be easy. You have endured and survived the most terrible torments for most of your life, Saeric, but your healing is past its most fragile, fledgling stage. You are a completely different man from the poor, battered thrall who collapsed nearly a year ago on my husband's floor. I know that we can never replace your family – God rest their souls – and nor should we wish to, but look around you. You are not alone anymore, Saeric. God has shone his light and love upon you.'

'But why?' he said. 'I am flawed beyond redemption thanks to Eanswith.'

'No man is perfect, for all have sinned and come short of the glory of God. Yet no man is beyond God's forgiveness, Saeric, not even you. And you must remember, you were but a child when you were drawn into sin. You have defeated that demon.' She looked down at Asaf, who had dabbed his finger in the salve and was sniffing it. 'And every life you save is another step towards salvation, whether they be your enemy's children, the woman you love, or even an innocent slave.'

'That child is not innocent,' Brother Cuthbert interjected, 'and his salvation will only come when he rejects his infidel beliefs and embraces the light of Christ.'

'Exactly,' Carwyn said, undeterred by Brother Cuthbert's censure. 'He has been saved once to be saved again.'

'I not need saving anymore,' said Asaf, gazing up at his hero. 'Anzar asab⊠ra has save me.'

Saeric looked at the boy, surprised. 'What does that mean?'

Brother Cuthbert crossed himself. 'A heathen invocation, no doubt.'

Asaf struggled to find the Saxon equivalent. He pointed at Saeric, clenched his fists, making himself look like a wrestler, then mimed thrusting with the sword and hacking with the ploughshare.

'Angry?'

He shook his head and reached out to pat Saeric's broad chest and shoulders, then puffed himself up again.

'Oh. You mean strong?'

Asaf's eyes lit up. 'Yes. Strong… fighter.' Then he frowned again, not sure of the next word. He pointed at a bird in the tree.

'Like him.' He flapped his arms and looked over his shoulder, then winced as it stretched his burned skin.

'A strong Blackbird?' Saeric asked, confused.

Hildelith laughed, realising what the boy meant. Had the men not said it themselves? 'No, dalcop. Angel. He means angel.'

'Angel,' Asaf said, trying out the word. He beamed back at Saeric and nodded. 'My warrior angel. Yes.'

Saeric found himself blushing, embarrassed by the accolade, then a darker thought occurred to him. *Strong perhaps, but I am no angel.*

No, you most definitely are not, the Devil agreed.

And yet, Saeric thought, looking around him, *here are people who believe in me and accept me, despite my flaws.* He frowned to himself, still unable to reconcile this fact. For so long, he had known himself to be unlovable, unworthy, even worthless. But as Carwyn had said, that was all the doing of the witch Eanswith and her whisperings of ill thoughts as she had tortured him and drawn him into her sordid grip. *But she is dead now, and her brother and father too. They are all dead. No more looking over my shoulder, wondering when they might come for me.*

He spotted Eadwald and Heremund standing over by the oak, deep in conversation. *I should be glad to have two of the most powerful men in Westseaxna Ríce aiding me in my quest, and a fearless woman who likes me–despite my broken body and soul–and who seems to have no desire to extract cruel payment in return for her attentions. Perhaps Carwyn is right: I have a better future after all. Maybe I might even achieve some measure of happiness, whether or not I manage to fulfil my promise to my kin, because here I have found a new home, a new family, and through them, hope.*

10
A bird in the hand

Scirburne, Wessex

'He broke the ring with his bare hands?' Heremund asked Eadwald, incredulous, making the action with his fists. The two men were watching Carwyn administer her attentions to Asaf and Saeric.

'Not quite,' Eadwald said, 'but he did break it with raw strength, yes. He wrapped the chain around himself then quite literally pulled it away from the post, running as hard as he could, given the building was burning down around him.'

'Really?' Heremund asked, dubious.

Eadwald nodded.

'Poor quality workmanship, iron, or both,' Heremund muttered.

Eadwald laughed. 'That's exactly what Saeric said. You're rubbing off on him, the poor fellow.'

'Then he is fortunate, is he not?' Heremund smiled back.

He nodded at the bronze-skinned boy. 'He did all that for a slave?'

Eadwald drew in a breath. 'Word of advice: keep that question to yourself. That boy was Saeric's replacement. Saeric would likely have died in the blaze trying to free him had that band not broken. That tells us a lot, does it not?'

'About him or his sadistic masters?'

'Both.'

Heremund raised his eyebrows. 'Well, I hope Saeric doesn't start a one-person slave emancipation campaign. I could barely afford the mountains of food he ate before he brought Gerard along, then came his daughter, and now he's found himself a new retainer. I'll have to open an inn to accommodate them all!'

'Don't worry,' Eadwald grinned, 'I'll take the lad to the garrison. There's always work for a boy his age, and you never know, he might become a fine soldier one day. He hides a bevy of remarkable skills and is surprisingly strong and courageous for one so small. He certainly proves the point that size isn't everything. You should see what he can do on a horse.'

'You'll have difficulty prising him away from Saeric.'

'He'll accompany his hero to Sceaptesburh, and then he'll stay when he realises that we don't mean him any harm. In the meantime, you could do with the extra pair of hands, and don't tell me Saeric hasn't helped you fill your coffers. You've got an order of swords to fulfil, remember?'

'Speaking of which, what happened to Saeric's own sword?' Heremund asked. 'That was good quality iron and a good blade.'

'Ah yes, that's the bit of the story the men have chosen to leave out. He used his sword to try to prize the ring loose.'

'What? He must have known it would have bent or snapped.'

'I'm sure he did, but he was trying to save the boy.' Eadwald raised his hand. 'Don't say it. I know what you're thinking, but really, don't say it. He and the boy share a bond whose price we can't even begin to measure. I'm just glad that he has come out of this alive, and he will now need to stay some while longer to save up for another batch of quality iron to make a new sword.'

Heremund smiled at that. 'You're devious; you know that? I always said you'd go further than me.'

'Further? I've not even caught your scent, you wily old goat.'

Heremund did not smile at Eadwald's jest, and the ealdorman knew his former master well enough to see that something was troubling him. 'What is it, old friend?'

Heremund didn't answer, prompting Eadwald to ask again. 'Heremund?'

The burly smith let out a long sigh, then he withdrew his gaze from Saeric and turned to the ealdorman. 'You jest about my past aspirations of greatness and glory, but they are spent now, Eadwald, you do know that, don't you? I had thought myself freed of my past misdeeds, but then Saeric arrived. Now I find myself being drawn back into the trouble and uncertainty that I had worked so hard to escape. I'm not sure I'm up to this, Eadwald. I meant what I said last spring. I like this simple life.'

'So what *are* you saying?'

'It was one thing to have Gerard in my brother's service – as both punishment and protection – but Dunstan is firmly in Ecgberht's camp now, which means Gerard has lost another ally. I am also troubled to learn that Baldwyn was behind the attack on Leo. Was it actually a ruse to hide an assassination attempt on Gerard? He was badly wounded after all, and it is sheer fortune that Saeric happened to be there to save him. Having failed in that attempt, Baldwyn then kidnaps Hildelith, presumably to draw Gerard into his trap once again. This whole situation reeks of conspiracy, Eadwald.'

The general rolled his eyes and then refilled his tankard from the jug on the table. 'You see intrigue around every corner and in every shadow,' he said. 'It was not Baldwyn who attacked Leo. It was a gang of thugs hired by his daughter. She wanted Saeric, not Gerard. She kidnapped Hildelith because she knew that Gerard's daughter and Saeric had eyes for each other. Eanswith did it for much simpler reasons: she was jealous and decided to force an exchange to get Saeric back.'

'And yet you kept Gerard away from there, didn't you? You made sure he was surrounded by your fyrd instead.'

'I'm not a fool, Heremund. Of course, I considered all of this and took measures, but you're wrong; this was not some elaborate plot to murder Gerard. And anyway, it's immaterial now. Baldwyn, his son, and his daughter are all dead. That threat is gone.' He paused, considering his friend for a moment. 'All this agitation is unlike you, Heremund. Something else is troubling you. What is it?'

Heremund took a long breath, then helped himself to more ale. A crow squawked loudly from the tree above, and Heremund crossed himself instinctively. 'I have been wrestling with myself about whether to speak to you about it, but following that business with the summons, I said I would look into whatever was bothering Talec's reeve, remember? Well, I got my answer.'

'If this is about the rebel who appeared in Escanceaster late last summer, I already know about it.'

'You do?' Heremund asked, surprised, then he rolled his eyes. 'Of course you do. Well, that's just it, Eadwald. He wasn't a rebel. Word is that the Kernowyon are just as keen to find him as Talec because they haven't a clue who he is. What does that tell you?'

'That it's yet another false sighting, a mistaken report.'

'Is it? Witnesses said the man put on a wolven tunic in front of a band of fyrdsmen and was shocked when they attacked him. Who would do such a thing, Eadwald?'

'An idiot?' Eadwald suggested. 'Or a rebel wanting to make a point.'

'Or it could be someone else.'

Eadwald let out an exasperated sigh. 'Not this again, Heremund. There has been no word of the mystery dissident ever since, and none of my spies has reported anything out of the ordinary. All they've heard is that a young rebel appeared one day in Escanceaster, as they do, then disappeared just as promptly, which they also do if they're lucky enough not to get caught.'

Heremund shook his head. 'This is different. Have you not stopped to wonder why this sighting has caused such agitation in Talec's camp?' When Eadwald did not reply, Heremund pressed on. 'At around the same time as this incident, there was a report of a young man appearing on the northern coast of Dumnonia, carrying a large chest and wearing a wolven tunic. Those who reported it swore the visitor did not understand them, nor did they, him. Hearing my agent's report about it made my spine tingle.'

'Well, tingles are a sure sign of truth,' Eadwald scoffed. 'Why are you, of all people, falling to superstition in your old age? You were Wessex's most successful military commander because you scoffed at such nonsense. "All that matters is what you see before you," you used to preach. "Rumours and hearsay have as much value to a military tactician as magic and minstrels' songs."'

'It has to be Caelin! Saeric himself says that he can feel his brother.'

'For God's sake, Heremund. He "feels" him? Why are you so desperate to believe that Caelin is alive? You just said you don't want any of this, so how is chasing a ghost going to help you fade into quiet obscurity?'

'Evidently, God has other plans for me,' Heremund said angrily. 'We should tell Saeric... Aneurin. We've gotten so used to calling him by his Saxon name that we forget who he is.'

'A damn good fighter is what he is,' Eadwald said. 'I know I mock him and his ploughshare, but he is terrifying. And watching him with that big bow sends jitters up my spine. He is a perfect figurehead for our cause.'

'Your cause. We must tell him,' Heremund repeated.

'What exactly? That his little brother might have shown up, only we can't be sure because no one has any idea where he is. I have heard the same reports as you, Heremund. More rumours that lead to nothing. It's been months. Where is he?' He changed tack. 'Can I remind you that we have a plan, Heremund, which centres around us putting Saeric on Dumnonia's throne, and I don't give a damn whether or not he is one of the lost princes.'

'You still don't believe him?' Heremund asked, astounded.

Eadwald let out a long sigh. 'You know I don't. The boys' boat was found wrecked on the shore after a host of heathen raiders had just finished sacking St Germanus. The chances of either of the boys having survived are nil. Could Saeric be of noble blood? Almost certainly. I think he is someone who has, like us, seen an opportunity and grasped it. And the longer he plays along, the more he becomes beholden to us. Loyal to us. Loyal to Westseaxna Ríce. He will make the ideal vassal regent.'

'He *is* Prince Aneurin,' Heremund said stubbornly, and it is not *our* plan. It's yours.'

'On what basis can you prove he is the ætheling? Dare I remind you of your own advice about evidence?'

'He knows the truth behind the story of the lost princes, for one.'

'As do we, and many others,' Eadwald challenged. He paused. 'What if, and I'm just speaking hypothetically, what if this mysterious newcomer *is* Caelin or even the real Aneurin, God forbid, and he possesses the regalia of Dumnonia in that trunk with which he was supposedly seen? What claim would Saeric – and therefore we – have to the Dumnonian throne then? Don't be so quick to see joy in this news, Heremund. Saeric is our bird in the hand, and we don't need to be diverted from our path by chasing phantoms.'

'Christ almighty, you've given a lot of thought to this.'

'Of course I have. There's too much at stake.'

'I knew I would regret raising this,' Heremund said.

'It makes no difference. I have people out looking for that rebel and the lad he was seen with, but as I said, it's been two months without any word of either. It was nothing.'

Heremund let out a sceptical snort. 'And what if you're wrong and they do find him? What then?'

'We will capture him, find out who he is, and if he turns out to be the real Aneurin and has the missing regalia, we'll put him to the sword and throw his body into a pit. Soon afterwards, one of my men will make a miraculous discovery: found hidden somewhere near Sanctus Germanus will be the regalia of Cadwyr. I will hand them to Saeric, and he will take the throne from Mael, as planned.'

'And if it is Caelin?'

'The same.'

Heremund stared at his friend, appalled.

'We know nothing about him,' Eadwald reasoned. 'He'll just as likely be some sort of demon if Northmen took him. Or he could be a fanatical idealist who dreams of Dumnonian independence. What if he turns Saeric against us? What if he harbours greater ambitions than his brother and kills him to gain the crown for himself? I believe such things have been known to occur in history,' he added pointedly. 'He could even be an imposter with the same intent; remember that we have no idea what Caelin looks like, nor indeed Aneurin. But all of this is inane speculation. Caelin was a bairn, and there is no way he could have survived. He drowned along with the rest of them.'

'For Christ's sake, Eadwald, how can you stand there and say such things with so little compassion? Caelin might actually be a fine young man who would be delighted to join his brother's cause. Has your time with Saeric not left any mark on you?'

'Of course it has, but the fact that I have grown to like him is immaterial. I don't care about the restoration of Cadwyr's line. I want Dumnonia's army and their loyalty. That was the reason we supported Mael, but we misjudged him. He used us to help him get rid of his brother, and now he's only interested in feathering the comfortable little nest we made for him. Thanks to Mael's reneging on our deal, Ecgberht has grown stronger. God has handed Saeric to us on a plate, and I will not allow some capricious usurper to wreck this opportunity to fulfil our promise to King Beorhtric, God rest his soul. Prince Ethelheard will accede to the Westseaxna throne.'

'You are beyond reproach,' Heremund said. 'What you are proposing is vulgar opportunism. Does it not occur to you that Saeric's quest and yours are strikingly similar, yet both of you fail to understand that the time for restitution is long past? Gerard has already paid a severe price for contesting the throne. He will never be accepted as king, certainly not now that so much time has passed, because Beorhtric's successor has proven himself a good leader. Ecgberht also happens to have a legitimate claim to the Westseaxna throne.'

'Legitimate?' Eadwald's eyes narrowed. 'Should I be concerned about your loyalty, Heremund?' he asked, his tone menacing.

Heremund looked back at his former second-in-command, his expression equally hostile. 'I would be very careful who you threaten, dear friend. Few others would stand by and allow such treasonous talk to pass unheeded. I will help you restore Aneurin to his throne because I believe him to be who he claims, and I wish to right a wrong. But I will not support you in your wider ambitions. You know this.'

'Why would God have sent Saeric our way if not to support our cause?' Eadwald said, becoming exasperated. 'You swore the same oath as me to our true king, remember?'

'Sixteen years have passed since then, Eadwald. I'm an old man now. Westseaxna Ríce prospers under Ecgberht's rule. You speak of restoring our kingdom to some sort of former grandeur. Ecgberht seems to be doing a good job of that, don't you think?'

'He tore up our alliance with Mercia.'

'Hardly surprising, given that Mercia drove him into exile.'

'Which is where he belongs, Heremund. I cannot believe that I have to justify myself to you. This was all your damned idea in the first place!'

'And our plan failed, which, on balance, appears to have been fortuitous for us all. We have grown rich on the back of Ecgberht's successes, none more so than you, for God's sake. Would you really throw all that away? Mercia is no friend to us now. You wish to depose usurpers who murder their kings? Then turn your attention to Beornwulf, who poses the real threat to our security.'

Eadwald backed down, knowing this was a fight he would not

win, and he needed Heremund to watch his back, but it rankled him all the same, particularly as Heremund was right. The new self-proclaimed king of Mercia was unquestionably their greatest threat now, having deposed the rightful king and their ally just months ago. Beornwulf had immediately begun building up and arming his fyrds in obvious preparation for war. In his arrogance, he was not hiding the fact that invading Westseaxna Ríce was his goal.

'Do not be tempted to tell Saeric about this,' Eadwald warned Heremund, 'because it will likely send him into another of his fits, and I don't know whether you've noticed, but they are getting worse each time. One day he's not going to return to himself, and what will you do then? He'll have your head off in a flash with that ploughshare of his; only I won't be there to save you.'

'No, I expect you'll just stand by and watch. Another potential adversary out of your way in this ridiculous crusade of yours.'

'You swore you would see this through,' Eadwald snapped.

'We made our play to install Gerard on the throne and failed,' Heremund growled back. 'You cannot seriously believe that in his current state, Saeric will make a better ruler than Mael. He needs more time to mend, Eadwald. He is only just now showing glimmers of the decent man hidden behind all the layers of hurt. Push him too hard now, and he will sweep through Dumnonia and slaughter them in a horrendous bloodletting to punish them: firstly, for their failure to protect him and his family; and secondly, for accepting his uncle's rule. As you just said yourself, he's a man on a very tight cord, and we can't risk setting him off on some kind of killing spree against those he blames for what has happened to him. Are you confident you'll be able to control him once he has what he wants? He could turn against us, and he'll be a far greater threat than that tub of lard, Mael. You must know this!'

'You are making no sense, Heremund! Why the Hell are you helping him on his quest if you fear this as the outcome?

Why not stick a sword into his guts and return to your sarding ironmongering? Your motives are as clouded as your reasoning. At least I am clear about mine. I refuse to wait another ten years to fulfil our plans. If you have it your way, Saeric will become as soft as Mael.'

'At first, I wondered whether I should do as you say and put a sword through Saeric's heart,' Heremund said. 'He is so badly damaged, riven by rage and hatred, very much like you.' He took a long breath. 'But we have all been used and manipulated by people far more intelligent, powerful and unscrupulous than you or I could ever aspire to be. And while I am in my old age and beyond saving, I do not believe the same to be true for you or Saeric, which is why I persist with you both, and Gerard too. I see a change in Saeric for the good. He is improving, and his slaying of that woman will bring him another step closer to healing his wounds. But his recovery is still in its infancy, and he could so easily be tipped back onto his self-destructive path. Sard it, Eadwald, you all deserve better from God and life, and I will keep doing whatever I can to steer you away from the darkness that resides in you. That is *my* motivation.

The ealdorman let out an exasperated snort and stalked off, leaving the smith standing alone by the oak. Eadwald went over to Saeric and the others, clapped his hand on his acolyte's shoulder, laughed at something, and then gave his goodbyes. He did not look back as he left the inner yard, so he did not see the grim, thoughtful expression on his former commander's face.

11

The heirs are dead

A hall near Dinuurin, Dumnonia

Aethelred stumbled through the doorway of the old council hall and paused as instructed just inside the threshold, his arms tied painfully behind his back. He wanted to lie down and sleep. How could these men keep going like this? Were they not exhausted too? They had ridden for days, resting only when the horses could go no further. He had been trussed up and blindfolded the whole time, but they hadn't mistreated him; certainly nowhere near as poorly as Earl Talec's men had done after the rebel had fled. In the tumult of the chase, he'd managed to escape the guards before he could be tortured and questioned, and so had headed eastwards into Westseaxna Ríce, figuring he would be safer there. He'd never know how in God's name he'd been found so long after the incident in Escanceaster, but here he was, presumably back in Dumnonia and probably so far west that he'd never see his home again.

His captor pushed past him while another man grabbed Aethelred's arm and led him forward. His cloak hung sodden and mud-spattered across his shoulders, and his hair lay slick against his forehead. The reek of horse dung and damp wool rose strongly from him, and for a brief moment, he flinched, wishing they had let him clean himself before presenting him to their leader. The rain thrummed loudly on the thatch above him, and he felt a steady drip, drip on his neck. He glanced up at the decaying straw and saw that water ran in thin streams to the floor in many places, gathering in glistening puddles and turning the packed earth to mud. A fire burned in the centre of the room, but it did little to warm it. A narrow trestle table stood at an odd angle near the fire, presumably placed to avoid the worst leaks. Five men stood around it, earnestly discussing some matter. Their faces showed exhaustion and concern. Aethelred had expected the headquarters of the Dumnonian rebel camp to have been a grand place, a great fortress built atop a high mount, ringing to the sounds of marching soldiers and rumbling war carts – not this lonely, run-down hovel that had seen more cattle than people within its smoke-blackened walls.

The rebel leader stood leaning on a crutch, his left arm hanging limply by his side. An old scar ran from his cheek to his eyebrow, and where his right eye should have been was a dark socket of gnarled scar tissue. His clothing bore traces of regal beginnings, but the colours in his tunic had faded with age. Looking at him now, Aethelred could scarcely believe this was the same legendary warrior who had, nearly ten summers ago, rallied the people of Dumnonia to rise against King Mael. Could this truly be Camus, master-at-arms to the former king? How could this maimed and weary old man have led such a defiant quest? He'd failed, of course, thanks to the intervention of King Ecgberht and his well-armed and disciplined fyrds. Yet the rebel still wore a pair of wolves on his tunic; the outlawed standard of those few Dumnonians who continued the fight to maintain their honour and heritage. Aethelred shook his head in sadness. Those days of past glory were clearly long gone, and this was a rebellion in name only. Aethelred looked to his escort. Perhaps his news might do some good and provide a small glimmer of hope for these tired old men.

The escort cleared his throat and stepped into the room. 'My Lord, we have found the one you seek.'

The men turned and looked upon the newcomer with both surprise and disdain. Aethelred watched their faces as they took in his dirty, unkempt appearance. The man standing to the right of the scarred leader spoke first.

'That's him? Bring him into the light.'

The man beside Aethelred shoved him in the back and growled at him to move forward. Aethelred did as instructed, but his escort pushed him in the back again, and he stumbled forwards.

The rebel leader stepped around the table and moved closer to his prisoner. 'What is your name?'

'Aethelred of Twyvertun, my Lord.'

'Aethelred is a Saxon name,' the tall, powerfully-built man who had spoken first said. He spat on the floor at Aethelred's feet.

'I am Dumnonian, but I have this name because my father is a Saxon settler.'

'Thief, you mean,' the rebel corrected.

'My mother is Dumnonian, and I too was born here. We have a smallholding this side of Twyvertun. I do not claim to support the rebel cause, but I am still Dumnonian.'

'Dumnonian?' one of the other men said, astonished at their captive's bold claim. 'Your father took the land of one of our own by the sword. Dumnonia is forced to pay taxes to the Westseaxna king, and worst of all, we must send our young men - the likes of you, mind - to Wintanceaster to fight in Ecgberht's wars against other Britons! And you would deign to call yourself Dumnonian?'

'That's enough, Pedyr,' the rebel leader said, then he turned his gaze back to his captive.

'My father received my family's lands as part of my mother's bride price,' Aethelred flared. 'He is no thief.' He paused, glowering at the ignorant Dumnonian rebel called Pedyr. 'And King Ecgberht fights other Saxons, not Britons.'

'All the same,' the rebel leader interjected, 'you must admit that your heritage does little to inspire confidence.' He changed tack. 'You've been a hard man to find. My men think I'm mad for wasting precious time and risking valuable lives looking for you, but I am glad you are here. There are some questions I wish to ask you.' He paused, his eyes not once leaving Aethelred's. 'We true Dumnonians make the odd gesture now and then, sometimes quite bold, to remind the Traitor that we are still here. You must think yourself unlucky to have gotten caught up in one such gesture.'

Aethelred nodded, not entirely understanding where this was going.

'When the rebel revealed himself, you ran,' the rebel leader said. 'Why?'

Aethelred let out a snort. 'Would you have stayed, my Lord? You know what Earl Talec is like. He would have strung me up and tortured me, accused me of being a rebel, then cut off my head anyway when he realised I was just a simple farmer's son who knew nothing.'

'And yet he seeks you still, which tells me that you have something he wants.'

'I've already told your men everything I know,' Aetheldred said. 'We met in the tavern. I shared dinner with him, my sleeping place was next to his, and then he put on the wolves and fled. I wish I'd never gone to Escanceaster that day. I just want to go home, but I can't, can I?' He saw the rebel exchange glances with the one named Pedyr, and his heart skipped a beat.

The rebel leader let out a sigh. 'No, you can't. Talec has been there.'

Aethelred paled. 'What does that mean?'

'That your fears are justified. Earl Talec believes you hold important information about that rebel, and so do I.'

'But I don't understand,' Aethelred said, becoming more distressed. 'I only met him that day. I know nothing about him. I don't know why he did what he did. He is your man!'

'That's just it, Aethelred. He isn't. We haven't a clue who he is.'

Aethelred blinked, taken aback by the unexpected revelation.

'My men think this is all an elaborate plan to lure me out

of the shadows; that the "rebel" was just pretending and that you "escaped" so that we would come looking for you, at which point you would bring Talec down upon us. Are they right?'

Aethelred stared at the rebel leader, shocked and frightened. 'No, my Lord. I swear to you, I'm not part of any plot, and your men kept me blindfolded all the way here. I have no idea where we are. I swear to you, I wish I'd never met that wealh, but he was so..., so lost.' He paused, his eyes momentarily taking a far-off gleam as he remembered the evening and Rathulf's introspection.

'Wealh? You just claimed yourself Dumnonian, yet you use that offensive Westseaxna word to describe this rebel?'

'Not because he was British, but because he was obviously foreign. He had no idea what he was doing. It was as though it was the first time he had been in a tavern, let alone a town. His eyes were as big as plates, and he had no clue how to order a drink or find food. When I tried speaking with him in our tongue, by which I mean Dumnonian *and* Saxon, he understood none of it, and I none of his speech.' He paused, frowning as he recalled the youth's inexplicable actions the following morning. He looked back at the rebel leader, who was staring at him, an odd expression on his face. 'That was why I was so surprised when he took out a wolven tunic the next day and put it on in plain view of the guardsmen. Why do that? I swear it was not an act of defiance. He was completely startled when the guards flew at him, and he barely came to his senses in time to defend himself. He took his trunk and fled into the alleys. I don't know what happened to him after that because I was fleeing myself. I suppose I felt pity for him because he was so sad and alone and maybe even a bit frightened. I liked him. He was so grateful I was being kind to him. My Lord?' The rebel leader seemed to have gone a shade paler.

'His name?' the rebel said urgently. 'What name did he give you?'

Aethelred frowned. 'It was unusual, difficult to pronounce.

Frankish maybe? Rar... Rardoof, or something like that.'

'You say he was foreign, yet he had a wolven tunic?'

'In fine, wine-coloured cloth with hems of gold and the standard itself woven in solid gold thread, my Lord. And he had two swords, one of which was the finest I've ever seen. He was very wealthy, to be sure.' On seeing Breoc's disbelief, he added, 'I'm not making this up, Lords. He showed me what he had in his travelling chest. It was filled with riches. I'm surprised he could lift it on his own.'

'Lord Camus,' Breoc warned again. 'Two swords? A chest filled with treasure? Really?'

Camus silenced the tall warrior, and then he turned back to Aethelred. His expression softened. 'You must pardon our rudeness, for we have forgotten our manners. Come and stand by the fire lest you catch a chill in those wet clothes. I would offer you a seat, but as you see, we have none. Breoc, pass me that mug and the wine, then untie him.'

'Is that wise, my Lord?'

'Do it, please,' Camus said.

Breoc reached across the table and poured a mug of wine from a clay jug and handed it to his leader, who then waited patiently for Aethelred's hands to be unbound. Aethelred rubbed his wrists, and then he took the wine. The pleasantries seemed so ludicrous to Aethelred in this bare hall with its collapsing roof and muddied floor, but he drank the wine gratefully and raised his mug in thanks. Meanwhile, the sounds of the storm outside underscored the stillness within the room, and the drone of the rain on the thatch provided a steady accompaniment to the silvery melody of water dripping on the floor.

The old rebel smiled pleasantly. 'Now then, Aethelred of Twyvertun, I want you to tell me everything that passed between you, from when you first met him to when you fled. Leave no detail out.'

'It was the very end of summer, my Lord, in that hot week before the rains came. The start of Holy Month. That's why I was in the city. I was bringing my village register to the mynster.'

'Where did you meet him?' Camus asked.

'In a tavern in Escanceaster up by the mynster. The Boar. It was early evening. Sunny. I remember how warm it was. I shared a meal and ale with him. I could tell he wanted company and that he was..., lonely. But he was frustrated that he couldn't understand our language.'

'Describe him,' Camus said, fixing his gaze on Aethelred.

'He was about my age and height but stronger than me. I think he was a warrior of some kind.'

'His face?'

'The face of a leader, like yours. Young. Strong. Handsome.' He smiled. 'The girls in the tavern were most taken with him.'

'Eyes?'

'Brown. Light brown.'

'Hair?'

'A sort of light brown too. Not blond, but not dark either. He wore it very long, below his shoulders in a braid like a girl's. I've only seen that once before.'

Camus was suddenly overwhelmed with a hot rush of excitement, but he immediately stamped it down. *I cannot afford this. I cannot bear another disappointment. The boy is a clever trickster, sent by Talec to inveigle his way into our band so that he can betray us. I should listen to Breoc and have the lad put to the sword.* 'His clothing?' he demanded instead. 'What did he wear? How was he armed?'

'I've told you. His dress was that of a nobleman or at least a man of wealth. He wore rich russet cloth trousers and a dark green tunic, with embroidered hems woven in orange and purple thread. His sword belt was decorated with silver and bronze studs and marked all over with intricate patterns. As I said, he had two swords.'

'Describe them,' Camus said.

'I'm no warrior, Lord, nor have I a sword of my own, but I know good weapons when I see them. The first one had a finely crafted pommel and a scabbard decorated with lots of writhing beasts. The other one, well, was exceptional. The first I could imagine he might wear in battle; the other was too fine for that. He let me hold it, Lord Camus,' Aethelred said, his eyes glistening. 'Its hilt was of burnished steel, with an ivory grip and fine gold and silver inlay, and gemstones set in the top of the pommel. Its blade was strange. It seemed to have been made from two different metals; they swirled into one another like the muddy waters of the Tamar mixed with the sea after a storm. I cannot imagine how it could have been crafted by a human hand. It was beautiful.'

Camus stared at the boy, astonished, and then he turned to Breoc. The wiry Briton frowned and shook his head.

'Come now, Camus. Everyone knows what Cadwyr's sword looks like.'

Aethelred looked at Breoc, stunned. *Cadwyr's sword? Did I hold the Sword of Dumnonia? How is that possible?*

Camus turned back to the alleged spy. 'The Sword of Dumnonia was fashioned by a unique smithing technique, mastered by the royal Frankish swordsmiths in Aachen. These rarest of swords are possessed of great power, bestowed upon them by the late Holy Roman Emperor Charlemagne himself. Cadwyr's father had been presented with such a sword by the Emperor himself, and second to the ring of kingship, it is the most prized treasure in all of Dumnonia. At least it was until it was lost during the overthrow of the kingdom by the traitor Mael.'

'You think the man I met is one of the lost princes!' Aethelred realised, astounded.

'They were all burned in the fires, God rest their souls,' Breoc reminded him. The tall warrior crossed himself.

'But there is a rumour that the youngest two survived,'

Aethelred said, excited. 'My mother spoke of it. She said that they were taken to safety and the reason King Mael does not have the regalia of kingship is because the lost princes have them.' He looked up at Camus, his eyes gleaming. 'I held the king's sword!'

'How old are you?' Camus asked, finding it hard to speak.

'Eighteen.'

'No,' Camus said involuntarily. 'That's not right. You must be older than that.'

Aethelred looked back at him, confused. He shook his head. 'No, Lord. If anything, Rardoof was a little younger than I.'

Breoc acted immediately. With a nod to the others, he pounced, grabbing the startled Aethelred and throwing him up against the wall. The other men pressed around and held him pinned to the flaking daub. Breoc drew his dagger and held it to the young Briton's throat.

'Who sent you, traitor?' Breoc snarled. 'This is another trick of Talec's to catch us out, isn't it?'

'No!' Aethelred cried, his eyes wide with fear. 'You found me, remember? What did I say wrong?'

'Every word, half-breed scum,' Breoc responded. 'I say again, who else is a part of this?'

Aethelred shook his head, too frightened to speak.

'Fool!' Breoc spat. 'Prince Aneurin would be twenty-five summers' old if he was alive as you claim; a fact that others before you managed to get right. You are nine years out.'

Camus had already turned away, losing himself to the bitterness that had risen to crush the blossom of hope, but his heart skipped a beat at Breoc's mention of the number nine. Aneurin had been nine when the kingdom had fallen, and his brother barely a year old. He and the other men of the rebellion had always assumed that Aneurin would be the one to return; the boy was heir to the throne after all and old enough to understand his duty. But what if – and Camus shuddered at the thought – Aneurin could *not* return? What if he had perished, leaving his younger brother in his stead? Camus frowned and looked again into Aethelred's eyes for any sign of deceit. He saw a young man with the fear of death in his heart.

'Breoc,' Camus said, trying to keep his voice calm. 'Let the boy go.'

'What?' Breoc half-turned to his master. His expression warned Camus not to push him.

'Hold him if you will then, but let him speak.'

Breoc lowered his dagger but did not loosen his grip on Aethelred's shoulder.

'Tell me about his tunic again,' Camus asked Aethelred quietly.

Aethelred glanced at Breoc, then he spoke haltingly. 'The two wolves were embroidered just like yours; only his were woven in gold thread, with little garnets for eyes. The gold in his tunic alone could have fed my town for a whole year.' He stopped then, seeing the look of utter disdain in Breoc's eyes.

One of the other men snorted and shook his head, smiling. 'Are you sure they were only garnets? Surely a man of his great wealth would have chosen rubies?'

'Whatever they were, they were certainly not in that tavern,' Breoc said coldly. 'A fine story, lad, but a pack of lies nevertheless.'

Camus frowned at Aethelred. *A standard of gold? Cadwyr's Carolingian sword? The story was extraordinary, in fact so unbelievable it could almost be true. Why then does my hair stand on its end, and my stomach twist into a knot as I listen to his words?* 'You said he seemed lost,' he said. 'Why?'

'My Lord, I implore you,' Breoc broke in. 'This is so obviously a trap, set by Mael and baited with this boy and his fantastic story to lead you into it. It has too many holes! If I am to understand this Saxon, the man he has reputedly seen is an imbecile! Why would he do such a stupid thing as to show his standard in the presence of a patrol? How could he not understand the consequences of such an act of defiance?'

'He wouldn't know if he had been raised in a place far away

from here,' Camus said.

'For the love of God, Camus,' Breoc spat. 'What can be more implausible than what we have already heard? Don't let him do this to you. You know it cannot be true.'

Camus stepped up and stood directly in front of Aethelred, his face uncomfortably close to the young Briton's. 'And yet I have long ago learned that the truth in most matters lies with the inexplicable. There is something else, isn't there, that you're not telling us,' Camus said to Aethelred. 'I can see it in your eyes.'

'Lord, I don't..., that is...,' Aethelred stammered, again glancing at Breoc.

'Breoc, go and stand over by the fire,' Camus ordered, firmly keeping his gaze on Aethelred. 'Do it!' he roared when he sensed that Breoc had not moved. When Breoc had complied, Camus nodded to Aethelred to continue.

Aethelred's words came in a rush. 'I don't know how it could be, Lord, but I think I have heard that language he spoke once before. It was a wealh captive sentenced to execution, and he had the same braided hairstyle – but it makes no sense.'

Breoc snorted loudly. 'Of course it makes no sense. Are you claiming the prince is a foreigner? From what land does he hail then? Could he be a courtier of Charlemagne; he wore a splendid Carolingian sword, after all. But nay, a man as fantastical as you describe must have come from a more exotic clime. A Northman raider perhaps!' The men all laughed at this, and Breoc turned to Camus, shaking his head in disbelief. His smile vanished when he saw Camus' expression. The rebel leader stared back at him, his face as white as a sheet. The mug that Camus had been holding slipped from his hand and fell to the floor with a loud clatter.

'A Northman,' Camus muttered hoarsely. 'Mother of God!' His eyes flew from Breoc back to Aethelred. 'That is what you cannot reconcile! How can a man who is supposedly heir to the Dumnonian kingdom be a heathen Northman? That's why he was so lost, had no idea what he was doing, and knew nothing of our language or customs: he was raised as a heathen! He could not know how dangerous it is to show his standard here!'

Aethelred nodded at Camus, wondering how in God's name the rebel leader could have known what he'd been thinking. 'But how can it be so, Lord Camus? A heathen?'

'Camus?' Breoc began, staring at his leader, astonished. 'How can you believe this preposterous lie?' He turned to Aethelred's escort. 'Pedyr, our leader has taken leave of his senses. Get rid of this traitor.'

Pedyr drew his sword, but he didn't get to use it. Camus stepped in front of Pedyr and put up his hand. 'Sheath your sword, Pedyr,' Camus barked, his voice revealing no trace of insanity. 'Aneurin may be in God's hands, but Caelin is not.'

'Caelin?' Breoc said, his brows arching with surprise.

'He will be eighteen next autumn,' Camus responded. 'As for Aneurin...' He trailed off, unwilling to ponder the fate of Dumnonia's rightful heir.

'The boys perished in the attack on Sanctus Germanus!' Breoc argued. 'Your very face bears witness to it! I am so tired of this ridiculous quest of yours to find them. They are dead, Camus. Dead!'

'Perhaps Aneurin is dead, Breoc, but not by Mael's hand. We have fed and fostered the tale of Mael's cruelty all these years because there is no better way to stir the hearts of a people than to tell of the cold and senseless slaughter of defenceless children.'

Pedyr stared at his leader open-mouthed. 'The boys perished in Caer Uisc!'

Camus shook his head slowly. 'Breoc was there when we cast off in our little boat. He stood on the shore and saluted, wishing us God's speed in our flight to safety in the west.' Camus paused, seeing doubt and confusion cross his companion's face. 'We made our way towards the monastery of Sanctus Germanus. After two days of flight, we thought we were at last safe, but when we arrived in the estuary under cover of a dawn mist, we found the place afire. I thought that Mael had got word of our escape and had somehow made his way to the mynster ahead of us. I left the boys in the boat while I assessed the situation. The tide was turning, so I instructed them to move out into the channel and wait in the safety of the mist until I returned. I made my way up the river banks toward the monastery, but I found it overrun by heathens when I arrived. I intended to make my way back to the boys, but the heathens found me and cut me down. Aneurin and Caelin drifted straight into the path of the departing heathen fleet.'

'But you received those wounds defending the boys against Mael!' one of the others protested.

'Defending the boys, yes, but against Mael? Many weeks passed before I was well enough to sail, but sail I did, into the north to find the boys.'

Pedyr blinked. 'But you were held captive. Talec tortured you for months, but you managed to escape with the help of guards sympathetic to our cause.'

Camus shook his head. 'No. All the while everyone believed I was in Talec's torture chamber, I was searching for the boys. It was hopeless. I had no idea where to look and no real way of finding the heathens. I returned empty-handed the following autumn to find the terrible destruction that had been wreaked upon our land and people by Mael in punishment for our defiance of his tyranny and for his failure to find the two youngest princes. It was then that I resolved to concoct the story of the boys' death at their uncle's hands. That atrocity would become for the Dumnonian people the symbol of Mael's base cruelty and his unfitness to rule this great land.'

Only the steady dripping of water on the floor could be heard in the room as the principals of the rebellion stared at their leader, speechless. All except Breoc, who shook his head at Camus.

'For a long time,' Camus went on, 'I lived in the hope that somehow the boys may have escaped the heathens, but as the weeks became months, and the months finally years, I came to accept that they had perished, most likely on that same day. We found the wreckage of their boat washed ashore, you see, but there was no sign of the boys. That's why Breoc thinks me mad. But it seems that Caelin at least was raised by the heathens. I don't know what has befallen Aneurin, but I believe that Caelin has come of age and has returned.'

Pedyr said, 'then we must get the word out. He will be here in the west somewhere.'

'Or he has returned to the northlands,' Camus said. 'Having received such a hostile welcome, it would be little wonder.' A thought occurred to him, and he turned back to Aethelred. 'You said he was alone. Did he not have any travelling companions with him?'

Aethelred shook his head. 'No, Lord.'

'That's odd.'

'Odd?' Breoc snapped. 'It's a sure sign this is all a ruse. If he really was raised by Northmen from a bairn, then brought back here sixteen years later, why did they not accompany him? In fact, having raised him all this time as heir to a kingdom, would they not have sailed in a fleet of ships filled with warriors to help him in his quest? Imagine the reward in return for their aid!'

'Perhaps they *have* come in a fleet of ships, and Caelin was simply checking the lay of the land,' Camus countered. 'Perhaps they are making ready for an assault on Escanceaster as we speak. Or perhaps it is not as we think, and Caelin has instead escaped them and has made his way here alone. Who knows what manner of torments he has experienced during all those years in the hands of the heathen demons? Did he come here by choice? Was he thrown out when he came of age, dumped back here where they found him or did he make his own way here?'

'This is the desperate talk of a senile old man who has finally succumbed to his delusions,' Breoc said coldly. 'Can you not hear yourself, clutching at so many farfetched explanations for the implausible? The heirs are dead. They've been dead ever since the fall of Caer Uisc!'

'So you keep saying,' Camus growled.

Breoc shook his head again, and then he snatched up his travelling cloak. 'I'm going to Lannaled. Good luck in your fool's errand, but don't think I will come running to rescue you when you get caught by the Traitor.'

'You must tell–'

'No! I'm riding to Sanctus Germanus to protect him from your madness, Camus. Hasn't he been through enough already?' Breoc stepped up to his leader, his face black with fury. 'Instead of chasing these ghosts, perhaps you should try attending to your nephew, who *is* alive.' He swept out the door, and soon afterwards, they heard a whinny and the sound of hoofs splashing in the mud outside.

Camus let out a long breath, then he said to Pedyr, 'we are the only ones who know of this. The Turncoat suspects something, but we mustn't attract his attention any more than Caelin already has. The only rumour I want out there is that the rebel seen in Escanceaster was one of our men. He was reminding Talec of his impotence and that we hold the Traitor in such contempt that we brazenly wave the wolves in front of his face knowing that he will never catch us.'

Pedyr smiled. 'I look forward to spreading that tale far and wide,' he smiled.

Camus waved his finger at his subordinate. 'Under no circumstances must there be any hint that his quarry might be Prince Caelin, do you understand? If Talec gets even the slightest whiff of the truth before we find the boy...' He left the sentence unfinished, but they all knew what would happen if Talec learned that one of the lost princes had appeared. The Earl would raze every building and crop from one end of the land to the other in his quest to find his enemy.

'My Lord?' one of the other men said. 'What about this Saeric of Scirburne we've heard reports about? We still haven't got to the bottom of his story yet.'

'We don't need to. Saeric is Earl Eadwald's bastard son – half Dumnonian by all accounts – and while we don't yet know what that means, he is not what matters right now. We must put all our efforts into finding Caelin, but we must do it quietly and carefully. If Caelin has gone to ground, we don't want to scare him off.'

'What about me, my Lord?' Aethelred asked nervously.

Camus considered him, then said, 'You must decide: join us in our quest, or I will stand aside and let Pedyr cut your throat.'

Aethelred swallowed. 'That's not much of a choice.'

'True,' Camus said. 'Choice is a luxury that was ripped from our hands when the traitor took power. In the matter of Mael, I will offer no such option as live or die. He will die. And I doubt that Talec gave your parents such a choice before he slashed their throats.'

Aethelred stared at the aged rebel leader, shocked. *How can you speak so plainly about my family's murder?*

'Make your decision, half-blood.'

'I... I will join you.'

'Good. Let us find prince Caelin. He has a two-month head start on us, so we must pray he is still here in Dumnonia and somewhere safe from harm.'

Part II

Kingdom of Dumnonia
Tvímánuður (Late Summer) 823 AD

Two months earlier

12

Arrival

Near Piltun, Northern Dumnonia

The old woman shouted at Rathulf, thrusting her broom at him as she would a yard hen. Rathulf stumbled onto the pathway, confused. *What have I done?* She had flown into a panic the instant she had come upon him, and then her husband had appeared, armed with a wooden spade. Now, the old man stood barefoot and bow-legged beside his wife, brandishing the weapon. A grim scowl twisted his mouth, and it would have been a comical sight but for the genuine fear that Rathulf saw in their eyes. They stared at him, their faces showing an odd mix of astonishment and alarm, and when Rathulf still had not moved, the old man poked his spade at him and shouted in an unintelligible language. The Norseman bent down to retrieve his heavy sea chest, then he turned back to the narrow path, faced with little choice but to leave.

So began Rathulf's third day in Dumnonia.

Twice exiled, Rathulf Thorvaldarsson had sailed here hoping that it might hold something familiar in it for him; some sign to indicate that all that had happened this past year had been somehow fated. But Dumnonia obstinately refused to offer even the slightest hint of welcome. The arrow wounds in his back and arm attested to that, to say nothing of the calamity that had befallen the rest of the *Storm Beater* and her crew.

His first night found him huddled under a rocky overhang near the shore, shivering not from the cold but from the accumulated shock of all that had happened since the Leap and Alrik's death.

It was hard to accept that it had only been a few weeks ago; it already felt like a lifetime away.

He had spent his second day wandering the beach, walking barefoot in the waves, reluctant to turn inland and face the reality of his exile. It was especially tough knowing that Ottar and the *Storm Beater* were within half a day's sail away on the puffin island. *Will I remember how to get back here, to this beach?* he wondered. The ocean was also his only link with home – it stretched unbroken back to Norvegr, and he had imagined the water lapping on the beach at the head of his fjord and his father's face gazing down the sheer-walled inlet. Rathulf had crouched down and dipped his fingers into the sea. *I am here, father,* he had thought. *But I wish you were here with me. And Alrik.* He had broken down then, unable to quell the feelings of desolation that had swept up from the water into his heart. *This is where I was born*, he had later tried to assure himself. *I am not a stranger here.* But as the day had worn on, the feeling of isolation had grown within him.

Then had come this final humiliation. As the sun sank below the western horizon at the close of the third day, Rathulf had come upon a group of huts huddled in a deep, narrow valley just inland from the shore. He had waited until twilight had faded into darkness, then he had snuck like a thief into the byre nearest him. It had seemed sensible to do; he felt little inclined to introduce himself to new people and had no idea how they might respond to him knocking on their door and requesting a night's hospitality. The byre had not been empty as he had hoped, and instead, he was forced to share the tiny space with a group of smelly sheep, which shuffled about for most of the night and stank of damp wool and decay.

It had seemed he'd just fallen asleep when he was wrenched awake by the startled cries of an old woman – the woman who had then shooed him away with her broom. Rathulf had leapt up, apologising and offering her his name, but she had backed away in fear. Soon her husband had joined her with his shovel, and so Rathulf had found himself on this road that took him up and away from the sea. He squinted into the rising sun, swallowing back the hunger pangs as his stomach protested the lack of food. *What strange, unfriendly people*, he thought. *All I did was sleep in their byre. In Norvegr, I would have been offered a place in their house to rest along with food and ale.*

The path swam as tears returned, but he angrily rubbed his arm across his eyes, refusing to give in to despair. *Perhaps I offended them by not seeking out their hospitality*, he wondered. *Perhaps they thought me the thief I feel.* He stopped. *Or maybe this is not Dumnonia after all.*

He had already begun to doubt Ottar the Doughty's assertion that this was Rathulf's homeland even before they had landed. Sigvald's master shipwright had plainly got them lost, which should have come as no surprise, for what were the chances that anyone, no matter how good a seaman, would remember how to get back to a faraway place they'd last seen sixteen years ago, with only their memory to guide them?

The journey had certainly begun well enough with the crossing from Norvegr to the Hjaltland archipelago. Ottar had confidently steered them over the perilous western ocean straight to the tiny group of islands. How Ottar managed that feat was beyond Rathulf's comprehension, for there seemed to be nothing at all in the vast open sea to give a clue as to their direction or destination. Clearly, Ottar held some sway with the sea Gods, Aegir and Ran. Rathulf was an excellent sailor himself, but his travels had always been limited to cruising the fjords alongside his best friend Alrik, and even they had managed to get lost from time to time, despite being surrounded by mountains and valleys that each bore their own unique shapes and forms to identify them. Out here on the open sea, there was nothing at all to orient you, and Rathulf found the experience deeply unsettling. The dark, turbulent water beneath their tiny wooden ship harboured all manner of monsters, chief among them Jörmungand – the terrifying sea serpent that encircled Midgard – and Rathulf had expended a generous quantity of silver in his offerings to Aegir and Njord to keep the dire sea terrors at bay.

❧

They arrived at Hjaltland on the heels of a waning storm, seeking shelter at the far end of a long inlet culminating in a wide, shallow beach, perfect for landing the knarr. The ship's crew ate the evening meal in relieved but awkward silence; no one able to find words of comfort or solace for their passenger. Later that evening, Rathulf wandered away from the tents to sit at the other end of the beach amongst the foam and driftwood, staring northward beyond the arms of the inlet to where his home lay unseen, far away over the ocean. With the death of Alrik and his subsequent betrayal by his other friend Leif, Rathulf's heart had been wrenched from his breast, leaving in its place a terrible, aching emptiness as broad and deep as the ocean over which he had just sailed. Rathulf gazed longingly across those cold waters, outcast and forsaken, while above him, the setting sun painted the storm clouds a majestic wash of pink and orange.

Gunnar came looking for him, but to Rathulf's surprise, Eirik's son did not mock or pester him. The youth simply sat nearby in silence, gazing out to sea. Gunnar's radical change in attitude towards his rival continued to confound Rathulf, but right then, he was grateful for the boy's quiet companionship.

Rathulf and his escort reluctantly left the bleak Viking outpost early on the third day, after Ottar had completed some minor maintenance to the ship's caulking. How quickly they had all come to appreciate firm land and an escape from the ever-moving, salty dampness of travel in an open boat, where sea spray was a constant irritation. It had surprised and worried Rathulf when Ottar had told him they had travelled a mere quarter of the distance and that the majority of the journey still lay ahead.

Rathulf's concerns eased somewhat when Ottar added that the rest of the trip would mostly be within sight of land.

The weather remained fair and warm as they coasted down the length of Bretland, Ottar keeping land in sight, as promised, to their port side. Occasionally the cliffs disappeared as the sea swept inland to meet a bay or inlet, but always the land returned, peeping above the grey-blue swell to their left. The occasional squall passed over them, but these showers were nothing like the frigid rains of home; summer clearly lasted longer this far south.

Some days later, they arrived at the new Norse outpost of Mannin, having spent an uneventful journey sailing southwards, spending the evenings ashore in tiny coves nestled within the rugged shoreline. They had encountered no one whenever they had made landfall, which Ottar said was a good thing, as the Norse were not well-liked in this land on account of their raiding. Rathulf had looked around him, bemused, wondering what a Viking raider might find of any interest or value in this bleak, uninhabited place. On the third day out, they had spotted two longships far to their starboard side, moving north under sail, but that had been the sum of their sightings.

Mannin was a large island that rose to an impressive mountainous spine. They tacked their way across its top and then down its eastern coastline, eventually pulling ashore on a sweeping beach fed by a good-sized river at its southern end. Three other longships lay on the strand, two of them abreast, and a third, some distance away up the beach. This had seemed to bother Ottar, and he suggested they proceed with caution. He drew up a polite few lengths away from the pair of longships, but his concerns had been unwarranted. The men welcomed the sea-weary crew of the *Storm Beater* with much jollity and insisted Rathulf's party share their evening meal.

Rathulf was in no mood for company or merriment but had little choice than to join the festivities. It emerged that the two ships were on their way back home after successful raiding in a land to the west of Mannin. There they had found gold, silver and ivory treasures and, most importantly, a goodly collection of slaves – men, women and some fresh-faced youths – who they had left bound in the longships. The raiders came from the southern part of Norvegr, from places whose names Rathulf didn't recognise. The other ship on the beach belonged to a crew from far to the north of Sognefjord and, according to Rathulf's hosts, were not especially friendly and were a little bit strange.

Talk inevitably turned to the purpose of Ottar's journey, particularly as they were heading in the wrong direction in a lightly-crewed knarr at the closing of the raiding season. Rathulf felt the prickling weight of the sideways glances and muted whispers of the men as they learned his tale and of the dark shadow of Fenrir that pursued him. He read from their expressions what they thought of him. Most felt pity, some fear, and others were indifferent to his fate. For what did they care about a blighted young orphan other than to ensure he stayed well away from their encampment lest his misfortune overspill onto them. Rathulf and his escort left the Viking waypoint early the following day, Rathulf heavy-lidded from lack of sleep.

That evening they struck their first resistance from the native peoples. They sailed south from Mannin under a strong breeze and made landfall near dusk, beaching the ship in a small cove with a beck providing fresh water. They had barely unloaded the tents when there were shouts from the hinterland above the beach. They managed to haul everything back on board and push off by the time a small band of men appeared on the clifftop above them. Ottar ordered everyone to the oars, having no interest in engaging a group of agitated Britons. They made away safely without incident. The watchers on the shore appeared to be unarmed, choosing instead to hurl insults in their unintelligible language and making various signs at them which were no doubt rude, warding or both.

'Can't they see we're not Vikings?' Gunnar said, using the

proper term for a Norse raiding party. 'This is a knarr with a crew of eight. Stupid erlendar.'

Aware of the failing light, Ottar decided to sail further west to find an alternative landing spot. He ordered the sail raised, hoping to catch the last of the evening breeze and outrun the watchers on the shore. To Ottar's consternation, four horsemen appeared on the clifftop a short while afterwards, and these men were armed. Ottar kept the ship out of bowshot, but the British riders tracked them along the coast, easily keeping up with the *Storm Beater* on their horses. Faced with little choice, Ottar turned further out to sea and sailed toward the sunset. He kept land in sight but well off their port side, hoping their followers would lose them or lose interest. Well into twilight, the land vanished altogether, and Ottar hauled on the steering board to bring the *Storm Beater* back onto a southeasterly heading. For a time, they saw nothing, and Rathulf began to feel uneasy as clouds gathered on the western horizon, bringing twilight to an abrupt end. Just as the light was failing, he spotted a darker, jagged line above the swell to their left. The wind was picking up, and Ottar let out a curse, ordering the sail reefed to slow their pace.

He gathered the men together. 'I was hoping to heave to out here, but the wind and swell are building, and rain is on the way. I'm not sure Ran and her nine daughters have our best interests at heart, so we'll have to make for shore.'

It seemed only moments later that the *Storm Beater* came to a crashing stop and tipped sideways, throwing the crew off their feet. 'We've struck rocks!' Torsten shouted, and Rathulf and Gunnar sprang up to drop the sail. Whether the Britons were still out on their horses seemed unlikely, but Rathulf nevertheless wondered whether his crew's shouts could be heard from the shore because on some nights back home, it was astonishing how far sound travelled up and down the fjord. *Probably sitting around a warm fire, celebrating our impending deaths*, Rathulf thought as he worked with Gunnar and the others to free the ship. By moving their cargo to the stern and pushing with the oars on the unseen rocks below the prow, they managed to free themselves. Their next worry was how much damage had been inflicted upon the *Storm Beater*. They deployed the oars and rowed parallel to the land, Ottar having abandoned the steering board and instead leaned out over the high prow to look for a landing place ahead and rocks below, using variable rowing force to steer. He spotted a pale strip at the base of the otherwise black cliffs and pointed the ship towards its middle, praying to Aegir and Ran to be kind to them. In response, the fickle Gods threw more rocks at them, and the ship crunched and bumped sideways as they pulled into the small cove. Ottar roundly swore as he tried to guide the boat through the darkness, unable to see what lay beneath the black, churning water. They ran aground about a ship-length from the shore, and for what seemed like the rest of the night to Rathulf, the small crew wrestled to drag the boat onto the rocky beach. They set the anchor between some large boulders above the high waterline, then spent a wakeful night on the ship's deck, taking turns to keep watch. They could not light a fire on the boat, but it was probably just as well, for they had no idea whether or not their pursuers were nearby.

The following morning brought grey skies, blustery wind and light rain, but their situation was better than Rathulf had feared. While there was some damage to the hull, only one strake had been badly split in the hull. Ottar made temporary repairs with a wooden patch and a slathering of tar, but the shipwright felt confident it would hold until they found somewhere safe to haul up and mend it properly. A second good tiding was that they had come ashore at the ebbing of the tide, so they simply needed to wait until the water was high enough, and they would clear the rocks.

They set sail as soon as the tar had set sufficiently to repel water and the tide had risen to allow them to escape the cove. They continued along the coastline under a strong northerly wind that drenched them with rain, making good, if soggy, progress. The party were soaked through by the time they pulled into shore for the night, convinced that they were now well beyond the range of the riders. Gunnar and Rathulf erected the two tents while the others made fast the ship and checked her over. The *Storm Beater* had taken on quite a lot of water, and they took turns bailing out the shallow hold. Only when Ottar had declared the ship ready to take back out to sea did he allow them to eat a cold meal of salted pork and the last of the very stale hard bread – just in case they were taken unawares again. The rain continued through to the next day, and they made for open water under a strong nor-easterly that drove them swiftly southwards. They missed the next landmark due to the poor visibility, and for the first time in their journey, Ottar seemed uncertain about their bearings.

'That's not right,' he had muttered, peering through the rain to their starboard side.

Rathulf fancied he saw glimpses of a strip of darkness on the horizon between the swell, which he presumed to be land.

'We've gone too far west,' Ottar said and ordered his crew to change tack. They sailed southeast for the rest of the day, and their reward was a return to sunshine in the late afternoon. The wind gradually decreased as the day wore on, and a new problem arose: becalming. None of the crew fancied spending the night in the middle of the open sea, particularly given the hull's fragile state; it had been harrowing enough in the passage to the Hjaltlands, but the Gods were determined to make Rathulf's journey a trial of patience. The *Storm Beater* bobbed listlessly in the gentle swell as the sun set on a warm, still evening.

'Well, we can't row our way to shore,' Ottar said, frowning to the east. 'We should be able to see land by now.'

Rathulf could see nothing but ocean in all directions, and a sense of panic began to creep into his bones, a fear that he knew he shared with the others. He decided to pose the question he had wanted to ask from the moment they'd left the mouth of Sognefjord. 'How do you know where to go?'

Ottar smiled back at the young Norseman. 'Memory, gut, and a knowledge of the stars, sol and the clouds.' When this did little to reassure Rathulf, Ottar tilted his head and added, 'I trust the Gods to guide us. So long as we make our offerings and remain faithful to them, they will protect us. You needn't worry so.'

They've not been very helpful so far, Rathulf thought, not at all reassured.

'I bet you didn't think you'd get this far only to be eaten by a sea Jötunn,' Gunnar grinned. He punched Rathulf in the shoulder. 'Or maybe Ottar's got us so lost that we'll sail off the world's edge.'

Rathulf could not hide the bolt of fear that shot through him with those words. He'd heard plenty of tales of intrepid explorers setting off to discover new lands only to perish when they came to the world's edge, where they would plummet to their deaths over the great waterfall. Some spoke of a worse fate – to sail into Niflheim, Jötunheim or one of the other realms, never to be heard from again.

Gunnar laughed mockingly at him, but Rathulf knew the boy was just as scared as he was.

'Aye, if we keep sailing south, we will just as likely stumble upon Muspelheim,' Ottar confirmed unhelpfully. 'I've not known anyone who has tried it to return. Same for those who have sailed west of Hjaltland.'

'But we're safe for now,' Rathulf said, more as a question than a statement.

'Aye, but there's a strong current,' Ottar countered, then he winked at Rathulf, seeing the young man's alarm. 'Worry not. It's taking us back the way we came..., for now. Best get the sail down and settle in for the night, although we will have to keep bailing, lest we sink in our sleep. Hakon, have we any food left? We'll need to go hunting soon. I hope your kingdom has some decent game, Ra.'

'I'm sure they have plenty of sheep,' Torsten said.

'Each to his own,' Hakon grinned, 'but I'd rather find me a proper young woman,' and he cupped his hands for emphasis. That prompted hearty laughter and lightened the mood.

A breeze out of the northwest welcomed them at dawn, and Ottar turned the ship eastwards, figuring they'd be bound to strike land again soon. He was right. First came the gulls, wheeling noisily around the boat, then mid-afternoon, Gunnar shouted, 'land ahead!' Sure enough, a low coastline became visible on the port bow; more of the same low, rocky shoreline punctuated by the small coves they had seen for much of their journey. They occasionally passed long, wide beaches, but these were far too exposed for overnighting.

'Where are their fjords?' Rathulf asked, taking a brief rest from bailing. His arms ached thanks to the constant scooping of water from the hold. The leak was getting worse, and he was relieved they were back in sight of land.

'There are none,' Ottar said, shaking his head. 'Your land is completely different from Aurlandsfjorden. There are fells, certainly – you'll have seen them rising inland beyond the coast – but they have none of the confining walls of home, Ra. Yours is a kinder, broader land.' He stretched his arms for emphasis. 'Feel how warm it is here. We are in our shirtsleeves today, and the sun beats warm on our shoulders and faces. That is what a Dumnonian summer holds for you, and I envy you for that.' He turned back to the approaching shoreline. 'But what we should be asking is whether that's Dumnonia?'

'You're not sure?' Rathulf asked, shocked. 'You can't just dump me anywhere!' He noticed Gunnar grinning to himself as he bailed, and Rathulf felt a flare of anger at the youth's heartlessness.

Ottar looked at Rathulf awkwardly. 'I plan to take you back to the estuary where we first found you. That way, we will know you are in the right place. But that's around the other side of Dumnonia, and in the meantime, we need somewhere to lay up for food, water, rest and repairs.'

It had been easy to say, but they spent the rest of the afternoon seeking somewhere suitable to land. The unwelcoming shoreline presented steep, jagged cliffs as far as the eye could see in either direction. Spurs of rock thrust out into the sea, making for dangerous inshore sailing and cutting off otherwise ideal landing places. In the clear light of day, Rathulf could now understand how lucky they had been the other night not to have smashed their little boat to pieces. Ottar steered them westwards, explaining that if this were Dumnonia, they would come to the end of it in time because it was a vast peninsula that jutted out into the great ocean of Midgard. At the peninsula's tip, they would turn left and sail right around underneath to where Rathulf had initially been found. Ottar spoke with his customary poise, but Rathulf detected a slight note of doubt in the shipwright's tone.

As they sailed southward to come around underneath, Ottar became increasingly agitated. 'This is wrong. It isn't how I remember it. That bay should not be there.'

'It was a long time ago,' Rathulf offered, trying to be helpful and also quell his own fears, but it only poured oil on Ottar's ire.

'My memory is not so unreliable,' Ottar snapped. 'We continue eastwards.'

Ottar grew more concerned, however, as the afternoon wore on towards sunset. He refused to admit they were lost, but it was apparent to everyone that they were. Rathulf stayed out of the way – difficult to achieve on such a small craft – busying himself with keeping the sail in trim to the unpredictable wind. He was starkly aware this was all his fault, and he began to wish that he had stayed home in Thorvaldsby. *Home*, he thought. *Funny that it's Thorvaldsby I automatically think of.* He looked out at the rocky shoreline to his left and wondered what in Odin's name he was doing. *How will I manage this on my own?* he wondered with a flash of uncertainty. *I haven't a hope of surviving here without Sigvald and the others. I'm an idiot for thinking I could.*

His self-doubt must have been written on his face because Hakon put a hand on his shoulder and said, 'it's not too late to change your mind, Rathulf. Remember, this is your choice. You are imposing this exile upon yourself. If you want to turn around and go back, no one will think less of you for it.'

'Yes, they will,' came Gunnar's scornful voice. The youth caught Rathulf's eye and threw him a derisive shake of the head. 'We're nearly there, for fuck's sake, and you can't return anyway. Ivar's men will cut you open from your chin to your cock and hang you up by your entrails. That's if these erlendar don't do it first since he's got no idea where we are.' He scowled at Ottar, who was standing by the steering oar.

'That's enough, Gunnar,' Hakon warned.

Eirik's son shrugged, unconcerned, and said, 'you know we're lost, and I know you're scared.' The last was directed at Rathulf, but the youth left it at that and moved to the front of the boat.

'He's right,' Rathulf said, fighting the knot of despair tightening in his gut. 'I have to keep going, whether I want to or not. It's what the Gods demand, and we all know what happens when I defy their will.' He glared at the decking under which his trunk lay protected in the shallow hold.

'Good landing spot ahead,' Gunnar called from the prow, pointing to a broad, sandy cove enclosed by two wooded headlands.

'I don't like it,' Ottar said. 'Too exposed. So far, we've been lucky, and I don't want to test Ran's patience.'

'We're running out of daylight. There's a high point at this end. We can climb up there and get our bearings,' Hakon suggested.

'It's quite sheltered under that headland too,' Rathulf added, 'and the trees will be useful for repairing the *Storm Beater*.'

Ottar let out a long breath, but he capitulated, and they turned ashore. They drew up onto the sandy beach, such a contrast to the rocky, shingle coves they'd recently been overnighting on. However, before they were permitted to relax, Ottar had them unstep and stow the mast and sail so that their ship would appear less threatening to anyone who chanced along. They could always make their way out to safety under oar if the need arose.

Leaving Torsten to watch the boat, the others made their way onto the headland to survey their surroundings.

'Not much to see,' Gunnar said disparagingly, gazing inland over the broad, windswept landscape.

Rathulf could only agree, and a part of him hoped this wasn't Dumnonia, for if it was, it was profoundly disappointing. Except for the grove of trees on this headland, the rest of the place was mostly treeless, and low, thorny plants grew along many of the other clifftops. He was heartened to see some grassy meadows further inland, though, which looked to be farmed. Rathulf was certain he could see little white dots that were surely sheep? He pointed in that direction, but Gunnar shrugged. 'Looks all the same to me. No people though, which is fortunate,' he added.

'Hel's thighs, I was right,' Ottar said, facing the opposite direction and peering out to sea. He pointed to the far southern horizon. 'Can you see that reddish-brown line between the sea and the sky?' he asked Rathulf.

They could see a goodly distance in the evening light, and by squinting, he could just make out a golden line way to their south. Or at least he imagined he could.

'That's Dumnonia,' Ottar said, but he sounded tense.

'Which is good, isn't it?' Rathulf asked, surprised that Ottar did not appear pleased.

'He's worried about the days we've wasted going the wrong way,' Gunnar offered, scowling at the shipwright. 'My father wouldn't have made so many mistakes.'

'And yet your father is not here,' Ottar replied pointedly.

'Now then, both of you,' Hakon growled. 'Can we not fight amongst ourselves? We know where we are now, and that is excellent. Let's rest here tonight, repair our ship tomorrow, then set out with gay hearts knowing we are on the homeward leg.'

'Homeward for him,' Gunnar objected, pointing at Rathulf. 'We've to get all the way back to Sognefjorden, and unless you hadn't noticed, winter is on the way. Don't any of you remember what happened to all those ships last winter?'

'No one forced you to come along,' Hakon reminded the youth, 'and any more words like that, and I might think you are afraid.'

That shut Gunnar up, but Rathulf felt Hakon was being hypocritical. *Of course, Gunnar is afraid*, he thought. *We're all afraid!*

Gunnar muttered a curse under his breath, then turned and stomped away.

'Where are you going?' Ottar said.

'To earn my passage and hunt us some dinner. I don't think I could eat another piece of salted pork or tørrfisk.'

'Well, night is falling soon, so don't venture too far. We've no idea what kind of Jötunn roam these parts. Go with him, Rathulf.'

Gunnar rolled his eyes but didn't say anything, so Rathulf followed him down to the ship and chose a spear, aware of his shortcomings in the face of Gunnar's talent with a bow. He also wasn't entirely sure that he'd be able to shoot with his injured hand. The two of them turned inland in search of some fresh meat.

'If you get lost, don't ask the natives for help,' Ottar called down to them. 'They'll likely skewer you. And if you do manage to catch something, remember to bring back firewood because there's not much to burn up here.'

As it was, they found both and not too far from the beach. They walked inland for a short distance to find themselves overlooking a deep, narrow vale that sheltered a small wood. Gunnar spotted the goat long before Rathulf saw it, hiding in the undergrowth. They crept towards it, moving in a wide arc around the animal to ensure the breeze remained in their faces and their scent was carried away from their prey.

'Gonna be hard to shoot through all these bloody bushes,' Gunnar whispered, frustrated by the screen of spiky shrubs and brambles.

Suddenly the goat lifted its head and looked straight at them, some sixth sense alerting it of danger. Gunnar loosed his arrow immediately, hitting the beast in the rump. It let out a loud, startled bleat, then sprang for cover.

'Spear it, quick!' Gunnar shouted.

Rathulf stood and hurled the heavy weapon at the retreating animal and, to his joy and not some little wonder, struck it in the flank, bringing it down. Gunnar barged through the undergrowth and pounced on it. He quickly slashed its neck, determined to prevent their dinner from escaping.

The goat was old and had a tattered length of rope trailing from its neck. It was a runaway, clearly, but old or not, it was fresh meat. Gunnar proceeded to gut it expertly. 'Don't just stand there watching,' he said, annoyed. 'Fetch some firewood.'

Rathulf did as instructed and found a decent supply of dead branches in the scrappy woodland that crowded the little vale. By the time he had stacked his arms as high as possible, Gunnar had finished his work, and he hoisted the carcass over his shoulder. He scooped up his bow, quiver and Rathulf's spear and led the way back to the cove. He beamed triumphantly as Ottar and the men heaped praise upon him for his success, and Rathulf said nothing, allowing the boy to feast on the accolades. To his credit, Gunnar noted that it was a joint effort and then, to Rathulf's surprise, added that it was Rathulf's accurate spear throw that had finished the job.

Hakon joined Rathulf on a second trip to gather more firewood, this time from the woods atop the headland, while Gunnar stayed behind to finish preparing the goat for cooking and then clean the blood from his skin and his clothes. Ottar, meanwhile, set up the portable spit and frame. As they were walking back to camp with an armful of firewood each, Hakon wondered at the transformation of Gunnar. 'For all your life, he has been your enemy, and now he is your friend?'

Rathulf paused, looking the older man in the eye. 'What are you saying? I don't deserve friends?'

'No, I was wondering at his change of heart.'

'Sigvald says it is because he wants a share of my treasure and power. By helping me now, I will be obliged to reward him when I get my kingdom back.'

Hakon nodded, clearly having thought the same, then he smiled at Rathulf's challenging expression. 'Yes, my young jarl,' he said, answering the unasked question. 'All of us expect the same.'

'Well, I think it is more than that,' Rathulf said, choosing not to rise to Hakon's bait. 'I think it is because he knows he was in the wrong over Alrik, and he is trying to make amends.'

Hakon stopped, surprised, and then he frowned. 'I doubt it. Watch your back, Rathulf, is all I'm saying. You have many friends, but he is not one of them.'

'Then he is smart because too many people close to me have paid the price for being my friend,' Rathulf reminded him. 'Better that none of you suffers their fate. And anyway, Gunnar's not *that* friendly.'

Hakon let it lie, but the conversation soured what should have been a cheerful evening for Rathulf, filled with the mouth-watering aroma of roasting goat over a fire, complemented by the sweet taste of warmed mead. After the meal, when the conversation had dulled to contented murmurings, Rathulf moved away from the fire and lay down on a broad slab of rock at the base of the headland to gaze up at the sky. It was a warm, clear night, and the embers of Muspelheim glittered brightly in the heavens above. He felt a sudden rush of grief as he remembered lying beside

Alrik two summers ago, swapping increasingly outrageous tales about the giants and monsters who had stirred up the fires that had spewed out the beautiful twinkling stars which now shone above Midgard – and what it might be like in that hot, burning land of the fire giants. He felt a tear form in the corner of his eye, and he brushed it aside, determined not to show weakness before these men. *The time for tears is past. I am a Dumnonian prince. I must be strong.*

The following morning, after checking they were still alone, Ottar took advantage of the spell of warm, sunny weather and their apparent isolation to properly inspect his previous hasty repairs to the damaged hull. He was concerned that the split planks might not last the return journey, for the weather would soon turn foul as autumn set in. Rathulf knew that the seaman was taking an enormous risk setting out this late in the season, and even if the weather was good down here, it was bound to grow worse the further north Ottar and his crew travelled.

The break also gave them the chance to wash their salt-encrusted bodies, hair, clothes, ropes and sail in the beck that flowed into the sea at the opposite end of the beach. Despite the sense of security offered by the sheltered little cove, they maintained a lookout throughout. Ottar refused to allow the boys to wander away from the beach, unwilling to test their luck with the Gods and figuring that the provision of fresh meat and plenty of firewood was enough to ask of them. As it was, they saw no one on land or at sea, although Gunnar had insisted that he'd seen three horse riders in the far distance inland. Hakon, who had been with him above the cove, hadn't seen them, but he had crouched down low beside Eirik's son just in case.

At the close of the day, Ottar declared the hull irreparably damaged, which was not the news anyone had expected or wanted. Three strakes would have to come off the port bow and be replaced with new ones, which could only be done safely in his shipyard back in Sigvaldsby. He'd done the best he could with fresh wood cut from the trees above, but he'd used up all the spare nails, caulking and tar in the repairs, leaving them with the bare minimum to cover another emergency. 'We'll leave tomorrow and make haste for Dumnonia. I hope they're a friendly bunch, Ra, because we may have to come with you. I'm not sure the *Storm Beater* will make it back in this condition.'

'Well, if the weather down here really is this warm, I'm definitely staying,' Gunnar said.

'Can't say I blame you,' Ottar said, 'but in the meantime, I need you to fetch us some more firewood.'

Rathulf started climbing up the headland, realised Gunnar wasn't following, so he turned around and called down to him.

'Nah, you go up there. I'm gonna look around,' Gunnar said.

Rathulf heard Gunnar's shouts and immediately knew that something was wrong. He leapt onto the boat and grabbed a spear, then jumped back down and ran towards Gunnar's warning shouts amid the dunes beyond. He crested a sandbank to see Gunnar running toward him, pursued by at least half a dozen armed men, their weapons drawn. There were more behind them. Rathulf spotted an archer on the headland to his left taking aim at Gunnar. Rathulf let out a wild yell and threw his spear at the man. The archer ducked out of the spear's path, but it was enough to distract him and let Gunnar pass safely. Rathulf turned on his heels and ran as hard as he could after Gunnar, following the other's lead by dodging and weaving as he leapt over the grass tussocks on the dunes.

'There are too many of them!' Gunnar shouted, glancing over his shoulder. He turned back to the shore and yelled at Ottar to ready the boat.

The shipwright was already pushing the *Storm Beater* back into the water with the help of Hakon and the other crew members. Ever the cautious captain, Ottar had ensured his boat sat just on the threshold of the beach so that it would be a relatively quick task to make for the sea. It was just as well because there was no time to lose. Abandoning much of what they had unloaded, they pulled themselves aboard and took to the oars, frantically shoving them through the oarports and hauling hard and fast to get clear of danger. Progress was far too slow, for this was a trading vessel, not a longship, provisioned with only six oars intended for inshore paddling, not outrunning attackers.

A dozen men appeared over the low dunes, shouting encouragement to one another and yelling insults at the fleeing Norsemen. Several others were making their way along the headland to get a better angle for their bows. They fired a succession of rapid volleys at the departing ship, and there was nothing Ottar, Rathulf or their crew could do to protect themselves on the open deck. One arrow found its mark, hitting Thorkel in the thigh. He cried out but kept rowing, yelling at the others to pull harder on their oars. Another arrow caught in Ottar's sleeve, and he let out a curse and ducked lower in the lee of the high sternpost. Other missiles slapped into the hull or skittered along the deck, and then they began to fall short as the *Storm Beater* cleared the bows' range. The crewmen continued pulling until they were well out of bowshot, then Ottar jumped down from the steering deck to check on Thorkel.

'I'll be fine,' the lanky Viking growled, gripping the shaft to rip it out of his leg.

'No!' Ottar said, grabbing the sailor's wrist. 'We are far from help, so let us do this properly. Rathulf, bring a knife so we can cut away the cloth. We'll ease it out.'

'But what about Vidar–' Rathulf began, staring with alarm at the sailor sitting in front of him.

'I'm alright,' Vidar said, although he clearly wasn't, because Rathulf could see blood seeping between the man's fingers where he was pressing his hand to his side. A bloodied arrow lay on the deck beside him.

'No, you're not,' Rathulf said, ignoring Ottar and pulling Vidar's hand away.

'It's just a graze,' the man snapped.

Rathulf heard Ottar swear, then the captain was there, lifting Vidar's shirt. The arrow had slashed a deep cut in the sailor's flank, and blood ran freely from the wound.

Ottar swore again. 'Rathulf,' he said. 'Help Thorkel get that arrow out of his leg while I attend to Vidar here. Be careful not to tear his skin overmuch. Fenrir's fangs, we don't need this!'

They heard cheering from the shore, and Rathulf offered the triumphant Britons a rude gesture in return. *I'm one of you, drittsekkar*, he thought angrily, repeating his gesture. It only made them laugh and cheer more loudly.

Rathulf got out his knife as instructed, but the injured sailor snatched it from Rathulf's hand and said, 'I'll do it myself. It'll be my luck for you to cut open an artery.'

Rathulf left him to it. He glanced back at the shore and saw that two riders had joined the party upon the clifftop. He silently cursed them, his people. *Bacrautar*, he thought angrily, taking up the steering oar. Then, out of the corner of his eye, he noticed Gunnar wince. Rathulf looked down at Eirik's son in time to see the youth staring in disbelief at his scarlet-smeared right hand. Blood was coursing down the side of his head and neck and running into his eyes. The young Norseman let out a croak, and then he flopped forward over his oar.

13
Puffin Island

Off the southern coast of Dyfed

'Gunnar!' Rathulf cried, his heart constricting with disbelief. *How could things have gone so badly wrong? And how could just a clutch of archers cause so much harm?* He jumped across an oar to Eirik's son and pulled Gunnar upright, slapping his face to bring him around. Gunnar blinked and looked at Rathulf, his eyes wide with panic and fear.

'Where were you hit?' Rathulf said, trying to find the source of the bleeding. It was hopeless. There was blood everywhere, in Gunnar's hair, on his neck, and spreading over his face. *Where is it coming from?* he wondered, trying to calm his own sense of panic. He grabbed a bailing pot, scooped up seawater, and then dumped it over Gunnar. He swiftly followed with another. 'Ottar!'

'Hel's thighs!' he heard Ottar curse, and the shipwright hurried over to Rathulf's side, calling to Hakon for help. Hakon wrenched Gunnar's oar from the oarport and threw it onto the deck behind them to give them more space. Rathulf was still cradling Gunnar in his arms, but the dousing had done the trick. He could see where the arrow had struck the youth on the top of his scalp in a glancing blow, and blood pulsed steadily from the deep gash.

Gunnar let out another croak and fainted again.

Ottar snatched up a cloth and told Rathulf to keep it pressed firmly on the wound. 'It looks worse than it is,' the sailor assured his charge. 'It doesn't seem to have pierced his skull. Scrapes to the head always throw out scads of blood. Keep him upright and keep that pressed on the wound. I need to get back to Vidar. Hakon, with me, please.'

Rathulf shuffled to the boat's edge, noticing that they had begun to drift back towards the shore. He didn't want to say anything to Ottar because Vidar was clearly in trouble, and the captain didn't need to be distracted right now. He looked across the water to the men lining the shore and clifftop, bows at the ready, waiting for the current to bring the *Storm Beater* back into range or, even better, aground on the rocky headland. Rathulf propped himself up against the hull, Gunnar in his arms, holding the cloth to the youth's scalp. At least Ottar had been right about the wound. The blood flow was slowing, but Gunnar remained pale. A few feet away, Ottar was working on the injured crewman. They had no fire to cauterise the wound, so things would go badly for him unless they could act soon.

Gunnar's colour improved, and he awakened, groggily realised who was holding him, swore rudely and shoved himself away from Rathulf.

'Gunnar!' Ottar snapped from the other side of the ship. 'He's trying to help you, and you haven't bled to death thanks to him.'

'I don't need coddling,' Gunnar said, his voice slurred. He tried to stand, but he swayed on his feet. Rathulf sprang up and caught him as he fainted for the third time.

'Forget him,' Ottar said to Rathulf. 'I need you to help Hakon and the others get the mast stepped and the sail up, then I want you to take us out to sea.'

Rathulf eased Gunnar onto the deck and propped him against the shield rail. Gunnar's head was still bleeding, so Rathulf tightly wrapped a strip of cloth around his scalp and tied it under his chin to keep the bleeding at bay. Gunnar moaned, and his head lolled on his shoulder, but it was the best Rathulf could do for the time being. He then worked with Hakon and Hjalmar to step the heavy mast and prepare the sail. It took far too long with just the three of them, and Rathulf barely managed his end of the yard with the sail attached. One of the archers ashore launched a speculative arrow which splashed into the water alarmingly close to them. The inshore current was now pushing the *Storm Beater* back toward the headland, which gave Rathulf the extra burst of energy he needed to haul up the sail. Thorkel joined them, taking up one of the lines to help raise the large, square sheet.

Rathulf took the helm immediately they'd hoisted the sail. No sooner had he done so than he felt something hit him in the back with a sharp prick, then an arrow clattered onto the deck beside him. He whirled around in a fury and saw the archers straining on their strings, trying to eke as much range out of their weapons as possible. A second arrow flew towards him, forcing him to duck sideways to avoid it, although it had lost its potency this far out. Nevertheless, it gave the men on shore cause to cheer and heckle him.

'I'm Dumnonian, you fuckwits!' Rathulf shouted back at them in Norse.

Hakon and Hjalmar finally got the sail rigged into the wind, and it filled with a reassuring whump. The ship surged forward, and Rathulf leaned on the tiller, turning them back out to sea. Their passage would take them close to the cliff and briefly into bowshot, but Rathulf had no choice, and he yelled at the crew to watch out. Arrows fell around Rathulf as the bowmen concentrated their fire on the man at the steering board. Rathulf stayed at the tiller, leaning hard on it to turn them away as fast as possible. An arrow caught him on the forearm, and he yanked it out and tossed it aside, swearing in pain as he willed the ship to turn.

Ottar had always boasted that the *Storm Beater* was light and fast, and she proved him right. The wind caught her and pushed her swiftly away from the men on the shore. Rathulf lifted his finger at them in a parting gesture, and then he turned his attention back to the occupants of the little knarr. No one else seemed to have been hit, although an arrow stuck out of the hull beside Gunnar, who was staring wide-eyed at Rathulf, fear writ all over his face. That surprised Rathulf, but he hadn't time to consider it just then; his priority was to get the *Storm Beater* away from shore as fast as possible. It had occurred to him that they must surely come across a British longship at some point, and these well-organised assailants seemed as likely as any to have a ship or two at their disposal. The wind was blowing from the southeast, forcing Rathulf to steer them westwards away from land and into the setting sun, but he had little choice. He was expecting Ottar to take command, but the shipwright was still attending to Vidar, clearly content to entrust their welfare to the young Norseman.

Meanwhile, Hakon, a seasoned seaman, tidied up the deck, knowing how important it was to keep the boards clear of anything that could lead to a mishap. He took care to gather up the arrows and stash them for future use, and then he stowed the oars on their rack in the centre of the ship. He also closed the oarport covers to prevent water from coming through onto the deck.

'What have we lost?' Ottar asked him.

Hakon shook his head and grimaced. 'Too much. The large tent, blankets, the cooking irons, a small water barrel, the last of the salted pork, and some other utensils. Oh, and the mead. On the upside, we still have our goat. How is Vidar?'

'Bad. We need to find somewhere to lay ashore. Rathulf, it's a clear night with a decent breeze, at least for now. See that bright star yonder? Aim for it. One advantage of being so far south is that we can see the stars earlier in the night. If I'm right, we'll hit Dumnonia around ótta. But before you do all that, you'd best check on your friend.'

He meant Gunnar, of course, so Rathulf went over to the seventeen-year-old, who was huddling in the shelter of the shield-rail. Gunnar shook violently, his eyes following Rathulf as he came over to him. Rathulf reached up, wrenched the arrow from the strake beside Gunnar's face, and put it aside. 'We're safe now,' Rathulf muttered. He peered into Gunnar's eyes, but the boy didn't seem to recognise him. He called Ottar over. The shipmaster took one look at the boy and let out a sigh.

'He's in shock. Perhaps he saw the Valkyries coming for him. There's not much we can do for him right now, besides tying him up to the mast so that he doesn't fall overboard. Oh, and you'd best put us back on course. You need to use the storm rope if you're going to step away from the tiller.'

Rathulf flushed at the gentle reprimand and saw that they were, indeed, veering off course. He moved to go back to his post, but Ottar caught his arm, then let out an expletive when he saw the blood. Rathulf winced in pain.

'Hel's thighs, Rathulf,' he said, pulling up Rathulf's sleeve to inspect the wound.

'It's not bad,' Rathulf said.

'Yes it is,' Ottar said. 'That will fester if it is not mended. Let me check you over.' He turned Rathulf around, tutting at the two places he had been struck in the back. Rathulf hadn't even felt the second arrow. Neither were deep cuts, but they would also need attending. 'Next time you decide to be someone's pin cushion, put on a gambeson or chainmail first, yes? Do you have a coat in that kist of yours?'

Rathulf shook his head.

'Well, it's too late for it now, anyway. Will you be alright?'

Rathulf nodded, looking down at his arm, which had started to hurt now that he was aware of it. 'I don't understand,' he said, struggling to maintain his composure. 'Why are the Gods still punishing me? I'm doing what they want. Why did they do this?'

'I don't know, Rathulf,' Ottar said gruffly. 'We'll make another offering as soon as we're at a safe distance. Now help me with Gunnar.'

Rathulf assisted Ottar in wrapping a rope around the mast

and under Gunnar's arms to prop him safely out of the way. 'Now set us back on course, and don't worry about Gunnar. He'll come to his senses soon enough, although I doubt he'll be in a cheerful mood.'

'I'm sorry,' Rathulf said as he began to understand the implications of their perilous situation.

'Let's worry about all that later,' Ottar said, moving to check on Vidar.

Rathulf returned to the tiller and pulled on it to bring the *Storm Beater* back into line with the lodestar, which shone brightly in the deepening dusk. He watched Ottar fetch a cloak and drape it around Gunnar's shoulders.

'Funny how matters turn out,' came the voice of Thorkel, who was busying himself adjusting the halyards now that they were out of the line of fire. 'I had always imagined a different outcome between you two, yet it is Gunnar who rolled over and you who has held his ground. You should have more faith in your path, Thorvaldarsson.' He shrugged. 'The Gods are testing you. So far, you're doing alright.'

It was the closest thing to a compliment that Rathulf would receive from the gruff sailor, and he allowed himself a smile before glancing at Gunnar and immediately feeling guilty. Fortunately, Eirik's son seemed unconscious, so he had not heard what Thorkel had just said. *Poor Gunnar*, Rathulf thought, although it should not have come as a surprise to him that Gunnar was craven since Alrik had always said as much. 'The noisier they are off the battlefield, the less you can trust them on it,' Alrik had once proclaimed, quoting a line from the Hávamál. Rathulf frowned to himself. *How would you have reacted had you been here, Alrik?* he wondered. Oddly, the answer that came was not favourable, for was Alrik not over-boastful himself? He'd not taken the Leap until forced to, and he'd not exactly been brave with Ivar. Reckless, yes, but when faced with a real threat, Rathulf had saved them, not Alrik. Unsettled by that realisation,

Rathulf turned his attention back to the sea and the lodestar that showed their way.

The weather remained clear and the wind fair, so Ottar set up the fire bowl on the deck near the prow. He made a small fire with their gathered driftwood, careful to place the grate over it to avoid any accidental spills of burning wood or coals, a hazard for a deck slathered with tar and whale oil. Rathulf hoped that there were no reefs or rocky islets ahead because he could see very little now, thanks to the light from the fire illuminating the sail and blotting out their surroundings. Ottar heated an iron poker to sear Vidar's wound. Despite his best efforts to remain valiant, Vidar bit down hard on the leather belt between his teeth and let out an anguished cry. His breathing grew rapid then he fainted when Ottar began to stitch up his cauterised wound with a length of fine fishing cord.

Rathulf winced in sympathy.

Ottar then turned his attention to Thorkel, who sat on a sea chest on Rathulf's side of the sail, holding one of the stays to help keep the sail in trim.

'I told you, I'll be alright,' he growled at his captain.

'I agree you probably will, but if you don't want to walk with a limp the rest of your life, I need to sew up the wound because it is deep, and you know what will happen if I don't.'

Thorkel gave his grudging consent, and Ottar scooped up a fresh pail of saltwater and doused the leg thoroughly, clearing away the blood which might otherwise become tainted if left in the wound to fester. A festering sore was an invitation to ill spirits, especially with such an inviting hole through which to enter the soul. Rathulf had seen the effects of those malignant spirits on a slave once, and that poor man had died a lingering, writhing, screaming death after a slight wound in his side had grown black with poison, and the malignancy had rapidly eaten through to his heart.

Rathulf looked away when Ottar threaded the fishhook again,

and it was then that Rathulf noticed Gunnar was awake, the boy's pale eyes glittering in the light of the fire as he frowned or scowled up at him; Rathulf couldn't be sure. This time Rathulf looped the storm rope around the tiller to keep the knarr's course steady, then he went to the mast to untie the youth. Gunnar's eyes followed him as he undid the bonds, but the boy remained unnervingly silent.

'We tied you up so you wouldn't fall overboard in the swell,' Rathulf explained. 'You lost a lot of blood. That's why you've got that bandage on. An arrow struck you right on top of your head, but your skull's so hard it bounced off.' Rathulf tapped the top of his own head to indicate where Gunnar had been hit. Gunnar paled, and for a moment, Rathulf feared the boy would faint again, but Gunnar took a deep breath and nodded.

'You got hit three times,' Gunnar said, in a strange, disbelieving voice, as though what he had seen had been a dream, 'but you're not hurt. Are we dead?'

Rathulf looked down at his forearm, which was bleeding badly and most definitely hurt. He was also all too aware of the cuts in his back.

'And you really know how to handle a ship,' Gunnar went on, 'so we must be dead.'

Gunnar's odd tone unsettled Rathulf. 'Thanks for that,' Rathulf said, 'but we're not dead. We got away.'

'But I saw the arrows hit you. You didn't flinch or duck or scream.'

Rathulf, who was beginning to feel aggrieved, wasn't sure what to say. 'I was just luckier than you,' he said.

'One day, I'll be lucky too,' Gunnar said, still thoughtful and speaking as though he was entirely someone else.

'You're Eirik's son. You don't need luck,' Rathulf said. He had meant no insult by it, but Gunnar scowled at the mention of his father.

Gunnar opened his mouth to respond but stopped, then said,

'I don't feel so good.'

Rathulf took a step backwards, fearing Gunnar was about to vomit.

'You'll be off-colour for a while yet,' Ottar warned, stepping over and peering into Gunnar's eyes. He took Gunnar's chin and turned the boy's head from side to side. 'That was a nasty strike, and you're lucky to be alive. I need to seal up your wound now.'

Gunnar let out a cry of alarm when he saw the fire iron in Ottar's hand, and he scrambled backwards out of the way. He had nowhere to go on the little ship, and Hakon grabbed him and held his arms behind his back. Rathulf untied the bandage.

Gunnar cursed them and tried to wrench himself free, forcing Ottar to slap him hard across the face.

'We're trying to save your life, lombungr,' Ottar growled, then he pressed the hot iron onto Gunnar's scalp. Gunnar screamed, and the air filled with the sickening smell of burning skin and hair. Rathulf scooped up a pail of cold seawater and poured it over Gunnar's head while Hakon soaked the cloth bandage and then tied it back around Gunnar's skull. Gunnar didn't faint this time, but he let out a sob, crawled back to the mast, drew his knees up under his chin, and wrapped his arms around them, crying softly.

'Stay there and rest,' Ottar said. He turned to Rathulf. 'You're next. Take off your shirt. Hakon, take the tiller.'

Rathulf did as he was told and stood by the brazier, steeling himself for the firebrand. He clenched his eyes shut and nearly burst his heart, suppressing the scream that wanted to explode from his mouth when Ottar applied the hot iron to his skin. He bit his lip when Ottar followed with the needle and stitched the wound shut. Rathulf kept his eyes closed and managed not to utter a sound. He opened them again when Ottar was binding a bandage tightly around it.

'That will heal well. It's a clean wound. Now let me look at your back.' He tutted again at the two puncture wounds, but a single stitch in each was all that was required to close them up. Unfortunately, they'll likely pop open again, but neither is too deep. You'll live.' He stepped back in front of Rathulf, smiling wryly. He handed Rathulf his shirt. 'Take over from Hakon. He's got a terrible sense of direction.'

Rathulf returned to the tiller and again saw Gunnar frowning up at him. Rathulf was unsettled by the speed and ease with which Gunnar's arrogant self-assurance had unravelled in the face of a potentially mortal injury. *Hel's thighs*, he thought. *I need to get off this knarr before Gunnar comes back to his senses and takes out his humiliation on me.*

As if to answer his call, the breeze stiffened a short while later and veered nor'westerly, driving the ship southwards at a faster pace. Under normal circumstances, Rathulf would reef the sail – especially in this darkness – but he wanted to get to Dumnonia as fast as possible. It earned him a questioning look from Ottar, but the experienced captain clearly had faith in Rathulf's judgement because he left Rathulf to it, busying himself with making Vidar comfortable on the deck, then dousing the fire.

'Land ho!' Rathulf shouted as soon as his vision adjusted to the darkness. 'Turning to port!'

He wasn't sure what it was, but he could see a dark, looming bulk ahead of them, with a pale line of breaking waves at its base. Oddly, either side of it was clear, so it must be a narrow promontory sticking straight out from the landmass.

'Well spotted, Rathulf!' Ottar praised, gripping one of the halyard ropes as they came around.

Rathulf set the storm rope on a heading that took them away to open water, then helped Hakon and Hjalmar reef the sail to slow them down. 'I hope there aren't any rocks out here,' he said uneasily.

'I'll keep watch upfront. Bring us back alongside but keep the shore well abeam so we can see if there's someplace to land. I confess I was not expecting us to make such good progress, but obviously I have no idea about anything anymore.' He sounded more amused than worried, but relief was the principal emotion behind Ottar's words. Rathulf knew they were in bad shape now, and he had already noticed that the *Storm Beater* was becoming more sluggish, despite the quickening breeze. He suspected the hold was filling with water, but no one was available to bail, so the sooner they found a beaching place, the better. He prayed that wherever they pulled ashore was free of cursed Britons.

They cruised southwards along the coastline, but all they saw was a continuous line of hulking cliffs, all at the same height with nothing rising behind them. Rathulf spotted some rocky pinnacles thrusting out of the water to their right, so he steered further away from the cliffs, worried there may be more of them further afield.

'Ahead, does that look like a beach?' Ottar called, pointing in front of them. 'There, inside the lee of that headland.'

Rathulf leaned out over the side to get a better look past the bulk of the sail. It would be low tide or thereabouts, judging from their previous days' sailing, and he prepared for a bumpy ride in. They had to go in under sail, for there was no longer a crew to row. Rathulf came in at an angle then steered for the middle of the beach, grimacing as he readied himself for the crunching and splintering of the hull on unseen rocks in their path. But there was nothing in their way, and they rode up a little too fast onto the gravelly beach, coming to a stop with a shuddering lurch. The boat slowly tipped sideways, gently settling on her port side. The list was not overly steep, so all in all, it was an excellent landing under the circumstances.

Rathulf couldn't help himself, and he let out a whoop of relief, closely followed by Ottar, who came and slapped him on the back, then immediately apologised for disturbing Rathulf's wounds. 'Fine work Rathulf. Right, let's drop the sail and tie her up, as the tide will be rising soon, and we don't want her to float away. We'll leave the mast up and the sail furled in case we have to get away fast. I'm afraid you and I will have to do all the hard work.'

'I can help,' Gunnar offered, but Ottar gave him a curt instruction to stay put.

The boat was stuck fast in the coarse sand, which did not seem to perturb Ottar, although he did throw Rathulf a wink and said, 'on second thoughts, let's hope we don't need to make a swift exit.' He lifted the heavy iron anchor from the prow and handed it down to Rathulf. They carried it together up the beach, trailing the sturdy landing rope behind them. A jumble of rocks protruded from the beach to their left, and they managed to wedge the anchor in tight between two of them. 'Now, we aren't going anywhere,' Ottar said. 'All the same, I think it best we camp aboard until we know where we are.'

'I'll take a look,' Rathulf offered. The moon was out and only occasionally hidden by the scudding clouds.

'What? Now?'

'I think I can see a way up to the top,' Rathulf said, peering up at the cliff above them.

Ottar stared at him. 'Don't be a fool, Rathulf. How will you see what you're doing? We can wait until morning.'

'No,' Rathulf replied, shaking his head. 'I need to know we're safe.' He could see how to get up; he was sure of it.

'Well, it would be helpful to know where we are, but for Odin's sake, be careful,' Ottar warned, frowning up at the steep slope behind the beach. 'You're short on sleep, and that will make you clumsy. Stay nearby. The last thing we need is another hoard of Dumnonians coming after our blood or for you to fall and break your neck. As Gunnar said, we haven't come all this way to have you fall to your death.'

Rathulf took his time, aware that the poor light made it difficult to spot danger on the treacherous climb to the summit. He tested every foot- and hand-hold. He didn't have to scale the sheer cliff, for there was a narrow, grassy wedge that rose along the face of the rock. He made it to the top without incident, and he peered over the crest, half expecting to see a British face appear in front of him. Instead, he saw a grassy hill rising gently away from him, then falling steeply away to his left. There was no sign of habitation at all. He offered a little prayer of thanks to his patron God, Thor, and then he carefully made his way up the hill and over to where it fell away. He laughed with relief because his hunch had been correct. They had landed on an island! He peered through the gloom along the spine of the flat-topped isle and again could find no evidence of habitation; at least nothing recent. He came upon a ruined circular stone building that looked quite old and then another further afield, beside a tumbled stone wall marking what had once been some kind of enclosure. He reached a high point and turned all the way around. Looking out to sea in every direction, he could see nothing but inky black water.

He offered some more words of thanks to the Gods, and then he made his way back to the cliff above the beach. It was much harder to get down, and his spine tingled as he started the steep descent. The tide had risen quite markedly while he had been topside, and the ship floated at the edge of the beach, held in place by the anchor. Seeing the *Storm Beater* led to a lapse in concentration, and he slipped and lost his footing. He grabbed the tussocky grass and scrabbled to find his feet, letting out a yelp of alarm.

'Rathulf!' came a startled call from below.

'I'm alright,' he called back, his left foot finding purchase. He took a long breath, heaved himself up, and tried a different route, giving full attention to his task. He finally set foot on the stones that lined the top of the beach, but he felt light-headed, and he found that his hands were shaking. *I'd best stop testing Gefion's patience*, he thought, wondering how long he could trust the goddess of luck to look out for him.

He received a scolding from Ottar for his efforts. The shipwright laid out the gangplank, which didn't quite make it to dry ground, so Rathulf had to make a running jump to keep his feet dry. Back on deck, Ottar shook his head and growled, 'you had me worried sick. You've been away most of the night! I was just getting ready to come after you. It'll be dawn soon.'

That surprised Rathulf, and he looked to the east, and, sure enough, the sky was beginning to lighten. He turned back to Ottar. 'We're safe. We've landed on an island, and there aren't any people here as far as I can see. I couldn't smell any hearthfire smoke.'

'The nine daughters be praised,' Ottar said. 'Let us pray to our Gods that you are right and that we have this refuge all to ourselves. I think you have earned yourself some sleep.' He paused, then frowned at his charge with an unusual intensity. 'I know that you believe yourself unsuited to your destiny, Rathulf, but today you have again shown the spirit and grit required if you are to succeed in your quest, and these things cannot be taught. You will leave the ill-fated curse of Fenrir behind you here, I am sure of it.'

Rathulf slept long into the morning, despite the sun being out and the deck awning flapping noisily in the breeze above him. He woke to find Vidar lying beside him in a fitful sleep. The injured seaman's face was pale and twisted in discomfort. Rathulf sat up and looked about. He was aware of a pain in his back where the arrows had nipped him, but his left arm hurt most, his healing not helped by his nighttime climb up the cliff. Ottar, Hakon and Torsten sat on the beach talking in quiet voices, and a little further away, he saw Gunnar fishing off the rocks. Eirik's son looked better as he frowned into the surging water at his feet. He still wore the bandage that Rathulf had tied on his head after Ottar's cauterising, and Rathulf could see a dark patch of blood on top. Rathulf jumped down onto the beach, startling the two men, who had been lost in their conversation.

''Morning Ra,' Ottar said. 'Sól shines his face upon us again today. How are you feeling?'

'Hungry,' Rathulf said. He looked over at Gunnar. 'Has he caught anything?'

'He has,' Ottar said, 'but we can't decide whether it is safe to light a fire.'

'Then I'll go back up and take a proper look,' Rathulf said. 'I'll be quicker this time,' he added, 'because it's daylight, and I need breakfast.'

Ottar looked down at Rathulf's forearm. 'Let me check that first.' The sailor unfurled the bandage and nodded with satisfaction. I'll recheck it when you're back down.' He rubbed a little honey in the wound and bound the dressing tight. 'Don't take too long up there. I want to know if we can light a fire.'

Rathulf went back aboard the *Storm Beater* to retrieve his dagger and sword, having no desire to be caught alone and unarmed. Then he started back up the cliff, following the same route he had climbed last night.

'Hey Thorvaldarsson, wait for me!' Gunnar shouted.

Rathulf stopped and waited while Gunnar took all his fishing paraphernalia back to Ottar. From above, Rathulf could see the silvery sheen of the catch in Gunnar's pail. His stomach growled at the thought of fresh-cooked fish.

Gunnar armed himself with his sword and bow, then came scrambling up after Rathulf.

'Are you alright?' Rathulf asked, nodding at the other youth's head.

Gunnar said nothing to Rathulf as he passed, continuing up to the top. The two of them made quick work of the climb, which was straightforward in the daytime. When Rathulf crested, he saw to his relief and satisfaction that the grassy plateau was as clear of people as he had reported last night. There were, however, the ruins of the buildings, and the two youths explored the round stone bases of the huts, wondering who had inhabited them and where they had gone.

'Let's go to the top of this rise and see if we can get a better view,' Rathulf said and set off towards the high point in front of them, a small part of him now worried that the island might, in fact, be inhabited after all. Gunnar trailed behind him, taking more time to look around. It was easy going in the warm sunshine, and they soon reached the top of the low hill, which gave them an excellent view in all directions. The island was much longer than it was wide, covered in low heath and tussocky grass and dropping precipitously on all sides to the sea. From this vantage point, they saw land in the far distance to the south and east. *Could that be Dumnonia?* Rathulf wondered, feeling an odd tingling in his spine at that thought.

'I fucking hope that's Dornmoonia,' came Gunnar's voice, thinking the same but getting the name wrong.

Rathulf turned to the raven-haired youth, who stood squinting out to sea. He looked ridiculous with his grimy bandage tied around his head and under his chin, reminding Rathulf of the old crone who did Helga's washing.

'I'm sorry about your head,' he said on impulse. 'If it's any consolation, I'm glad you came.'

'I'm fine,' Gunnar said curtly, 'and I wish I hadn't.'

Rathulf wasn't sure how to respond to that, so he remained silent. As Rathulf had feared, Gunnar was angry that Rathulf had witnessed his cowardice.

As if reading his mind, Gunnar turned to him and said, 'I suppose you think it's funny. Gunnar, brave son of Eirik the Black, the most feared Viking in all Sognefjord, gets a scratch and faints at the sight of his own blood. Then he squeals like a girl when he is treated for his wound.'

'No, I don't,' Rathulf replied, genuine in his denial. 'It's a bad wound, and if the arrow had been any better aimed, you'd be dead.'

Gunnar's scowl deepened. 'How long were you hugging me

like that, getting a hard-on with me in your lap, huh? Well, let's get one thing straight: I'm *not* Alrik, so don't even think about me becoming your new rassragr boyfriend. That's not why I came, trust me.'

'So why *are* you here?' Rathulf asked, annoyed that Gunnar still wouldn't accept that Alrik and Rathulf had been friends and no more.

Gunnar's eyes narrowed into a cold glare. 'It's not because I fancy you or want to be your friend, kuksuger. It's because I know that your dirty little ergi boyfriend will be writhing with envy knowing that it's me going to Dumnonia with you and not him.' His mouth twisted into a sneer. 'It was all he talked about. It made us sick the way he fawned over you so that he could be the one to share in your glorious return. And we all know what he expected in return for his unfailing loyalty.' He shook his head with disgust, then he turned and stomped off, leaving Rathulf staring after him, stunned.

Rathulf's immediate desire was to run up to the spiteful youth and punch him, but he stayed where he was, trying to control his breathing as he struggled to hold in a scream of raw fury. *He is angry because he fell short in front of us all*, Rathulf reminded himself. *Of course he's going to take it out on me.* He sighed. *Why did I let him come when I knew it would be like this?*

Once he had calmed down, he followed Gunnar northwards along the highest part of the plateau, keeping a sensible distance between them, all the while wondering if there could ever be anything he might do to lessen the other's hatred of him.

Gunnar was waiting for him on the next rise. He frowned at Rathulf and said, 'what's the matter with you?'

'What's the matter...? I want to know why you're so horrible to me. What have I ever done to make you hate me so much? You've never liked me.'

'Do you really want me to answer that?' Gunnar asked. He pointed northward. 'There's the end of the island. You were right, for once. There's no one here. But there are masses of seabirds, so I'm gonna catch us some.'

It occurred to Rathulf that they already had plenty of food in the form of a pailful of fresh-caught fish, but he said nothing and followed Gunnar to the very tip of the island.

'Look, seals!' Gunnar said quietly, crouching down and nodding at the rocks below them.

This end of the island teemed with wildlife; hundreds of sea birds wheeled around them, screeching and keening, and a sizeable herd of seals lay sunning themselves on the rocks. Further around the point was a large colony of puffins, and scattered among them were the nests of gulls and other birds in the cliffs above the waterline.

'If it weren't for the lack of safe harbour and shelter, this would be a good raiding base,' Gunnar observed.

'Answer my question,' Rathulf said, unwilling to allow Gunnar to ignore him. 'What have you got against me?'

'You really want to do this?' Gunnar said. 'Alright then. For a start, I'm better than you at *everything*,' he snarled, jabbing Rathulf in the chest with his finger, his pimpled face uncomfortably close. 'I'm better with the bow, the sword, swimming, wrestling, hunting. Everything! And I know how to steer a ship just as well as you.'

'So?' Rathulf asked, taking a step backwards.

'So how come *you're* the one who steered us out of danger, even though you were shot three times while I was cowering in a corner, shitting myself? You're the kuksuger. You're supposed to be pathetic and unmanly, but you're not. You rode your fucking Jötunn horse the wrong way over Odin's Breach, for fuck's sake! No one's ever done that! No one! Ever! It's all people talk about now. Valiant Rathulf this, fearless Rathulf that. Everyone loves you, including my fucking father. You're not even a proper Viking! It makes me sick.'

Rathulf blinked at Gunnar, lost for words. *Are you still jealous of me? Is it really that simple?*

'The main reason I came with you was to make sure you never come back. I need you out of my way, Thorvaldarsson.'

'What?'

'Shall I cut you to ribbons and push you over the cliff for the seals to feast on you? Your body will be gone by the time the others come to find you. I'm sure I'll be able to cry some tears for you; how you slipped and fell and got attacked by the bull. It won't be a heroic death, of course. You'll lie with a broken leg, screaming in terror and pain as the bull comes for you. Who knows what I'll say? Who cares? You'll be dead, and that's all that matters.'

Rathulf punched Gunnar in the face for that, swearing roundly at him as he landed his blow. Gunnar staggered backwards but managed to dodge Rathulf's second punch, then he launched himself at his rival, swinging both fists furiously. Rathulf had missed Gunnar's nose, so the boy could come in hard, and he quickly proved his earlier assertion that he was the better fighter. Gunnar held nothing back, and Rathulf suddenly found himself on the defensive, holding up his arms to protect his face as Gunnar pummelled him with powerful blows from both fists. Gunnar took advantage of Rathulf's capitulation and aimed two heavy punches into the middle of his opponent's chest and solar plexus. Rathulf cried out as his ribs exploded in pain, and he stumbled backwards to get away from Gunnar. He'd not been aware that Gunnar was backing him toward the edge, and suddenly his left foot found air, and he let out a yelp of fright as he lost his footing and toppled backwards.

Gunnar grabbed Rathulf by his injured arm just in time to prevent his enemy from falling. Their eyes locked together, Gunnar holding Rathulf's life in his hands as he teetered on the cliff's edge. Rathulf's chest burned as he struggled to breathe.

'Feel familiar?' the raven-haired youth growled, his face twisted into a cruel sneer. 'Who will let go first? You, or me?'

For a moment, Rathulf feared that Gunnar would do just that.

'I told you I was better than you,' Gunnar said, his voice cold, unwavering. 'Remember that when you are king.' His mouth twisted into a cruel smile. 'I will come back here one day with a warhost so large you'll wet yourself. I will sweep through your land and raze every steading, rape all your men, women and children, then take every able-bodied person still alive into slavery, so you'll be left with *nothing*. And then people will speak of me in their firehalls: Gunnar Konungsefni of Lustrafjorden, vanquisher of kings.' He hauled Rathulf back to safety and stood in front of him. 'Go back and bleat to Ottar,' he said. 'I'm not afraid of you. I'm not afraid of him. I'm not afraid of anyone.' Then he punched Rathulf hard in the kidneys, followed up with another to his stomach, then turned away and walked towards the island's tip.

Rathulf sank to his knees, gasping for breath as tears of pain and fury welled in his eyes. He desperately wanted to rip out his sword and shove it into the ugly dritt's stomach, but he knew it would be he who would end up gutted like a fish and left as fodder for the seals because Gunnar was right: he was a far better fighter than Rathulf would ever be, as he'd so brutally demonstrated. *How could I have been so stupid to think that maybe you'd changed?* he thought, primarily angry at himself for his naivety. *And you've only gotten worse, thanks to your humiliation.* He watched Gunnar drop over the cliff edge at the other end of the point. *Well, it doesn't change the fact you're a coward*, he thought, finding solace in that small truth.

He was still angry when he arrived at the little cove where the *Storm Beater* lay at anchor. While he had been away, Ottar had laid a fire and gutted the fish in anticipation of good news.

'What's happened to you, and where's Gunnar?' The shipmaster asked, alarmed. He looked up at the cliff, clearly worried that Rathulf had done something he might regret.

'Who cares,' Rathulf muttered, walking to the water barrel

to take a drink. He'd only realised how thirsty he was now that he was back at the beach. 'He's still alive, if that's what you're worried about.'

'What passed between you two?' Ottar asked.

'What do you think?' Rathulf snapped, wincing as his bruised face and ribs objected to his shouting. 'The drittsekk attacked me.'

'Is there ever going to be a day when you two don't pick a fight with one another?' Ottar asked impatiently. 'You both need to grow up.'

'I'm not the one being a bacraut,' Rathulf said, 'and he's the one who pissed himself at the first sign of danger. I'm just trying to be nice to him, but he can't help himself. It's little wonder he has no friends.'

'Is he truly still alive?' Torsten piped up, 'I thought you might've finally cracked and run him through.' He seemed hopeful that was the case.

'I wish,' Rathulf said, scowling at the injured sailor. 'He's hunting birds.'

'So,' Ottar said, attempting to calm tempers and change the subject. 'I take it we can light the fire?'

Rathulf nodded. 'There's no one here. Other than more birds than you can count and a herd of seals at the far end. And some ruined old buildings.'

Ottar's eyes lit up. 'Then this would be a good place to camp on our journeys between Dumnonia and home. What kinds of birds?'

'All sorts. Lots of puffins. Gannets. Gulls. But we didn't find much water. Although,' he added, 'there was a small tarn about halfway along the island. I suppose you could camp there, but there's no shelter at all. It's just flat and open from end to end.'

'Aye, and this little bay would be no haven with a nor'easter blowing. Still, it suits our purposes nicely.'

'How is Vidar?' Rathulf asked, looking over to the *Storm*

Beater, keen to deflect the conversation away from his altercation with Gunnar.

'Bad,' Ottar said. 'We've not the skills or salves to help him.' He sighed when he saw the young man flinch at the news. 'He knew what he was getting into, Ra. Of course, no man wishes to die on an expedition, but he played his part in getting us away from those erlendar. He would rather this death than fade away in old age by the hearthfire.' He cocked his head and smiled in sympathy at his young charge. 'You must not take all these hurts and responsibilities upon yourself, Rathulf. As a jarl, you must be tougher-skinned. It will be even harder as king.'

'What if I don't want to be a king?' Rathulf said, anger rising again. 'I didn't ask for any of this. I was happy back in Aurlandsfjorden before Thorvald dug up the trunk.'

'Were you? Your father often spoke of your frustration at being cooped up in that little farmstead. You couldn't wait to come of age and join a raiding party.'

'Which would have been perfect! All I've ever wanted is to be a Viking, or better still, an explorer like you and Sigvald. I want to see Byzantium and the great cities and deserts of Myran's homeland. I don't care about Dumnonia. I can't even speak their language! And he's *not* my father.'

'Be careful what you say, Rathulf, and of course Thorvald is your father. He adopted and raised you as his son to become the fine young man you are today so that you can fulfil your destiny.'

'I just told you that I don't want this destiny,' Rathulf said, 'and I hate the Gods for forcing me on this path.'

'Mind your words!' Ottar said again angrily, making a warding sign. 'We are not yet in Dumnonia. Once you've landed, you can abuse the Gods all you like.'

'Well, it's over there,' Rathulf said, pointing to the southeast, 'and I'd like to go as soon as possible. Don't bother taking me back to where you found me. I'll work it out for myself.' He walked away from the shipwright and climbed the small promontory at the beach's southern end, seeking time and space alone. He stared eastwards to the land of his birth, wishing he had not behaved so ungraciously to Ottar, who, of all people, least deserved it. He also knew he had no choice in this quest, which annoyed him, but he was most frightened about what might become of him. It was old ground that he had trudged countless times already; a pointless waste of time because there were no winners, and the outcome was always the same. But it didn't make it any easier to accept.

He was soon drawn back to the campfire by the fabulous smell of grilling fish. Ottar said nothing to him, silently offering the first plate to Rathulf. Rathulf muttered his thanks, sat down on his stool by the fire, and ate hungrily, not even bothering to pick out the smaller bones.

'Look out!'

Rathulf started at Ottar's cry, and he looked up just in time to see a seal tumbling down the cliff straight at him. Rathulf sprang out of the way as the animal bounced on the rocks above and landed with a heavy thud beside him. He shouted an expletive up at Gunnar, who stood at the top of the cliff, grinning down at him. 'Sorry,' the youth called in an insincere voice.

'Jötnahreðr,' Rathulf muttered, and he walked to the other side of the fire and helped himself to another fillet of fish.

Gunnar clambered down the slope to the beach and stood over his prize; the triumphant hunter returned. 'I've brought us some *proper* dinner,' he proclaimed.

'Well done,' Hakon said, his eyes feasting on the carcass.

'Where did you find it?' Torsten asked.

'At the other end of the island. I had to drag it all the way here by myself since cry-baby Rathulf left me to do it on my own.'

'Go fuck yourself,' Rathulf said.

'Gunnar, what happened up there?'

Eirik's son looked at Rathulf, his expression smug, a wicked smile playing in the corners of his mouth. 'The sansorthinn wanted to know if I'd be his new boyfriend,' Gunnar lied. 'I said no.'

Ottar looked at Rathulf, his eyebrows raised in disbelief.

Rathulf shrugged, not even bothering to rise to Gunnar's bait. 'I want you to take me to Dumnonia as soon as the tide allows,' he said, 'and he can stay here.'

'Nuh-uh,' Gunnar said. 'I'm coming too. Ottar hasn't the manpower to make it back without me.'

He was right, of course, and so early the following morning, under a favourable breeze, Ottar, Gunnar, Rathulf and Hakon set sail due east from their island sanctuary into the rising sun towards what Rathulf hoped was his birthland.

They made landfall shortly before midday on a broad, sweeping beach that Gunnar spitefully noted would be a perfect landing place for a large Viking warhost or raiding party.

'We won't dally Rathulf, lest more of your fellow countrymen take exception to our arrival,' Ottar said, not understanding the meaning behind Gunnar's observation. He helped Rathulf down the gangplank with his heavy sea chest. They dumped it on the sand, and Ottar shook his head at its weight. 'You're going to struggle with that trunk on your own.' He looked down at Rathulf's freshly bandaged arm and hand. 'And those wounds will never heal with you hoisting that box around.' Ottar had sewn up the deep cut in his forearm again earlier that morning, but his palm had, at least, not needed further mending.

'I'll find a horse,' Rathulf said. 'I've enough money to buy a whole herd of them.'

'Even so, it's too heavy. Why don't you leave your kist with me and just take your father's trunk?'

Rathulf knew that Ottar was right. He wouldn't be able to carry the heavy box far on his own. He let out a sigh. 'No, I'll keep my sea chest because it has handles and a lock. You look after my father's one. It's the stuff inside it that matters. He pulled out the Dumnonian trunk and transferred the contents into the sea chest, then gave the Dumnonian box to Ottar.

Ottar looked up at the shore beyond the beach, then frowned. 'This is a long way from where we found you. The estuary is on the other side of Dumnonia. I don't know how far south it is from here, and I think it is maybe more east than west.' He frowned. 'I'd rather take you there.'

'No. It will take us days to get all the way around, and who knows what resistance we'll meet along the way. Vidar is in bad fettle, and I can't be the cause of any more hardship or death. You need to get back home while you have a chance. It may be too late already.' *And I couldn't bear to spend another day stuck on a boat with that jerk.*

'But what will you do? Where will you go?'

Again the enormity of what he was doing struck Rathulf like a charging bullock, and he looked over Ottar's shoulder at the *Storm Beater*, wondering what in Odin's good name he was doing. He drew in a breath to steel himself. 'I'll put on my wolven tunic, the sword and ring, and tell them my name. Someone will recognise them, if not me. Hopefully, they won't skewer or shoot me on sight.'

Ottar held Rathulf's gaze, and the seasoned warrior saw the doubt and fear in Rathulf's face. 'I will go back to the island to repair the ship. By my reckoning, Mani will be showing us his full face in five days. I will return to this beach on the tide's turning the following day.' He raised his hand when Rathulf began to object. 'It's in the Gods' hands whether Vidar lives or dies, and there is plenty of food and enough water to sustain us. Hopefully, it will give you enough time to take your first measure of the place. We can then decide whether you will stay here or return to Sognefjorden with us. Who knows, perhaps you will find your kin, and they can help Vidar. We could even stay with you over the winter, and you would at least have someone from your northern home to keep you company?'

Rathulf glanced back at the *Storm Beater* at Gunnar, who sat on the shield rail, watching them with a sour expression on his face. Gunnar spread his hands in question. 'Are you going or what?' he said.

Ottar sighed. 'I don't know what passed between you and Gunnar yesterday, but you mustn't let him spoil this day. He is jealous of you, pure and simple. You are everything he wants to be and more, but he will never come close to you, Rathulf. You are one of a kind and, more importantly, a prince. Don't ever forget that. Now, help me push the ship back so we can cast off.' He called to Gunnar and Hakon to take up an oar each, and as they backpedalled, Rathulf and Ottar heaved the prow off the sand. As soon as the *Storm Beater* was free, Ottar deftly vaulted over the shield rail and took his place at the tiller. Hakon and Gunnar worked together to turn the boat around to point back out to sea. It would be a slower return trip as they'd be sailing across the wind, and Rathulf watched Ottar's diminished crew stow the oars and haul up the sail.

'Remember to be here on the day after the full moon,' Ottar said. 'Whether it is good tidings or bad, you must come, and if the outlook is poor, you can sail back to Thorvaldsby with us, knowing that you can return next summer to try again. But if we miss each other for some reason, this is where we will be, come next Lithasblot. I'm sure everyone will join me – either to take you back home or to join you in your triumph. Remember this place; it is the bay that is due east of our puffin island.' He raised his hand in salute. 'May Thor bring good luck and good cheer, and may your sword and wits stay sharp.' He turned back to the prow, barking orders at Gunnar and Hakon to bring the sail into trim.

Rathulf watched them sail away, then he bent down and hauled the heavy trunk onto his shoulder, wincing in pain as the action inevitably troubled the arrow wound in his arm. *I can do this*, he told himself, taking his first step towards dry land. *I am home.*

14

Run, you idiot!

Escanceaster, Dumnonia

Now, as Rathulf trudged up the narrow path that led out of the tiny Dumnonian village with its broom-wielding peasants, he wondered whether he shouldn't just accept defeat and go back to await Ottar's return. The journey back to Sognefjorden would be unbearable, of course, especially with Gunnar there to mock him for his spinelessness. That alone spurred him to continue up the track and away from the coast.

It was not long before he came upon a group of ill-clothed men standing in conference further up the track. They held various farming implements – hoes, spades and forks – but before Rathulf could avoid them, one of the men spotted him and immediately caught the others' attention. They all turned and stared at Rathulf, their faces showing surprise and alarm. Rathulf tensed. He had seen the same narrowed eyes and dark frowns earlier in the old woman and her husband. His hand automatically fell towards the hilt of his sword, and with that action, the men scattered into the fields like frightened sheep. However, one of them stood his ground, though his knuckles showed white where he gripped the handle of his hoe. Rathulf glanced to his right in time to catch a row of faces ducking below the top of the low stone wall that ran beside the road.

Rathulf lifted his hand in greeting to the man with the hoe. Precisely what good it would do him, he was unsure, but at least he might garner a name, a destination, a purpose. 'I mean no harm,' he said in Norse. 'I am Caelin, jarl of Dumnonia. Can you tell me the way to Kair Uisk? Or Sankus Jermus?'

The man's frown changed to astonishment, then he opened his mouth and spoke a torrent of gibberish. Rathulf tried again, but the response was the same: another stream of words that made no sense whatsoever. The peasant farmer's brow knitted in confusion.

This is hopeless, Rathulf thought, realising the futility of this exchange. *Why did I think he would understand me?* Angry with himself, he retrieved his trunk and hoisted it onto his shoulder. The man with the hoe stood aside to let Rathulf pass, but as Rathulf went by, the man said something. 'I don't understand,' Rathulf replied helplessly, and the man just stared after him, unable to hide that he thought Rathulf mad.

Rathulf continued along the road, gritting his teeth as he forced back his frustration. *What am I doing wrong?* he wondered. *Apart from the obvious fact that I can't communicate with them, what am I doing that so offends these people?* He searched his mind for an answer, but he could think of nothing he had said or done that could be considered insulting. Perhaps there was a custom of greeting here that he had missed. But how did that explain the farmers' apparent fear of him?

After that, Rathulf made a point of moving off the road whenever he chanced upon other travellers. By midday, he had walked many miles, resisting his desire to stay near the coast and instead choosing paths that led him further inland. The day was uncommonly warm – Ottar had been right about summer lasting longer down here, no doubt because Dumnonia was closer to the fires of Muspelheim. Rathulf swapped the sea chest to his other shoulder for what seemed the hundredth time, roundly cursing its weight and awkwardness. One part of him wished he had left it hidden somewhere by the shore, but he knew the prospect of ever finding it again would have been remote. He paused and looked about him, feeling hungry, thirsty and tired.

Lush pasture rolled away in every direction, and here and

there, footpaths and hedges slashed the fields; the neat lines interrupted by the occasional clump of thatch-roofed huts marking a farmstead. Dense green forest intruded in swathes, particularly along the waterways. Here, the trees were all broad-leaved and tall with luxurious crowns; he could not see a firtree of any kind anywhere. There was the occasional birch, but these too were rare. The land stretched away to the east as far as the eye could see, and in the far distance, a line of hills shimmered in the heat haze. There was not a mountain or ice cap anywhere. Rathulf laughed ruefully to himself. *Ice wouldn't last a day here. How different it is!*

Even the breeze carried with it all the strangeness of this foreign place. In Norvegr, the wind was sharp-edged and pure, born of glaciers and fjords and snow-fringed pine trees, but here the air pressed warm and heavy on his chest, thickly laden with myriad alien scents. How Rathulf craved the cold fjords of home! He felt exposed and vulnerable in the face of all this endless open space, and he yearned for the encircling walls of his own little valley.

Memories of Alrik came riding on the wings of his thoughts of home, and Rathulf again found himself wishing that he could somehow step back in time to prevent Alrik from making the Leap. The heart-wrenching image of his friend's apologetic shake of his head just before he let go of Rathulf's hand to fall to his death flashed into his mind; a memory that would haunt Rathulf for the rest of his life.

The young Viking let out a strangled cry and screwed his eyes shut, desperate to exorcise the distressing images from his mind. *Why did you have to die?* he thought wretchedly. *You should be here. You should all be here: Alrik, Leif, Ingrith, father, Sigvald and me, exploring my homeland together. I should be riding Tariq, and Myran would be in the party too. Instead, Alrik is dead, and I'm alone because I was too weak to bear a moment's pain.*

Rathulf spat out a stream of profanities, hating the Gods,

hating Alrik, but most of all hating himself for his inadequacy. *Why couldn't I have just held him?* he demanded angrily of himself. Rathulf knew that Alrik would have saved him if their places had been reversed. His friend would never have allowed so small a thing as a cut shoulder to overcome him at such a critical time.

Rathulf shook his head slowly, grief threatening to consume him entirely. *I can't afford to think this way*, he told himself. *I can't change what happened. I must look forward. I have a new world to explore, a new life to live—a brother to find.* But Myran's words of solace rang hollow in his mind now, for what good was an exciting new world to him when it held nothing but emptiness and sorrow? And how could he be sure his brother was alive? He'd only ever seen him in dreams. Not for the first time, Rathulf wished he had met his death at the bottom of the ravine beside his friend. Unconsciously he shifted the trunk to his other shoulder and trudged on, unsure where he was going or why.

Later in the day, he heard the gentle murmur of running water ahead. The road turned and dipped into a wooded vale, and there, under the dappled shade of an alder grove, ran a little brook, its clear waters sparkling in the sunlight. Exhausted, Rathulf dumped the trunk and sank gratefully onto the grassy bank, cupping his hands and drinking thirstily. Then he tugged off his shoes, settled against a tree and closed his eyes, easing his aching feet into the healing waters. The brook's friendly banter soothed Rathulf's frayed nerves, and he soon drifted into sleep.

His moment of peace was soon shattered, however. Voices – foreign voices – intruded into Rathulf's dream, and he woke with a start to find a man dressed in rough-woven trousers and a plain shirt standing over him. Rathulf instinctively reached for his sword, but the man held up his hand and shook his head, speaking to him urgently. Behind him stood a pony laden with bales of what looked like seaweed. A runny-nosed boy looked on, holding the pony's bridle loosely in one hand. The man spoke in a continuous stream at Rathulf, sounding most urgent, most concerned. Some words sounded vaguely familiar, but the pedlar spoke too quickly for Rathulf to catch their whole meaning. Nevertheless, it was clear that he wanted Rathulf to get up and leave. Rathulf pulled on his shoes and angrily scooped up his kist, annoyed that no one in this wretched land would leave him be. He turned to continue along the road, but the man pulled at Rathulf's sleeve and shook his head vigorously. *What now?* Rathulf thought.

'I want to find Kair Uisk,' Rathulf said. 'Or Sankus Jermus. Is this the way?'

The man shook his head and pointed in a different direction, back the way Rathulf had come. He still spoke in an unbroken diatribe, seemingly unaware that Rathulf understood nothing of it. Rathulf pulled his arm away, but the man grabbed him again, his face showing confusion and anger. He jabbed his finger at Rathulf's chest, shook his head, and spoke more gibberish.

All at once, the frustration and despair that had been simmering just below the surface rushed to the fore. The young Viking wrenched his arm free, and he shoved the man hard, pushing him back towards the cart. Rathulf ripped out his sword and thrust it toward the hawker, succumbing to a base desire to inflict pain upon someone to relieve his own hurt.

'Can't you see I don't understand?' Rathulf shouted in Norse. 'I don't understand any of it!'

The seaweed hawker stumbled into his cart and lifted a hand to defend himself, cowering in the face of Rathulf's fury. His boy stood silently beside the pony, watching Rathulf without rancour or fear. Rathulf stared at him for a moment, and then he turned back to the man, his anger all at once diffused by the witless lad's unguarded expression. Rathulf shoved his sword back in its scabbard, scooped up the heavy trunk, and marched up the hill to get away from the man and his boy as quickly as possible. The hawker called after him urgently, but Rathulf resisted the temptation to look behind him. He felt both ashamed and frightened, for the encounter had proven to Rathulf that very little lay now between him and a madness borne from grief. *I must stay in control*, he warned himself. *My sanity is all I have left. Lose that, and I may as well throw myself off a cliff.*

He continued inland, but back up on the open ground, the sun shone fiercely, and the air held a thick, humid closeness that forewarned an evening storm. Rathulf sweltered under his heavy tunic, and the suffocating heat was eased only slightly by the light breeze that blew at his back. He paused by another beck and helped himself to a drink, then, before setting off again, he peeled off his wolven tunic. He paused, looking down at the golden wolves, and wondered at the man's earlier reaction. *Is it the wolves he was objecting to? And the others before him? Could it be that they were not welcome here? Is that what they were trying to tell me?* He stowed it in his trunk and lifted the heavy burden, determined that he would find himself a horse and some saddlebags so that he could throw this damn box away. *I am such a daufi. Why did I think this would be a smart way to carry my things?*

Presently the path he followed met up with a larger and more travelled one, and Rathulf pressed further southeastwards. As the afternoon wore on, the countryside became increasingly wooded, with swathes of dark forest sweeping over the tops of the hills between the hedged fields. Far in the distance, Rathulf saw the arched back of a vast, barren moor rising high above the surrounding woods and farmland. Its cover of gorse and heather shone like burnished copper above its yellow-green skirt of fields, and behind it towered the white mass of a storm-head. Heavily laden wains and oxcarts rumbled past him in either direction, but the greater flow of traffic travelled Rathulf's way. He was astounded at both the size of the road and the sheer number of people travelling along it. He had never seen so many people – other than the summer Althing assembly and markets perhaps – but there definitely weren't any thoroughfares like this in Sognefjorden. A narrow trackway might zig-zag its way up the valley wall and across the uplands, but the challenging terrain meant that the vast majority of travel was by boat on the fjords between the little farms that clung to the odd bits of arable land squeezed in amongst the towering cliffs.

Here, the sky and land were as broad as the ocean itself, farmed land stretched as far as the eye could see, and every bit of it was filled with livestock, thatch-roofed houses and people. At first, he tried to avoid the other travellers, but the volume of traffic grew so great that Rathulf eventually had little choice but to join the throng. To his surprise and relief, he was left alone for the most part, and he began to wonder at the concerns the seaweed hawker had held for his welfare. *So if it was my tunic,* he thought, *then what does that mean for me and my family?* He finally risked asking people if this was the way to Kair Uisk, and they nodded, pointing in the direction he was going, although some did frown at him and said something like eskankesta. *Maybe I'm saying it wrong*, he thought.

Late in the afternoon, at a junction with a still larger road, Rathulf came across a small roadside stall selling food. He pointed hungrily to a pile of large barley cakes and held up five fingers. The stall-keeper responded with what must have been the price, but Rathulf had no idea how much they were worth, so he dug into his money pouch and handed the woman the smallest piece of silver he could find. He had clearly over-estimated their value, for the stall-keeper grinned her toothless grin and gave Rathulf two extra cakes and a chunk of honeycomb to sweeten their taste. Rathulf offered his thanks, then settled down on his chest by the side of the road and devoured the cakes hungrily, watching the passers-by. No one gave him a second glance; indeed, their disinterest in him was as surprising as his previous encounters.

It must be the wolves, he thought again. *And I thought they were just offended because I couldn't communicate with them! What does it mean, I wonder? Could Cnut be right?* It didn't bear thinking about, but the prospect that he and his kin had been outlawed – or worse – did seem to be growing more likely.

He was distracted by the sounds of an argument off to his right, and he turned in time to see a small wooden bowl skitter out onto the road. It rolled on its rim around the legs of a passing ox and came to a stop in front of Rathulf. A man appeared before him and bent down to retrieve it with an apologetic smile.

He was quite old and dressed in the simplest of garments, little more than a brown hessian sack, which was of inferior make to Rathulf's eye, being fashioned in a very coarse weave. The sack was tied loosely around the man's waist by an equally plain belt of twined rope, and his over-large sleeves flapped about like a gosling's wings. His only adornment was a large ivory object embellished with silver in the shape of an uneven cross hanging around his neck, which Rathulf presumed to be a poorly-wrought rendition of Thor's hammer. A hood finished off the garment, which today was pulled back, revealing a rather large head with a shaven crown cut into an otherwise thick mop of greying hair. The hairstyle was absurd and entirely impractical in this heat, and Rathulf wondered why a man might want to wear such a silly fashion. Any man in Norvegr who dressed like that would be laughed out of the hall. He realised that the subject of his musings was looking back at him with raised eyebrows, and Rathulf flushed. The man chuckled and turned away.

Rathulf watched the stranger return to the stall and hold out his bowl for a second time. The woman shouted at him again, then, when the stranger did not go away, she snatched the bowl from his hand and threw it back at him. It hit him in the chest with a loud slap then clattered off onto the road. To Rathulf's astonishment, the man simply bowed and smiled, said a word of thanks, and then turned to collect his bowl. Unfortunately, a team of oxen beat him to it, and Rathulf watched as the bowl splintered into fragments under their hooves. The man let out a sigh, then, without the slightest hint of anger, turned and picked up his little travelling bundle and proceeded on his way.

Rathulf stared at him as he walked past, amazed at his ability to contain his temper. In fact, the Norseman found it difficult to suppress his own anger over the woman's appalling behaviour, and he knew that had it been him, he would not have walked away empty-handed. Rathulf called to the sack-garbed man to wait. He gathered up the remaining three cakes and handed them to the man. In the background, he heard the woman berating him, but, inspired by the man's example, he ignored her.

The man took only one cake, but Rathulf shook his head and pressed the others into his hands. 'You have them,' Rathulf said, realising his Norse probably could not be understood.

However, his intent was clear, and the man responded with such a gentle, gracious smile that Rathulf's heart warmed. 'You should take the honeycomb too,' Rathulf said, darting back to his chest to retrieve the delicacy. He added it to the pile in the man's hand, then the man smiled and gestured at Rathulf's sticky fingers. Rathulf shrugged, then set about licking them clean, grinning like a boy. The man laughed and indicated to Rathulf to sit down. The Norseman offered the man his trunk, and then he settled down on the ground cross-legged next to him. The kindly man carefully smeared honey onto one of the cakes and handed it to Rathulf, his eyes and tone insistent. When it became clear he would not rest until Rathulf did as he was bidden, Rathulf took it and indicated that the man must do the same for himself. He did, and the two ate in silence as the wains rumbled by.

Rathulf polished off his cake in no time, but the bald-crowned man ate his slowly, savouring every bite. Rathulf again felt self-conscious in the presence of this remarkable person, and he wondered what kind of craft or position he held in society. The man turned and saw that Rathulf had finished his cake, so he offered the other. 'It's yours,' Rathulf said, shaking his head. 'I've already eaten five, so stop trying to give it away.'

The man smiled and had half-turned back to his cake when he suddenly stopped, frowned, and looked squarely into Rathulf's face. He stopped chewing, his brown eyes widening for a moment, and then Rathulf found himself again the subject of the same shocked and suspicious expression. He bit back his frustration and disappointment and rose, stunned that this man too would be turned against him. *What in the name of Odin about me is so intolerable? Not the wolves, after all. Could it be my hair?* He had noticed that no one else seemed to wear it as he did, short on the sides and long at the back, tied into a braid. He felt a light hand on his arm, and he turned to meet the questioning gaze of the strange man.

'I'm sorry,' Rathulf said, 'but whatever it is I've done to offend you, I honestly didn't mean it.'

The old man looked up at him, apparently surprised by Rathulf's tone, then his face softened, and he said something that was clearly meant to soothe. Rathulf hesitated, then he realised that as the man sat on his trunk, he could go nowhere unless he tipped him off into the dirt. He sat back down.

The stranger pointed at Rathulf's bandaged hand and asked a question, concern in his voice.

'I cut myself,' Rathulf said, looking down at his hand, 'but the rest are from you people.'

The stranger then nodded at Rathulf's sword, and he indicated that he wanted to look more closely at it. Rathulf hesitated. Could he trust this man? What if he made off with it? He smiled to himself. *And I could not run him down if he did?*

The Norseman drew the weapon from its scabbard and handed it to the man, who turned it over in his hands, peering at the hilt intently, then at the blade. If anything, he seemed disappointed. He then looked again into Rathulf's face. Rathulf blinked, but the stranger held the Norseman's gaze. Again, Rathulf felt uncomfortable, and he shifted uneasily under his scrutiny. The man's expression suddenly lost its intensity, and he laughed and handed back the sword. Rathulf took it back, wondering what was so funny. The man said something soft, confidential. The words sounded familiar, almost recognisable, but still, they were frustratingly foreign to him. Rathulf shrugged and shook his head, wishing he could understand even one word of this man's speech.

This meeting was important – Rathulf knew that with absolute certainty – but where could it lead when neither could hold even the simplest conversation? The man laughed again, shook his head, stood up, and then gestured in an invitation for Rathulf to join him. Rathulf nodded and moved to pick up his trunk, still wondering what had passed between them both just now. *Should I show him my tunic?* he wondered on an impulse, but he scolded himself for being rash. *He's the first person I've met here who has shown me kindness. Why would I risk wrecking that?*

'Osbert,' the man said, placing his hand on his chest, then holding it out in greeting.

Rathulf hesitated. *Do I use my Dumnonian name? So far, it hasn't done me any good, but this man seems different.* The tonsured man tilted his head in waiting, the moment turning awkward.

'Rathulf,' the Norseman said, choosing caution. He shook the other's hand. 'Rathulf Thorvaldarsson of Aurlandsfjorden.'

The old man smiled, and then his eyes slid to the bandage on Rathulf's forearm.

'Oh yeah, that's an arrow wound from being shot by you people,' he said, knowing the man could not understand him. 'And yes, it hurts.' Inexplicably, tears came to his eyes, and he angrily rubbed them away. *Hel's thighs, what is the matter with me?* he wondered, embarrassed and angry at himself.

The other nodded, grabbed one of the rope handles, and hoisted his end of the trunk. Rathulf told him not to bother; he was so old, it would just as likely break his arm, but the other was insistent. So Rathulf picked up his end, and the two men – one at the beginning of his journey, the other nearing the end – walked side by side in silence at a comfortable pace, Rathulf's companion bowing and smiling in greeting at all the passers-by. Rathulf noticed that, unlike the mean-spirited stallholder, most travellers nodded their heads respectfully in return. Even more interesting was the fact that they all nodded at Rathulf as well, as though his being with this man miraculously removed whatever stain he had been carrying with him.

Some while later, the man pointed ahead and said something in Dumnonian. Rathulf could not understand, but he could make out what appeared to be a large stone building surrounded by a low wall. Perched atop the building's gable was a wooden cross, much like the one worn by Rathulf's companion. The road passed right by it, and the man paused by the gate. He muttered an incantation, then made a sign with his hand, which Rathulf realised was in the shape of a cross. So, was this a temple to the God he worshipped? Rathulf was curious about it and indicated they should go in, but the old man shook his head. His face bore a troubled frown, so Rathulf nodded respectfully, and they continued. *Perhaps I cannot enter because I'm not initiated into his sect*, he thought.

It was late in the day now, and most of the traffic was moving in the same southeasterly direction that Rathulf and his companion walked. The roadway dropped gradually into a valley through which a wide estuarine river flowed. Rathulf saw what appeared to be the ruins of a bridge crossing the broad mudflats, its parallel rows of jagged timber stalks protruding like pleading hands from the mud. The old man said something, presumably about the bridge, and then he indicated that they would continue to follow the river downstream. This they did for a time before the road climbed gradually from the river to a crossroads at the crest of the hill.

The man pointed to their left. Rathulf turned and stared at the view that opened before them, astonished. Below ran the river they had been following, and spanning it was an impossibly long and substantial bridge of stone and wood. On the far bank and sprawling out towards the fields beyond was the largest town Rathulf had ever seen. The young Norseman dropped his end of the trunk and gazed in wonder at the place, unaware that his travelling companion had also stopped to look, not upon the town, but instead at Rathulf and his reaction to this new wonder.

Nothing of this scale existed in the northern lands, nor had Rathulf ever seen such massive defences. A great fort stood at the town's core, perched atop a mound that rose from the river. Its thick stone walls enclosed a cluster of buildings, the tallest of which was a square-sided tower rising many times the height of the rooves beside it. Rathulf stared at it, astounded. Its lines were so square, so exact. How could such a construction stand so high? What held it all together? In Norvegr, the largest building was Eirik's fortified hall, vast by Norse standards, but a peasant's barn beside this place.

Rathulf felt a flush of pride. *My people built this*, he thought to himself, *a place of rock and stone that will stand here forever.* No wonder the raiders speak with such awe of the southern lands, and how impermanent Eirik's wooden hall and Rathulf's tiny turf-roofed farmhouse seemed in the shadow of this magnificent place! *Here lies civilisation, wealth, and hope*, Rathulf thought. *Surely this will be the right place to begin my search for Aneurin.* He turned back to the old man, filled with excitement and apprehension. *Could this be the town that Tegen had spoken of*, he wondered. *The place of my birth?*

He pointed at the city and asked, 'Is that Kair Uisk?'

The sack-clothed man stood patiently beside him, his expression one of curiosity. He nodded and repeated, 'Caer Uisc.' He then said something else: the same word that the others had used – 'eskankesta.'

Rathulf frowned back at him, not understanding. *Does this place have two names?* 'I've never seen anything this big or so… so solid!' Rathulf explained. *I've found it! I've found my home!*

The old man smiled and said something in response, holding his hand out towards the road that led down to the river.

On an impulse, Rathulf asked about the other place, Sankus Jermus.

The old man frowned, not understanding, so Rathulf tried again. The man's expression changed, and he smiled. 'You mean Sanctus Germanus?' he said.

Rathulf smiled back, delighted that he had understood. 'Sanktus Jermarnus,' Rathulf said slowly, trying the name out.

The old man nodded, then pointed in the other direction, away from the city towards the southwest. This surprised Rathulf. *How far away is it?* he wondered, thinking about how many days he had been travelling thus far and how long he had left before returning to the beach opposite puffin island.

'I follow that road?' Rathulf asked, pointing to the one that led up the hill from the crossroads to their right, away from the city.

The man nodded, then asked Rathulf something about Sanctus Germanus.

Rathulf had no hope of understanding, so he gave an apologetic shrug. 'It's where I was taken,' he said, looking down the other road. *Well, if I have no luck here, then at least I know which route to take now.*

They picked up their respective trunk handles and began their descent to the river, Rathulf keeping his eyes fixed on the enormous town. Surrounding the fortress was the settlement itself: a disorderly assortment of wooden buildings so closely packed that Rathulf could not distinguish one from another. It took him a few moments longer to realise that much of the town on the fortress' side of the river was also encircled by a stockade. At first, he had not seen it because the jumble of rooves sprawled continuously on either side of the wall; the stream of people funnelling through the high gateway had drawn Rathulf's eye. Columns of smoke rose from scores of evening cooking fires, and Rathulf fancied he could smell the roasting meat even from this distance. His stomach grumbled noisily.

They came to the bridge, which was defended by an imposing guard tower at either end. Rathulf noticed a couple of men atop the tower, but the gates were open, and no one was being challenged as they passed onto the crossing.

The town grew more imposing as they approached, and Rathulf gazed up at the massive fortifications. Even the most determined Viking host would have difficulty taking this place, and Rathulf smiled to himself as he remembered Gunnar's mean-spirited boast back on the island. *Let's see you try to attack this, my town*, he thought smugly. *You'll dash yourselves against my walls, and we'll pick you off one by one until you all lie dead beneath us.*

A haze of dust and woodsmoke hung over the town, and its different scent again struck Rathulf. He had seen many new trees on his long walk from the coast, and he knew this to be the source of the sharp, spicy smitch that tickled his nose. Other smells: a stew simmering on the fire, freshly cut thatch, and fish left too long in the sun were familiar, but there was another, pervading odour, which Rathulf had first noticed when he had passed the outlying huts: the smell of human waste. As the road led him closer to the town wall, the stench grew in strength, and Rathulf soon saw why. The narrow pathways between the densely packed houses ran with dark streams of wastewater, and Rathulf watched, astonished, as a woman stepped from her doorway and threw the disgusting contents of her pail into the middle of the street. Rathulf stepped around the sticky muck, holding his hand over his mouth and nose to stifle the smell and prevent himself from throwing up. *Do they not have toilet pits here in Dumnonia?* he wondered, disgusted.

The town gates rose ahead of him, and Rathulf tapped his guide on the arm. 'Let me take it now,' he said, 'you must be tired of its weight.'

His companion gave him a wry smile and let go of the heavy chest, and Rathulf immediately felt a pang of shame. *Am I so transparent?* he wondered, knowing the man thought that Rathulf feared he might make off with his possessions. 'I'm sorry,' Rathulf said. 'I didn't mean to offend.'

Rathulf indicated for the man to take up the handle again, which he did. They walked single-file, the man leading the way to a pair of imposing gates beneath a substantial, stone-built watchtower. Two warriors guarded either side of the portal, each armed with a heavy spear. They also wore swords and daggers. They wore identical clothes, sporting tabards with an emblem that Rathulf did not recognise. One of them stepped forward and challenged Rathulf, holding his hand up in the universally understood order to halt. Rathulf began to speak, but his travelling companion interrupted and spoke sternly to the guard. The latter paused, casting Rathulf a suspicious glare, but he stepped back and indicated that they could pass through. Rathulf offered thanks to his companion, wondering what he had said and who he was that he could dismiss the guards so readily. A man of authority, certainly. Rathulf offered a silent prayer of thanks to the Gods for placing him in this man's care. *Perhaps my luck is finally turning*, he thought.

They passed through the gatehouse into a large market square beyond. Rathulf stepped into a different world. On the side from which he had just come, the houses had been so densely crammed together that the street had been in shadow, but here the evening light streamed into the open square, tinting the swirling dust in shades of amber. He blinked, his eyes taking a moment to become accustomed to the brightness. Traders in colourful tunics hovered about their stalls; bare-chested slaves hoisted bags of grain and other provisions onto carts and donkeys; groups of women stood by a well with pails in hand, laughing and chatting. The shadow of the fortress darkened the middle of the square, but when Rathulf looked up at the tower's stone bulk, the setting sun shone back at him through its uppermost windows.

Rathulf's companion spoke, and the young Norseman turned to see the old man pointing at one of the buildings across the square. His companion then said something else to Rathulf, and they moved off up the street towards the heavy gates of the fortress above. *Does he come from there?* Rathulf wondered, amazed. *Could he be one of the warrior class then? No wonder he is so interested in my sword.* As the older man still held one handle of his trunk, Rathulf followed him up to the fort, anticipating a wash and decent meal. Four more warriors, all wearing identical tabards over their chainmail armour, stood guard on either side of the enormous oak gates, each holding a spear. A small, human-sized door cut in the larger gate opened, and another warrior wearing the same emblem stepped out. He took one look at the two visitors, shook his head, and said something to Rathulf's bald-crowned companion in an obviously rude tone.

The bald-crowned man spoke back equally forcefully, which prompted a testy reply. Their discussion continued in increasingly angry exchanges until the bald-crowned man let out a long breath, then he turned to Rathulf. He led Rathulf away from the gates and spoke to him in a quiet, apologetic voice. He pointed down into the square.

Will they not have me as their guest? Rathulf wondered, hurt. In Norvegr, there would have been no question that Rathulf would join him at his hearth for the night. The man looked back at Rathulf apologetically, and although he clearly understood Rathulf's confusion, he again indicated that Rathulf would need to find lodgings elsewhere. He then turned and stepped through the small gate. Before the door closed, the man turned and looked back. His expression was again questioning, doubting, then he turned away, and the door closed. Rathulf was left standing before the imposing façade, uncertain whether to bang on the gates and demand to be let in or do as the man had suggested and go back to the square. As it was plain he was not welcome, he hoisted up his trunk and turned and walked back down the hill, convinced there must be another reason he could not join the man inside.

Rathulf and his companion had attracted a following of young children when they had entered the outskirts of the settlement, but Rathulf had been so enthralled with the town that he had barely noticed them. They sprang and danced about him now, tugging at his pants and chattering in an excited rabble. A couple of them gestured at his trunk, offering to carry it. Rathulf held onto it firmly, knowing just how easily the scruffy band could make off with it and disappear for good amid the maze of narrow alleyways that led from the square.

His immediate desire was to find a place to eat and sleep, and he glanced around the marketplace, wondering how and where he might find lodgings. He walked towards the group of men nearest to him, intending to ask for help. The men stopped talking and turned away from him, their faces clearly showing their disapproval. Rathulf stopped, annoyed by their reaction. *Not again*, he thought. *I have not even spoken, yet you shun me?* Rathulf knew he stood out as a foreigner; his long, braided hair had already drawn many curious glances, to say nothing of his inability to speak their language. But why this manifest aversion to him, which had begun with the woman by the sea? If not the wolves, then what?

Rathulf made his way across the square to another gathering of men, fighting off the knot of despair that rose again within his heart. The men stood in a loose huddle, laughing at something one of them had just said. They were better dressed than the previous group; perhaps the others had been slaves, and Rathulf had broken some taboo by approaching them. The man told the tale looked up, shook his head, and frowned. He pointed at Rathulf, shook his head again and said something.

'What have I done wrong?' Rathulf demanded in exasperation,

despite knowing they could not understand him. 'What is so wrong with me that you all stare in horror?'

He swore under his breath and turned away, wondering how he would survive here. His first instinct was to go back up to the fort and ask the old man for his hospitality. He had decided that he would do just that when the eldest of the boys tugged at Rathulf's pants, almost tripping him over. Rathulf snapped at the lad, waving his hand to shoo them away. The boy persisted, tapping his hand on Rathulf's scabbard and shaking his head. Rathulf paused, the realisation finally dawning. He glanced around the square, and, sure enough, no one carried a sword. A few men wore daggers in their belts, but Rathulf alone wore a long blade.

Rathulf pointed at the hilt and raised his eyebrows at the boy, and the lad nodded his head vigorously. Rathulf grunted in understanding and unbuckled the weapon, and bent down to stow it in his chest. How am I to ever learn the foolish customs of this land? Rathulf muttered to himself. He pulled the cord that held the key from around his neck, and the boys crowded around while he unlatched the padlock of his trunk, their curious faces fixed on the quiet, long-haired stranger. The eldest boy reached out and gingerly touched the sword, but he snatched his hand away when Rathulf looked up at him.

Rathulf had meant to tell the youngster to keep his hands off, but the boy had already read the rebuke in the Norseman's scowl, and he looked at Rathulf through wounded eyes. Rathulf sighed. The boy must have been no older than seven or eight and most likely the child of slaves, judging from the state of his clothing. It was doubtless his dream to be a warrior one day, and what harm could be brought in letting him have a look? Rathulf slowly drew the weapon from its sheath and held it up for the boy to see. The lad made a soft cooing sound and tentatively ran his fingers along the flat surface of the gleaming blade. He smiled in wonder, tracing the carved pattern on the grip, occasionally glancing up at Rathulf as if to ask permission to continue his exploration.

One of the other children reached out to grab the sword, but the boy snarled, and the younger one drew away, frowning.

Someone shouted a stern command from somewhere behind them, and the boy lifted his hand and pointed urgently at the chest. Rathulf quickly slid the blade back into its scabbard and stuffed it in the trunk. He had just rammed the lock into place when a tall, barrel-chested man with thick, hairy arms appeared, brandishing a leather belt. The boys scattered like startled mice, leaving Rathulf kneeling alone in the dust, staring up at the strap-wielding giant. The man shrugged in what Rathulf presumed was an apology for the unwarranted attention of the street rabble, then he turned away and went back to his stall. Rathulf felt naked without his sword – a sensation heightened by the sudden loss of his entourage – and he drew little comfort from the knowledge that most of the other men went about unarmed. *Do they leave their swords at home by choice or direction?* Rathulf wondered. He heaved his chest onto his shoulder and returned to his quest to find a place that might offer him a bed and a bath.

In Norvegr, Rathulf had always stayed with friends or family when travelling, but he knew that no matter where he might find himself at the end of a day's journey, he could always be sure of at least one night's welcome in a stranger's home. Rathulf had no idea whether this was the case in Dumnonia, so he strode towards the nearest building, hoping he might receive a warmer reception now that he had removed his sword. A group of plainly garbed men stood near the doorway, chatting and drinking. Rathulf was about to hail them when he spotted his new young friend standing in the shadows on the far side of the square. The boy shook his head and pointed to a different building. Rathulf paused, then tilted his head and rested his hand on his cheek, hoping this meant sleep in Dumnonia too. The boy flashed a grin and nodded, still pointing to the other building. Rathulf walked across the square, silently thankful that he had found this unexpected guide.

The boy joined Rathulf at the door. He pointed to himself and said, 'Wilfred.'

Rathulf responded with his own name. Wilfred repeated it thoughtfully, then nodded to himself once he had mastered the unfamiliar Norse sounds. Then he took Rathulf's wrist and led him inside.

Rathulf stood in a large room with a high, open ceiling and crisp, whitewashed walls. Sputtering oil lamps hung from the thick oak beams, casting warm, subdued light. The inn had an air of neatness and calm about it, a quiet haven from the grime and noise of the market beyond. Rathulf glanced down at the boy gratefully.

A long bench stood near the wall opposite the door, with flagons of what Rathulf presumed to be wine and ale sitting on a wooden shelf above. Tables and benches were neatly arranged within the central part of the room, while curtained bunks lined the walls to the sides. A group of finely dressed men sat at a table near the centre of the room, but they took little notice of Rathulf. The man behind the bench smiled when Rathulf entered, but his face turned sour when he spotted the boy. He waved his arm and ordered the boy out, but Rathulf put his hand on the lad's shoulder and said in Norse, 'he means no harm,' hoping that at least his tone would be understood.

The innkeeper glanced at Rathulf dubiously, but the boy started talking, pointing towards the bunks. The innkeeper nodded in understanding and said something to Rathulf. Rathulf looked back at him blankly, and the innkeeper smiled and apologised, speaking more slowly his time. It made no difference, and Rathulf looked down at his young friend for help. The boy grinned and tapped Rathulf's money pouch. Rathulf looked back, surprised. *Must I pay for this man's hospitality?* he wondered. *What kind of place is this?* As he lifted the leather bag from his belt, it occurred to him that he had no idea how much the man might want for a night's sleep, so he held the pouch out to the boy, indicating that he should take out the correct amount of silver. The boy's eyes widened at the sight of the immense wealth contained in the little bag, and upon seeing Wilfred's expression, Rathulf's heart stopped. *What am I doing?* he thought in a panic, realising his mistake too late. Wilfred took one look at Rathulf, and then his eyes flew to the door. The innkeeper let out a belated shout of warning, but the boy was quicker. He snatched the purse from Rathulf's hand and ran out the door.

Rathulf cursed and lunged at Wilfred, but he was far too late. The young rascal vanished, and although Rathulf was only moments behind him, he could find no trace of the boy whatsoever when he emerged into the evening sunlight. He looked about the square, wondering which way he should go, but it rapidly became apparent that any pursuit would be futile. Humiliated and cursing his stupidity, he returned to the inn. He almost yelped in surprise when he saw Wilfred framed in the doorway, a broad grin lighting his face.

For a moment, the Norseman was confused, and then he saw the rebuke in Wilfred's mischievous eyes. The boy thrust the pouch at Rathulf, shaking his head and rolling his eyes, no doubt at Rathulf's immense stupidity. 'That was not funny,' Rathulf growled, taking back his purse. Nevertheless, Wilfred had taught him an important lesson. He had given no thought to the consequences when he had offered the little thief what amounted to a small fortune. *How would I have survived here without money?* he wondered. The thought of being penniless in this strange land made him shudder. *I am tired*, he decided. *I need to rest and recover my senses.*

The innkeeper was waiting nearby, a disapproving frown creasing his otherwise pleasant features. The boy held up two fingers, and Rathulf took out two small pieces of silver and handed them to the innkeeper. The innkeeper's eyes lit up when he saw how much Rathulf was willing to pay for a night's accommodation, but Wilfred put his grimy hand on Rathulf's arm and shook his head. Rathulf turned to the innkeeper, his eyebrows raised, and the Briton hesitated, then he nodded and handed back the silver. In the background, Rathulf caught one of the merchants smirking at him. Wilfred dug about in Rathulf's purse and pulled out the smallest piece of silver he could find, then gave that to the innkeeper along with a stream of instructions. The Briton muttered something under his breath, turned away, and handed back a small pile of copper coins, which Wilfred put into Rathulf's purse. Again, Rathulf flushed with embarrassment.

Wilfred retook Rathulf's wrist and led him to the bedplace. The sleeping arrangements were simple: a long wooden bench ran the length of the wall, and each sleeping place was defined by a thin straw mattress and a coarse woollen blanket folded at its foot. A plain curtain, drawn back for the daytime, was the only concession to privacy. Although the inn was almost empty, Rathulf noticed that most of the sleeping places had already been taken. He set his trunk down to mark a spot, then turned to the innkeeper, rubbing his hands over his body in the sign for washing. The Briton responded and pointed outside. Wilfred tugged at Rathulf's arm, indicating that he could take him to the washing place. Rathulf dug into his trunk and found a clean shirt, then he locked his moneybag inside and glanced back at the innkeeper, wondering how safe it would be to leave his possessions in the hands of a person who demanded payment for a bed. He was faced with little choice, so he turned and followed the young scamp out into the square.

The marketplace was entirely in shadow now, but the air was warm and pungent with the smells of cooking and ale. Rathulf followed Wilfred into one of the dark alleys, and soon they plunged steeply down towards the outer wall. They passed through a narrow gateway, and suddenly Rathulf found himself surrounded by his young retinue again. They shouted, jostled and pranced around him, each vying for his attention, but whenever one of the noisy rabble ventured too close, Wilfred snarled at them, and they backed away.

Their path took them past the last houses and through a strip of carefully-tended vegetable plots. The river lay before them, its slow-running waters glistening in the rich yellowing light of sunset. Two men stood on the grassy bank drying themselves, and they nodded in greeting at Rathulf. Rathulf acknowledged them in kind, then began stripping off his clothes. He tugged at his belt, then paused, feeling a little self-conscious. He glanced down at Wilfred, who shrugged and said something, then pulled off his own shirt and trousers and sprang into the water. Rathulf smiled and followed the boy's example. He was joined by the other boys, who tore off their tattered rags and plunged into the river shouting and laughing.

The air was still heavy with the heat of the day, and Rathulf sank gratefully into the cool water. Here the river was waist-deep at best, but Rathulf didn't care a jot. Only now that his tired body was given time to pause, did Rathulf realise the extent of his exhaustion. He had not had a moment's rest since the Althing, and the strain of his self-imposed exile had worn him to the point of collapse. For a long time, he just swam lazily about in the swimming hole, enjoying the cooling effect of the water and the warmth of the last rays on his face. It felt wonderful, too, to rid himself of the last traces of sea salt at long last. The boys shouted and splashed in the water nearby, but they kept a respectful distance, wary, no doubt, of the watchful eye of Rathulf's self-appointed protector, who had left the water and now sat cross-legged on the bank beside Rathulf's clothes. Rathulf came out of the water feeling refreshed and clean. He wiped himself dry with his old shirt, then he pulled on his pants and settled down beside his new friend. Wilfred pointed at the bandages on Rathulf's hand and arm, and the Norseman told him the latter was an arrow wound, and although Wilfred understood none of it, the boy nodded wisely. Wilfred leaned around behind Rathulf and tapped the two cuts in his back. 'My welcome to Dumnonia,'

Rathulf said. Then Wilfred tapped Rathulf's shoulder, which was almost fully healed now. 'That marks the worst day of my life,' Rathulf said.

Wilfred was perceptive enough to leave it there, and they sat in silence for a while, watching the gently swirling water as the lengthening shadows of the willows reached out across the river towards them. Leaves and other flotsam flashed in and out of view as they floated through slivers of golden sunlight. A wide, flat-bottomed boat drifted by, its pilot leaning lazily on his pole, oblivious to the watchers on the bank. Rathulf lay back in the grass and gazed into the pale blue sky with its russet-stained fringe. Feathers of cirrus floated high above him, reflecting the soft pink hues of the westering sun. *There is hope for me here, after all*, he thought. *All I needed to do was shed my sword! Such a simple thing, yet for the fact that I cannot communicate with my people. But I will learn, I will remember. I knew this language once, for had not Tegen taught it to me?*

He sat up to find Wilfred and the other boys waiting patiently for him. Wilfred handed Rathulf his clean shirt, and the Norseman nodded in thanks and pulled it on. They made their way back to the town to find that the stallkeepers had packed up for the day, making way for many long benches that spilt out from the taverns bordering the square. Men who had worked the fields in the hot sun all day now sat with their friends, swapping jokes and swigging large mugs of ale. Rathulf's inn was no less crowded, but Wilfred remained outside by the door, even though Rathulf beckoned for him to come in. Wilfred shook his head, flashed Rathulf a grin and a wave then disappeared into the crowd.

Rathulf went straight to his sleeping place to check on his trunk. A young man with mouse-brown hair sat on the next paillasse, and Rathulf nodded in greeting. The Briton looked to be about Rathulf's age, and he thrust out his hand and said something in greeting. Rathulf realised that he was offering his name, but it took Rathulf a couple of tries to get it right. The Briton, on the other hand, found it near-impossible to pronounce Rathulf's name. Aethelred laughed and shook his head, then chatted on for a while before realising that Rathulf could not understand a word. He laughed again, rolled his eyes and clapped the visitor on the shoulder, obviously apologising. He started again more slowly, and Rathulf did manage to catch a word or two. Rathulf wished he had paid more attention to Tegen as a child, and again he shook his head with frustration. Nevertheless, the words sounded almost familiar, and Rathulf smiled back. Although he was annoyed that he could not converse with this young man, he was grateful and a little bemused by this sustained change in fortune.

The two young men managed to share that Rathulf had arrived by sea, and then they embarked on a game of charades to determine Rathulf's profession. Merchant? Trader? Farmer? Finally, the Briton made to pull out an imaginary sword from its scabbard and thrust the invisible weapon at Rathulf. Ra smiled and nodded. *Yes*, he thought, *I suppose I am whatever a sword-bearer is in this land. Perhaps warriors are rare here. Maybe they are a particular class of people.* The Briton was pointing at Rathulf's hip and raising his eyebrows. 'It's in my sea chest,' Rathulf said in Norse, forgetting that Aethelred was as little able to understand him as he was a Briton.

Wondering what might be the cause of their odd aversion to wearing a sword, he took his Norwegian blade from the trunk and handed it to Aethelred. A little warning voice reminded him of his recent experience with the money pouch, but it simply wasn't in Rathulf's nature to suspect every new person he met of ill will. While Aethelred tested the weapon's balance in his hand, Rathulf reached back into the trunk to check that his Dumnonian blade still lay in its place beneath the tunic. He heard a low whistle beside him and glanced up to see the Briton peering at the precious sword. It was evident that Aethelred wanted a better look, but Rathulf was torn between the need to protect this most valuable possession and a reluctance to ruin this fledgling friendship. He chose friendship and indicated to Aethelred that he might hold it. This the Briton did with much reverence, turning the magnificent weapon over and over and marvelling at the fine artistry in the blade and hilt. He looked from the sword to the chest and then to Rathulf, clearly impressed.

His expression suddenly changed when he saw something over Rathulf's shoulder, and in a smooth action, he slipped the sword back into its scabbard, scooped up Rathulf's other sword and dropped both carefully back into the chest and closed the lid. Then he laughed at Rathulf, indicating with his eyes that Rathulf should respond in kind. For a moment, the Norseman was confused, but then he heard the tramp of boots and the clink of swordbelts. He turned to see a group of six men filing into the tavern. They glanced over at Ra and his companion, but they seemed more interested in ale than visitors. Rathulf locked the chest and put the key back around his neck, then Aethelred took Rathulf's arm and led him to a table on the far side of the room, taking care to keep some distance from the newly arrived visitors.

Rathulf noticed that the atmosphere in the tavern had changed with the coming of the six men. People spoke in lowered voices, and more than one patron shot a sideways glance at the group of newcomers. The six were dressed in the same costume: long, dark riding breeches and short, dusty brown tunics over plain long-sleeved shirts. An emblem was embroidered in yellow cloth on their breasts, a beast that Rathulf did not recognise and a motif that appeared to be some form of leaf or flower. All wore identical swords sheathed in matching scabbards, and Rathulf wondered if they were all brothers, perhaps the sons of a local chieftain. Perhaps only jarls were permitted to carry swords here. Nevertheless, this jarl could not have been particularly wealthy; the weapons appeared relatively poor in manufacture, and the scabbards were surprisingly plain and utilitarian. One of the men caught Rathulf peering at his weapon, and he cast the Norseman a narrow-eyed glare and spoke in a dark tone. Aethelred piped up and offered an explanation to deflect the man's attention, then he jabbed Rathulf in the ribs and glared at him, wanting to know what Rathulf thought he was doing. Rathulf apologised and made a point of avoiding the men after that.

They sat in comfortable silence for a time, and Rathulf felt a calmness settle over him as he shared ale with this stranger. Gradually his exhausted mind drifted into a strange half-sleep. The world became a confusing jumble of disjointed voices and images of the inn intermixed with flashes of his life from the Leap to his swim in the river this very evening. It was some time before he realised that Aethelred had disappeared, and immediately he came back to his senses in a flash of panic. His concern subsided when he noticed that his companion had left a half-drunk mug of ale on the table, marking his intention to return. Aethelred did a short while later, clutching a roasted chicken and two large slabs of bread on a wooden plate. He dumped them down on the table in front of Rathulf and laughed when he saw the Norseman's hungry eyes. Rathulf felt immensely grateful to this young man, and he thanked him in Norse, knowing that Aetheldred understood the meaning behind the words. Behind the teasing glint in Aethelred's eyes was gentle humour that held no reproach, and all the while Rathulf devoured the food, Aethelred watched him with a half-amused grin. The Briton ate very little for his part, content to leave the largest share of the pickings to Rathulf.

After the meal was over and they'd tossed the bones into the hearth, Aethelred pointed to Rathulf's empty mug. Rathulf smiled and nodded. The Briton scooped up the cups, and it suddenly occurred to Rathulf that Aethelred had to date paid for everything, so he rose to fetch some coins from his trunk. Aethelred looked surprised, then frowned, shook his head, and went off to the bar. They tried a little more conversation, and Rathulf learned by trial and error that Aethelred was the son of a landowner; one who was reasonably well-off judging from his clothes and generosity.

After a time, Rathulf drifted into his private world again. *How different this place is to home*, he thought, wondering how he might start a life here, where he might go, and what he would do to clothe and feed himself. During his darkest moments, he had entertained the thought that he would throw his life to the Gods and find the person responsible for his pain and kill him. At least if he were to die in the attempt, then his life would not have been completely wasted, and he might, in some part, redeem himself in the eyes of his family. But how could he take his revenge? He knew nothing of the man save his name. Where he lived, if indeed he lived at all, Rathulf might learn in time, but then what? Stride up to him and thrust a dagger through his heart? This enmity seemed so disconnected from Rathulf's own life, yet by Tegen's account, his entire family had been slaughtered by this person, thus setting in motion the train of events that had ultimately led to Rathulf's life in Norway being smashed to pieces by the Gods so that he had no choice but to leave.

Is that not enough reason to hate him? he wondered. And, of course, as a Norseman, he was honour-bound to avenge the deaths of his murdered kin. Yet he found he could not hate a person he'd never met or known.

Rathulf's thoughts inevitably turned to Ivar, and he shuddered. *That* had been hatred. *That* had been vengeance. He never again wished to experience that horror, that frightening loss of control that had unleashed a monster that could kill with such cold violence. Rathulf still could not accept that it had been he who had plunged his dagger over and over into the disgusting slave trader's heart. He had hoped it was his fylgja taking its revenge, for Rathulf had been raised to respect the law, to choose the assembly over the sword. No matter how much Ivar may have deserved such a fate, Rathulf had never imagined he would allow himself to sink to the level of a base murderer. But murder Ivar he had, in front of hundreds of witnesses, and although cleared of the crime by the Assembly thanks to the many mitigating circumstances, Ivar's kin had vowed to have their revenge. Rathulf knew they would not rest until they took his life in return for Ivar's. Worst of all, he could not rid himself of the taste of Ivar's blood in his mouth, just as the slaver had promised.

Rathulf was snapped from his thoughts by a gentle touch on his arm. He twisted around to find a young woman standing beside him, holding out a jug of ale and raising her eyebrows in question. Before he could say no, she swept around his chair and sat down in his lap, circling one arm around his neck and pouring ale into his mug with the other. Rathulf glanced at Aethelred, somewhat taken aback by the sudden appearance of this amorous girl. His British companion grinned back at him, then he lifted his eyes and said something to the girl. She giggled, relinquished the jug and moved her hand to rest on Rathulf's upper thigh. Embarrassed, Rathulf pushed her off him and shook his head. Attractive though she was with her ample bosom and seductive eyes, a romp with a stranger was the last thing on his mind. He glanced self-consciously around the room and noticed that a few other men had attracted similar womanly attention. Perhaps the girl was provided by the host of this place for Rathulf's pleasure. She was certainly dressed like one of the thrall girls from home. Her gown barely contained her; indeed, it accentuated the plunging line of her cleavage, and Rathulf was unable to take his eyes from the pearly skin of her breasts. But his memories of Alrik and Ingrith were still too raw, and he shook his head again, so she moved on to another prospect without even a backward glance.

❧

He woke early the following morning to find Aethelred snoring softly in the bedplace beside him. Another sound slowly registered: the drumming of rain on the thatch. The Norseman let out a resigned sigh and settled back in his bed; he would do little travelling today. *Perhaps that is for the best*, he thought. *My feet are tired, and I've yet to explore the city. Maybe I won't need to go anywhere else. Perhaps Aneurin is here.* The steady drone of the rain soon sent Rathulf into a doze, and his dream sent him back to the grove on his birthday and Alrik's mischievous face smiling down at him. Rathulf sighed and lifted a hand to stroke his cheek, but his knuckles grazed the post beside him, wrenching him from his dream. He blinked, confused, and then the sound of water dripping noisily on the other side of the wall dragged him back to the cold reality of the inn, Dumnonia, and his exile. He stared into the soot-darkened rafters, feeling a sudden, painful longing for his own bed in Thorvaldsby, with Alrik lying beside him.

No, he told himself. *I'm confused. This is home: here in Dumnonia.* But another part of him immediately refuted the notion. *Aurlandsfjorden is your home*, it said: *the little turf-roofed farm nestled on the shores of your fjord. Sigvald, Thorvald: they are your family.* Another scornful voice laughed at him coldly. *That is not your home. You are an exile now, unable to return to the people you know and understand.*

'No!' Rathulf railed, half speaking aloud. He tugged on the thong around his neck but found only the key to his padlock there. He had cast his amulet of Thor into the fjord upon his departure from Aurlandsfjorden, angry that his patron God had abandoned him. *How have I wronged you?* he wondered. *How may I make amends and return to my world?* He felt the cold sting of a tear on his cheek, and he brushed it away quickly. *I must remain strong*, he reminded himself for the hundredth time. *I am Dumnonian, if not by upbringing, then at least by birth. It is who I am, who I am destined to be. Here is where I will find my family; my true kin are here, in this inn, in this city, all around me.*

He realised that Aethelred was no longer snoring, and he turned to see that the Briton was looking at him. Rathulf quickly turned away, ashamed. *He has seen me weeping*, he thought. *What must he think of me?* Aethelred rolled onto his back and put his hands behind his head, and he too stared into the thatching above, deep in thought. Rathulf watched him for a moment, then turned away. They lay in silence while the inn came to life around them. Some while later, when the delicious aroma of bacon filled the air, Aethelred sat up, scratched his head sleepily, and reached around for his clothes. Rathulf followed the Briton's example and opened his trunk and retrieved his clean shirt, then, feeling cold in the damp morning air, reached in and drew out his tunic. Without a thought, he pulled it on. It was not until he was tightening his swordbelt that he realised Aethelred was staring at him, wide-eyed.

The young Briton's mouth moved, but no words came from his lips. His eyes were fixed on Rathulf's standard, and he pointed at it and shook his head. Behind Aethelred, the other men who shared their sleeping space stared too. Rathulf instinctively looked down at his tunic, but at first, his sleep-blurred mind saw nothing but the familiar golden wolves. Then Cnut's mocking words came crashing into his thoughts. "How can you be sure you will be welcome there? If the account of your heritage is true, then your fellow Dumnonians will be as keen for your head as Ivar's kin shall be here."

The wolves: the mark of his lineage, the mark of the family to be expunged from Dumnonia forever. One of the men began shouting and pointing at Rathulf, and Aethelred slammed the lid on Rathulf's trunk, rammed home the lock and shoved the chest into Rathulf's arms. 'Run, you idiot!' he yelled. 'Run!'

Rathulf turned towards the centre of the room, and the innkeeper, who had just appeared from the cellar, saw Rathulf's standard and stopped mid-step. Behind him, one of the jarl's men was halfway through pulling on his breeches, and he too stopped mid-way, astonished. His eyes leapt from the standard to the Norseman's face, then back to the golden wolves. For a moment, no one moved, then the guardsman gave a hoarse shout, the innkeeper dropped his wine jar, and Rathulf plunged for the door.

15

Watch for the full moon

Escanceaster, Dumnonia

Rathulf burst from the inn and splashed across the rain-doused square. He saw the dark opening of an alley and steered towards it. Behind him came the shouts of the men gathering themselves in pursuit. He flew down the narrow passageway, running as fast as he dared. The streets were slick with mud and filth, and the added burden of the unwieldy trunk on his shoulder tested his balance at every turn. He was also conscious that he was unarmed. His sword and dagger lay out of reach in the chest. He swung into a lane that led him uphill, hoping that it might throw his pursuers off his scent.

'No!'

At the sound of the urgent warning, Rathulf swung around to see young Wilfred running up the passage towards him, pointing to Rathulf's left. The boy stopped in his tracks and flashed Rathulf a startled look when he saw the Norseman's wolven standard, then he came to his senses and dashed past Rathulf and disappeared into the side alley, just as the men from the inn appeared on the street corner below. Their leader shouted triumphantly, prompting Rathulf to spring after Wilfred. An arrow thudded into the wall by his head, and then he was gone, half running, half sliding down the alley after his young guide. Here the houses stood so close to one another that their thatched rooves overlapped, forcing Rathulf to run at a crouch. He fell twice, landing heavily on his rump on both occasions, unable to throw out a hand to steady himself because of the accursed trunk. After the second fall, Wilfred scrambled back to help Rathulf onto his feet. The boy paused for a moment, his eyes again falling to Rathulf's tunic, then to Rathulf's face. He shook his head in wonder, then grabbed the trunk's handle and was off again, urging Rathulf to keep up. The sounds of their pursuers could always be heard, sometimes distant and muffled, sometimes frighteningly close.

Wilfred took a sharp turn and ducked through a doorway. Rathulf followed blindly, having little choice but to throw his life into the boy's hands. He collided with one of the house's occupants; it was too dark to see who it was, and he crashed to the floor for the third time. A woman screamed, then Wilfred was dragging at Rathulf's sleeve. The Norseman staggered onwards, dimly aware that he was utterly lost in this confusing maze of streets. They took a few more turns, always heading downhill away from the tower. Then Wilfred stopped in a doorway and stood panting as he waited for his urgent knocking to be answered. The door opened, and a poorly-dressed man appeared. His swarthy face turned to a scowl when he saw who stood on his doorstep, and then it changed to astonishment when he saw Rathulf. Before the stranger could utter a word, Wilfred had bundled them all back through the doorway and slammed the door shut. Rathulf couldn't help but notice that it hung on only one hinge and the gaps between the boards meant that it did little to shield them from either wind, rain or sight.

Man and boy engaged in a heated discussion held in rasping whispers, none of which Rathulf understood, although the man's consternation was evident. On numerous occasions during the debate, Rathulf found himself the subject of their attention, and at one point, their unwilling host fired a stream of questions at Rathulf, all of which went unanswered. The discussion came to an abrupt halt at a hissed command from Wilfred, who held his hand up for silence at the sound of approaching footfalls. Rathulf instinctively reached for his sword but, with a pang of alarm, remembered that both were locked in his trunk. Wilfred shook his head, and the sound of running feet passed by, quickly receding into the distance, to be swallowed by the drumming of the rain outside.

The sounds of pursuit had barely receded when the stranger led Rathulf and Wilfred out through a narrow yard behind the house. He paused at the alleyway and looked up and down before indicating they should follow him. He hurried down a steep pathway that skirted the town wall, then ducked behind a pile of broken lumber and disappeared. Rathulf plunged after him and saw a ragged hole in the stonework at the base of the wall. He dropped to his knees, shoved the trunk ahead, and then crawled through the ancient drain. He had to twist awkwardly on his side to avoid the rusted stumps of the iron grating that had long ago broken away. On the other side, the man grabbed Rathulf's arm and roughly hauled him to his feet, then he pointed down towards the river. He issued a stream of unintelligible instructions, then ducked back to the hole. Wilfred collided with him as he came through. The man cursed and cuffed the boy over the head, and then he was gone.

Rathulf and Wilfred stood beneath the bulk of the wall, catching their breath as the rain lashed down around them. Rathulf's clothes were soaked through, and his sodden tunic dragged heavily on his shoulders. There was a muffled yell from above. The Norseman glanced up and saw a warrior leaning over the parapet.

Wilfred shouted at Rathulf and pushed him down the hill. Rathulf barely had time to scoop up his trunk before an arrow came whistling past them, striking a rock nearby and skittering into the mud. Rathulf half ran, half slid down the slope, just managing to keep up with the boy as he sprang over a low wattle fence and through a fishmonger's yard. They scrambled over an upturned barrel and out onto the muddy street beyond. More shouting came from behind as they careened through an empty marketplace – little more than a slight widening of the road – ducking and weaving around the stalls shut up against the rain. A spear tore harmlessly into a woollen awning to their right, and then they were clear.

Neither Rathulf nor Wilfred saw the bowman standing down the hill ahead of them, crouched beside a cart. Unlike the other soldiers before him, this man took time to aim, ignoring the water streaming down his forehead, neck and arms. He pulled the cord taught, waited for his quarry to come within range, and released his arrow.

Wilfred must have seen the movement out of the corner of his eye, for he changed direction mid-step, springing sideways and backwards, causing Rathulf to lurch out of the way. The missile struck Wilfred in the chest with such force that it lifted him off the ground. He flipped head over heels backwards and landed at Rathulf's feet. It was pure luck that saved Rathulf from the same fate. The shaft of the next arrow slipped on the bowman's wet finger as he fired, sending it whistling past the Norseman's elbow. Rathulf let out a yelp of surprise and looked around in a panic, wondering from where it had come. Seeing that Rathulf was unarmed, the bowman stood up and drew another arrow from his quiver.

Instinct took over, and with a shout to Thor for protection, Rathulf snatched up his trunk and, holding it like a shield, ran straight at the soldier. The bowman loosed an arrow, but it slammed harmlessly into the wood, and then he sprang to the side. In his haste to move, he tripped on his bow as it tangled in the spokes of the cart's wheel. Rathulf shoved the trunk into the soldier's chest, knocking the wind from him and bowling him over. The soldier lay on his back, gasping for breath. Rathulf snatched up the dropped arrow and, yelling profanities, rammed it into the soldier's throat. Then he turned and ran back up to Wilfred, wondering why the boy hadn't got back up. 'Let's go!' he said urgently and grabbed Wilfred's hand. Only when his hand met resistance and he looked down did he see the pool of blood beneath the boy, already forming a grisly stream as it mingled with the muddy water washing down the path.

'No!' Rathulf cried, dropping down beside Wilfred.

Wilfred looked up through wide eyes, panting in shock, his tears mingling with the rain. Further uphill behind them, Rathulf saw more soldiers stumbling and sliding down the slope. One paused to throw a spear. It fell short, but the next would doubtless fly true.

Wilfred ran his fingers over Rathulf's breast, tracing the golden wolves of Dumnonia's kings, his eyes showing his wonder and pride. He tried to speak but instead coughed up blood. He turned his head weakly in the direction of the river. Rathulf understood the instruction but had no intention of leaving the boy. Another arrow slammed into the ground beside him, the shaft slapping against his ankle.

Rathulf tried to lift Wilfred, but the boy fought him off, shaking his head. The effort proved too much for him, and his eyes flew wide. Then he let out another cough and slumped in Rathulf's grip, his pale young face dropping limply onto Rathulf's forearm. Rathulf glanced behind him and saw that the men were almost upon him. He laid Wilfred back down in the mud, hoisted up his sea chest and ran towards the river. As he passed the cart, he saw the Dumnonian guardsman slumped beside the wheel, his eyes open in death. *At least you have been avenged, Wilfred.*

Rathulf plunged into the huddle of the low-roofed buildings that lined the bank, clattering along the boardwalk beside the wharf. He saw an open doorway and sprang inside, shoving it closed behind him, praying to Thor that the men hadn't seen him go inside. He carefully moved away from the entrance, struggling to control his heavy breathing as he scanned the cramped space. As far as he could tell, he was alone, sharing the space with odd-sized barrels, piles of rope and other ship-related equipment; perhaps the storeroom of a fisherman or trader, who,

Rathulf hoped, was out in his boat and well away from here. There was a commotion and shouting outside, and suddenly the men were there. Rathulf held his breath, but they pelted past the Norseman's hiding place and away down the riverside. Rathulf carefully set his trunk down on the earthen floor and crouched down to peer through a gap at the bottom of the wall by the door. Rain still thundered down outside, spattering mud up into Rathulf's face. In the background, Rathulf heard the frustrated voices of his pursuers. Soon they would realise what he'd done and double back, searching the rows of storerooms and sheds until they found their quarry.

Rathulf looked out over the river and saw that the tide was out. A wide, grey mudflat, slick and greasy under the heavy skies, lay between the shore and the channel. Rathulf knew there could be no escape that way; he'd become stuck fast in moments, an easy target for the spearmen and archers. He twisted his neck and peered further downstream. Through the grey curtain of rain, he spotted the sturdy bridge spanning the river. His moment of elation turned to dismay when he followed the bridge back to the shore and remembered the guard tower that straddled the crossing.

He swore at Thor under his breath, cursing his ill luck and reckless stupidity. *Why didn't I leave this tunic in the trunk where it belongs?* He angrily tore it off, struggling with the sodden garment and swearing at it as it tangled in his arms, in his furious despair, forgetting that he was pursued. Finally, it was off, and he threw it onto the floor. The golden wolves glinted back at him in the dim light, and Rathulf swore again and stamped on them, hating them and all they stood for. Anger swiftly turned to sorrow, and he sank to his knees, sobbing quietly, remembering Wilfred's grin as the scruffy boy handed back the stupid traveller's moneybag and Wilfred's wry chuckle as he pointed out the women watching Rathulf bathe. Then came the wonder and intense pride in the young boy's eyes in the moments before he died, when he realised who it was he had led to safety: none other than one of the Lost Princes of Dumnonia.

Rathulf brushed away his tears and reached down to smooth the golden embroidery, feeling the precious thread cold under his fingertips. *Ah, Wilfred*, he thought, *what did you do in your short life to deserve such a fate? And what did I do to deserve so loyal a guide? Well, you shall not have died in vain. I will find a way out of here, no matter what it takes, and in the name of Thor, I promise to avenge you. Know that when I am king, all the people will hear of your bravery and how a grubby street urchin saved a kingdom.*

Rathulf wrung out the tunic as best he could, and then he folded it tightly. He pulled the key from around his neck and unlocked his chest. He took out his Norse sword and scabbard, strapped them on, and then placed the still-wet tunic back in the trunk. He drew the strap around the box, set the lock, and then dropped the key around his neck under his shirt. For a moment, he wondered whether he should leave his chest here but thought better of it and hoisted it up onto his shoulder. He took a deep breath, gingerly opened the door, and peered out.

Nothing happened. No one shouted, and no arrows came his way. He stepped out onto the boardwalk and drew his sword. Despite having a weapon now, he still felt vulnerable in the open. He hurried along the wooden pathway, keeping as close to the buildings as possible, but he struggled to maintain his balance with a sword in one hand and the sea chest on his opposite shoulder. In the end, he re-sheathed the weapon, as it was more a hindrance than a help. He turned away from the bridge, heading back the way he came, hoping to find his way up to the hole in the wall. He avoided the place where Wilfred lay, not because he couldn't bear to look upon the dead boy, but for fear he would lose his resolve upon seeing him and seek out the soldiers in a crazed desire for revenge, thereby throwing all this to waste.

He spotted a group of men and women ahead and ducked

into the gap between two wattle fences barely high enough to crouch behind. He immediately felt stupid and hoped they'd not seen him, for what better way to arouse suspicion than to behave like a brigand? With little choice but to make his way along the fence line, he came out in a narrow alleyway behind the marketplace. There were more people here, huddled together in the paltry shelter of the eaves, waiting for the rain to ease. Rathulf did his best to appear normal and strode across the market and into another narrow laneway, fast realising he was running out of options and time. There were more shouts from the waterside below as the men realised their quarry was behind them somewhere. Rathulf hurried uphill, trying his best to avoid watchful eyes, his mind working furiously to conjure his next move.

Rathulf's means of escape arrived unexpectedly. He stepped around a muddy corner and all but walked into the path of a man riding a fine horse. The mare started and took a step backwards, throwing her rider off-balance. At that moment, Rathulf saw his chance. He dropped his trunk and grabbed the rider's arm. His Norse boyhood coming into play, Rathulf hauled the man from the saddle, while with the other hand, he grabbed the reins to prevent the horse from bolting. His victim hit the ground hard, the fall winding him. The rider opened and closed his mouth soundlessly, croaking for help. Remarkably, no one else was present, so Rathulf worked quickly. He lifted his trunk onto the back of the saddle. The grey mare snorted, but Rathulf held the reins tight in the crook of his arm, pulling on the bit whilst he lashed the trunk behind the saddle. He was silently thankful to Myran for having taught him this, among other valuable one-handed skills essential to a caliphate cavalryman. As soon as he was done, Rathulf thrust a foot in the stirrup, mounted the horse and pulled her around. He plunged into the street without a backwards glance, choosing the direction from which the rider had come. With one hand steadying the bouncing trunk behind him and the other holding the reins, he leaned forward and urged the mare into a gallop. In the way of his journey so far, his fortunes once again veered wildly – this time in his favour – for this was a fine horse indeed; strong, obedient, and well-trained.

The road led straight to the bridge and its guard post. He could not recall if there had been any kind of barrier last evening, so he charged up to it and was through before the startled guards had time to react. Horse and rider clattered over the bridge at full speed, Rathulf urging the mare as hard as she could run. A guard sprang out of the other gatehouse ahead of them and hurled a spear, but the mare dodged it skilfully without any prompting from her rider, and then they were through. An arrow whizzed by Rathulf's head and fell harmlessly behind them as they charged past the scattering of houses near the bridge and into the countryside beyond.

Rathulf fancied he heard distant shouts from behind him as he came to the crossroads, but his own triumphant war cry drowned them out as he stormed past a startled shepherd, leaving a scattering flock in his wake. He turned in the direction of Sankus Jermus and followed the road as it led inland towards a dark swathe of woodland. Rathulf knew that this victory would be short-lived, so he urged the mare on. She answered his call with enthusiasm, undeterred by the pace Rathulf set or the driving rain that seemed to have no end.

Soon afterwards, he came upon a way-marked junction in the road. He had no idea what the markings meant on the stubby stone plinths, so he turned southwestwards, choosing the smaller of the two roadways because this led directly to the forest. He passed through a village, its inhabitants scattering as Rathulf hurtled through. He planned to make for Sankus Jermus, the destination that Tegen had told Sigvald should be safe. She had thought Kair Uisk might be dangerous, and she had been right. *Let's hope I get a warmer welcome there*, Rathulf thought, *and if I don't, I can make it back to the beach in time for Ottar.*

He counted the days again in his head, praying that Ottar would remain true to his word. Rathulf had no hope of seeing the moon in this weather. At least he had this excellent horse and could therefore travel far more swiftly than on foot.

The track soon degraded as the trees swallowed horse and rider, and he was forced to dismount as the path narrowed to little more than a passage winding between the trees. Rathulf told himself this would be good because the tangled roots and undergrowth would hinder his pursuers. *If it doesn't hinder me too*, he thought, picking his way carefully over a moss-covered log. He paused and looked behind him, grimacing at the trail of deep hoofprints. With any luck, the men from the fort would follow the more obvious path – at least for a while – which would give him some advantage.

The track dropped down to a fast-running stream, its brown, churning waters swollen by the rain. Rathulf led the mare into the water and then turned her upstream. It took a considerable amount of encouragement to get her to walk through the water, but the riverbed was wide, and she eventually found her feet. For his part, Rathulf struggled to stay upright, gripping the harness with one hand and waving his other to keep his balance. Their slow progress was mainly because of his clumsy feet as he slipped on unseen rocks and other obstacles in the muddy water. All the while, Rathulf kept his ear open for any sound of pursuit, but mercifully the only noises he heard were those of the forest under rain and the crashing and burbling of the beck.

He had no idea how much time had passed when he finally decided to plunge back into the trees, choosing a place where the undergrowth was thick beside the bank. He led his mare up out of the water and through the hazel shrubbery for some distance before tethering her to a stout tree. He then followed their tracks back to the water's edge to cover all evidence of their passage, filling in the little craters left by her hooves with soil and leaves. He stood by the horse when he had finished, nodding with satisfaction. Whilst far from perfect, it would be unlikely now that anyone would find the place where they had left the river. He continued in what he hoped was a south-westerly direction, always walking slightly uphill, again believing that this would tire any pursuers.

The forest's edge came suddenly, with the crossing of a small brook and a short, steep climb up the other bank through thinning trees. Rathulf paused under the shelter of a stunted oak, surveying the landscape ahead of him through fast-moving sheets of rain. A vast moor rose beyond him, stretching westwards into the grey distance, its highest reaches shrouded by cloud. He wondered whether this might be the same moorland that he had seen on his way to Kair Uisk.

How far away is it? he wondered, feeling suddenly uneasy that he was riding further away from his rescue. *What if I can't find my way back in time?* Fear of being left to fend for himself in a hostile land threatened to overwhelm him, but then his horse let out a little snort, and he reminded himself that he had this wonderful mare, and all he needed to do was turn north and ride until he struck the coast. His main problem was that it was difficult to know where he was in this utterly foreign land, especially in the driving rain, which completely hid the sun.

He scanned both ways along the edges of the forest and saw, to his surprise, that a roadway emerged from the trees a short distance above him. Leaving the mare by the oak, he made his way up to the road. It was much too substantial for comfort, and Rathulf ruefully wondered whether he might even come up behind his pursuers after all the effort he had gone to avoid being seen. Knowing his luck, this road probably led straight back to the Kair Uisk. For the time being, therefore, he decided he had no choice but to join it. At least the mare was well-rested. Rathulf went back and checked the bindings on the trunk, then he mounted the fine steed and pointed her westwards onto the moor.

They made good time, coming across very little traffic as they cantered along the well-kept road. He soon learned why it was so quiet. The road took a sweeping turn and rose upwards. Suddenly they were surrounded by dense fog. Rathulf cursed and pulled the mare back to a walk. He peered into the grey mist ahead, barely able to see the path ahead of them. He had no idea what lay on either side or behind him, and he soon felt unsettled by the quiet, damp gloom. He murmured encouragement to his horse and pressed on, praying that he would not suddenly appear amid a patrol, or worse, come across a fog Jötunn. He shuddered at the thought of it, and the mare skittered nervously in response to his uneasiness.

He maintained a steady pace, straining to keep his eyes on the path ahead. Even so, he twice led them off the track, which rapidly dwindled into sticky bogland on both occasions. To add to his suffering, the light was beginning to fail. Clearly, he had spent more time in the forest than he had reckoned, and now he faced the prospect of spending a miserable night on this exposed, fog-bound moor. He had little choice but to continue westwards, regretting his decision to aim for high ground. His only consolation was that surely no one would find him in this mire.

Some while later, a low shape loomed out of the fog, and then another crouched nearby. Rathulf stopped, peering ahead while carefully reaching for his sword. They were the size of a large dog but did not appear to be moving. The mare seemed untroubled, so he gently nudged her forward. The dark shape stayed motionless, and then more appeared in a line ahead of them, on either side of the pathway. Rathulf felt his neck prickle, and he drew in a breath to calm himself, realising that they were rocks. *What is the purpose of this place?* he wondered. It felt like witchery to him, and his discomfort grew as the mist swirled around him, revealing that the row of grey stones continued into the gloom. *Where is this leading me? Straight into the maw of a Draug, just as likely.* He drew his sword, kicked the mare's flanks, and ordered her into a gallop. Yelling at the top of his lungs to scare away the Jötnar, he charged down the row of stones, swinging his sword wildly about his head. No sooner had they reached full speed than the row of sentinels ended abruptly in a bog.

'Thor, protect me!' Rathulf cried as his horse stumbled in the mire. It was a trap, just as he'd feared. He wrenched on the reins and turned her to the right, hoping to find firm ground, but they only sank deeper. 'Fuck!' he swore, expecting to feel the sharp bite of fangs or claws tearing into his back at any moment. His horse was as frightened as he was, and she backed up out of the squelching moss and turned for the line of stones.

'Don't go back there,' Rathulf cried, 'they'll be waiting for us!'

But she ignored him and flew back the way they had come, knowing this led to safer ground. They thundered past the last stones, but she galloped on, forcing Rathulf to lean back and haul on the reins to pull her up. 'Steady now,' he said, patting her neck. He realised he was panting, and he sat still for a long time, trying to calm himself. He peered into the mist, expecting a monstrous shape to materialise, but none came.

He was aware darkness was falling, so he turned the mare around and pointed her westward, this time paying closer attention to the path ahead. They came upon the stones again, but they stood to his left, and he realised they must have inadvertently strayed off the trail earlier, unconsciously drawn to the stone passageway, as was no doubt the Draug's objective. Rathulf wondered why they had been allowed to escape. Had the monster eaten already, its hunger sated by some earlier hapless traveller?

Whatever the case, Rathulf had no intention of waiting to find out, nor did he relish the idea of spending the night in the open up here. He urged the mare onwards, and soon enough, the road began to dip into a small swale. To Rathulf's relief, the fog thinned as they dropped below the cloud. The moor stretched away in all directions around them, and the path soon began to rise again towards the mist. Rathulf stopped, searching either side of the track for any sign of shelter. He spotted a low, grey shape some distance away and decided anything had to be better than curling up beside the road. He didn't dare imagine what unnamed horrors roamed these parts in the night. He dismounted and led the mare along the road a short distance, and then they followed a narrow, brown-stained beck downhill, Rathulf carefully watching where he placed his feet to avoid plunging into a bog. They came to no harm and arrived at a ruined building made from rough-hewn stone. It was circular, with the floor lying at some depth below the surrounding ground level. It had no roof, and the wall barely stood higher than Rathulf on the road-facing side, but once inside, it would be sufficient to hide them from passers-by. However, as for the fell monsters of the night, it offered no protection at all.

Rathulf unstrapped the trunk and the previous rider's bundle and placed them in the lee of the wall, then let the mare's reins drop. She let out a snort of thanks and wandered a short distance away to chew on the lush grass beside a small spring; perhaps the reason this place had been built. For his part, Rathulf sank gratefully to the ground, his back to the cold, wet wall. The rain had stopped for the time being, and from this high perch, Rathulf could see a fair distance away to the south. Nothing about this bleak landscape felt familiar to him, and he shivered with fear, cold and hunger. He reached down and unwrapped the rider's bundle, finding an excellent woollen blanket, a spare shirt, a dagger (plain but of good quality), a tinder box (of no use to him here) and a small cloth bag containing some chunks of salted pork and hard, dry bread. He ate the food hungrily and then made his way to the spring. The water was clear and pure, and Rathulf realised that he'd drunk too little this day despite being so wet from the rain. Once he'd satisfied his thirst, he took up the mare's reins and tied them around his trunk, not at all convinced it was a good idea, but he could see no other way of tethering her.

He then wrapped himself in the blanket and leaned against the wall, his drawn sword resting across his knees, ready to defend himself if the need arose. Night fell quickly, and the rain picked up again in a steady drizzle. Despite his determination to stay awake, Rathulf soon succumbed to exhaustion and drifted into a fitful sleep.

A day's ride further to the north, Ottar and his reduced crew of four settled in for the night, dropping anchor just beyond arrow-shot off the beach and offering a prayer to Njord to stop the rain. He was soaked through and didn't fancy the chill night ahead, but he'd made a promise to Rathulf and so had returned to the beach, and now he would wait. He offered another prayer, this time to Rathulf's patron God Thor to let Rathulf know that Ottar was ready to take him home should he wish it.

The door slammed open violently, and the startled Abbot let out an involuntary expletive, then he crossed himself for his blasphemy.

'Where is he?' demanded the tall, finely dressed man standing in the doorway.

'Earl Talec,' the abbot said, putting down the parchment he had been reading. He stood and bowed to the nobleman. 'I am very sorry, my Lord, but to whom do you refer?'

Talec let out an impatient snort and entered the room. He was followed by two armed guardsmen who took position on either side of the doorway. 'You know who. I was told that Brother Osbert was seen entering the mynster yesterday evening. Where is he?'

'He... he left early this morning, my Lord,' the Abbot said.

'And where did he go?' Talec snarled.

'I... I'm sorry, my Lord, I did not speak with him. He was gone by the time of Lauds. It was still dark.'

'And that did not raise your suspicions? A known rebel

sympathiser sneaking off before daylight, in the rain, no less?' Talec walked up to the Abbot, his eyes narrowed in anger. 'No doubt you've heard about the dissident who showed himself this morning?'

The abbot nodded.

'Well, that same rebel walked hand-in-hand into the city yesterday afternoon with your monk, Osbert. Scores of people saw them together. A convivial pair full of good cheer, apparently.'

'He's not *my* monk, my Lord. He was excommunicated for his offences. You bore witness.'

'He still wears a fucking habit.'

'It is the cloak of a heretic, My Lord.'

'And yet you allowed him into your mynster.' Talec stepped up to the monk and stood face to face with him. Being somewhat taller than Hendra, Talec looked down his nose at him. 'Where is Osbert?'

'I truly do not know, my Lord,' the Abbot insisted. 'He took his leave without my knowledge. I naturally refused him permission to stay in our guesthouse, so he chose to sleep with the lay kitchen staff. Someone met him before dawn, then the two of them went off in the direction of the docks. I presume they had a boat there.'

'Obviously,' Talec snapped, 'he was meeting that dissident. My men chased the shit down to the river, but he vanished.' Talec let out a frustrated sigh. 'So Osbert said nothing about his plans or these rebels?'

The Abbot shook his head. I expect they were Kernowyon, wanting to impress someone back west. They do it from time to time, don't they? Some sort of initiation, I've heard. Go to Escanceaster and stir up trouble for Earl Talec. It is quite the sport, I believe.'

Talec's eyes narrowed. 'Take care, Abbot.'

The Abbot spread his hands in entreaty. 'I am sorry, My Lord. I did not mean to offend.'

Talec decided not to press the matter. 'Well, the man who put on that tunic was not Kernowyon. They say he was a foreigner. I want to know what they are up to and what Osbert's young companion was carrying in his chest. I believe their disgraceful act at the inn was a diversion, but for what?'

'If I were to hazard a guess, My Lord, I imagine they carried weapons. We all know the Kernowyon are receiving help from their cousins over the sea in West Francia. That foreigner was probably delivering money and swords, and they decided to enjoy a little sport whilst they were here.'

'And that amuses you, does it, to have my nose rubbed in it by rebel filth?'

The Abbot shook his head. 'Of course not, My Lord. They are sinners and traitors.'

Talec let out a long breath through his nose, evidently deciding that the Abbot was telling the truth. 'You're wrong. They were up to something.' He turned to leave. 'If you do hear anything – anything at all – you will report it to me immediately, do you hear?'

The Abbot nodded. 'Of course, my Lord.'

Talec swept from the room, followed by his two guardsmen. The Abbot listened to their receding footsteps and the sound of the outer door opening and closing, then he shut his own door and leaned against it, crossing himself. 'Lord God, deliver me from my sins, for I have lapsed most gravely this hour.'

'Oh, for God's sake, Hendra, stop all this self-flagellation,' came a voice from behind the wall on the opposite side of the room. A door creaked open, and Brother Osbert stepped from behind the tapestry.

'What the Hell are you up to?' Hendra hissed, 'and why would you do something so inflammatory? You're unwelcome here as it is. I presume that foreign boy is from Francia bearing gold and blades for the cause? Where is he now? On his way back home?'

Brother Osbert raised his eyebrows. 'What makes you think it was my idea? I didn't have anything to do with it.'

Abbot Hendra gave him a sceptical look. 'Lies fall from your tongue like rain from the sky. You were seen entering the city with that rebel, claiming him as your bodyguard. Who is he?'

'What would you say if I told you that I met that young man for the first time on the road to Crediantun yesterday afternoon?'

'I would not believe you. What exactly is going on?'

Osbert laughed. 'You think I'm going to tell you so that you can scuttle off to squawk to the Turncoat and earn your keep?'

The Abbot let out a snort of disgust. 'I'm no traitor, brother, as you know, but I do not support your reckless campaign. I told Talec what you wanted him to hear. Now get out of here before I change my mind and turn you in.'

Osbert knew better than to argue, so he bid farewell and left the Abbot to stew in his self-reproach. At least he had learned that Hendra knew nothing of the mysterious rebel either. *But if he isn't one of Hendra's disciples, then who the Hell is he?* The answer that came to him was the one that had kept him awake most of the previous night, and again Osbert cursed himself for not trusting his instincts and going down to the inn to confront the boy directly. He'd almost done it earlier while they were on the road, but it hadn't felt safe or wise given the short time of their acquaintance. It was impossible, of course, and yet....

'Damnation,' he muttered as he hurried through the cloister garden to the gate that led out into the city. A light mizzle had set in, and he drew his cowl around his head. *Well, at least I know where you are going next, he thought. Let's just hope you don't reveal yourself to those sycophants before I can get word to Camus, although he'll not believe me, like as not.* He let out a sigh, then carefully eased open the gate to the alleyway outside.

Rathulf woke with a start to darkness. He scrabbled around for his sword and found it lying by his side. He couldn't recall falling asleep, nor did he remember his dreams. He looked up to see the curious face of his borrowed mare, who had remained obediently by his side all night. He smiled back at her and again thanked Gefion for her kindness in his time of need. He had no idea what time of night it was, but the clouds had thinned, and Mani's face shone brightly behind a ragged shroud. Rathulf stared at it, horrified. Was it waxing, full or waning? The veil of cloud blurred the disc, so he could not be sure, but it certainly looked full to him. Fighting off a sense of panic, he looked back up to the roadway and saw that the mist had cleared, so he quickly rolled up his blanket and lashed everything back onto the horse. He led her back up to the track, and they set off westwards, keen to take advantage of the cover of night to draw further away from trouble but further away from Ottar. Soon, he found himself looking for any kind of road or trackway that might lead north, and he prayed that this moor would end soon. *I can't afford to miss Ottar,* he told himself. *What if I receive just as cold a welcome in Sankus Germus. Then what do I do? Where do I go?*

Shortly before dawn, the rain came again, carried by a stiffening breeze out of the west. The weather steadily worsened, and Rathulf rode hunched low over the mare's neck, shivering with cold and exhaustion, but he pressed on, knowing that he had very little time to make it back to where Ottar had dropped him; assuming, of course, that he could even find it again. He knew he was hopelessly lost, but he hung onto the hope that once he'd found the sea, he could look for the island, then turn east or west, depending upon where it lay.

He came to a crossroads and took the smaller track leading to the north. It led to a ford, but the river ran too high and swift due to the heavy rain. He carried on, his sense of alarm rising at the thought that he might be left behind. The trail petered out into another bog, so he turned around and returned to the crossroads as the sky began to lighten, although the rain did not ease. He took the original path further westwards at the crossroads and was rewarded shortly afterwards by another trackway leading north.

He almost missed it in the driving rain. He kicked the mare into a gallop, knowing with increasing certainty that he had to get away from this unwelcoming land and return to Aurlandsfjorden, back to the place he knew, the place he belonged.

He rode recklessly, fear of abandonment driving his carelessness as the path narrowed and entered a thickly-wooded forest. All that mattered was that it led north. He had convinced himself that it had been a full moon, meaning that Ottar was already at the beach, waiting for him. He paid little attention to the path ahead, focused only on his rescue. The track rose steadily beside a deepening gorge, through which a river roared.

In the gloom of the rainy dawn, neither he nor his mare saw the landslip ahead of them. One moment the path was there, then they rounded a bend, and there was nothing; just a wide, deep gouge in the earth. They shot out into space at full tilt, only this was not Odin's Breach, and there was nowhere to land on the other side.

Horse and rider crashed into broken trees and branches as they tumbled with flailing limbs down the slope. It was all over within a few heartbeats, the two of them coming to a stop amid the jumble of uprooted trees and shrubbery near the base of the hillside. Rathulf had mercifully been knocked out early in their fall, so he did not suffer when he landed on the sheared stump of a sapling. Nearby, the river thundered through the steep-sided gorge, carrying away the debris swept into its path, turning the water a pale muddy brown. Above them, the rain cleared, and the clouds briefly parted, revealing the full moon at its zenith; the pale blue disc shining like a great eye against a pink dawn sky.

Arann, a teenage novice from the newly-established Hlidaford Mynster, made his way along the narrow path that clung to the riverbank, carefully treading so that he didn't slip in the mud and fall into the fast-flowing waters beside him. It was just after morning prayers, and he'd sloped out after Lauds to avoid the Prime mass. It came at the cost of missing breakfast, but he didn't feel like singing today. He'd get into trouble for sure, but he needed to escape the confining walls of the mynster, for he loved the strong, invigorating smells of the forest after rain.

And there was also the small matter of his snares.

It had been a hard week, and Brother Caedmon had been particularly cruel in his punishment for Arann's spontaneous improvisation during one of the psalms. It was so hard to stick to the monotonous drone required of the service when his heart wanted to express his joy in the music through a melodic counterpoint! It was not as though he did it on purpose. It was God's will, surely? Brother Caedmon had, of course, said that was nonsense and that Arann had instead surrendered to his sinful indulgences. Arann had stupidly spoken back and, as a result, received a flurry of lashes from Caedmon's birch.

Why keep punishing me for my gift? he wondered. *Am I to be denied even that small joy? What am I saying? Those old soaks relish inflicting punishment; on themselves as much as we novices. Perhaps they are jealous of my talent? God knows, none of them can hold a note, except for Brother Joseph, but he doesn't count because he is nice to me. Remarkable, really, since I'm one of the most hated people in the kingdom. But then Brother Joseph is a decent man, unlike all those other fart-filled bags of wind.* He sighed, knowing that he was deluding himself. *No, it's because of my Great Sin, for which I am to be forever punished and purged of any moments of happiness in my life. So much for forgiveness,* he thought angrily, but at the end of the day, his actions had been devastating in their consequences, resulting in the near destruction of an entire kingdom. *Well, at least I got something good from their harsh sentence for my mistake.* He smiled to himself. God obviously disagreed with their judgement, for why else would He have given him this spectacular compensation?

He glanced warily at the surging torrent, knowing an

unpleasant death lay in those turgid waters. None of the monks could swim, of course, and Arann was no different; not that anyone would survive if they fell in there. He turned his attention away from the river and focused on finding his traps. His snares had all been washed away in the downpour as expected. He had set them by the water's edge across the little paths the rabbits and voles used. He let out a sigh. *Ah well, at least I managed to get out for a bit.*

Above him, the fast-moving cloud parted briefly, and the early morning sunlight speared down the gorge and sparkled brightly on the myriad droplets on the leaves, briefly transforming the forest into a jewelled fairyland. *Not that fairies exist, of course. That would be blasphemy.* Arann paused, struck by the scene's beauty, and then he burst into song. He sang for the sun, the rain, the leaves, the birds, and the lucky voles that had escaped to live another day. In his more fanciful moments, he would imagine the various animals pausing in their scrabbling and fossicking to listen to his singing. The forest was his most appreciative audience, for here, he could let his voice soar and swoop and dive without fear of reprisal. Here, there were no grumpy monks critical of his timing or timbre, and here he was free of the daily reminders of his Great Sin that stung him in so many little ways; the unfair apportioning of unpleasant chores, the serving of lesser helpings at mealtimes, or finding that the only bench available in the calefactory was the one furthest from the fire.

As suddenly as it had appeared, the sun vanished behind more clouds, and Arann fell silent. He sighed and turned to go back to the monastery, but he heard an unfamiliar noise in the silence. A sound that didn't belong. His mind could do that; fade out all the other noise, like the angry river beside him, to focus on one thing, be it a lark in song, the chirruping of a cricket, or the heavy breathing of an animal close by. He froze. That was undoubtedly no rabbit. Swallowing hard, he slowly turned to look behind him.

Standing just six feet away was a terrifyingly large grey wolf, its golden eyes fixed intently on him.

'Jesus, Mary and Joseph,' Arann whimpered, standing dead still.

The wolf took a step towards him.

'Nice wolf?' Arann whispered, holding up a hand and wondering how far the river was behind him. He suddenly became aware of the river's noise. It roared so loudly in his head that it was impossible to know whether he was yards from it or his next step would send him to a watery grave. *Better that than being torn to shreds and eaten alive by a slathering wolf?* he wondered.

The beast did not growl, nor did it sink low in an attacking stance – it just stared at him, its gaze impossible to avoid. 'What do you want?' Arann asked it while praying in his head for God to conjure a miracle to save him. He'd seen what a pack of wolves could do to sheep, and he'd even seen a shepherd come in with his arm shredded by one of the beasts, his forearm hanging by skin alone from the severed elbow. This was not how Arann imagined he'd die. An assassin's knife, perhaps, but not being eaten by a wolf in the forest that he had thought was his friend. Given how many powerful enemies he could list, it would be ironic if it were a wild animal that ended up killing him. Still, it would be cause for celebration for many.

Why did I go out this morning? he wondered in desperation, his eyes still locked on the wolf. I should have stayed indoors. I was warned not to go wandering alone in the forest.

The wolf let out a low growl, which startled Arann into a high-pitched yelp. Then the animal unexpectedly released the novice and trotted down the path. Arann didn't dare move, although he badly wanted to run as hard as possible in the other direction.

The wolf stopped and looked back at Arann as though it was waiting.

'I'm not following you if that's what you want,' Arann said. 'I'm not an idiot. There's a pack of you around that corner.'

It started walking back towards him. Arann glanced over his shoulder. He was running out of ground. The path here turned and made its way up over a rocky hillock, and Arann wondered whether he could make it up there in time. The wolf stopped and sat down, watching him.

'What do you want?' Arann asked, frustrated.

The beast tilted its head and let out a little whine, then it rose and walked away again, looking behind him.

'Be strong and courageous,' Arann muttered in prayer. 'Do not fear or be in dread of them, for it is the Lord my God who goes with me. He will not leave or forsake me.' *I must be mad*, he thought, nevertheless following the animal, for it was plain that was what it wanted. He felt an odd tingling in his chest, a sense that the wolf meant him no harm. *No doubt a devilish trick to lull me*, he thought, crossing himself.

They walked along the riverbank for a short distance as the path rose over a small knoll, where the wolf stopped. Arann gasped when he reached the top and saw what lay before him. A broad swathe of the forest had been swept down the steep wall of the gorge by God's Great Hand, leaving an ugly scar in its wake. Below them lay a jumbled mass of wreckage; trees that had been torn in half mixed with boulders, earth and mud. The landslip had partially blocked the river, which was swirling and gnawing at its edges, and as Arann watched, a tree slipped into the torrent and was snatched away, tumbling and rolling as it was flushed downstream.

Arann heard a strange, anguished sound from somewhere in the tangled wreckage. The wolf sat down, looking from Arann to the debris.

'Jesus, my Lord and Protector, you want me to go down there? What manner of monster is hiding in wait to make me his dinner? Do you get the scraps as a reward for luring me here? Is that it?'

The wolf settled down on the wet ground, resting his muzzle on his forepaws, his eyes holding Arann's gaze. It was all bizarre and unsettling.

Shaking a little from nerves, the novice cautiously picked his way down the slope, partly for fear of the fate that awaited him but also because the ground was all broken up and slippery. He struggled to maintain his footing, and soon enough, his habit was covered in mud, rotting leaves and twigs. *Brilliant*, he thought, flicking off the worst of it but knowing that he was compounding his impending punishment.

He pushed his way through a patch of uprooted undergrowth and came upon a shocking sight: a horse, wild-eyed and shivering, with its broken hind leg still caught up in the crook of a split tree so that the beast hung upside down with its head and flank resting on the ground in front of Arann. The youth gasped and looked away, taking a deep breath to calm himself. He moved to the side to avoid the mare's gaze and saw that the horse was saddled, but there was no sign of its rider. He looked up the steep hillside and wondered what on Earth had possessed them to come out last night in that terrible storm. *What did you do to deserve this fate?* Arann wondered. He squinted up the hill. *Is that a box up there by that tree? I wonder if it came loose when you fell?* There appeared to be a travelling roll too, but with all the muck and debris, it was difficult to tell. Everything is blurry beyond my outstretched hand, he thought ruefully. Still, his eyesight was a good deal better than most of the cranky old monks of Hlidaford, where squinting was a typical facial expression.

On an impulse, Arann turned and checked the horse more carefully. It was then that he found its rider on the other side, pinned beneath the near-dead animal. The rider was barely a man, with a handsome face and unfashionably long hair tied in a braid. He lay so still that Arann thought he must be dead. The rider wore an impressive-looking sword, and his richly-dyed clothes implied wealth or nobility, as did the fine mount, of course. *What were you doing out here?* Arann wondered again as he checked for signs of life. To his surprise, he felt a pulse.

'Jesus Christ!' he swore. 'You're alive?'

He slapped the young man's face to rouse him, but the rider did not respond. Arann tried to move the horse off him, using a broken branch as a lever, but the mare was stuck fast and far too heavy, and all that Arann achieved for his efforts was a further faceful of leaves and muck when the branch broke under strain. What he did find, however, was the terrible wound in the rider's thigh where he had been impaled on a broken branch.

'Merciful mother,' Arann muttered, shaking his head. There was nothing he could do for the poor fellow on his own. The rider was barely alive and would need urgent help if he was to survive. Arann put his hand on the youth's shoulder. 'I'm going to get help. You stay alive, do you hear me?' He muttered a quick prayer of salvation for the youth, and then he turned to climb back up to the wolf. The ground moved underneath him. 'Christ!' he called, grabbing at a branch to steady himself as he heard a cracking and splintering of wood behind him. Another fallen tree was being engulfed by the raging waters, taking a slab of ground with it.

I can't leave you here, Arann thought. *You'll get washed away.*

Cursing, he went back to the horse and searched for a better lever. He found a more substantial branch and worked to wedge the unwieldy thing under the horse. This time it worked, and the horse slid a little closer to the river. It was enough to free the injured young man, but Arann nearly vomited when he pulled the rider off the branch that had impaled him.

'Mother of God,' he muttered, avoiding looking at the dreadful wound as he dragged the young man uphill towards the wolf. He slipped and landed in the muck more times than he could count, and by the time he had reached safe ground, he was covered from head to toe in mud. He flopped down beside his patient, no longer frightened of the wolf, which sat and watched him in silence.

'Thanks for your help,' Arann said, lying on his back, panting.

A heavy burst of rain arrived, prompting Arann to sit up. He rechecked the rider and was rewarded with a weak pulse.

'There is no chance I can drag you all the way to the mynster by myself,' he said. 'You're too heavy.'

He stood, and the wolf rose with him.

'I can't do anything,' Arann told it, then he pointed down at the rider. 'You must wait here and keep an eye on him while I get help. Will you do that?'

The wolf seemed to nod in understanding, and then it settled down next to the injured young man, flicking its ears in the rain.

'I'll be back as soon as I can,' Arann said to it. 'Promise.' Then he turned and ran.

'He's not coming,' Gunnar said. 'I'll bet he got himself killed on the first day.'

Ottar threw him a dark glare. 'We don't know that.'

'So what do you plan to do? Wait here for another week? We've already wasted three days on this beach. Even he's not so dumb that he can't see when the moon is full.'

'You'd like that, wouldn't you? Your nemesis dead and out of your way? Well, it won't make anyone like you any more than they already don't,' Ottar said harshly.

'He's right, much as I hate to say it,' said Hakon from the other side of the boat. 'We've attracted the erlendars' attention staying out in the open for so long, so we can't wait here anymore. They'll be back in force soon enough. And with the weather turning sour, we'll have no hope of getting home if we don't leave now. You can read the signs as well as I. Ran is not going to waste any more of her time on us. You have the lives of seven other men to consider, remember?'

'Six,' Gunnar reminded him, for Vidar had died two days before they'd set out to return to the beach.

Ottar knew all of it to be accurate, but he also knew that Rathulf would be completely alone if they left now. If Rathulf were somehow still alive, he'd have to fend for himself until next summer, which felt like a lifetime away as Ottar looked out over this deserted beach here at the other end of the world. He heaved a long sigh. 'Very well,' he said. 'Let's go home.'

'About time,' Gunnar said, jumping over the side to retrieve the anchor and heave the boat into deeper water.

In a flash of anger, Ottar grabbed an oar from the rack above, intending to slam it into the ugly dritt's face as he climbed back aboard. *Let him stay here too and see how he fares.*

'No!' Hakon shouted, grabbing his skipper's arm as he swung the heavy beam at Gunnar.

Gunnar let out a startled cry, and he grabbed the oar blade as it came to a halt in front of his face. He spat out an expletive and used the oar to clamber aboard. 'I wouldn't do that if I were you,' he snarled. 'You need me to get back to Sognefjorden.'

'I'm willing to take my chances,' Ottar said. 'Get off my ship.'

'No.'

'Ottar,' Hakon warned. 'Don't do this. He's Eirik's son.'

'Eirik will never know.'

'You're putting us in an impossible situation, damn you. Yes, I think he's a repellent bag of shit, but it's not his fault that Rathulf hasn't come back. You can't take it out on him. Rathulf's fate is with the Gods now. We've done our bit. We delivered him back to his homeland as was meant, and it is our fulfilling of that part of his destiny that will give us leverage with the Gods when we ask for their help to guide us safely home.'

Ottar threw the oar onto the deck and stalked back to the tiller. When no one moved, he roared at them. 'What are you waiting for? Get the damn sail rigged and hauled up that mast!'

As the wind caught the sail and the *Storm Beater* surged away from Dumnonia, Ottar peered back along the beach, desperately wanting the seventeen-year-old to appear from the hinterland on his horse and gallop out to meet them. But of course, Rathulf didn't come. The beach remained as deserted as it had been when they'd pulled up three days ago.

'May the Gods of Asgard look out for you, Rathulf, whether in life or death,' Ottar prayed. 'If you have perished, then I pray you died with your sword drawn and that you are now sharing tales of adventure with Alrik in Valhalla. If you are alive, I pray that you are safe in the hands of your family and that you are surrounded by such joy and contentment that you have already forgotten us.'

He tossed a piece of silver into their wake, then he turned for'ard and steered them toward home.

END OF BOOK 4

READ ON IN BOOK 5 OF
THE WOLVES OF DUMNONIA SAGA:
THE MONK'S SWORD

MAPS, GLOSSARY AND HISTORICAL NOTES

Warning: *These notes contain information which may spoil the reader's enjoyment of the books if read in advance of the story. You are advised to consult only those words in the glossary relevant to the passage you are currently reading. You will also find plenty of other information, including more background to the characters, the Viking Age, and the inspiration for this series at: www.wolvesofdumnonia.com*

As a work of historical fiction, *The Apprentice Prince*, and indeed the whole *Wolves of Dumnonia* series, is the result of many years' research into the period we know as the Viking Age. As always, I apologise for any historical errors or inaccuracies that have crept into the story, and I'm happy to receive your comments and corrections at: feedback@wolvesofdumnonia.com

Dumnonia in 823AD

While the characters and their deeds in this book are imagined (with the exception of the Saxon King Ecgberht of Wessex), the historical context of the *Wolves of Dumnonia* saga is authentic.

All of the locations mentioned in this book existed in Rathulf's time, and where possible, I have used the contemporary names for those places. For instance, Escanceaster = modern-day Exeter.

On the following pages, you will find maps showing the places mentioned in the text. You can find high resolution, colour versions of these and all the other maps from the series (Maps 1 to 5) on the *Wolves of Dumnonia* website.

Following the maps is a glossary of place names mentioned in this book listed in alphabetical order under the name by which they were known 1,200 years ago. I have also provided a glossary of terms that are used in the book. Once again, for the complete glossary of words used throughout the series, please pop across to the Wolves of Dumnonia website.

MAP 6: Rathulf's Sea Journey to Dumnonia
Route of the Storm Beater in late summer 823 AD
Attack on the Storm Beater
0 50 100 150 200 250 Miles
0 50 100 150 200 250 300 350 Kilometres
N
From Sognefjorden
Hjaltland (Shetland Islands)
Orkneyjar (Orkney Islands)
Suðreyjar (Hebrides)
VESTRSAE (ATLANTIC OCEAN)
STRATHCLYDE
NORTHUMBRIA
Lindisfarne
Jarrow
Mannin (Isle of Man)
Eoforwic (York)
ÍRLAND
Dubhlinn (Dublin)
Weisfjord (Wexford)
Hlymrekr (Limerick)
Cork
Vadrefjord (Waterford)
Tamoworthig (Tamworth)
WEST WEALAS
MERCIA
EAST ANGLIA
Lundenwic (London)
WESSEX
KENT
Wintanceaster (Winchester)
Lundi / Puffin Island (Lundy)
Scirburne (Sherborne)
DUMNONIA
Escanceaster (Exeter)
St Germanus (St Germans)
Syllingar (Isles of Scilly)

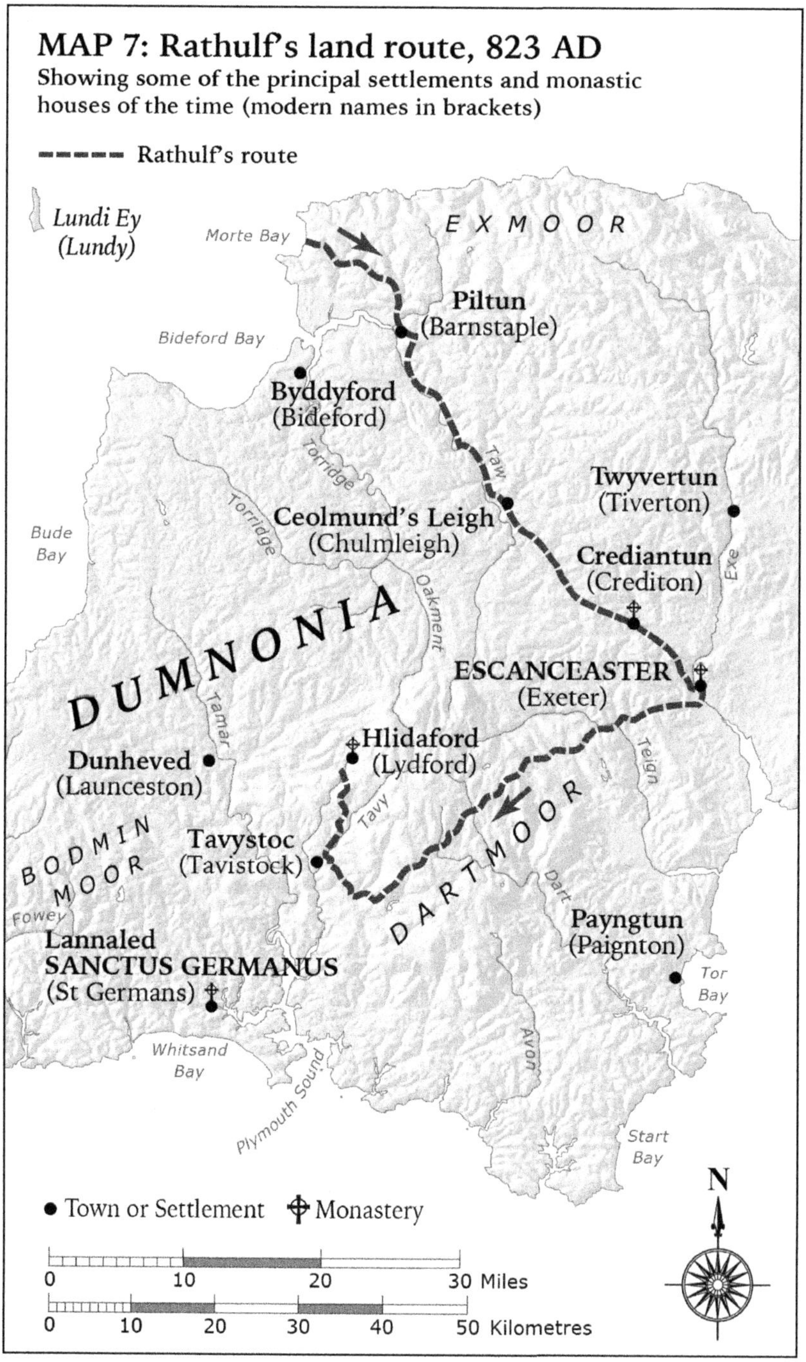
MAP 7: Rathulf's land route, 823 AD
Showing some of the principal settlements and monastic houses of the time (modern names in brackets)
Rathulf's route
Lundi Ey (Lundy)
Morte Bay
EXMOOR
Piltun (Barnstaple)
Bideford Bay
Byddyford (Bideford)
Torridge
Taw
Twyvertun (Tiverton)
Torridge
Ceolmund's Leigh (Chulmleigh)
Bude Bay
Crediantun (Crediton)
Exe
Oakment
DUMNONIA
ESCANCEASTER (Exeter)
Tamar
Hlidaford (Lydford)
Teign
Dunheved (Launceston)
Tavy
DARTMOOR
BODMIN MOOR
Tavystoc (Tavistock)
Fowey
Dart
Lannaled SANCTUS GERMANUS (St Germans)
Payngtun (Paignton)
Tor Bay
Avon
Whitsand Bay
Plymouth Sound
Start Bay
N
Town or Settlement
Monastery
0 10 20 30 Miles
0 10 20 30 40 50 Kilometres

Glossary of Place Names

Throughout this series, you will encounter names and terms that may be new to you, principally because most of the unfamiliar ones are Old Norse (the language of the Norwegian Vikings; abbreviated to 'ON' in the glossary) or derived from Old Norse. There are also a number of Old English (abbreviated to 'OE' below) place names which have since evolved into the different spellings by which we know those places today. The glossary will hopefully shed some light on them for you. There's also the odd Latin term in there too. Remember you can hop over to the searchable online version at: www.wolvesofdumnonia.com

A note on historical place names

Where possible, I have used the name and spelling by which a settlement was known in the early- to mid-ninth century (i.e. the 800s AD). In some cases, this has been quite difficult, however, because spellings often vary between sources, or in some cases, there isn't a record of the name by which that settlement was known at that time. You might also be surprised how much a place name can change over time; sometimes to a completely new name altogether. This is especially the case where a place has changed hands through history (e.g. Eboracum > Eoforwic > Jorvik > Yerk > Yourke > Yarke > York). I have also chosen to use the 'er' suffix (rather than 're' written in some sources) for names like ...mynster and ...ceaster. I am sure I have been inconsistent from time to time, for which I apologise to those purists amongst you.

Likewise for my Old Norse spellings, where I suspect I have also been inconsistent, for instance using 'th' instead of 'ð'. Again my apologies to any who are offended by my misspellings or my mixing of accents and modifiers.

ON = Old Norse. OE = Old English (Anglo-Saxon). L = Latin

Name	*Description*
Armorica	Home of Mael ap Caradoc in exile, Armorica is the Roman name for the province of northwestern Gaul and Spain. In the context of this story, specifically the lands known today as 'Brittany' in western France. It is no coincidence that the area is called Brittany (and its inhabitants 'Bretons'), as these lands were settled by the Britons of Cornwall following the collapse of the Roman Empire in AD410. Indeed, by the middle of the 6th Century, this area of Armorica was known as Britannia, and within this division were the minor kingdoms of Dumnonia and Cornouaille, reflecting their direct origins across the channel. The Breton and Cornish languages were also identical in those times, and even today are the most closely related of the surviving Celtic languages. It isn't known why the migrations took place, for certainly a large number of people left old Dumnonia for Armorica, and this occurred over a period of centuries. The most popular theories centre around the Saxon expansion into British lands; as the Saxon influence extended westward, more people left for the "free" lands of the south. It is even possible that the settlement was originally started by a few adventurous souls, and as 'New Dumnonia' became more secure and viable, perhaps more people came, lured by the travel brochures which promised warm sun, fertile lands and, most importantly, no Saxon overlords. [Todd: 238-240]
Bretland **Bretlander**	A Norse term for Britain / an inhabitant of Britain. ON.
Caer Uisc	Capital of Dumnonia, now known as modern-day Exeter. See the entry for Escanceaster below.
Cornubia	The ancient Latin name for Cornwall, as recorded by the Romans. The name also refers to the related British kingdom in Armorica (the Breton peninsula in West Francia). Ancient Cornubia occupied a territory coextensive with the later Breton kingdom of Cornouaille, south of the River Elorn to the Elle. L.
Cornwall	The modern name for the land that was once part of the kingdom of Dumnonia. While some sources claim that the present-day name of Cornwall is derived from 'Cornovii' (the Celtic name for the people inhabiting the far west of the

Name	*Description*
Cornwall (cont'd)	land), unfortunately it is more likely to have originated from Old English. The Saxons referred to the Dumnonians as the Cornwælisc or Cornwealhas; the direct translation being the 'Welsh of the Horn' (horn referring to the promontory which the Dumnonii inhabited). Innocuous enough until one learns that 'Welsh' (wælisc) is, in fact, a less-than-kind term derived from the Old English word 'wealh' (plural wealhas), meaning a foreigner, stranger or borderer, and also serf or slave. No wonder the Welsh prefer to describe themselves by their Celtic name, Cymru (pronounced coom-ree). Some Medieval maps also show the area now covered by Cornwall and Devon as 'West Wales.' [Source = Brewer's Dictionary of Phrase and Fable 1898 + others]
Cridiantun / Crediantun	Saxon name for an important monastic settlement a few miles northwest Escanceaster (Exeter), its modern name being Crediton. OE meaning is "town on the River Creedy." It is perhaps most famous for being the birthplace of Winfrith or Saint Boniface, who was born there in c. 672 and then took his Christian mission across to the Frankish Empire (where he became patron saint) and to the heathen lands beyond. OE.
Dumnonia	Birthplace of Rathulf and his brother Aneurin ap Cadwyr, an ancient British kingdom in the far southwest of what is now England, occupying the rough land area of present-day Cornwall, Devon and some of Somerset. Also home to Tintagel, claimed by many as the birthplace of legendary King Arthur. After two centuries warding off the inexorable expansion of the Saxon Kingdom of Wessex, Dumnonia eventually fell to the Saxon King Ecgberht in 838AD. Thereafter the people inhabiting the area became known by the Saxons as the West Welsh, or 'kernow-wealas', from which the modern-day name 'Cornwall' is derived. 'Wealas' is a somewhat derogatory Saxon word meaning 'foreigners or strangers.' Wealas, or Wales as we know it today, thus means 'foreigners or strangers,' which is why, unsurprisingly, folks from this country prefer the original British term Cymru (pronounced 'cum-ree') to describe themselves today.
Escanceaster / Caer Uisc	The Anglo-Saxon walled city now known as Exeter. Originally built by the Romans as the administrative centre of Dumnonia and named Isca Dumnoniorum. When the Romans left, the British moved back in, named it Caer Uisc, and it remained the capital of Dumnonia until the Saxons took the city from the Dumnonians some time in the 600s AD.

Name	*Description*
Escanceaster / Caer Uisc (Cont'd)	The first part of the name, 'caer' is the British word meaning 'stronghold', 'fortress', or 'citadel', in this case referring to the roman walls that enclosed the town. The Saxons kept the Roman name of Isca and added the suffix 'Ceaster.' Ceaster (also 'chester' or 'caster') is an Anglo-Saxon word meaning 'a nice, strong, walled town or fortress kindly built for us by the Romans.' Chester/caster is a common element of many place names in Britain to this day (e.g. Chester, Dorchester, Manchester, Lancaster, Silchester), indicating their Roman origin. Evidently the medieval scholars tired of the mouthful that was Escanceaster, however, and eventually shortened it to the much punchier 'Exeter.' OE.
Fjordlands	In this series of novels, the area that comprises the southwestern edge of Norway, stretching from modern-day Stavanger north up to Trondheim. In Rathulf's day, anything beyond Trondheim was so cold, remote and full of monsters that no one with any sense would venture there.
Francia / Frankia	Also known as the Kingdom of the Franks or Frankish Empire, Francia was a vast kingdom that in Rathulf's time roughly covered the areas now occupied by modern day France, Germany, Austria and northern Italy. Its most famous monarch was Emperor Charlemagne (Charles the Great). OE.
Hjaltlands	ON name for the Shetland Islands.
Ljóthús	ON name for the Isle of Lewis, Outer Hebrides, Scotland.
Lundenwic	Saxon name for present-day London. OE.
Lundi / Lundy	A small island (5km long and 1km wide) in the Bristol Channel off the north coast of Cornwall. The name means 'puffin island', from the Old Norse lundi meaning 'puffin'. ON.
Mannin	Early medieval name for the Isle of Man.
Mercia	One of the principal Anglo-Saxon Kingdoms, covering a large area of central Britain. OE.
Norvegr	The original name from which modern-day 'Norway' comes, from the Norse meaning 'the north way,' (Norðr vegr) referring to the sheltered sea route up the west coast of that country.
Petrocstowe	Saxon name for an important Dumnonian monastic town, famous for being founded by St Petroc, one of the early Irish Christians missionaries who brought the Celtic brand of Christianity to Dumnonia and far beyond. Modern-day

Name	*Description*
Petrocstowe (Cont'd)	name is Padstow. Cornish name is Lannwedhenek. Home of St Petroc's Priory before it moved inland to Bodmin, most probably as a result of Viking raids.
Sanctus Germanus	A monastery, also known by its Cornish name as Lannaled, founded by St Germanus ca. 430AD by the banks of the River Lynher, southern Dumnonia. Modern-day name is St Germans, Cornwall. L.
Sceaptesburh	Saxon name for modern-day Shaftesbury in Dorset. 'Sceapt' is from the OE name meaning 'a point' and 'Burh' is the OE word for a fortified settlement. OE.
Scirburne	Saxon name for modern-day Sherborne in Dorset. OE name meaning 'bright, clear stream.'
Sogne-fjorden	Sognefjorden is the longest fjord in Norway (and second longest in the world), cutting 205 kilometres (127 miles) inland from the Atlantic Ocean. It is exceptionally deep for much of its length: at around 1,000 metres (3,300 ft). Anything lost overboard is definitely not going to be retrieved.
Tonetun	The Anglo-Saxon name for Taunton, in present-day Somerset. OE, meaning town on the River Tone.
Tottaness	The Anglo-Saxon name for Totnes, in present-day Devon. OE.
Twyvertun	The Anglo-Saxon name for Tiverton, in present-day Devon, meaning town on two fords. OE.
Westseaxna Ríce	OE name for the Kingdom of the West Saxons (Wessex), whose capital was Winchester. King Alfred the Great is perhaps Wessex's most famous Monarch. In Rathulf's time, it was King Ecgberht (reigned 802 – 839) who was causing all the trouble for Dumnonia.
Winburne	Important Saxon monastic town in Wessex, modern name Wimborne. The Minster is dedicated to Saint Cuthburga (who was sister to Ine, King of Wessex and wife of Aldfrith, King of Northumbria), who founded a Benedictine abbey of nuns at the site of the present-day minster in c.705.
Wiltun	The Westseaxna name for Wilton, located just to the west of Salisbury in present-day Wiltshire. In Rathulf's time, Wiltun was the principal town in Wiltunscire (now Wiltshire). OE.

Name	*Description*
Wintanceaster	Capital of the Saxon kingdom of Westseaxna **Ríce** (Wessex), and later all of England. There has been a settlement on this site for millennia. It came to prominence during the Roman Era, when it was named Venta Belgarum. It was later renamed by the Saxon settlers to Wintanceaster, with the 'ceaster' suffix being the Saxon word for 'former Roman fort'. The city has retained its Saxon name (with a minor spelling alteration) as present-day Winchester. OE.
Worgemyn-ster	Old Saxon name for present-day Warminster, Wiltshire. Also recorded in some texts as Worgemynstre. OE.

Glossary of Terms

Listed below are some potentially unfamiliar names and terms you will encounter in this book. In many cases, you will find even more detail about these and other terms in the comprehensive glossaries on the *Wolves of Dumnonia* website.

ON = Old Norse. OE = Old English (Anglo-Saxon).
ME = Middle (medieval) English. L = Latin. B = Brythonic.

Name	*Description*
Addlepate	A foolish or dim-witted person (addle = confused; pate = head). OE.
Aegir	The ill-tempered Lord of the Ocean, God of the sea. Married to the Goddess Ran and father to the Nine Daughters (who are in turn representations of different aspects of the sea). The bringer of storms and big seas, Aegir lives in an underwater hall and from time to time rises to the surface to wreck ships and drag their crews back down to the bottom. Captains and crews make offerings to Aegir prior to a voyage to ensure a safe passage. ON.
Ætheling	Saxon title of nobility, meaning "crown prince" or heir to the throne. OE.
Althing	Also 'Thing'. The annual assembly of free men in the fjordlands (and indeed all of Scandinavia), presided over by a Lawspeaker. ON.
Anglo-Saxon	See entry for 'Saxon' below.
Anglo-Saxon Chronicle	The Anglo-Saxon Chronicle is an ancient collection of annals written in Old English that recount the history of the Anglo-Saxons. The original manuscript of the Chronicle was created late in the 9th century, most probably in Wessex, during the reign of Alfred the Great (r. 871–899). .
Asgard	One of the nine Norse realms, Asgard is located in the highest, sunniest branches of the world-tree Yggdrasil. It is home to the Aesir community of Gods. Valhalla, the 'hall of the slain' is located here. It lies on a plane above Midgard (realm of the mortal humans), and the two are connected by a magical rainbow bridge called Bifrost. ON.

Name	*Description*
Bacraut	ON slang meaning 'arsehole.' (Plural = Bacrautar.)
Baedling	An effeminate man. OE.
Bairn	'Baby.' This is actually the Scottish spelling, from the original ON 'barn.'
Beck	From Norse 'bekkr', meaning stream. ON.
Beorhtric	Beorhtric was King of Wessex from 786-802. He contested the throne with Ecgberht, whom Beorhtric (with the help of Offa of Mercia) drove to exile. Beorhtric married one of Offa's daughters, Eadburh. According to the annals, Beorhtric died from being accidentally poisoned by Queen Eadburh, who subsequently fled to a nunnery in Francia.It was during Beorhtric's reign that the Anglo-Saxon Chronicle recorded the first Viking raids in England.
Beornwulf	Beornwulf was King of Mercia from 823 to 826. His short reign saw the collapse of Mercia's supremacy over the other kingdoms of the Anglo-Saxon Heptarchy.
Brazier	A container, usually fashioned from iron and often with legs, intended to hold a fire. Normally found in large spaces such as halls, they are designed to provide both heat and light. They were used by all peoples across Europe during the Viking age and beyond (you will find them in beer gardens even today) and come in a multitude of shapes and sizes.
Burh / Burg	OE word meaning fortified place or fort. Also spelt 'Burg' in some sources. A modern town name that contains the element burg, burgh, bury or borough hints at a fortified past.
By / Byr	ON word meaning 'farmstead,' 'hamlet,' or 'village,' but can also be applied to larger settlements. In virtually all cases it appears as a suffix to a name, such as 'Sigvaldsby,' meaning: 'Sigvald's place.' In England, there are thousands of place names ending in 'by' which indicates a Scandinavian origin or influence.
Byre	Not to be confused with the Norse word 'byr', a byre is a building in which farm animals are housed, particularly cattle. Strictly speaking it is actually a British term, meaning 'cowshed.' An equivalent Norse word is 'hlaða,' meaning barn.
Ceorl **Churl** **Carl**	All variations on a term meaning an Anglo-Saxon freeman of the lowest class, ranking below a thegn. OE.

Name	*Description*
Charlemagne	King of the Franks (born 742AD), ruler of the Carolingian Empire (769 to 814) and Light of the West, Charles the Great (or Charlemagne) was a high point in the otherwise bleak Dark Ages of Europe. He established the Holy Roman Empire and brought stability and learning to Europe. His Royal seat was in Aachen (present day Germany), and the kingdom extended across most of what is present day France (which takes its name from the Franks), Belgium and parts of Germany.
Daufi	ON slang meaning 'stupid.'
Drakkar	ON meaning 'dragon ship' (a posh longship).
Draug	ON name for a monster of the night; an undead creature possessing superhuman strength, often guarding a treasure hoard. Plural = draugar.
Drittsekk	Old Norse slang, literally meaning 'bag of shit.' Our equivalent is 'scumbag.'
Eadburh	Eadburh (also spelled Eadburg) (fl. 787–802) was the daughter of King Offa of Mercia and Queen Cynethryth. She was the wife of King Beorhtric of Wessex, and, according to Asser's Life of Alfred the Great, she killed her husband by poison while attempting to poison another. She fled to Francia, becoming an abbess until she was eventually expelled from the monastery and ended her days begging in the streets of Pavia. OE.
Ealdorman	Anglo-Saxon term. An ealdorman was a high-status individual in Saxon times, appointed by the king as his representative. They were originally drawn mostly from ancient and powerful families and commanded armies on behalf of the king. Thegns (a lower rank) served the ealdormen.
Equerry	An officer of the household of a prince or noble who has charge over the stables. Actually a medieval French term, probably derived from Latin 'Equus' (horse).
Ergi	Norse word (definitely a slur) describing the recipient of a homosexual act. Homosexuality was at best frowned upon in Scandinavian culture during the Viking Age, but one thing we do know from the writings preserved in the sagas is that being the recipient of a homosexual act was a cause for severe derision; not because it was seen as perverted, but because it was regarded as the ultimate act of submission. ON.

Name	*Description*
Erlendar	Foreign, not native. ON.
Fenrir	Also Fenris in some sources. The most fearsome of the Norse wolven monsters, father of the wolves Sköll and Hati. He is the 'great devourer,' who, at the commencement of Ragnarök, breaks free of his bonds and runs throughout the world with his lower jaw against the ground and his upper jaw in the sky, consuming everything in his path. He kills the god Odin before finally being killed himself by one of Odin's avenging sons, Víðarr. ON = "Fen-dweller."
Fjord	ON word describing a long, deep, narrow seawater inlet with steep sides or cliffs, originally created by a glacier scouring a pathway through the landscape to the sea. When the ice melted and the glaciers retreated, the gouges filled with seawater to create the fjords. The entire west coast of Norway is deeply cut by fjords (many of which pierce scores of kilometres inland), resulting in a unique and spectacular landscape. Sognefjorden, where Rathulf and the main players in this book live, is exceedingly deep at 1,308m (4,291 feet), and stretches just over 200 kilometres inland from its mouth. On the other side of the world, the South Island of New Zealand also boasts a smaller number of similarly impressive fjords, as does Chile.
Fjordlands	In this series of novels, the area that comprises the south-western edge of Norway, stretching from modern-day Stavanger north up to Trondheim. In Rathulf's day, anything beyond Trondheim was so cold, remote and full of monsters that no one with any sense would venture there.
Fletching	The feathers on the tail of an arrow.
Frank / Frankish	A person or thing that comes from Francia.
Fylgja	A spirit which accompanies a person in connection to their fate or fortune, and which often represents some aspect of the person's character. Usually a carnivorous animal. Similar in concept to the 'totem' animal found in other cultures' belief systems. Rathulf's fylgja is, unsurprisingly, a wolf. ON.
Fyrd	An early Anglo-Saxon term, describing an army that was mobilised by the local Lord from amongst his freemen to defend their estate or shire in times of trouble or war. The Saxon Kings had their own fyrd too, who were select representatives from the higher levels of Saxon society and who would join him on royal expeditions

Name	*Description*
Gambeson	A thick, padded coat worn under armour. Also spelt Gambison. ME.
Gefion	An ancient Norse goddess of agriculture, fertility, abundance, and prosperity. Her name is derived from the Old Norse verb gefa, "to give," and her name can be translated as "Giver" or "Generous One." ON.
Gryphon	Also spelt Griffin or Griffon. A mythical beast: half-lion, half eagle. Commonly seen in medieval coats of arms, including Sherborne's. OE.
Hauberk	A shirt of mail, usually reaching at least to mid-thigh and including sleeves. ME.
Hávamál	ON word meaning "sayings of the high one." Attributed to Odin, the Hávamál is a collection of Norse poems from Viking Age Iceland. They are effectively Norse proverbs, providing advice about good living, proper conduct and other general wisdom about how to be a good Viking.
Hel	The Goddess of death who presides over a realm of the same name; the place where people who die of old age and sickness go. Her face and upper body are those of a living woman's, but her thighs and legs are those of a corpse's, mottled and mouldering or rotting away. Hence the curse 'may you rot between Hel's thighs.' ON.
Jötunheim	ON, literally meaning "land of the giants".
Jörmungand	ON, literally meaning "huge monster", Jörmungand is a giant sea-serpent, the most feared of all sea-monsters, who in Norse mythology is so large that he encircles the earth and grasps his tail in his mouth. It is said that when he releases his tail, Ragnarök (the great battle at the end of everything) will begin. Jörmungand is an arch-enemy of the God Thor.
Jötunn	In Norse mythology, a race of giant, nature spirits with superhuman strength. Trolls belong to the Jötunn race. Their name means "devourer". ON.
Jötnar	A group of Jötunn. Generally something best avoided. ON.
Jötnahreðr	A Jötunn's penis.
Karve	An inshore pleasure craft; a yacht. Wealthy Norsemen used them to show off, and some were very ornately carved (carving was the bling of the day) and very much prized. Much like the supercars of wealthy young footballers and social media stars today. ON.
Kernowyon	The Brythonic term for the people of Kernow (modern-day Cornwall). B.

Name	*Description*
Kist	From ON 'kista,' being a chest or trunk for storing clothing or linen.
Knarr	ON word for a cargo ship, essentially the same open-decked design as a longship but with wider and deeper sides suitable for carrying cargo across the open seas. Also spelt Knørr in some sources.
Kuk	ON slang meaning 'cock.'
Kuksuger	ON slur meaning 'cock-sucker.'
Kuktryne	ON slur meaning 'cock-face.'
Liðasblot	Viking late summer (harvest) festival, giving thanks to Urda (Ertha) for her bounty. A "Blot" represents an offering made to the gods. It can take the form of an animal, food, or other goods. In Norse rituals, the people accept and eat the offering. Therefore, a feast is usually associated with a Blot. ON.
Longship	The Viking warrior's sleek means of passage to the southern lands for raiding. ON = 'Langskip.'
Midgard	'Middle Earth': the place where mortal humans live. The Norse believed that the universe was comprised of nine worlds or realms, of which Midgard was one. ON.
Muspelheim	One of the two primordial Norse realms, Muspelheim is the Realm of Fire, land of the fire giants. Not a very nice place. The embers from the fires of Muspelheim formed the stars in the night sky. ON.
Mynster, Mynstre, Minster	In the 9th century, a mynster was a monastic settlement, centred around a church, in which the community devoted their life to Christian observance. A mynster may have been either a community of monks (male) or nuns (female). Over time, these monastic settlements often grew into towns in their own right, as the monasteries rose in wealth and stature. Scirburne (Sherborne) is one such example. The modern term 'Minster' to describe a very important church (e.g. Westminster) is derived from this term. OE.
Niflheim	One of the two primordial Norse realms, Niflheim is the realm of ice and cold, with the frozen river of Elivágar and the well of Hvergelmir, from which come all the rivers. It is the abode of the Goddess Hel, who presides over those poor Viking souls who are unfortunate enough not to die a heroic or notable death (and thus were refused entry into Valhalla). ON.

Name	*Description*
Nine daughters	These are the nine daughters of Ægir and Rán, a giant and goddess who both represent the sea in Norse mythology. The names of the nine daughters are poetic terms for different characteristics of ocean waves, such as 'frothing wave,' and 'foam-fleck'. ON.
Njord Njörðr	Njord is a god among the Vanir. He was the Norse god of the wind and of the sea and its riches. His aid was invoked in seafaring and in hunting, and he was considered the god of "wealth-bestowal," or prosperity. He was the father of Freyr and Freyja by his own sister. ON.
Norse Norsemen Northman	The name of the people who lived during the Viking Age primarily in the area covered by modern-day Norway and Iceland (but also settlers in Western Britain and Ireland who originally hailed from Norway). The term 'northman' is one of the many names used by the medieval historians to describe the Viking raiders from the North. Latinized as 'Nortmannus' (recorded in Medieval Latin, 9th century).
Odin	In Norse mythology, Odin is the father of all Gods and men. He is associated with wisdom, healing, death, royalty, the gallows, knowledge, battle, sorcery, poetry, frenzy, and the runic alphabet, and is the husband of the goddess Frigg. His two ravens, Huginn and Munin (Norse, meaning 'thought' and 'memory' respectively) fly over the world daily and return to tell him everything that has happened in Midgard. He is also accompanied by two wolves, Geri and Freki (Norse, meaning 'greedy one' and 'ravenous one' respectively). ON.
ótta	The time of the day roughly from 3:00 am to 6:00 am. ON.
Ran	In Norse mythology, the goddess Rán and the jötunn Ægir both personi-fy the sea, and together they have nine daughters who personify waves. Each daughter's name reflects poetic terms for waves. ON.
Rassragr	ON slang (very crude) for a man who allowed himself to be sodomised. Literally means 'arse-unmanly.' This was one of the most grievous insults that could be dealt in Viking times.
Sansorthinn / Sansorðinn	An extremely offensive insult in Norse–considered by many to be the most offensive slur possible–meaning the receiver of a homosexual act. ON.
Sard, Sarð, Sarding	OE profanity, predating the word 'f*ck' but having the same meaning. OE.

Name	*Description*
Saxon / Anglo-Saxon	Following the departure of the Romans from British shores in 410AD, a new group of invaders began to harry the island, sailing across the channel from what is now Germany and Denmark. They were the Angles, Jutes and Saxons, and it is after the Angles that England is named. These 'Anglo-Saxons' gradually conquered the Romano-British tribes over the following two centuries, so that by the time Rathulf was born in 807AD, most of southern Britain was under Anglo-Saxon control. Only the far western corner remained in British hands, but it would not be long before this remnant kingdom of Britons–known as Dumnonia–would face the Anglo-Saxons' wrath. In Rathulf's day, the Anglo-Saxons were more commonly referred to collectively as 'the Saxons.' (Much as the Viking invaders from Norway and Denmark were collectively labelled 'The Danes' by the Anglo-Saxon chroniclers.) There remains considerable debate amongst academics as to whether the broad-brush term 'Anglo-Saxon' is an appropriate label to apply to the diverse peoples who raided and settled the British Isles at this time, and who subsequently went on to establish independent kingdoms across the land. Most likely those people would have referred to themselves by their kingdom name, such as "I am Mercian," or, in the case of Wessex, "Wesseaxna." It was the Wessex King Alfred the Great who began to collectively call the Anglo Saxons 'the anglcyn' (a precursor to 'the English').
Scortum	Latin term, meaning sex slave or prostitute. L.
Solmonath	The Month of February (approximate) in the Saxon calendar. OE.
Sorðit	Norse profanity, similar to "f*ck". ON.
Starboard	Viking ships did not have rudders of the type we typically see on the stern of boats today; rather, they attached a broad paddle-like oar–called the 'steering board'–to the outside right-hand side of the hull at the stern; thus lending its name to that side of all ships today (starboard). ON = stýri (rudder) + borð (side of a ship).
Strake	A horizontal line of planks that make up part of a longship's hull. Longships were 'clinker-built', which means that the adjoining strakes were held together on an overlap by rivets. In more recent times, the topmost strake on a ship's hull became known as the 'gunwale' because in medieval times this was where guns were attached. Vikings didn't have guns

Name	*Description*
Strake (Cont'd)	of course, and in their days it was called the 'Ripr'. In larger fighting longships, the topmost strake was constructed with an outer plank so that the Viking's round shields could be slotted into the gap for stowage while at sea, hence the term 'shield-rail.'
Swale	A low or hollow place, especially a marshy depression between ridges. ON.
Tabard	A simple, sleeveless overtunic or heavy overmantel, carrying the colours and/or crest of the wearer's thegn or fyrd. Generally worn over a tunic or armour.
Thegn / Thane	Anglo-Saxon term, meaning "servant, attendant, retainer." It generally referred to an aristocratic retainer of a king or nobleman in Saxon England. Commonly a thegn was a Lord who held an estate and had his own retainers (a 'fyrd') who could be called to arms in times of war or trouble. OE.
Thor	One of the Aesir–the principal Norse Gods–Thor is considered to be the protector of all Midgard. Thor is strength personified, and he wields the mighty hammer Mjöllnir. His battle chariot is drawn by two goats (named Tanngrisnir or "teeth-barer/snarler" and Tanngnjóstr or "teeth-grinder"), and his hammer Mjöllnir causes the thunder and lightning that rumbles and flashes across the sky.
Thrall	ON word for 'slave.' Slavery was an everyday norm in Viking times, with all cultures and kingdoms maintaining an active trade in people as saleable commodities. Slaves were seen as little better than cattle–advanced domestic animals at best–who typically lived in the darkest end of the longhouse with the other domestic beasts. If slaves did not behave properly then they were beaten. An owner could punish his slaves as much as he wanted. Slaves' bodies were also available for sexual exploitation. Historical and archaeological evidence suggests that the Vikings were not particularly kind to their slaves, but that could also be said of their Saxon and British counterparts.
Tiller	The handle on a ship's steering board or rudder.
Tørrfisk	Stockfish; unsalted fish, especially cod, dried by cold air and wind on wooden racks. ON.
Valhalla	Hall of the fallen heroes, located in Asgard. All good Viking warriors desired entry to Valhalla when they died, for there they would fight and feast into glorious eternity.

Name	*Description*
Valkyries	Valkyries are the warrior maidens who attended Odin, ruler of the gods. The Valkyries rode through the air in brilliant armour, directed battles, distributed death lots among the warriors, and conducted the souls of slain heroes to Valhalla, the great hall of Odin. Their leader was Brunhilde.
Viking	Strictly speaking, a person from Scandinavia (modern Sweden, Norway and Denmark) who partook in ship-borne raids and piracy (to 'go a-Viking'). However we tend to use the catch-all term 'Viking' to mean anyone from that part of the world during a particular period in history known as the Viking Age. There were three main groups of Vikings: the Norse, Rus and Danes. Rathulf was raised by Norse Vikings, i.e. folk who lived in the fjordlands of present-day Norway. In many of the early Saxon and English texts the Viking raiders are all referred to as 'the Danes,' regardless of their actual origin (they all looked terrifyingly similar to the poor monks who were often subject to the raids).
Viking Age	The period of European history generally defined as beginning in 793 with an attack by Vikings on the monastery of Lindisfarne in present-day Northumbria, and ending in 1066, with the invasion of England by William the Conqueror. The Battle of Hastings marked the beginning of the Norman period of British history; Norman referring to William's Viking ('Northman') ancestry.
Villein	A tenant farmer who was tied in servitude to their landowning Lord. Synonymous with the term 'peasant.' The majority of people in early medieval Britain were peasants. OE.
Weala **Wealas** **Wealh**	'Weala' (and its variant spellings) is a somewhat derogatory Saxon word meaning 'slaves, foreigners or strangers.' Wealas, or Wales as we know it today, was the term many Saxons used to describe native Britons, which is why, unsurprisingly, folks from this country prefer the original British term Cymru (pronounced 'cum-ree') to describe themselves today.
Wergild	A wergild was a defined value placed on every man, graded according to rank, and used as the basis of a fine or compensation for murder, disablement, injury (or certain other serious crimes) against that person. It was payable as restitution to the victim's family by the guilty party. It was also a levy (tax) imposed by the kings of Wessex to their vassal states, such as Dumnonia. OE.

Acknowledgements

Where is *The Monk's Sword*, you may be wondering? Well, much of the action in that book has moved to the right (I seem to have a habit of doing this) and will now appear as book 5 in the series. In the meantime, this fourth book in the Wolves of Dumnonia saga has taken way too long to come to fruition, disrupted by house renovations followed by the arrival of Covid and the consequent stresses and financial pressures of both. I therefore apologise to those patient readers who have been waiting for this next instalment.

Like its preceding volumes, *The Apprentice Prince* is the result of many people's hard work and support, without whom Aneurin and Rathulf's story would never have been told. In addition to those who I have thanked previously – and whose contribution continues throughout this series – I would like to call out Hamish and Rebecca from the Garsdale Retreat for providing such a fabulous environment for writers like me. I've enjoyed my two stints in the Yorkshire Dales over the past few months, sharing the crisp air, great food and wonderful company with other like-minded people. Being able to get away from it all to focus on one's creativity has been a precious gift. It has certainly helped me get this book finished.

As always, I continue to be supported by our fantastic team at Strengthening Practice and Elterwater Press. Thanks especially to Katy, Erica, Liz and Shane, who continue to pick up the pieces I leave behind in my chaotic wake. Thanks also to my outstanding voice actor, Toby Gaffney, and sound engineer, Nick Smith, for their terrific rendition of the story in audiobook form.

Finally, my wife Jo remains my rock and my love, and keeps me and my increasingly complex saga on track with her wise counsel and continuity checks. And, of course, there is Ethan, our brilliant son, and I'd best not forget our greying whippet, Lola.